# TIDES
## *of* WAR

### A NOVEL OF ALCIBIADES
### AND THE
### PELOPONNESIAN WAR

### STEVEN PRESSFIELD

**Doubleday**

LONDON · NEW YORK · TORONTO · SYDNEY · AUCKLAND

TRANSWORLD PUBLISHERS
61–63 Uxbridge Road, London W5 5SA
a division of The Random House Group Ltd

RANDOM HOUSE AUSTRALIA (PTY) LTD
20 Alfred Street, Milsons Point, Sydney,
New South Wales 2061, Australia

RANDOM HOUSE NEW ZEALAND
18 Poland Road, Glenfield, Auckland 10, New Zealand

RANDOM HOUSE SOUTH AFRICA (PTY) LTD
Endulini, 5a Jubilee Road, Parktown 2193, South Africa

Published 2000 by Doubleday
a division of Transworld Publishers

A catalogue record for this book is available from the British Library.
ISBN 0385 601646

Typeset in 11/14pt Goudy by Falcon Oast Graphic Art

Printed in Great Britain
by Mackays of Chatham plc, Chatham, Kent

1 3 5 7 9 10 8 6 4 2

**Steven Pressfield** is the author of the novel *The Legend of Bagger Vance*, which has recently been filmed by Robert Redford, and the bestselling novel about the battle of Thermopylae, *Gates of Fire*. He lives in Los Angeles and is now at work on his third historical novel, also set in ancient Greece.

# PRAISE FOR GATES OF FIRE:

'A breathtakingly brilliant reconstruction of the most heroic battle of ancient times. There have been many books about Sparta and its warrior code, but none have captured so magnificently the hearts, minds and spirits of the warriors who fought at Thermopylae. This is a work of rare genius. Savour it!'
DAVID GEMMELL

'With a sound grasp of strategy and ex-infantryman's understanding of comradeship and its grim wit, Steven Pressfield adds colour and a credible cast of soldiers and their wives to the historians' accounts. I couldn't put it down.' *Daily Telegraph*

'It makes one proud to be Greek, and especially proud to be half-Spartan. A great read.' TAKI, *Spectator* 'Books of the Year'

'Pressfield's imaginative and gory retelling of the combat is compelling, and his prose is clear and accessible.' *Sunday Times*

'Excellent . . . Pressfield has succeeded in recreating an ancient world and telling a rousing and moving story.' *Yorkshire Post*

'Unbearably suspenseful . . . Pressfield's descriptions of war are breathtaking in their immediacy.' *amazon.co.uk*

'Steven Pressfield brings the battle of Thermopylae to brilliant life, and he does for that war what Charles Frazier did for the Civil War in *Cold Mountain*. When you finish Pressfield's work, you will feel you have fought side by side with the Spartans. This novel is Homeric.' PAT CONROY

'Gripping and swashbuckling . . . written as a kind of heroic saga, drenched in the gore of battle and the dust of Spartan discipline . . . The war with Persia provides the occasion for *Gates of Fire*, but the conflicts within Sparta, caused by divided loyalties and private animosities, are the true stuff of this novel's drama . . . Herodotus, who made Mr Pressfield's story possible, would have enjoyed this book.' *New York Times*

'A tale worthy of Homer, a timeless epic of man and war exquisitely researched and boldly written. Pressfield has created a new classic, deserving of a place beside the very best of the old.' STEPHEN COONTS

'Incredibly gripping, moving, and literate . . . rarely does an author manage to recreate a moment in history with such mastery, authority, and psychological insight.' NELSON DeMILLE

FOR CHRISTY

# HISTORICAL NOTE

By their epochal victories over the Persians in 490 and 480/479 BC, Sparta and Athens established themselves as the pre-eminent powers in Greece and the Aegean – Sparta on land, Athens at sea.

For half a century the states maintained a tenuous equilibrium. At Athens these years inaugurated the Golden Age of Periclean democracy. The Parthenon was constructed, the tragedies of Aeschylus, Sophocles, and Euripides commenced performance; Socrates began to teach.

By 431, however, Athens' power had become too great for the free states of Greece to endure. War came – that struggle called by Thucydides 'the greatest in history', which lasted, as the oracle had foretold, thrice nine years and ended with the capitulation of Athens in 404.

One man set his stamp upon this conflict, for good or ill, beyond all others. This was Alcibiades of Athens.

Kinsman of Pericles, intimate of Socrates, he was, the ancient sources attest, the most handsome and brilliant man of his era, as well as the most lawless. As a general he was never beaten.

# THE FIFTH CENTURY BC

. . . the worst enemies of Athens are not those who, like you, have only harmed her in war, but those who have forced her friends to turn against her. The Athens I love is not the one which is wronging me now, but that one in which I used to have secure enjoyment of my rights as a citizen. That country that I am attacking does not seem to be mine any longer; it is rather that I am trying to recover a country that has ceased to be mine. And the man who really loves his country is not the one who refuses to attack it when he has been unjustly driven from it, but the man whose desire for it is so strong that he will shrink from nothing in his efforts to get back there again.

Alcibiades addressing the Spartan Assembly,
in Thucydides' *History of the Peloponnesian War*

She [Athens] loves, and hates, and longs to have him back . . .

Aristophanes,
on Alcibiades, in *The Frogs*

MACEDONIA

Potidaea

CORCYRA

Thermopylae

EUBOEA

BOEOTIA

ATTICA

Thebes

ACHARNAE

Gulf of Corinth

Patrae

Eleusis

Megara

Athens

Elis

Corinth

SALAMIS

Piraeus

PELOPONNESE

Ionian
Sea

ARCADIA

Argos

Mantinea

Tegea

LACEDAEMON

Sparta

GREECE
AND THE AEGEAN

430 B.C.

ATHENIAN EMPIRE

SPARTA AND ALLIES

THRACE
Selymbria
Byzantium
Chalcedon
Propontis
CHERSONESE
Lampsacus
Cyzicus
Sestos
AEGOSPOTAMI
Abydos
Doscylium
Hellespont
PHRYGIA
Methymna
LESBOS
Aegean
Sea
Mytilene
ARGINOUSAI ISLANDS
Cyme
LYDIA
Sardis
CHIOS
Smyrna
Clazomenae
IONIA
Notium
Ephesus
ANDROS
SAMOS
Priene
Miletus
DELOS
CARIA
NAXOS
RHODES

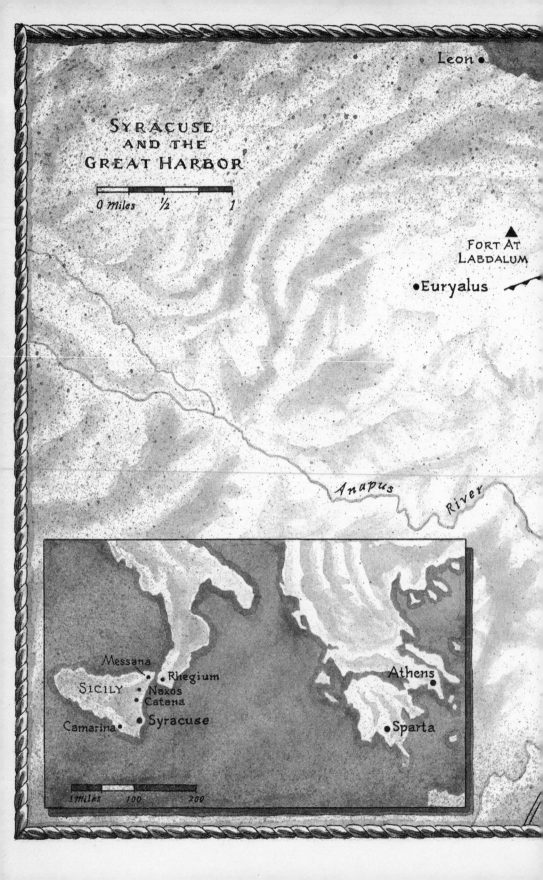

SYRACUSE
AND THE
GREAT HARBOR

0 Miles    ½         1

Leon •

FORT AT
LABDALUM

•Euryalus

Anapus        River

Messana
        • Rhegium
SICILY    • Naxos
        • Catana
Camarina•    • Syracuse

Athens

Sparta

1 Miles    100        200

# TIDES OF WAR

# BOOK ONE

## AGAINST
## POLEMIDES

# ONE
# MY GRANDFATHER JASON

MY GRANDFATHER, JASON THE SON OF ALEXICLES OF THE DISTRICT OF Alopece, died just before sunset on the fourteenth day of Boedromion, one year past, two months prior to his ninety-second birthday. He was the last of that informal but fiercely devoted circle of comrades and friends who attended the philosopher Socrates.

The span of my grandfather's years ran from the imperial days of Pericles, the construction of the Parthenon and Erechtheum, through the Great Plague, the rise and fall of Alcibiades, and the full tenure of that calamitous twenty-seven-year conflagration called in our city the Spartan War and known throughout greater Greece, as recorded by the historian Thucydides, as the Peloponnesian War.

As a young man my grandfather served as a sail lieutenant at Sybota, Potidaea, and Scione and later in the East as a trierarch and squadron commander at the battles of Bitch's Tomb, Abydos (for which he was awarded the prize of valour and incidentally lost an eye and the use of his right leg), and the Arginousai Islands. As a private citizen he spoke out in the Assembly, alone save Euryptolemus and Axiochus, against the mob in defence of the Ten Generals. In his years he buried two wives and eleven children. He served his city from her peak of pre-eminence, mistress of two hundred tributary states, to the hour of her vanquishment at the hands of her most inclement foes. In short he was a man who not only witnessed but participated in most of the significant events of the modern era and who knew personally many of its principal actors.

In the waning seasons of my grandfather's life, when his vigour began to fail and he could move about only with the aid of a companion's arm, I took to visiting him daily. There appears ever one among a family, the physicians testify, whose disposition invites and upon whom falls the duty to succour its elderly and infirm members.

To me this was never a chore. Not only did I hold my grandfather in the loftiest esteem, but I delighted in his society with an intensity that frequently bordered upon the ecstatic. I could listen to him talk for hours and, I fear, tired him more severely than charity served with my enquiries and importunities.

To me he was like one of our hardy Attic vines, assaulted season after season by the invader's torch and axe, blistered by summer sun, frost-jacketed in winter, yet unkillable, ever-enduring, drawing strength from deep within the earth to yield up despite all privations or perhaps because of them the sweetest and most mellifluent of wines. I felt keenly that with his passing an era would close, not only of Athens' greatness but of a calibre of man with whom we contemporary specimens stood no longer familiar, nor to whose standard of virtue we could hope to attain.

The loss to typhus of my own dear son, aged two and a half, earlier in that season, had altered every aspect of my being. Nowhere could I discover consolation save in the company of my grandfather. That fragile purchase we mortals hold upon existence, the fleeting nature of our hours beneath the sun, stood vividly upon my heart; only with him could I find footing upon some stony but stabler soil.

My regimen upon those mornings was to rise before dawn and, summoning my dog Sentinel (or, more accurately, responding to his summons), ride down to the port along the Carriage Road, returning through the foothills to our family's mains at Holm Oak Hill. The early hours were a balm to me. From the high road one could see the naval crews already at drill in the harbour. We passed other gentlemen upon the track to their estates, saluted athletes training along the roads, and greeted the young cavalrymen at their exercises in the hills. Upon completion of the morning's business of the farm, I stabled my mount and proceeded on foot, alone save Sentinel, up the sere olive-dotted slope to my grandfather's cottage.

I brought him his lunch. We would talk in the shade of the overlook porch, or sometimes simply sit, side by side, with Sentinel reclining on the cool stones between us, saying nothing.

'Memory is a queer goddess, whose gifts metamorphose with the passage of the years,' my grandfather observed upon one such afternoon. 'One cannot call to mind that which occurred an hour past, yet summon events seventy years gone, as if they were unfolding here and now.'

I interrogated him, often ruthlessly I fear, upon these distant holdings of his heart. Perhaps for his part he welcomed the eager ear of youth, for once launched upon a tale he would pursue its passage, like the tireless campaigner he was, in detail to its close. In his day the scribe's art had not yet triumphed; the faculty of memory stood unatrophied. Men could recite extended passages from the Iliad and Odyssey, quote stanzas of a hundred hymns, and relate passage and verse of the tragedy attended days previous.

More vivid still stood my grandfather's recollection of men. He remembered not alone friends and heroes but slaves and horses and dogs, even trees and vines which had graven impress upon his heart. He could summon the memory of some antique sweetheart, seventy-five years gone, and resurrect her mirage in colours so immediate that one seemed to behold her before him, yet youthful and lovely, in the flesh.

I enquired of my grandfather once, whom of all the men he had known he adjudged most exceptional.

'Noblest,' he replied without hesitation, 'Socrates. Boldest and most brilliant, Alcibiades. Bravest, Thrasybulus, the Brick. Wickedest, Anytus.'

Impulse prompted a corollary query. 'Was there one whom memory has driven deepest? One to whom you find your thoughts returning?'

At this my grandfather drew up. How odd that I should ask, he replied, for yes, there was one man who had, for cause to which he could not give name, been of late much upon his mind. This individual, my grandfather declared, stood not among the ranks of the celebrated or the renowned; he was neither admiral nor archon, nor would his name be found memorialized among the archives, save as a dark and self-condemned footnote.

'Of all I knew, this man could not but be called the most haunted. He was an aristocrat of the district of Acharnae. I helped to defend him once, on trial for his life.'

I was intrigued at once and pressed my grandfather to elaborate. He smiled, declaring that to launch upon this enterprise might take many hours, for the events of the man's tale transpired over decades and covered on land and sea most of the known world. Such prospect, far from daunting me, made me the more eager to hear. Please, I entreated; the day is well spent, but let us at least make a beginning.

'You're a greedy whelp, aren't you?'

'To hear you speak, Grandfather, the greediest.'

He smiled. Let us start, then, and see where the tale takes us.

'In those days,' my grandfather began, 'that class of professional rhetorician and specialist in affairs of the courts had not yet arisen. On trial a man spoke in his own defence. If he wished, however, he might appoint an associate – a father or uncle, perhaps a friend or gentleman of influence – to assist in preparing his case.

'By letter from prison this man solicited me. This was odd, as I shared no personal acquaintance with the fellow. He and I had served simultaneously in several theatres of war and had held positions of responsibility in conjunction with the younger Pericles, son of the great Pericles and Aspasia, whom both of us were privileged to call friend; this, however, was far from uncommon in those days and could in nowise be construed as constituting a bond. Further this individual was, to say the least, notorious. Though an officer of acknowledged valour and long and distinguished service to the state, he had entered Athens at her hour of capitulation not only beneath the banner of the Spartan foe but clad in her mantle of scarlet. I believed, and told him so, that one guilty of such infamy must suffer the supreme penalty, nor could I contribute in any way to such a criminal's exoneration.

'The man persisted none the less. I visited him in his cell and listened to his story. Though at that time Socrates himself had been convicted and sentenced to death, and in fact resided awaiting execution within the walls of the same prison, and to his aid I must before all attend, not to mention the affairs of my own family, I agreed to assist the man in the preparation of his defence. I did so not because I believed he could be acquitted or deserved to be (he himself readily ratified his own inculpation), but because I felt the publication of his history must be accomplished, if only before a jury, to hold the mirror up to the democracy which, by its conviction of the noblest citizen it had ever produced, my master Socrates, had evinced such wickedness as to crown and consummate its own self-immolation.'

My grandfather held silent for long moments. One could see his eye turn inward and his heart summon the memory of this individual and the tone and tenor of that time.

'What was the man's name, Grandfather?'

'*Polemides the son of Nicolaus.*'

*I recalled the name vaguely but could not place it in quarter or context.*

'*He was the man,*' *my grandfather prompted,* '*who assassinated Alcibiades.*'

# T W O

# MURDER IN MELISSA

THE ASSASSINATION PARTY [MY GRANDFATHER CONTINUED] WAS LED BY
two nobles of Persia acting under orders of the Great King's governor of
Phrygia. They proceeded by ship from Abydos on the Hellespont to the stronghold in Thrace to which Alcibiades had repaired in his final exile, whence,
discovering their prey absconded, the party pursued him back across the straits
to Asia. The Persians were accompanied by three Peers of Sparta whose chief,
Endius, had been Alcibiades' guest-friend and intimate since boyhood. These
had been appointed by the home government, not to participate in the murder,
but to serve as witnesses, to confirm with their own eyes the extinction of this
man, the last left alive whom they still feared. Such was Alcibiades' renown
for escape and resurrection that many believed he could cheat even that final
magistrate, Death.

A professional assassin, Telamon of Arcadia, accompanied the party, along
with some half dozen henchmen of his selection, to plan and execute the
action. His confederate was the Athenian Polemides.

Polemides had been a friend of Alcibiades. He had served as captain of
marines throughout Alcibiades' spectacular sequence of victories in the
Hellespontine War, had acted as his bodyguard when the conqueror returned
in glory to Athens, and had stood upon his right hand when Alcibiades restored
the procession by land in celebration of the Eleusinian Mysteries. I recall
vividly his appearance, at Samos, upon Alcibiades' recall from exile to the
fleet. The moment was incendiary, with twenty thousand sailors, marines,

and heavy infantry, distraught for their own fate and the survival of their country, enveloping the mole they called Little Choma as the longboat touched and Polemides stepped off, shielding his charge from the mob which seemed as ripe to stone as salute him. I studied Alcibiades' expression; nothing could have been clearer than that he trusted the man at his shoulder absolutely with his life.

It was this Polemides' duty now, some seven years subsequent, to draw the victim out and with his cohort, the assassin Telamon, perform the slaughter. For this his fee was a talent of silver from the treasury of Persia.

Of all this the man informed me, concealing nothing, within the first minutes of our initial interview. He did so, he stated, to ensure that I – whose family shared bonds of marriage with the Alcmaeonids, Alcibiades' family on his mother's side, and myself through my devotion to Socrates, whose link to Alcibiades was well known – would know the worst at once and could pull out, if I wished.

The actual indictment against the man made no citation of Alcibiades.

Polemides was charged in the death of a boatswain of the fleet named Philemon, who had been murdered some few years prior in a brothel brawl at Samos. A second impeachment was preferred against him, that of treason. It was under this rubric, clearly, that the jurors would read that more consequential slaying. Such obliquity was not uncommon in those days; yet its indirection was compounded by the specific statute under which his accusers had brought him to trial.

Polemides had been arraigned neither under a writ of eisangelia, the standard indictment for treason, nor a dike phonou, a straight charge of murder, both of which would have permitted him to elect voluntary exile, sparing his life. Rather he had been denounced (by a pair of known rogues, brothers and stooges of acknowledged foes of the democracy) under an endeixis kakourgias, a far more general category of 'wrongdoing'. This struck one at first as preposterous, the issue of prosecutors ignorant of the law. Further reflection, however, revealed its cunning. Under this category of indictment, the accused might not only be imprisoned before and throughout trial, without option of voluntary exile, but denied bail as well. The death penalty still obtained, and the trial would take place, not before the Council or Areopagus, but a common people's court, where such terms as 'traitor' and 'friend of Sparta' could be counted upon to inflame the jurors' ire. Clearly Polemides' accusers wanted him dead, by the right hand or the left. As far as one could predict, they would get their wish. For all those who hated Alcibiades and blamed him for the fall of our nation, yet many still loved him. These would raise no remonstrance to the execution of the man who had betrayed and slain their champion. Still, Polemides observed, his accusers were, he was certain, of the opposite party – those who had conspired with their country's enemies, seeking to purchase their own preservation at the price of their nation's ruin.

As to the man Polemides himself, his appearance was both striking and singular, dark-eyed, of slightly less than average height, extremely thick-muscled, and, though well past forty years, as lean through the middle as a schoolboy. His beard was the colour of iron, and his skin despite imprisonment retained the dark copper of one who has spent much of his life at sea. Scars of fire, spear, and sword crisscrossed the flesh of his arms, legs, and back. Upon his brow, though bleached by exposure to the elements, stood vivid the koppa slave brand of the Syracusans, token of that captivity endured by survivors of the Sicilian calamity and emblematic of unspeakable suffering.

Did I abhor him? I was prepared to. Yet in the flesh his clarity of thought and expression, his candour and utter want of self-exoneration, disarmed my prejudice. His crimes notwithstanding, the man appeared to my imagination much as might have Odysseus, stepping forth from the songs of Homer. Nor did he comport himself in the brutish or insolent manner of the soldier for hire; on the contrary his demeanour and self-presentation were those of a gentleman. What wine he had, he proffered at once and insisted upon vacating for his guest the solitary stool his cell possessed, pillowing it for my comfort with the fleece he used to bundle the chamber's single bare pallet.

Throughout that initial interview he performed as we spoke various calisthenics intended to maintain fitness despite confinement. He could place his heel upon the wall above his head and, standing flat on the other sole, set his forehead with ease upon his elevated shin. Once when I brought him some eggs, he placed one within the cage of his fist and, extending his arm, challenged me either to prise his fingers apart or crush the egg. I tried, employing all my strength, and failed, as he grinned at me mischievously the while.

I never felt afraid with the man or of him. In fact as the days progressed I came to embrace a profound sympathy for the fellow, despite his numerous criminal deeds and lack of repentance therefor. His name, Polemides, as you know, means 'child of war'. But he was not a child of just any war, rather one unprecedented in scale and duration and distinguished beyond all previous conflicts by its debasement of that code of honour, justice, and voluntary restraint by whose tenets all prior strife among Hellenes had been conducted. It was indeed this war, the first modern war, which forged our narrator's destiny and directed it to its end. He began as a soldier and ended as an assassin. How was I any different? Who may disaffirm that I or any other did not enact in the shadows of our private hearts, by commission or omission, that same dark history played out in daylight by our countryman Polemides?

He was, like me, a product of our time. As, to the harbour, high road and low follow their several courses along the shore, so his path had paralleled my own and that of the main of our contemporaries, only passing through different country.

# THREE
## IN POLEMIDES' CELL

YOU ASK, JASON [*THE PRISONER POLEMIDES SPOKE*], WHICH ASPECT IS most distasteful of the assassin's art. Knowing you as the paragon of probity you are, you no doubt anticipate some response involving bloodguilt or ritual pollution, perhaps some physical difficulty of the kill. It is neither. The hardest part is bringing back the head.

You have to, to get paid.

Telamon of Arcadia, my mentor in the profession of murder, taught me to pack it in olive oil and bring it home in a jar. In the early days of the war such proof was not required. A ring might do, or an amulet, or so my tutor apprised me later, as at that time I had not yet commenced employment in the 'silent art', but served as a common soldier like everyone else. The assassin's requirements grew sterner as the war dragged on. Those victims who got the chance invariably pleaded, some quite eloquently, for their lives. For my part I considered it dishonourable, not to say bad business, to yield to such blandishments. I honoured my commitments.

I see you smile, Jason. You must remember I was not always a villain. My family counted among its ancestors the hero Philaeus, Ajax's son, forebear of Miltiades and Cimon, he to whom the rights of the city were granted with his brother Eurysaces, from whom Alcibiades claimed descent. My father was a Knight of Meleager and bred racehorses, a number of exceptional lineage, including the mare Briareia, who was the pole horse on Alcibiades' team when it won the crown at Olympia, the year of his magnificent triple, when Euripides himself sang the victory ode. We were good people. People of quality.

That said, I make no pretence to innocence of Alcibiades' assassination or any other charge. But these scoundrels aren't after me for that, are they? They're still too happy to see him dead. Men hate nothing worse than that mirror held before them whose reflection displays their own failure to prove worthy of themselves. This likewise is your master's crime, Socrates the philosopher. He will suck hemlock for it. My own transgressions, I fear, remain unsullied by such aspirations to honour.

This murder charge, I say, the one of that luckless fellow Philemon . . . of this I'm innocent. It was an accident! Ask anyone who saw it.

But listen to me beg for my life! I sound like every other lying swine in here. [Laughs.] If I had gold in the yard, I'd dig it up. Yes, and have your way with my wife and daughters as well! [Laughs again.]

But hear me, Jason. I appreciate your coming. I am aware of the demands upon you from other quarters and grateful for your time. I know you despise, if not me, then my transgressions. As for my chances of acquittal, the betting man will long since have purchased the shovel to dig my grave. Yet remain, I beseech you. Track with me the course of this man I am said to have slain and our intertwined fates – yours, mine, and our nation's.

If I am guilty, Athens is too. What did I perform, save what she desired? As the city loved him, so did I. As she hated him, I did too. Let us tell that story, of the spell he cast over our state and how that bewitchment led us to ruin, all in the same basket. As I plead for my life like the dog I am, perhaps we may dig up some gold in the yard, the treasure of insight and illumination. What do you say, Jason? Will you assist me? Will you help a villain explore the provenance of his villainy?

# FOUR
# ORDEAL AND COMMISSION

WHEN I WAS TEN, MY FATHER SENT ME FOR MY SCHOOLING TO Sparta. This was far from unheard-of in the decades before the war, when fellow feeling still prevailed between the two great states by whose allied exertions Greece had been preserved from the Persian yoke. Periodic clashes and conflicts notwithstanding, the dominant disposition towards Sparta among the Athenian gentry was respect. Many of the older landed families, not alone of our city but of Greece entire, shared bonds of guest-friendship with clans at Sparta; such gentlefolk often felt keener kinship for their kind across borders than for the commons of their own states, whose increasing stridency and self-assertion threatened not only to overturn the old courtly ways but to coarsen and corrupt the rising generation of youth. What more satisfactory inoculation for these striplings, their fathers reasoned, than a turn or two in the Spartan *agoge*, the Upbringing, where a lad learned the old-fashioned virtues of silence, continence, and obedience?

Among my father's forebears were the Athenian heroes Miltiades and Cimon, the latter esteemed by the Spartans little less than their own kings, which affection Cimon returned in abundance, naming his eldest son Lacedaemonius, who himself trained at Sparta, though only to age sixteen. Through such ties and by his own exertions my father succeeded in enrolling his firstborn among that handful of foreigners permitted to 'stand, steal, and starve' beside their Lacedaemonian counterparts. Some twenty or thirty of us *anepsioi*, 'cousins', trekked in each year from all Greece, taking our places among the seven hundred homegrowns. Alcibiades himself, though he did not train at Lacedaemon, was *xenos*, guest-friend, of the Spartan knight Endius (who would stand present in Asia to oversee his friend's assassination). Endius's father was named Alcibiades, a Lacedaemonian name which alternated in both families. My own father's name, Nicolaus, is Laconian, as was mine at birth, Polemidas, but whose pronunciation and spelling I Atticized upon enlistment.

I was nineteen when war began, at Sparta, one season short of that commencement called O and C, Ordeal and Commission, the accession granted to non-Lacedaemonians, equivalent to initiation into the Corps of Peers for citizens, the Spartiatai, and their 'stepbrother' comrades, the *mothakes*.

Few believed then that the war would last more than a season. True, Athenian troops were in action, besieging Potidaea, but this was strictly an internal affair between Athens and one of her subject states, however vocally the latter might squeal, and did not violate the Peace. It was not Sparta's ox being gored. The Spartan army, egged on by her allies, had indeed invaded Attica in retaliation, yet so lightly was this regarded that I without demurral participated in the make-up of the two line divisions, to be reinforced by twenty thousand heavy infantry of Sparta's Peloponnesian allies, which comprised the invasion brigades. All the foreign boys helped too. We thought nothing of it. The army would march in, raise hell, and march out, to be succeeded by some form of negotiated settlement by autumn or winter. The idea that we lads in schooling might be sent home was never even broached.

It was on the eve of the Gymnopaedia, the Festival of the Naked Boys, that I learned my father's estate had been burned. I had been elected an *eirenos*, a youth-captain, and this night took charge for the first time of my own platoon of boys. We were at choral practice, just setting up, when one of the lads, a particularly bright youth named Philoteles, advanced in the scrupulous manner prescribed by the laws, eyes down, hands beneath his cloak, and sought permission to address me. His father, Cleander, was with the army in Attica and had sent a message home. He knew our farm. We had welcomed him as a guest more than once.

'Please convey to Polemidas my extreme regret,' Cleander's letter stated, employing my Laconian name. 'I exerted all influence I possessed to prevent this action, but the district had been selected by Archidamus, prompted by the omens. One farm could not be spared when all others were torched.'

I applied at once for an interview with my commander Phoebidas, the brother of Gylippus, whose leadership in Sicily, scores of thousands of deaths later, was to prove of such calamitous effect against our forces. Should I return or complete my passage to initiation? Phoebidas was a gentleman of virtue, a throwback to a nobler age. After much deliberation, including taking of the dream omens at Oeum, it was decided that duty to the gods of hearth and fatherland superseded all conflicting obligations. I must go home.

I trekked to Acharnae, a hundred and forty miles in four days, without even a dog to accompany my steps, oblivious of the sequence of sorrows of which this blow was the precursor. I expected to find vines and groves blackened by fire, walls toppled, crops laid waste. This, as you know, Jason, is no calamity. The grapes and olives spring back, and nothing can kill the land.

I arrived at my father's farm, Road's Turn, during the hours of darkness. It looked bad, but nothing could prepare me for the devastation which greeted my eyes at daybreak. Archidamus's men had not simply scorched vineyard and grove but sheared the living plants to the nub. They had poured lime into the open stumps and spread this brew across every square yard of field. The house was ashes, and the cottages and barns. All stock had been slaughtered. They had even killed the cats.

What kind of war was this? What manner of king was Archidamus to countenance such depredation? I was enraged; more so my younger brother Demades, whom we called Little Lion, when at last I located him in the city. Eluding our father by whose command he was to maintain his study of music and mathematics, he had enlisted in the regiment of Aegeis, outside our tribe and under false papers. My two younger uncles and all six cousins had joined their companies. I signed as well.

The war had begun. In the far north the Potidaeans, emboldened by the vigorousness of the Spartan incursion into Attica, had enlarged their revolt from our empire. A hundred ships and ninety-five hundred Athenian and Macedonian troops held them besieged. Alcibiades, the most illustrious youth of our generation, had mustered already. Too impatient to wait for his twentieth birthday and the cavalry trials, he had shipped as a common infantryman with the Second Eurysaces, that company which his guardian, Pericles, had claimed as his first command. When weather and the close of sailing season threatened to strand the last of our unembarked Acharnian companies, we were piggy-backed onto the penteconters of this unit. We sailed on the eighth of Pyanopsion, Theseus day, into a howling northerly.

Of the hundreds of passages I have endured in subsequent seasons, this was the worst. No mast was even stepped; sail was broken out only as weather-cover, pitifully inadequate, against the seas which pounded over the bows daylong onto the exposed backs and shoulders of us, serving as oarsmen as well as infantry, bereft of refuge in the undecked galleys. It took eighteen days to get to Torone, whereupon our Acharnian companies and those of Scambonidae were conjoined under the Athenian general Paches and, reinforced by two troops of Macedonian cavalry, sent back the way we had come, by sea, with orders to capture and occupy the Perrhaebian fortresses at Colydon and Madrete.

These sites were unknown to me, as was the region entire; I felt as one washed up at the extremities of earth. Surely such weather could prevail only at the verges of Tartarus. We made south, twenty-two ships – among whose companies now stood my brother, 'making the skip' from his original regiment – packed with puking neophytes greener even than ourselves, while enemy cavalry tracked the flotilla's progress from shore, barring all attempts at landing. Alcibiades was aboard our ship, the *Hygeia*. He had made a nasty name for himself by assigning his turn at oars to his attendant (when none other younger than twenty-five even dreamt of such extravagance) while he himself monitored the convoy's passage more like a fleet commander than an untried shield-humper like the rest. About his shoulders he wore a black woollen cloak with the design of an eagle in silver, of such superb workmanship that its worth could be no less than a year's pay for a colonel. Every item of his kit was the finest, and his looks . . . well, you know these as well as I. One was torn between jealousy, for all knew well of his wealth and lovers, and awe, that any of flesh could be so spectacularly gifted by heaven. For three days the squadron alternately ran before, then beat into, a gale which the locals described as 'moderate' but which to me was in-distinguishable from the hoarblast of hell. At last at the third sunset a storm of murderous ferocity struck. Paches' flagship signalled all vessels to make for shore, enemy be damned.

Do you know that headland, Jason, called the Blacksmith's Bellows? Its sound once heard may never be forgotten. The swifter vessels fetched the lee; those lumbering pots, as our own, were driven in and nearly dashed. The sole landing site was a splinter of gravel, walled on three sides by two-hundred-foot cliffs, and defended across its solitary channel of ingress by stone promontories exploding with white water and boom-ing beneath the thunder of storm-pounded surf. Only after a struggle titanic in its exertions and sustained throughout the terrifying descent of darkness did our severed remnant, six ships, succeed in beaching upon that site called the Boilers, a strand so slender that the vessels' prows (beaching stern-first being out of the question in such a tempest) were staring straight into the face of rock. Waves taller than a man crashed about their sternposts, seeking to suck them back into the sea. To augment the hospitality of the place, the foe had got above us, at the summit of a precipice too sheer to scale, and begun raining boulders and initiating rockslides. Two of six ships were holed at once, nor could the youths of our force be induced to respond to orders to preserve the others, but crouched in clefts at the base of the fall, drenched and dread-stricken.

Command had broken down. Paches and the Athenian officers had been swept beyond the headland; it took an eternity to determine the ranking senior of our shredded squadron, a captain of Macedonian infantry it turned out, and he, overcome by the extremity, had retreated to a cave at the cliff base, from whose shelter he could not be drawn.

Upon the strand boulders plummeted like hail. With each ship holed, our extinction became more certain; the enemy would simply close from above and take us down with stone and shaft. Beside *Hygeia*, a horse transport had broached to. A number of the beasts thrashed in the surf, drowning; two who had made land had been struck by rockfalls and back-broken; their cries unstrung the rookie troops further. The vessel herself pitched among the breakers, secured only by bow and stern lines, each manned by twenty lads, frantic themselves and buffeted chest-deep in the maelstrom. Alcibiades and his cousin Euryptolemus had hurled themselves into this rescue. I found my brother Lion; we joined too. After monumental exertions the transport was at last beached. Without a word Alcibiades had become our commander. He strode off, seeking a senior officer to report to, ordering the rest of us to follow as soon as the horses had been secured ashore.

The gale continued to scour the landing beach. Boulders plummeted from above; concussions of thunder never ceased. My brother and I had just reached the brow of the strand, seeking the command post; we could see Alcibiades ahead, addressing the Macedonian captain. Suddenly this officer struck him with his staff. We dashed forward. Even amid the cacophony of storm and surf, the content of the confrontation was clear: Alcibiades demanding orders, the captain incapable of giving them. He wheeled upon the youth, twenty years his junior, whose family and reputation he knew, as we all. 'Your kinsman Pericles is not here, young man, nor may you presume to dictate in his name!'

'I speak in my own and that of these who will perish, absent your deliverance,' Alcibiades rejoined. His gesture took in ships, gale, and the rain of rubble which continued to pelt from the enemy above. 'Take action, sir, or by Heracles I will!'

Only two fifties remained unholed. Alcibiades struck for them. The captain was shouting, commanding him to stay put and threatening hell if he disobeyed. The youth bawled no defiance, simply strode on; and we, my brother and two score others, followed in his train as if drawn by fetters of adamant. At breakers' brink he issued orders. No-one could hear a word. Yet we seized oars and launched into the teeth, ten at each bank, without even stepping the steering oars, so worthless were they in that sea. How the ships got off without loss of life I cannot say. What preserved the party, beyond heaven's clemency, can only have been the beaminess of the craft and the quantity of seas shipped as unintended ballast. Of four pulls at oars, only one found purchase. Gale-driven chop hammered the hull like a siege engine, while swells twice the vessels' length made them race like runaways. Plummeting into a trough, the bows nosed under, sending seas cascading into the bilges; ascending from a crest, the gale struck upon the exposed keel, elevating the vessels vertical as vine stakes. At oars we were literally standing on the thwarts of our comrades aft.

Somehow the two fifties managed to pull a half mile to sea. The lads communicated like dogs, by cries rendered mute in the blast; yet one understood the object: to make the first northward landing, scale the face, and get behind the foe.

Now Alcibiades rowed, with such a will as to impel all to emulation; his orders, shouted man-to-man down the banks, were to run into shore any way possible, taking no care for the vessels but only to land ourselves. The crest that bore us in unspooled with such velocity as to fling all bodily from their benches. We plunged over the gunwales. I was knocked senseless by the fall, coming to myself among breakers, shield filling with the weight of the seas, which hauled me under with a violence unimaginable. My forearm, seated through the sleeve to the elbow, bound me as a shackle; only the rivets' failure, wrenched from their sockets by the press of turbulence, loosed me to breach the surface. A boy drowned before my eyes, dragged under in the same way. On the strand our remnant collected, shattered with exhaustion and bereft, all, of shields and weapons. Both boats were splinters. Lads shook as if palsied, blue to the bone.

One turned to Alcibiades. Drenched and weaponless as he was, and quaking as convulsively as we others, yet he revelled in this. No other phrase may describe it. To the lads unnerved by the ships' loss he responded that had the vessels not sunk of their own, he would have ordered them holed and scuttled. 'Banish all thought of retreat, brothers. No avenue remains but to advance, and no alternative save victory or death.' He ordered count, and when three were discovered missing, drowned, he commanded our remainder to give meaning to their sacrifice. What we lacked accounted nothing beside the audacity of our stroke. 'Want of weapons is no liability in this dark. Our sudden apparition in the enemy's rear will be weapon enough. The foe will flee from the shock of our assault alone.'

Alcibiades drove us up the face. He was a horseman and knew in this wet that the enemy, being cavalry, would seek before all to get his mounts under cover. We were not lost, he repeated, however black the tempest, but must only follow the brink, employing heaven's bolts as our beacon, till we discovered such a site. Of course he was right. A crag appeared. There they were. We fell upon the enemy's grooms with stones and clubs and the shivered shafts of our oars. In moments our commander had us mounted and pounding along the precipice in dark as total as the tomb. At the crest the main of the foe fled, as Alcibiades had predicted. We chased a dozen into the fells, myself desperate to strip the shield from one. For the Spartan-trained, death was preferable to return from action, even victorious, empty-handed.

Here the first man fell beneath my blow. A plunge among rocks; I heard his skull crack on the stone in the dark. My brother dragged me off him, seeking to strip breastplate as well as shield. I was mad with the joy of my own survival and felt myself invincible, as so many young soldiers who in such states commit acts of barbarity. Lion hauled me back to the precipice. Our party had collected, masters of the site. We had won! Below, our troops cheered their deliverance. The face of the cliff had been roped, I saw; several from the strand had mounted and now stood before us. I recognized the Macedonian captain. He was berating Alcibiades, vehemently and with malice.

He declared the youth reckless and insubordinate, a disgrace to his country and the order of the Alliance. Three are dead by his defiance, two ships lost for his usurpation of command! Where are your shields and weapons? Do you know the penalty for their deficit? The captain's eyes blazed. He would see Alcibiades hauled up on charges of mutiny, if not treason, and by Zeus dance upon his grave!

Three Macedonian warrant officers, the captain's compatriots, reinforced him at arms. Alcibiades' expression never altered, awaiting only the harangue's termination.

'One must not make such a speech,' he declared, 'with one's back to the precipice.'

I will resist overdramatizing the moment, but report only that the three henchmen, considering their position, seized their commander and executed his precipitation.

The rest of us, who had just experienced for the first time in our young lives such a baptism of terror – and over such a sustained interval as we had never imagined – now discovered ourselves confronted with an even more extreme exigency. What would become of us? Surely those below must report Alcibiades' action. We were accessories. Would we not be tried as murderers? Would our names be blackened, our families shamed and dishonoured? Would we be returned to Athens in chains to await execution?

At once Alcibiades stepped to the three Macedonians, setting a hand

P69,837

on their shoulders to assure them he harboured no malign intent. Might they inform him, he enquired, of the name and clan of their fallen captain?

'You will prepare the following despatch,' Alcibiades commanded. He proceeded to dictate the text of a commendation for valour. Each act of heroism which he had himself performed, he now credited to the captain. He recited this officer's valour in the face of overwhelming peril; how he had, disregarding his own safety, put out into the storm, scaled the sheer face of stone to envelop and rout the enemy, preserving by his actions the ships and men of his company below. At the summit of triumph, as his sword slew the foe's commander, cruel fortune over-hauled him. He fell. 'The fame of this action,' Alcibiades concluded, 'shall endure, imperishable.'

This despatch would be sent, Alcibiades declared further, to the captain's father and presented personally by himself to Paches and the generals of Macedonia upon our squadron's return. He turned then to us youths, including Lion and myself, looking on.

'Which of you, brothers, will set his hand beneath mine on this citation?'

Need I recount, none failed to assent.

As to our unofficial company of infantry, it succeeded, reunited with the brigade under Paches, in its mission over a month and more of fight-ing, during which Alcibiades at nineteen, though by no means officially in command, was in fact deferred to by all superiors and permitted such latitude of action and initiative as to render him effectively its captain. When this unit at last reached Potidaea, our original destination, and joined the line troops engaged in the siege, it was disbanded as non-chalantly as it had been formed, and Alcibiades, undecorated but unindicted, was repatriated to his regiment.

It was my brother's observation regarding this incident that, though he, and I as well, served in subsequent seasons beside a number of the young men present at the precipice in that hour and had ample opportunity of converse, formal and informal, on this or any subject, never did one offer mention of this instance or confirm by word or allusion the actuality of its occurrence.

# FIVE
# THE INDISPENSABLE MAN

AT THE SIEGE OF POTIDAEA TWO YOUNG MEN ESTABLISHED themselves as indispensable: Alcibiades and my brother. By his bearing both in action and in counsel it had become patent that the former was

> *pre-eminent of hero's fire,*
> *without rival among the host.*

Within all the corps he was acknowledged the most brilliant and audacious, possessed of the most abundant genius of war. At Athens his fields of enterprise had been limited by youth to sport and seduction. Campaign overturned this, granting him a sphere commensurate to his gifts. Overnight he came into his own. It was deemed by no few that he, though not yet twenty, could have been elevated to supreme command and not only prosecuted the siege with greater vigour and sagacity but brought it to a successful conclusion with far less loss of life.

As to my brother, he had made his name among the hard heads and raw knots of the corps. Experience teaches that however numerous the brigade or army, the work of war is performed by small units, and each must possess to be effective one man like Lion who is unacquainted with fear, who arises cheerful each morning despite all hardship, ready to shoulder another's load with a laugh and turn his hand to all tasks, however mean or humble. A unit lacking a man like Lion will never endure, while one with such a mate may be beaten but never broken.

Our father's letters caught up to us at Potidaea. We were summoned, Lion and I, to the tent of Paches' adjutant, a captain of Aexone whose name I cannot recall. The officer read aloud two pleas of our father, confirming my brother's age at sixteen years three months and pleading for his immediate discharge, with a pledge to pay all fines and fees of transport. 'What have you to say, young man?' our captain demanded.

Lion straightened to his full height, such as it was, and swore by the waters of Styx that his years were not only twenty but twenty-three. Our father, he testified, though well-meaning, had come unhinged following the devastation of our district and now feared, understandably, the loss of his sons; thus this appeal from Athens, presented with such touching and plausible conviction. When the captain summoned witnesses from our home district who testified to the truth of the letter, Lion refused to buckle. It was not age that made a soldier, but passion and heart! Our commander cut him short. I have never seen one so inconsolable as Lion; the sight was almost comical of him slouching aboard the galley home.

Responsibility for my brother's misdemeanour fell upon me, as it should, his elder. I was fined three months' pay and banished from line duty, assigned command of a platoon of boys, foresters. We were issued not arms but axes and packed off with the mules and logging sledges.

You were at Potidaea, Jason. I remember you. You came in with Eurymedon in the terminal spring, the squadrons bearing the relief parties of the cavalry and the replacements for the assault troops carried off by the plague. You were lucky. You missed the winter.

Winter in our fathers' time was the off-season. Who even dreamt of fighting in the snow and ice? Summer was the time of war; in Sparta men didn't even have a word for summer; they called it *strateiorion*, campaigning season. But a siege cannot be prosecuted in sunshine only. Thus a new calendar for a new kind of war.

It was a porous siege. On the line the troops had more intercourse with the enemy than with their own countrymen. We sold food and firewood; the Potidaeans traded treasure. Gold first, then jewellery and linen. They sold their armour and their swords. From midwinter they were peddling their daughters.

By the gods, it was cold up there. Piss steamed on the air and turned to ice before it hit the dirt. To dress in armour made the skin peel in patches where it touched the freezing bronze. The glory of dying for one's country lost whatever pale lustre it had possessed, especially to succumb to plague or pestilence or some perverse mischance, a blind-luck bowshot lobbed from a battlement, only to have the campaign decided in spring by treaty and everyone suddenly allies again. We camped there, frozen and miserable, while the city of the Potidaeans loomed at the neck of the promontory, frozen and miserable as we.

The three northern gates, those that gave out upon the landward side, stood barred only in daylight. With nightfall they became avenues of skimmers, scavengers, and scum. You could see their tracks in the snow, broad as boulevards. Our company was commanded by a bribe-commissioned captain named Gnossos. Here is what we did. For every eight trees logged, we turned over four to the army; the other four went to the foe. They paid our captain in women. Not whores but respectable wives and daughters of the city. They were ploughing us for firewood. I refused to permit my lads to take part in these orgies, in which it was not uncommon for one female to service a dozen men before returning through and under the walls to the city. Such degeneracy, countenanced by their superior, would debase what little warrior spirit these striplings possessed. In addition, overscrupulous as this may sound from a man of my subsequent deeds, I could not bear to witness the ravagement of person this commerce inflicted on the women themselves.

I was hauled up for this. Behind my back my bucks began calling me 'the Spartan'. It was put about that I sided secretly with the foe and that my prudish intransigence was not only undermining the morale of youth but, defying as it did my commander's ordinance, was at best insubordination and at worst treason. In a clash with my captain the word 'procurer' escaped my lips. I was cashiered.

I went for aid to Alcibiades. The army had engaged the enemy in full strength that autumn, an attempted breakout in force requiring the mobilization of our entire corps; Alcibiades had distinguished himself in this action and in fact been awarded the prize of valour, judged the bravest of the six thousand upon the field. It took several months for the crown and suit of armour to be delivered. In fact he had just received the former this evening when I approached. He was celebrating with his tentmates.

Any encampment massed upon one site for a prolonged interval becomes, as you know, Jason, a city of its own. Its market becomes the agora, its training fields the gymnasium. The *polis*, battling boredom, throws up its own diversions and distractions, its characters and its clowns. There is a good part of town and a bad, a neighbourhood one enters at his peril and a precinct of privilege and fame, which exercises its spell over all. Invariably one tent establishes itself for the brilliance of its occupants as the epicentre of the camp.

Alcibiades' tent, Aspasia Three (the main streets of the seven fortified camps ringing the city had been named each after a famed courtesan of Athens), had become this nexus. This was in consequence not alone of his celebrity but of the wit and converse of his tentmates, who included in their number of sixteen your own master Socrates (renowned then less as a philosopher than a doughty and stalwart campaigner, forty years of age), the celebrated actor Alcaeus, Mantitheus the Olympic boxer, and Acumenus the physician. These fellows were the most fun. Everyone wanted to be with them. An invitation to dine at Aspasia Three was more highly prized than a decoration. For that reason I had avoided Alcibiades, not wishing to push myself uninvited upon him and also because I judged the status of our friendship to be cordial but remote.

Now, however, the gravity of my situation compelled me to come forward. I waited till that hour when the evening meal would be concluded, then hiked the mile to Aspasia Camp, seeking only a few moments of Alcibiades' time, perhaps to speak to him outside the tent and get him to put in a word for me with the brass. I had thought I could simply rap at the post and get it over with.

To my surprise, and in contrast to the other snug-battened precincts of the camp whose lanes stood dark and vacated save the odd trooper dashing from one shelter to another in the cold, the court fronting Alcibiades' tent burned bright with torch and brazier, the intersection of the lanes milling gaily with a motley of off-duty officers and infantrymen, wine sellers, jugglers, sweets bakers, a party of acrobats in midperformance upon a stage of logs, and a professional fool, not to mention a number of gap-toothed trollops from the whores' camp, loitering in high spirits. The aroma of spitted meat augmented the cheer; bonfires blazed upon the earth, which had thawed and was churned by the press of celebrants. As I wedged through the crush, the tent flaps parted and there emerged to the air the most dazzling specimen of womankind I had ever seen.

Her hair was russet; her eyes of such violet they seemed to flash like diadems in the torchlight. She was mantled crown to toe in sable and escorted by two cavalry officers, six-footers, clad in the ermine-fringed cloaks of the enemy. Of the besiegers none attempted to lay hands upon them; in fact our lads drew the party's mounts before them, boosting them onto the horses' backs. The lady trotted off not in the direction of the city, but up the slope towards that bluff called the Asclepium where, I later learned, a cottage of spruce had been erected for her use and her bodyguards'.

'That's Cleonice,' a fried-onion vendor volunteered. 'Alcibiades' girl.'

I would doubtless have remained marooned on the doorstep all night had not my host's cousin Euryptolemus chanced to pass, seeking the tent, and, recognizing me, tugged me forward. He informed me in merry spirits that the gentlewoman Cleonice was the wife of Machaon, the wealthiest citizen of Potidaea. Alcibiades had initiated a liaison with the lady, seeking through her husband to facilitate the betrayal of the town from within. 'Now she's fallen in love with him and refuses to go home. She even claims to be carrying his child. What can one do?'

Euryptolemus, whom his companions called Euro, instructed me to wait while he ducked inside. Moments later I heard Alcibiades' laughter; the flaps parted and I found myself tugged clear of the mob and welcomed to the warmth within. 'Pommo, my friend, where have you been keeping yourself? Not alone in the woods with those innocent boys!'

Alcibiades, I was informed, had appointed himself master of revels. He sat upon the bench of honour, with his crown before him, cheeks flushed with wine. He had been wounded; beneath his tunic one could see his wrapped ribs. He introduced me as his mate of the Boilers and ordered a seat and a bowl of wine. He had heard of my troubles. 'Is it true you called your commander a pimp?'

My arrival had interrupted a discourse; I sought to deflect attention from myself and let the talk resume. The party would not hear of it. I was asked by the Olympian Mantitheus to state my objections to a little harmless fornication. I replied that such acts were far from innocuous, but degraded the morale of the youths in my charge.

'I have a younger sister, Meri,' I found myself saying with passion. 'I would eviscerate the man who so much as laid a hand on her garment absent my father's leave. How then may I stand by and watch other maidens despoiled, even the daughters of the enemy?'

This elicited an ironic chorus of 'Hear, hear.' To my surprise the advocate who sprang to my defence was Alcibiades. His posture was greeted with amusement both wry and derisive, which he endured with good nature. 'You may laugh, gentlemen, to hear me, whose reputation as a seducer of women is not inconsequential, take up the cudgels on behalf of the fair gender. But I of all may claim to know how it feels to be female.'

He paused and, turning to me, declared that I must set aside all concern regarding the charges lodged against me. Strings would be pulled. For now I must drink, not moderately as the Spartans, but deep, Athenian-style, so as to overhaul the company which had got the start of me. Otherwise, my host asserted, the jests would not seem as droll or the discourse as profound. He turned to his companions and resumed.

'Consider, my friends, that a beautiful youth is much like a woman. He is paid court to, flattered, celebrated for virtues he does not yet possess, and in general acclaimed for qualities which are not of his own making but accidents of birth. And do not you smile, Socrates, for this is much to the point of that matter upon which you were presently discoursing. I mean the disparity between the true self of the political man and the *mythos* he must project to participate in public life. I was stating, nor did you impeach its veracity, that I or any other who enters politics must be two: Alcibiades, whom my friends know, and "Alcibiades", that fictive personality who is a stranger to me but whose fame I must fuel and fashion if my influence is to prevail in the arena of policy.

'A beautiful woman is in the same dilemma. She cannot but perceive herself as two creatures – the private soul known to her intimates and that external proxy presented to the world by her good looks. The attention she receives may be gratifying to her vanity, but it is empty and she knows it. She comes to resemble those urchins during the Festival of Theseus who wheel painted barrows with bulls' horns on the front. She recognizes that her admirers love her not for herself, that is, the wheeler, but for that fancy she wheels before her. This is the definition of degradation. It is why, gentlemen, I came very young to despise those suitors who paid court to me. I recognized even as a child that it was not myself they loved. They sought only the surface, and for reasons of their own vanity.'

'And yet,' Mantitheus the boxer put in, 'you do not rebuff the advances of our comrade Socrates, nor reject the friendship of ourselves, the remainder of this company.'

'That is because you are my true friends, Mantitheus. Even were my face as punched-up as your own, you would still love me.'

Alcibiades endeavoured to induce Socrates to resume his dissertation on that subject which my arrival had interrupted, but before he could, the actor Alcaeus returned the topic to the shamed women of Potidaea.

'Let us not employ lightly, gentlemen, the word "degradation". War is degradation. Its object is the ultimate degradation – death. These women have not been slain. Their bruises of the flesh will heal.'

'You surprise me, my excellent friend,' Alcibiades replied. 'As an actor you of all people should know that death takes many and far more evil forms than the physical. Isn't that what tragedy is all about? Consider Oedipus, Clytemnestra, Medea. Their wounds would heal as well. Yet were they not ruined utterly from within?'

Mantitheus spoke. 'If you ask me, it is not these women who suffer true debasement, but their fathers and brothers who permit them to be used in this hateful manner. These men possess options. They could starve. They could fight and die. In truth these young women are heroes. Consider that when a man risks all in defence of his country, he is crowned for valour. Are not these girls the same? Are they not sacrificing their most cherished possessions, their maidenhood and name of virtue, to succour their beleaguered countrymen? What if, when spring comes, their confederates the Spartans at last get off their arses and trek here to their aid? What if it is ourselves who are routed? By the gods, the Potidaeans should erect statues to these brave girls! In fact, taken in this light, our young gentleman here' (he indicated myself) 'is not delivering these noble lasses from shame, but denying them their shot at immortality.'

Laughter and choruses of 'Again, again' greeted this, accompanied by raps of wine bowl bottoms upon the wooden crates and trunks which served as tables for the banquet.

'But wait,' Alcibiades broke in, 'I see our friend Socrates smiling. He is about to speak. In all conscience we must warn our comrade Polemides, or perhaps as Odysseus approaching the Isle of the Sirens stopper his ears with wax. For once exposed to the sweet discourse of our friend, he will find himself enslaved for ever, as are we all.'

'You make sport of me as usual, Alcibiades,' the man Socrates declared. 'Must I endure such abuse, gentlemen, coming from this fellow who of all ignores my counsel, attending only to his own pursuit of popularity?'

Socrates the son of Sophroniscus sat across from me. Of all assembled, his appearance was far the least prepossessing. He was stocky, thick-lipped and pug-nosed, already at forty quite bald, and his cloak, blood-besmirched yet from a skirmish earlier in the month, was of a cloth coarse and pecunious as a Spartan's.

The men began chaffing him about an incident of several days prior. Apparently Socrates, standing outside in the bitter cold, had been seized midmorning with some enigma or perplexity. There he remained, in open sandals on the ice, pondering the issue daylong to the marvel of all who beheld him, themselves shivering indoors with their feet swathed in fleeces. The soldiers peeped out at intervals; there Socrates remained. It was not until nightfall that, his puzzlement resolved, he abandoned his self-imposed post and decamped to the fire for supper. Led by Alcibiades, the party demanded now to hear what riddle had with such tenacity occupied their friend's mind.

'We were speaking of degradation,' Socrates began. 'Of what does this consist? Is it not that apprehension of an individual according to a solitary quality, to the exclusion of all the manifold facets of his soul and being, then using him or her thereby? In the case of these unhappy women, that quality is their flesh and its utility in gratifying our own base desires. We dismiss all else that renders them human, descended of the gods.

'Note further, gentlemen, that this single quality by which we convict these women and sentence them to exile from humanity is one over which they themselves possess no authority, a quality thrust upon them willy-nilly at birth. This is the antithesis of freedom, is it not? It is the use one makes of a slave. We treat even our dogs and horses better, granting to them their subtleties and contradictions of character and esteeming or contemning them thereby.'

Socrates drew up and enquired of the company if any found fault with his meditation thus far. He was endorsed by all and exhorted to continue.

'And yet we who consider ourselves free men often act in this manner not only towards others but towards ourselves as well. We account and define our persons by qualities gifted to or deprived us at birth, to the exclusion of those earned or acquired thereafter, brought into being by enterprise and will. This to my mind is an evil greater than degradation. It is self-degradation.'

He glanced subtly towards Alcibiades. Our master of revels clearly discerned this look and returned it, amused and intrigued, and not without irony.

Socrates resumed. 'Pondering this state of self-slavery, I began to puzzle: what precisely are the qualities which make men free?'

'Our will, as you said,' put in Acumenus the physician.

'And the force to exercise it,' added Mantitheus.

'My thoughts precisely, gentlemen. You are running along with me, and even outpacing my poor ruminations. But what is free will? We must agree that nothing that does not possess free will may be called free. And that which is unfree is degraded; that is, diminished to a state lesser than that intended by the gods.'

'I think I see where this is going,' Alcibiades put in with a smile. 'I feel chastisement coming, gentlemen, of myself and us all.'

'Shall I break off?' Socrates enquired. 'Perhaps our master of revels is fatigued, worn out from heroism and the adulation of his peers.'

The company urged their comrade to recommence.

'I was observing the young soldiers of the camp. Conformity to the norm is their overmastering impetus, is it not? Each unprompted wears his curls like every other, drapes his hem to the same length, and strides about and even postures in the identical attitude. Inclusion in the hierarchy is all; exclusion the paramount fear.'

'This doesn't sound much like freedom,' volunteered Acumenus.

'It sounds like democracy,' put in Euryptolemus with a laugh.

'Would you agree, gentlemen, that these youths, tyrannized by the good opinion of their peers, do not possess freedom?'

All concurred.

'In fact they are slaves, are they not? They act not by the dictates of their own hearts, but to please others. There are two words for this. Demagoguery. And fashion.'

The company responded with whistles and cheers. 'To whose dictates you, Socrates, are mercifully immune,' declared Alcibiades.

'No doubt with my poor cloak and sword-barbered beard I am perceived throughout the camp as a figure of fun. Yet I maintain that, unfettered by the constraints of the mode, I am the most free of men.'

Socrates expanded his metaphor to include the Assembly at Athens. 'Does there exist beneath heaven a spectacle more debased than that of a demagogue orating before the masses? Each syllable screeches of shamelessness, and why? Because we discern, hearing this vile wretch pimp himself to the multitude, that his speech springs not from the true conviction of his soul, but is crafted cunningly to truckle to the whim of the mob. He seeks his own advancement by their favour and will say anything, however wicked or infamous, to promote his stature in their eyes. In other words the politician is the supreme slave.'

Alcibiades was thoroughly enjoying this give-and-take. 'In other words you would declare of me, my friend, that by pursuing politics I act the pimp and panderer, seeking to advance my station among my peers, and that by so doing, I neglect my nobler self in favour of my baser.'

'Is that what I would say?'

'Ah, but here I have you, Socrates! For what if a man seeks not to follow his peers, but to lead them? What if his speech proceeds not from the falsehoods of the flatterer, but from the truest precincts of his heart? Is that not the definition of a man of the *polis*, a politician? One who acts not for himself, but for his city?'

The conversation ran on with lively animation for most of the evening. I confess I did not, or could not, follow much of its twists and turns. At last, however, the discourse seemed to condense about one issue that the company had been debating before my arrival: could a man in a democracy be described as 'indispensable', and if so would this man merit dispensation beyond that of his lesser contemporaries?

Socrates took up his post on the side of the laws, which, however imperfect, he professed, command that all men stand equal before them. Alcibiades declared this preposterous and with a laugh claimed that his friend did not, and could not, believe it. 'In fact I nominate you beyond all, sir, as indispensable. I would sacrifice battalions to preserve your life, and so would every man at this table.'

A chorus of 'Again, again!' seconded this.

'Nor do I speak from affection only,' the younger man continued, 'but for the advantage of the state. For she needs you, Socrates, as her physician, to the tendance of her soul. Bereft of you, what shall become of her?'

The older man could not contain a laugh. 'You disappoint me, my friend, for I had hoped to discover love rather than politics sheltering beneath that devotion you so passionately proclaim. Yet let us not pass over this issue lightly, gentlemen, for at its heart lies matter which compels our most rigorous examination:

'Which takes precedence, do we believe, man or law? To set a man above the law is to negate law entire, for if the laws do not apply equally to all, they apply to none. To install one man upon such a promontory founds that flight of steps by which another may later ascend. In fact I suspect, don't you, brothers, that when our companion nominates myself as indispensable, his intent is to establish that precedent by which he may next anoint himself.'

Alcibiades, laughing, declared himself indeed indispensable. 'Were not Themistocles, Miltiades, Pericles indispensable? The state would lie in ruins without them. And let us not forget Solon, who gave us those laws in whose defence our friend stands with such steadfastness. Do not misunderstand me. I seek not to overturn law, but to adhere to it. To declare men "equal" would be absurd if it were not evil. In truth that argument which seeks to calumniate one man as "above the law" is false on its face, for that man, if he be Themistocles or Cimon, conforms by his actions to a higher law, whose name is Necessity. To impede in the name of "equality" the indispensable man is the folly of one ignorant of the workings of this god, who antedates Zeus and Cronos and Earth her-self and stands everlastingly as their, and our, lawgiver and progenitor.'

More laughter and rapping of wine bowls. Socrates was about to respond when a commotion interrupted from without. An overturned brazier had set the adjoining shelter alight; now all poured forth to assist in its extinguishment. The salon broke up. I found myself beside Alcibiades. He motioned to his groom to fetch horses. 'Come, Pommo, I'll escort you back to your camp.'

I secured the password of the changing watch and we set out into the cold. 'Well,' Alcibiades enquired when we had cleared the first line of pickets, 'what did you think of him, our Professor Baldpate?'

I replied that I could not quite make the man out. Sophists, I knew, grew rich from their fees. Yet Socrates, garbed as he was in homespun, appeared more like . . .

'A beggar?' Alcibiades laughed. 'That is because he scorns to profit from that which he pursues out of love. He would pay if he could; he considers himself not a teacher but a student. And I will tell you something else. My crown of valour . . . did you notice this night that I never set it, as one decorated ought, upon my head? This is because the prize rightly belongs to him, to our own coarsecloth master of discourse.'

Alcibiades related that at the height of the battle for which he had been honoured he had fallen, wounded and cut off, assailed on all sides by the enemy. 'Socrates alone came to my defence, dashing from safety to shelter me beneath his shield, until our comrades could rally and return with reinforcements. I argued vehemently that the prize belonged to him, but he persuaded the generals to award it to me, no doubt seeking to school my heart to aspire to forms of glory nobler than those of politics.'

We traversed the remainder of the crossing in silence. Beyond the battlements of the besieged city one discerned cookfire smoke.

'Do you mark that smell, Pommo?'

It was horseflesh.

'They're cooking their cavalry,' Alcibiades observed. 'By spring they will be done for, and they know it.'

At the foresters' camp Alcibiades made a show of his arrival, without words putting it clear to all that I stood in his esteem, and any who crossed me must deal with him. Sure enough, within ten days my commander received orders rotating him back to Athens, his replacement an officer with instructions to leave me free to run my platoon as I wished.

I dismounted now and handed the reins back up to my friend. 'What will you do with the rest of your evening?' he enquired.

I would write a letter to my sister. 'And you? Will you return to continue your discussions of philosophy?'

He laughed. 'What else?'

I watched him depart, trailing the companion horse. His track in the snow bore him back, however, not along the picket line towards Aspasia Three, but in ascent upon the slope called Asclepium to that cabin of spruce wherein awaited the lady Cleonice, she of the violet eyes.

# BOOK TWO

# THE LONG
# WALLS

# SIX

# A YOUNG MAN'S SPORT

THUS [GRANDFATHER RESUMED] CONCLUDED MY INITIAL INTERVIEW
with the assassin Polemides. I left him and made haste to Socrates. It
occurred to me crossing the Iron Court, which conjoined the wings of the
prison, that mention of this evening thirty years past might summon a smile
from our friend. In addition I was curious. Did Socrates recollect the young
soldier called Pommo? I decided against this, however, not wishing to further
burden one with so much already upon his mind. Also I imagined the crush of
friends and followers would prevent me from securing a moment apart with
our master.

When I arrived at his cell, however, I discovered him alone. The mode of
his execution had been established that day by the Eleven Administrators
of Justice: he must take hemlock. Though this method mercifully spared the
flesh from mutilation, its pronouncement this day, bringing home as it did
the imminence of our master's end, had cast his friends into such a state that
Socrates had been constrained to banish them, only to secure an interval of
peace. Of this the warder informed me on my approach. I anticipated a similar
dismissal and was relieved to see Socrates rising, motioning me warmly within.
'So, Jason, are you coming from your other client?'

He knew all about Polemides. Indeed he recalled the youth, he confirmed,
not alone from that evening of the siege but from subsequent service with the
infantry, and by report from Alcibiades' days of triumph in the East, in which
Polemides had served as captain of marines. Our master remarked upon the

conjunction of these two defendants, the philosopher sentenced for schooling Alcibiades and the assassin awaiting trial for slaying him. 'It would seem that a jury possessed of consistency must, having convicted the one, acquit the other. This bodes well,' he observed, 'for your client Polemides.'

At that time Socrates' summers had passed seventy, yet he appeared save his beard gone white and the noble amplitude of his girth much as Polemides described during the siege of Potidaea. His limbs stood hale and sturdy, his carriage vigorous and purposeful; it required scant imagination to picture the veteran snatching up shield and armour to advance once again into the fray.

Not surprisingly the philosopher evinced curiosity about his fellow inmate and even advanced counsel upon how best to defend him. 'It is too late to file a countersuit, a paragraphe, declaring his indictment unlawful, which of course it is. Perhaps a dike pseudomartyriou, a suit for false witness, which may be invoked up to the moment of the jury's vote.' He laughed. 'You see, my own ordeal has rendered me something of a jailhouse lawyer.'

We discussed the Amnesty, in place since the restoration of the democracy, which exempted all citizens from prosecution for crimes committed theretofore. 'Polemides' enemies have got around this cleverly, Socrates, by charging him with "wrongdoing". That rakes a lot of mud, and, as he admits, there is more than enough with which to tar him.' I narrated an abridged version of Polemides' story, what he had told me thus far.

'I knew several of his family,' Socrates remarked when this chronicle concluded. 'His father, Nicolaus, was a man of exceptional integrity, who perished in attendance upon the stricken during the Plague. And I enjoyed a cordial if chaste acquaintance with his great-aunt Daphne, who effectively ran the Board of Naval Governors through her second and third husbands. She was the first of the aristocratic ladies, in her widowhood, to conduct her affairs entirely on her own, with no male as kyrios or guardian, and not even a servant about the house.'

Our master expressed concern for Polemides' comfort. 'The heat is stifling on that side of the court, I hear. Please, Jason, take him this fruit, and that wine; I may imbibe no more, as they say it spoils the savour of hemlock.'

When the others returned with the evening, some measure of amusement was wrung from the coincident confinement of the murderer and the philosopher. Crito, Socrates' wealthiest and most devoted follower, spoke. In the days prior to our master's trial, he had hired detectives and set about acquiring intelligence of the philosopher's accusers, seeking to bring to light their private crimes and thus discredit them and their indictments. It occurred to me now that I might do the same for Polemides.

I had then in my employ a married couple of middle years, Myron and Lado. They were incorrigible snoops, both, who delighted in nothing more than digging up dirt on the high and mighty. I decided to set these bloodhounds to work. What had become of Polemides' family? What motivated his accusers? Had someone put them up to this, and if so, who? What covert agenda did they seek to promote?

Meanwhile, my grandson, I sense your assimilation of this tale wanting. You need more background. Polemides and I were contemporaries; he knew as he spoke that I understood the times and required no exposition as to their feel and flavour. You of a later generation, however, may benefit by a brief historical digression.

In the years before the War, that period of my own and our narrator's boyhood, Athens stood not in the state of faded glory within which she currently resides. Her best days were not behind her, but present, to hand, dazzling and incandescent. Her navy had routed the Empire of Asia and driven the Persian from the sea. Tribute flowed to her from two hundred states. She was a conqueror, an empire, the cultural and commercial capital of the world.

The Spartan War lay years in the future, yet already Pericles' vision had inspired him to prepare for it. He fortified the harbours at Munychia and Zea, reinforced the Long Walls along their entire length, and built the Southern Wall, the 'Third Leg', that, should the Northern or Phalerian Wall fall, the city would remain impregnable.

You, my grandson, who have known these adamant marvels or their restored rendition all your life, take their existence for granted. But at that time they were a feat of engineering such as no city of Greece had ever dreamt, let alone dared. To extend the city's battlements, four and a half miles on one side, nearly the same on the other, yoking the upper city to the harbours at Piraeus, bounding these as well on all sides save the sea, thus turning Athens into an island of invincible fortification . . . this was considered folly by most and madness by many.

My own father and the main of the equestrian class had stood in violent opposition to this enterprise, opposing first Themistocles, then Pericles implementing the former's policy. They discerned clearly, the landholders of Attica, that the Olympian, as Pericles was called, intended when war came to leave defenceless before the invader, and in fact abandon, our estates, farms, and vineyards, including this one above whose fields you and I now sit. Pericles' strategy would be to withdraw the citizenry behind the Long Walls, permitting the foe to ravage our farmsteads at will. Let them deplete their warrior spirit in the slave's tasks of chopping vines and torching garners. When they got bored enough, they would go home. Meanwhile Athens, which controlled the sea and could procure its needs from the states of its empire, would peer down contemptuously upon the invader, secure behind her impregnable battlements.

All revolved about the navy.

The great houses of Athens, the nobles of the Cecropidae, Alcmaeonidae, and Peisistratidae, the Lycomidae, Eumolpidae, and Philaidae, all prided themselves as knights and hoplites. Their ancestors and they themselves had defended the nation as cavalrymen or gentleman warriors of the armoured infantry. Now Athens had devolved into a nation of oar pullers. The fleet employed and emboldened the commons, and the commons packed the Assembly. They hated it, the aristocracy, but were powerless to resist the tide of change. Besides, the navy was making them rich. Reforms initiated by Pericles and others established pay for public service, appointing officials by lot rather than ballot, thus stacking the magistracies and the courts with hoi polloi, the many. To those of the 'Party of the Good and True' who expressed revulsion at the spectacle of our city's champions slouching down harbour lanes bearing their oars and cushions, Pericles responded that it was not his policies that had made Athens a naval power and an empire. History had done it. It was our fleet, manned by our citizen crews, which had defeated Xerxes at Salamis; our fleet which had chased the Persian from the seas; our fleet which had restored freedom to the islands and the Greek cities of Asia. And our fleet that was hauling in, and enriching us all with, the wealth of the world.

The construction of the Long Walls was no gauntlet flung into the teeth of history, Pericles argued, but recognition plain and simple of the reality of the time. We would never beat the Spartans on land. Their army was invincible and always would be. Athens' destiny lay at sea, as Apollo himself had decreed, declaring,

the wooden wall alone shall not fail you,

and as Themistocles and Aristides had proved at Salamis, and Cimon and all our conquering generals in the succeeding generation, including Pericles himself, had confirmed again and again.

Others inveighed against this policy of 'walls and ships', declaring that imperial expansionism would inflame, and had inflamed, mistrust of us among the Spartans. Leave them in peace and they will leave us. But push them into a corner, show up their pride by our ever-enlarging power, and they will be compelled to respond in kind.

This was true and Pericles never refuted it. Yet such was the brass, the crust, the arrogance of those years that Athens' citizenry disdained accommodation of other states as her tradesmen and even her whores scorned to vacate for their betters the public way. Why should they? They who had defeated the mightiest army and navy on earth, who had made the Aegean their millpond, by what dereliction should they leave their city vulnerable for fear of offending Spartan delicacy? Does not the husbandman secure his garden with a palisade of stone? Do not the Spartans themselves ring their camps with pickets and sentries at arms? Let them live with the navy and the Long Walls. And if they could not, then let come what may.

And come, war did. I served the first seasons as a sail lieutenant but was reassigned with the second winter to the northern siege, the same described by our client, of Potidaea. The hardship, if anything, was greater than he told. Plague had begun; fully a fourth of the infantry were carried off. We bore their ashes home in clay pots beneath the benches of our oarsmen and nested their shields and armour beneath weather-cover on our decks.

With the third spring Potidaea fell. The wider war was now two years old. Clearly it would not soon end. The Greek states had been split between Athens and Sparta, each compelled to side with one or the other.

Corcyra with her fleet had entered the lists, allied with Athens. Argos held aloof. Save Plataea, Acarnania, Thessaly, and Messenian Naupactus, every state of the mainland stood with Sparta – Corinth with her wealth and navy; Sicyon and the cities of the Argolid; Elis and Mantinea, the great democracies of the Peloponnese; north of the Isthmus, Ambracia, Leucas, Anactoria; Megara, Thebes, and all Boeotia with her mighty armies; and Phocis and Locris with their matchless horse.

The islands of the Aegean and all Ionia stood within Athens' hegemony; our warships still ruled the sea. But revolts flared in Thrace and Chalcidice, vital to Athens for her timber, copper, and cattle, and the indispensable Hellespont, the city's lifeline for barley and wheat.

Attica had become a Spartan playground. The foe rolled across the frontier at Eleusis, laying the Thriasian plain waste for the second time, then doubled Mount Aegaleus to scorch again the districts of Acharnae, Cephisia, Leuconoe, and Colonus. Spartan troops devastated the Paralian district as far as Laurium, ravaging first the side that looks towards the Peloponnese, then that facing Euboea and Andros. From the top of their Long Walls the citizens of Athens peered towards the shoulders of Mounts Parnes and Brilessus, beyond which rose the smoke of our last estates succumbing to the torch. At the city's threshold the invaders broke apart the shops and tenements of the suburbs, tearing up even the paving stones of the Academy.

Polemides served under Phormio in the Corinthian Gulf, first at Naupactus, then in Amphilochian Argos. In Aetolia he suffered among other wounds one of the skull, which rendered him sightless for an interval and required confinement at home for most of a year. This my bloodhounds reported, produce of their scourings. No member of Polemides' family could be located. His brother Lion's two daughters, now grown, had married and vanished into the sequestration of their husbands' households. Polemides had a son and daughter of his own, though my ferrets could discover no more than their names. These were the issue of an apparent second marriage, to one Eunice of Samothrace; though no registration of this union could be found.

Polemides had been married once, for certain, during the interval of his recuperation after Aetolia, to the daughter of a colleague of his father's. The bride was named Phoebe, 'Bright'. As many in that reign of war, Polemides married young, just twenty-two. The maiden was fifteen.

When I attempted during our next visitation to query him on this subject, he demurred, politely but with emphasis. I respected this and forswore further interrogation. My importunity had however recalled to our client's mind the matriarch of his clan who had arranged this union, for whom the prisoner clearly felt profound affection and to whose memory his thoughts now returned. He recalled an interview in her apartments upon his return after these campaigns. 'How odd,' he remarked. 'I have not thought of that day in twenty years. Yet much of its content may have bearing upon our tale, and at this very juncture.' I held my tongue; after several moments Polemides began:

I DIDN'T GET BACK TO ATHENS FOR TWO AND A HALF YEARS AFTER Potidaea, serving in one campaign and another. You know how it was.

The wound that packed me home didn't even come in action; I plunged from a scaffold and split my skull. I was blind with it for a while. My dear comrades in hospital rifled every item of kit I owned except three silver tetradrachms I kept up my arse; they'd have got shield and breastplate too if I didn't pillow my head on one with an elbow crooked round the other. The letters to my sister Meri that one crony wrote for me never made it back to Athens, so that when I tramped down the gangplank at Munychia, there was no one to greet me, and I couldn't even borrow a spit to hire a ride into town. I hiked alone, humping arms and armour, while the flaming poker inside my skull threatened at every step to drop me faint.

The Plague had begun. I could not believe the alteration it had wrought. The Circuit Road, whose breadth at my departure twenty-six months earlier had yawned so amply that young bloods used to race horses on it at midnight, now stood narrowed to a wagon-width, shoulders solid with stalls and shanties abutting the Long Walls, the hovels of refugees driven in from the country. In town, alleys teemed with the dispossessed. Civility had fled. Even the sight of one as myself, a young soldier suffering, elicited neither a kind word nor a hand to help one up a kerb. Upon familiar lanes one glimpsed only strangers, thumbing their few damp obols, borne not in purses, but, like bumpkins, in their cheeks.

In town again I rested a day, doted upon by my sweet sister. Meri had saved stone cherries for me, the year's last, against this homecoming her heart feared might never come. Her love was like sunshine to me; I wished to bask all day. For Meri's part, merely to look upon her brother was not enough. She must touch my face and hair and sit pressed to my side for hours. 'I must be sure it's really you.'

She and our father insisted that I visit, as soon as strength permitted, our aunt Daphne, in whose care I had passed my early years and who languished now alone and embattled, in her sixty-second winter. Meri sent a boy ahead and at the third noon I went over.

Daphne was really our great-aunt. She had been a celebrated beauty in her day. As a maiden she had led the basket girls of the Greater Panathenaea and borne to the Serpent of the Acropolis the sacred bowl of milk. Now five decades on, she yet set at the city's service all she possessed. Uncoerced she had let her lower floors to a family of the countryside. These had in turn opened their doors to others in straits and these likewise, so that the court when I entered shocked me with the mob of its tenants and the state of disrepair their privation had produced. Upstairs, however, my aunt's sphere remained unaltered, including my own boy's room exactly as I had left it. The old lady's looks survived as well, and bidding me sit in that chamber which had been her fourth husband's drawing room and now doubled as cupboard and kitchen, she yet projected the self-assurance of one to whom attention has been paid and who commands it still.

Had I seen the shanties in the streets? 'By the gods, were I a man, Polemides, the Lacedaemonians would rue their insolence!'

My aunt always addressed me by my full name and always with the same tenor of disapproval. 'What kind of a name is that to give an infant? "Child of War" indeed! What in heaven's name was your father thinking, and his wife to accede to such whim?'

She decried as always the untimely passing of my mother. 'Your father would not remarry, yet he was overwhelmed by the three of you young ones and the care of the farm. That is why he sent you abroad for your schooling. That and the fear that I might pamper you soft.'

She took my callused fists in hers. 'As a babe you had hands plump as a goose's breast and soft sweet curls like Ganymede. Now look at you.'

She insisted on preparing my lunch. I fetched bowls from the high shelves and charcoal from the scuttle. I could feel her eyes upon me, missing nothing.

'You have suffered a skull fracture.'

'It's nothing.'

'By the Holy Twain! Do you think I have learned nothing all these years?'

She had sounded each campaign I had served in, upbraiding me now for volunteering when I might have taken ship home a year and even eighteen months earlier. She knew the names of each of my commanders and had interrogated all, if not in person, then their lieutenants, and if not these, their mothers and sisters.

'What derangement possesses you, Polemides, to step forth undrafted before the line? You have not been stoned!' She meant conscripted, summoned from the *katalogos* to assemble for induction before the tribal stone. 'Do you volunteer just to break your sister's heart and mine?'

She spoke of Meri, whose betrothed, a lieutenant of marines, had lost his life at Methymna. My sister remained a virgin, seventeen now, with only the slenderest dowry, thanks to our straitened case. How many other maidens languished thus, all young men called to war?

My aunt did not wish me to shun hazard, she insisted, only to serve with prudence and forethought. 'The aim of your education at Sparta was to inculcate virtue and self-command, not to train you for the warrior's trade. You are a gentleman! By the gods, do you feel no call to the land?'

I squirmed.

'Your brother displays even less attendance than yourself. And your cousins care only for actors, horses, and their own good looks. Who will preserve us, Polemides? Who will keep the land?'

'It's all moot, isn't it, Aunt? With Spartan companies roasting stew over the sticks of our beds and benches.'

'Don't dish that cheek to me, boy. I'll still put you over my knee and tan your backside!'

She made a prayer and set the pot upon the coals.

I had two cousins, Daphne's grandsons, Simon and Aristeus, who had grown up on horseback; they had distinguished themselves with the cavalry and acquired, my aunt now informed me, a certain dubious celebrity. Did I know that they had taken to carousing about town with that pack of dissolutes and dandies that make up to the coxcomb Alcibiades? 'I have seen it with my own eyes,' my aunt declared. 'Your cousins dine with playwrights and whores.'

'The best playwrights, I'm sure.'

'Yes. And the most accomplished whores.'

She had observed this mob herself one dawn, she reported, as she stood opposite the Palladium in procession for the City Dionysia, awaiting the trumpet. 'Here they came in a pack, self-crowned and gambolling like satyrs, inebriated from some all-night debauch. And there my Simon and Aristeus! Do you know the baker's emporium on the corner by the General's Bench? When the postulants emerged with the holy offering, these sots waylaid it for their dinner! Yes, and carolled for us of the procession as well. All of them, your cousins included, disporting themselves in ribald mockery of heaven!'

My aunt reprehended the profligacy of that whole crowd, but before all its champion, Alcibiades. He had brought home from the north, she narrated, his bastards by that alien tart Cleonice – two boys – and set the lot up in apartments of the same quarter as his own, upon a lane down which his legitimate daughters by his wife Hipparete must pass each day on their nurse's walk. 'What shall these maidens say when they reach the age of reason? "There go our daddy's by-blows, aren't they handsome?"'

I made some remark that sought to make light of it.

'Is there nothing you and your generation cannot find to mock?' My aunt regarded me with resignation and rue. 'Perhaps your father named you more aptly than I gave him credit for. Tell the truth: you enjoy war. They are congenial to you, the stink of the cookfire and the tramp of comrades at your side. Your grandfather was like that. I admire it in you; it is manly. But war is a young man's sport. And none, not even you, may maintain that state for ever.'

She made the offering and served my plate.

'We must find you a bride.'

I laughed.

'You'll catch something from those whores.'

At last her handsome face lit with a smile. I clasped her to me, this noble lady who had ever been my benefactor and champion. When my embrace at last released her, I beheld on her face no longer mirth but sorrow.

'What shall become of us, Pommo?'

This cry wrenched from her, heartsore, with my name unwontedly colloquialized.

'What has become of our family? What will become of you?' My aunt began to weep. 'This war will be the end of all that was fair and gentle.'

Then turning as if in conformity to some impulse of heaven, she seized both my hands in hers and pressed them with a vigour remarkable in one so frail.

'You must survive it, my boy. Swear to me by Demeter and Kore. One among us must endure!'

From the street could be heard the rude cry of some ruffian, no longer that of one passing through as a drayman or teamster, but one who dwelt here, below, and called this once-noble lane his own.

'Pledge this, my child. Give me your oath!'

I swore it, the way you do to a dotty old lady, never thinking of this promise more.

# S E V E N
# A  S I G N I F I C A N T  S I L E N C E

I T WAS THIS LADY DAPHNE [GRANDFATHER RESUMED HIS NARRATION] who arranged the marriage of her great-nephew Polemides to the maiden Phoebe.

You may find it queer, my grandson, when I relate that our client, throughout all recounting of the events of his life, not once made mention of his bride by name. In fact, save a solitary confession towards the terminus of his tale, he cited her existence only thrice, and that indirectly. Did this indicate a want of affection? On the contrary, I find this omission extremely significant, indicative in fact of precisely the opposite. Let me explain.

In those days, more so even than today, a man made reference to his spouse rarely. The greatest glory of a woman was modesty and reserve; the less said of her, for good or ill, the better. A wife's place was within chambers, her role the rearing of children and the management of the household.

A boy raised in that period, particularly one as Polemides, schooled beneath the stern aegis of the Lacedaemonians, was taught primarily to endure. The virtues were those of men; beauty, men's beauty. Remark the sculpture of that era. Only in recent seasons has the female form – and that only of goddesses – come to rival the male in currency of bronze and stone. A youth of that era was schooled to idealize the form of other men, not in a manner prurient or lascivious, but as a model of emulation. To behold in marble the peerless physiques of Achilles and Leonidas, to admire like perfection in one's comrades or elders, fired the youth to forge his own flesh in the image of that *ideal, to embody inwardly the virtues such perfection of externals implied.*

The spell cast over his contemporaries by Alcibiades derived in no small part, in my opinion, from this impetus. His beauty was remarked, for those of noble mind, as an intimation of some loftier perfection inhering within. Why else would the gods have made him look like that? Another of our master's disciples was the poet Aristocles, called Plato. His Theory of Forms arises from that selfsame interpretation. As the material manifestation of an individual horse embodies the particular and the transitory, Plato suggested, so must there exist within some higher realm the ideal form of Horse, universal and immutable, of which all corporeal horses 'partake' or 'participate in'. To this way of perceiving, a man of Alcibiades' spectacular beauty appeared little short of the divine, his perfection in flesh approaching that ideal existent only upon loftier planes. This is why men followed him, I believe, and found it so reflexive to do so.

Thus to Polemides and those of our generation, his and mine, the male form alone embodied arete, *excellence*, and andreia, *virtue*. How must our client have responded, informed by his father of the identity of his bride-to-be? If he were like me, I doubt he had in his life considered the female form of especial beauty. In the carnal sense, yes, but never idealized as the male. How unappealing did she appear to him, this maiden of next door whom he had doubtless known since she was a drizzle-nosed runt?

Yet there is a telling allusion in Polemides' tale. His wife, Phoebe, he stated at one point, when she was seventeen and already mother to their child, requested initiation into the Mysteries of Eleusis. At another point in his narrative Polemides expressed his distaste for this conceit, which he regarded as little more than superstition, and effeminate at that. Yet he not only permitted his bride this favour but accompanied her upon its exercise, making the pilgrimage by sea and completing the full initiation himself.

Why would he do this? What could his motive be, save to honour his spouse and forge with her a deeper union? We may at this point be forgiven a venture into imagination. Let us picture Polemides at twenty-two or -three, already a veteran of twelve years of Spartan discipline and two and a half more of war. He returns home, wounded; he recovers, sufficiently for his father and great-aunt to provide a bride. Perhaps his thoughts turn towards mortality; he may desire children, if only to cheer the advancing age of his father. The Plague has begun. His countrymen are perishing for cause unknown; no abatement is in sight. Nor does he find his male companions to hand; all are off to war. He is cooped within the city, in the apartments he shares with father, sister, perhaps cousins, aunts, and uncles.

Our young soldier accepts his bride. She is of good family, friend to his sister Merope; no doubt she is possessed of wit, skilled in music and the domestic arts. She comports herself with modesty, self-effacing as all daughters of breeding; we may surmise that she is not without physical charms. Incapacitated as he is, the young husband finds he must rely on his bride for company and converse, perhaps even such necessities as to be brought his meals, to read or mount the stairs.

He finds his bride kind and patient, shrewd in her application of their straitened resources. She is younger, her heart is gay. She makes him laugh. Here is a man, recall, who all his life has been drilled in hardship and self-denial, to whom the supreme virtue is the sacrifice of his life in war. It occurs to him with the shock of revelation that there is another oar in the boat. He is not alone. Perhaps for the first time the steel of his heart relents. His wound makes him dizzy, in alarm he gropes for balance; to his astonishment he discovers his bride at his elbow, steadying him with a gentle hand. May we not envision her delivering to his bedside a favourite dish, setting flowers for him upon the sill, singing at his side in the evening?

He discovers her affection for his father, and the love this gentleman reciprocates. He hears the lass giggling with his sister in the kitchen. Does this make him smile? Despite the horrors without, the clan manages cheerful evenings at home in each other's company.

As for appetites of the flesh, our young Polemides has thus far slaked them only among the harridans of the whores' camp or in illicit liaison with women of the street. Now he finds himself in the marriage bed, beside his bride. She must be innocent. Her tender years inspire not the rough lust of the soldier, but the gentle passion of the husband. How do they discover their desire? Haltingly perhaps; doubtless deficient in skill. Yet together, each for the first time with the other.

He speaks of this never, as any gentleman. But in his heart affection grows. He has never known another, save his family, to treat him with tenderness, to look out if he is comfortable, if his needs have been attended to. May we not fancy his soldier's heart softening? Might not the occasion arise when our Polemides draws up upon the private instant and recognizes perhaps for the first time that he is happy?

Now consider her, the lass Phoebe. How does she find her husband? No *paragon for the sculptor's studio perhaps, but an athlete and soldier none the less; virile and disciplined, a young man of substance, beside whom she need never know fear. Unthinkable is it that he will abandon her. Should the worst come, he will die defending her and her children. Must not our bride, the Bright One, respond to this, beyond her schooling as an obedient wife, out of the uncoerced attachment of her heart?*

*And our bridegroom is vulnerable. He has been wounded, he knows fear. He needs her. While outside, the foundations of the firmament crack and crumble, within, a private cosmos conceives itself and grows. A child stirs within the bride's womb. With what joy must the couple, keenly aware of their own mortality, have responded? More than this one need not posit to imagine the pair, in the gentle darkness of their bedchamber, forging a union which the young husband, schooled to silence and close counsel, would not dream to disclose in words.*

*Perhaps I take licence, my grandson. I may read into Polemides' state of mind overmuch of my own. This, however, is what my heart tells me of the man.*

*So were we all, of that generation. Like Polemides we, too, were taking brides. We, too, had children growing and upon the way. Our steps should have been bearing us abroad in welcome to the spring; we should have been casting open portals to range with our darlings upon the vernal hills. Yet these stood shuttered to us now. We were walled in, compassed by the armoured corps of our enemies. We had asked for war and war had come. What none had foreseen, however, was the spectral henchman at his shoulder: the Plague.*

*Here advanced an invader more implacable than the myriads of Persia, more pitiless than the phalanxes of Lacedaemon. One could not treat with this enemy or buy it off for gold. It countenanced no quarter; tokens of submission could not induce it to draw back. It advanced in darkness and in daylight, and no sentry's cry could call the warning. Walls of stone could not keep it out. It answered to no gods, paid heed to no offerings. It took no day off, vacated upon no holiday. It did not sleep or pause for respite. And nothing could slake its appetite.*

*The Plague showed no favouritism. Its silent scythe cut down the illustrious and the obscure, the just alongside the wicked. Daily about us we perceived its mounting toll. In the gymnasium the comrade's cubicle, within which no hand hung street clothes more. The vendor's shuttered stall, the theatre patron's vacant seat. By day we inhaled the stink of the crematoria; at night the wagons of the dead rumbled beyond our gates. In sleep we heard the groan of their tread; their terror invaded even our dreams. In her self-legislated immurement Athens reeled beneath the scourge, soundless and invisible, to whose ravagement none stood invulnerable or immune.*

# EIGHT
# PROGNOSIS: DEATH

IN THOSE DAYS AS YOU KNOW, JASON [POLEMIDES RESUMED], THERE
existed few formal curricula in medicine; an individual could simply
call himself a doctor and offer his services for hire. More frequently a
private person found himself recruited, so to say, by his own facility for
succour. This was the case with my father. He had the gift. Stricken
friends sent for him. He made them well.

From his years upon the land my father had acquired expertise of herbs
and *kataplasmata*, poultices and purges, splints, bindings, even surgery,
all the folk-derived veterinary usages the husbandman learns seeking to
keep his stock sound and thriving. More beneficial stood his manner of
proffering comfort. One simply felt better in his presence. My father
revered the gods in the simple, straightforward manner of his age. He
believed; his friends believed in him; it worked. Soon their friends were
calling too. In this manner Nicolaus of Acharnae, bereft of the income
of his estate, found himself competent to support his new household in
the city. He threw away his farmer's boots and hung out the physician's sign.

With the rise of the Plague my father's services became much in
demand. My sister Meri took upon herself the role of nurse, accompanying him on his rounds. I was in the city then too. I had married and
had a young son. Often I, too, travelled with my father and sister, more
to provide security under arms in the remote precincts they were called
to than to assist in any medical capacity.

I detested the sick. I was afraid of them. I could not but feel that they had drawn their distress upon themselves by their own delinquent actions, concealed from mortals but known to the gods. And I dreaded contagion. I stood in awe of my father's and sister's intrepidity to enter these dwellings of the doomed. I recall one midnight, summoned to some shantytown quarter, a hive of tent cloth and wicker, where ventilation stood nonexistent and the vapours of the dying loitered noxiously, stinking to heaven. The madness of the street-spawned Theseus religion stood at its zenith then. The lane was plastered with crimson bull's horns. Every wall read *Proseisin*: 'He is coming.' The tenement itself teemed with immigrants, ancients and babes, those foreigners who had flocked to the city in her decades of abundance and now in her affliction remained marooned, dying like flies. Not all the gold of Persia could have induced me to enter that hellhole. Yet in they trooped, my father and sister, armed only with a hidesack of herbs and that handful of inadequate instruments of physic – the listening stick, the lancet, and the speculum.

Let me show you something, Jason. It is my father's casebook; I have kept it all these years.

*Female, 30, fever, nausea, abdominal convulsions. Prescriptives: foxglove and valerian, purge of strychnine in wine. Prognosis: poor.*

*Infant, 6 months, fever, abdominal convulsions. Prescriptives: tea of willow bark, astringent of comfrey and hellebore in beeswax suppository. Prognosis: poor.*

In the margins my father notes his fees. Those circled are the ones who paid. One may scan twenty and thirty cases without finding a mark. But skip down. The months pass. Economy now informs the notes.

*Male, 50. Plague. Death.*

*Child, 2. Plague. Death.*

I was twenty-three then. I was not ready to die, or to stand idly by while those I loved succumbed. Yet what could one do? The helplessness ate your guts. My mother's father took his own life, yet uninfected by the scourge; the patriarch could not endure to outlive yet another generation of those he loved. My father and I bore his bones away in a child's phaeton, out through that gate called Lionheart heretofore, now the Gate of Tears, to our tomb in the country. Half a hundred parties of the bereaved trekked with us; the queue stretched to the Anaceum. The Spartans, the season's ravagement completed, had withdrawn, save the odd cavalry patrol. One tracked us along the Acharnae Road. Their lieutenant called to us to see reason and seek peace. 'This is not war,' he cried, his knight's heart outraged at such horrors visited upon children and women. 'It is hell.'

For myself I had witnessed little of the nobility of war so eloquently advertised by this officer's countrymen, my schoolmasters. In Aetolia we burned villages and poisoned wells. In Acarnania our blades were employed to slaughter sheep, not staying even to strip the beasts of hide or fleece, but dumping them throat-slit into the sea. The only real battle I had seen was at Mytilene under Laches, the ablest amphibious commander of the war, save only the Spartan Brasidas and Alcibiades.

The latter had won his second prize of valour, in the raid on the Spartan harbour at Gytheium, and was to collect another at Delium, saving the life of your master Socrates, this time as a cavalryman – all in all a 'triple', on land, sea, and horseback. By then, too, he had entered his first chariot at Olympia, though his driver had spilled and failed to finish.

I saw none of Alcibiades during those days. The Plague had hit his household hard. In addition to Pericles, he had lost his mother, Deinomache, an infant daughter of his wife Hipparete, and both sons of his lover Cleonice, who herself had perished not long after. His cousins, Pericles' sons Paralus and Xanthippus, had fallen, and Amycla, the Spartan nurse who had remained loyal, even when her country called her home.

Without the walls awaited war; within, pestilence. Now arose a third scourge: one's own countrymen, made desperate by the first two. The poor cracked first. Driven by want, they took to plundering the homes of those of middling wealth, which stood vulnerable owing to their banishment of watchmen and stewards, all save the most trustworthy, who themselves took to crime to pay a physician or an undertaker, which professions amounted to the same thing. What good was money if you would not live to spend it? A gentleman would perish, bequeathing his treasure to his sons; these, anticipating their own imminent extinction, ran through their patrimony as fast as their fists could scatter it, abetted by every species of parasite and bloodsucker, seeking the juice as it spilled. You saw it, Jason. Disease would carry off a man's wife and children; bereft of hope, he sets his own flat alight, then lingers in numb *katalepsis*, nor disclaims his offence to the brigadiers hastening onto the scene as the blaze consumes the tenancies of his neighbours. Near the Leocorium I saw a man hacked to pieces for this felony. Others set fires purely out of malice. After dark, flame-spotting became a spectator sport.

My brother served then with the infantry under Nicias in Megara; he and others shuttled regularly with despatches. Again and again he urged me to get out. Enlist as a marine, take oars on a freighter, anything to vacate this antechamber of hell, the besieged city. He had sent his wife Theonoe and their babes to her kinsmen in the north; my own bride and child remained in Athens.

'They're dead already,' Lion addressed me with passion. 'Their graves are dug. Father and Meri too, and us with them if we're mad enough to stay.' This upon an evening when he and I drank alone, not for pleasure, but shamelessly, to render ourselves insensate. 'Listen to me, brother. You're not one of those pious nincompoops who see this scourge as a curse from heaven. You're a soldier. You know one does not make camp in a swamp or drink downstream from a shithouse. Look around you, man! We're kennelled like rats, ten crammed in space for two, the very air we breathe contaminated as a terminal ward.'

This was how one spoke then. You remember, Jason. One tolled the truth with the candour of the condemned. Civility rode the greased sluice into the gutter, succeeded by scruple and self-restraint. Why obey the laws when you were already sentenced to death? Why honour the gods when their worst was nothing beside what you already bore? As for the future, to turn to it with hope was madness, to contemplate it with dread only made your present plight more unbearable. What object was served by virtue? To conduct oneself with patience and thrift was folly; heedlessness and pursuit of pleasure, common sense. To defer desire was absurd; to succour the afflicted, the fastest way to bring on your own end.

Despair begat boldness, slow death the courting of extinction. Gangs roamed the streets, armed with paving stones and wagon staves, weapons they could cast aside or claim harmless when the constables collared them, which they never did. These thugs scrawled insults on the public halls, defacing even the sanctuaries of the dead, and none stood up to them. With each act of insolence uncondemned, this scum grew more brazen. They hunted foreigners, the weaker the better, and beat them with a barbarity unprecedented. More than once my father and sister, hastening to one in need, were compelled to tend some fellow bludgeoned in the gutter and left to die. The white robe of the sisters of mercy lent protection on their rounds, yet there arose those who donned this garment to gain access to a home, to ransack it even as the occupants cried out to them, dying. I saw one female stoned on the very threshold she had plundered, the mob making off with the villainess's loot while her blood yet ran upon the pavement. Arms had been out-lawed, and all firebrands, even courtesy torches to light one's way home. The penalty was death for those caught bearing firesticks and tinder.

The randomness of extinction brought out all that was worst in men, and all that was best. My sister Meri organized meetings in our home, clearinghouses for nurses and physicians seeking any diet, regimen, or curative that brought relief. No course was too outlandish. The fever that consumed the sick brought such torments that the sufferer could not stand on the skin the touch of even the lightest cloth. You entered a home and everyone was naked. The afflicted, on fire with fever, plunged into public fountains, then others, desperate with thirst, drank the water. Night's cool brought no surcease, as the pain merely of lying upon one's bed drove sufferers to madness. Physicians prescribed baths and diuretics; they bled some, purged others. Nothing worked.

The doctors looked worse than the dying. My wife would feed these scarecrows, growing more gaunt each day herself. Soon the search for remedials became supplanted by the quest for drugs to blunt the pain, then, whispered, merciful means of despatch. People drank bull's blood or swallowed stones. I myself became recruited to this dolorous trade. I scoured the sailors' markets for morphia and dogbane, hemlock and belladonna. My sister instructed me in the concoction of potions to carry off the dying. Soon these became too costly to secure.

My infant son took ill. His cries, heart-scoring, ceased not night or day. My wife rocked the babe, crooning, as she, too, weakened. When their pain became unbearable, Meri dosed them with nightshade, the last she had, to bear them away.

My cousin Simon, now a captain in the cavalry, had come to stay with us, bringing his wife Clymene and infant twins. Then his brow, too, began to burn. He fled one night, taking only his horse. Within days Clymene began to fail, crying for him; I scoured all his haunts, even those we shared in childhood. One midnight, despairing, I determined to seek out Alcibiades, at his town estate on the Hill of the Knights.

The streets then, even those of the wealthy, had become corridors of horror. Neighbours had perished, abandoning their pets; others who could not feed their animals or grew too sick to care had let them loose. Now packs of dogs ranged wild. These would not go after corpses, their beasts' wisdom prohibiting, but hunted the living, even indoors, clawing at shutters and pouring in over thresholds while their howls and snarls, ungodly, echoed down the vacant lanes. I ran this gauntlet for what seemed hours, at last drawing up before Alcibiades' gate.

Lanterns blazed; no watchman attended. Gay music sounded from within. Crossing the courtyard, I saw a man of my age, unknown to me, cavorting in a dry fountain, cupping from behind the ungirdled breasts of a prostitute. Another sprawled in the shadows with a *porne* on her knees before him.

I advanced into the interior. The place was torchlit and pullulating with revellers. Drums beat. A procession, chanting, jigged about the court. Upon a dais stood a congress of men and women clad as acolytes and bearing wands of willow. They enacted a burlesque of the rites of Thracian Kotyttos, the orgy goddess.

Here arose Alcibiades, at the fore, performing in mockery the office of priest, or should I say priestess. He was dressed in women's robes, lips painted, his curls bound in lampoonish caricature of the sacred style. He was barefoot, dead drunk. I advanced before him, demanding the whereabouts of my cousin.

Alcibiades stared. He had no idea who I was. The dancers capered wantonly about him. 'Who is this intruder who dares trespass, uninitiated, within the hallowed precinct? Kneel, supplicant, and show reverence of the goddess!'

I demanded again my cousin.

Alcibiades recognized me now. He elevated his staff, which I saw was a cook's stirring paddle, for soup.

'Bow, interloper. Display deference to heaven or, by my vested powers, I'll have you blown senseless.'

Two whores twined about his knees. He directed one forward; she lurched upon all fours, clutching at my cloak, beneath which from its baldric hung a *xiphos* sword.

'And comes this stranger armed as well? Impiety! What punishment for this?' Alcibiades flung his wine bowl in sham outrage. 'Attend, postulants, to this killjoy heretic! He has observed, as Menoetius says,

> *that which no mortal, unpunished,*
> *may look upon and depart.'*

Now I saw my cousin. 'Get out of here, Pommo,' he commanded me, emerging from the daisy chain of prancers.

'Not without you,' I replied.

'Pommo, you swine!'

This from Alcibiades, descending from his perch and draping a merry arm about my shoulders. 'Once upon a siege, my friend, you played the spoilsport and I commended you. But see, the tables have turned. It is our country now which stands embattled and immured.'

He tugged the whore before me to her feet. 'What do you think of this?' he pronounced, and tore her garment to the waist. 'Not impressed? How about this?' He stripped her naked. The girl made no effort to cover herself but faced me in the eye, prideful in her beauty.

'Let him alone, Alcibiades,' my cousin put in.

I noted Euryptolemus advancing to intercede.

'You're not queer, are you, Pommo?' Alcibiades declaimed. 'We can address those needs as well!' He motioned to the shadows, summoning boys.

'What of your famous *mythos*, Alcibiades? What will Athens think of these proceedings?'

'Who will inform her, Pommo? Not you, I know. Nor these others, for if Euphorion speaks true,

> *Which dare call him thief,*
> *whose fist resides within thief's purse?'*

Euro moved beside me, sheepish and ashamed. 'Pommo has lost wife and child,' he informed his cousin.

'And I mother and sons, daughter, and uncles and cousins. To say it with stone, as our friends the Spartans phrase it: "Who hasn't?"'

Fury seized me. 'You claimed once to be two – Alcibiades and "Alcibiades". Which are you now?'

'I am a third Alcibiades. He who cannot stand to be the other two.'

'That Alcibiades,' I declared, 'can go fuck himself.'

Anger flared within his eyes, quelled at once and mutated into an aspect of irony and despair.

'And can you call yourself friend to one Alcibiades and spurn the others?'

'I was never your friend.'

I turned upon my heel.

'Come back, Pommo! Take your vows. Be one with us!'

Striding out, I could hear him call after me, laughing. 'The good alone die young. Haven't the Spartans taught you that? Take care, old friend. Don't tempt the gods with virtue!'

In the courtyard I seized my cousin and pleaded with him for his children's sake to come home. He would not, but clasped me hard, brow glistening with that sheen of fever one knew only too well, and exhorted me to stay – here, where laughter and music yet obtained.

'Go home, then!' my cousin called as I stalked clear. 'Go home to death. I will stay here with life, for as long as I have to live it.'

Here, Jason, this entry in my father's log:

*Male, 54. Plague. Death.*

This was his own warrant of doom, self-diagnosed.

Within days he began to fail. My sister laboured, using all her skills. Then she, too, showed the signs. She would not drug the pain with those few *pharmaka* we yet possessed, preserving them for others.

My father grew desperate to release her. Twice I prevented him. How much longer could she last? Ten days, he said, in this hell of pain.

I sat all night with my sister while she writhed.

'Do you love me, Pommo?'

I knew what she wanted.

'You must not let Father do it.'

Again I stalked the streets. Let her go, I prayed. But always, returning, she lingered. Her agonies redoubled.

'You are a soldier, Pommo. Be strong like one.'

We bore her, my father and I, to the tub. Her frame was light as a child's. 'May the gods bless you,' she said. I instructed my father to seize her, hard, when I gave the nod. At this instant my edge sliced the artery.

'May the gods bless you,' my sister repeated.

She clutched my hand and my father's, his own as weak as hers.

'May the gods bless you.'

[*The man Polemides here broke off. Emotion cracked his voice. With great effort only could he continue, his phrases broken with sobs.*]

How may one's tongue give voice to such utterance? 'I watched my wife and child die.' Was it for this the gods gifted us with speech, to pronounce such unholy idiom? 'I opened my sister's veins.'

[*The man buried his face in his hands. I rose and embraced him. His arms clutched me, while piteous sobs convulsed his breast.*

[*He turned away. I understood and rose to absent myself.*

[*Departing, I glanced back. The man stood in his cell's corner, cheek pressed against the stone of the wall, while both arms clutched tight about his person as he broke down with this remembered grief.*]

## NINE
# A  CALLING  ACQUIRED

M Y FATHER DIED THAT NIGHT. WITH THIS ALL WHOM I LOVED HAD been carried off save my aunt, my brother's wife and babes sent north for their safety, and Lion himself. He was absent with the fleet; I conducted the obsequies, attending upon our father's brothers and the gentlewomen of the clan. Enemy incursion had cut off access to the country, to our family tomb. We must inhume Father's and Meri's bones beside my own wife's and infant's, beneath the stones of our city house. As I voiced the terminal invocation,

*May the earth rest lightly upon you,*

my soul was animated by one object only: to see the remains of these I loved interred on the land, where they belonged and would find peace. That meant returning to war, to drive out the foe. I would find a vessel or infantry company and ship out.

Waking alone several days later, I determined to empty the house and commenced before dawn to set its contents at the kerb. Before I had stacked three items a crowd had collected. I began to laugh. 'Just leave me armour and something to cook with.' The place was picked clean in five minutes. Believe it or not, the mob respected my wishes. I found my wife's kitchen intact, and my military gear. They left my bedding as well.

A day later, or perhaps that same forenoon, I was approached by a gentleman of our country district, a friend of my father's. He looked bad. We spoke of happier seasons, of childhood games played with his sons and daughters upon the land. Would I, in remembrance of these bonds, perform now a service for him?

'It's my wife,' he said, and spoke no more.

Moments passed before I realized what he wanted. I was appalled and fled.

Two nights later this countryman returned. 'My wife delivered you, Pommo. By the gods, I beg you now: deliver her.'

There are frontiers one crosses, my friend, without understanding of what one does. This was not one of them. With gravity I acceded and performed the service this man requested.

Within days two more such assignments were set before me. I performed them as well. Why not?

The good alone die young.

I continued to apply for service with the fleet, but must have looked so bad the officers took me for sick. I could not find a berth.

More haunted figures, strangers as well as acquaintances, presented themselves, requesting my abetments of mercy. I began to get good at it. It was like being a doctor, I told myself. Like my father, I delivered the afflicted from their torment. In fact my physic was superior; my cures took. No client complained. And business kept getting better.

Another night a different rap came at the post. It was Euryptolemus, on horseback. When I stepped out I saw, also mounted, in the shadows, Alcibiades.

'Don't worry,' I told him before he could speak. 'I have said nothing about your ritual observances.'

'Do you think that's why I came?'

'I have no idea why you do anything.'

In that moment I hated him.

'And you, my friend,' he queried, perceiving. 'Are you yourself so free from sin?'

'It seems sin has become less handy of definition.'

'Indeed.'

Euro led a third mount. 'We're going to the harbour. Come on, take a ride.'

We proceeded at a walk through the silent lanes.

'Pericles' spit has gone dry,' Alcibiades announced in the detached tone of the bereaved. So the scourge had found even the Olympian. 'He will stand with Theseus, Solon, and Themistocles among those who have shaped our nation, and none shall surpass him.'

He spoke no more, nor did his cousin, all the way to Munychia. The naval base, when we reached there, churned with a cacophony of ships' chandlers, expeditors, and stevedores hastening to beat the tide, which was due, one of their number informed us, an hour before dawn. A fleet under Phormio was rigging out for Naupactus. The troop transports lay along the embarkation quays, while the triple-bankers, the men-of-war, waited like great stingered hornets, sixty in all, hull by hull in their torchlit sheds, each obscured beneath a swarming mantle of ship's joiners and riggers, sailbenders, cordwainers, and sparhandlers. Petty officers bawled orders amid a din of shoring jacks and carpenter's mawls, windlasses, winches, and cranes. The slipside catwalks, themselves a maze of hawsers and mooring cables, stem and stern stays, warp lines and every form of brace, sheet, shroud, lift, hoist, and ratline imaginable, seethed with battalions of administrators, admiralty clerks and supply secretaries, registrars of the *katalogos*, Council members, priests, merchants and recorders, curators of the *neorion*, the shipworks across whose teeming timbers now advanced the *nautai* themselves, packing their seabags and oars and scrambling in orchestrated chaos to 'sign in, sign off, and sign over' in time to beat the *apostolei*'s trumpet. Stacked arms lined the quays beneath the unit guidons, with the infantrymen and their attendants sprawled out in the blaze of cressets and their own meagre fires, oiling their bronze against the salt and securing their shields within fleece coverts.

At the foot of the pier Alcibiades spoke apart with Phormio and several of his captains, while Euryptolemus and I mounted the limestone steps carved with sailors' graffiti, lewd drawings, and the ubiquitous footstep-and-fanny ikon indicating the route to the nearest house of ill fame, to that open-air tavern called Ouros, Fair Wind, which overlooks the embarkation quays. Euro asked if I had ever seen a lodestone of Magnesia, a magnet; how it attracts irresistibly the filings of iron. He meant his cousin.

Below on the dock we could see the stir Alcibiades created simply by his presence, how the infantrymen manoeuvred as they had in camp at

Potidaea only for a glimpse of him. Many seemed to address him as they passed; we could hear several, urging him to speak out more boldly, don't let youth hold him back, seek command and seize it. The main of the soldiers were young, our age. They had grown impatient with the dilation of their elders. 'Lead us, son of Cleinias!' more than one cried with a raised fist and a gesture of affirmation.

In the mariners' tavern where his cousin and I waited, anticipation of Alcibiades' arrival had electrified the colony. Serving girls and laundresses of the abutting lanes scurried up, pinching the flush into their cheeks and dressing their hair with their dirty fingers. Do you know that dive, Jason? It serves food as well as wine. The proprietor is a Phoenician of Tyre; he decks his place with maritime kit and affects to give seafaring names to the plates of the day, which he now, as Alcibiades entered, rattled off to his guest while escorting him to table. Might he recommend the 'Top o' the Catch'? Perhaps the 'Smack o' the Sea'?

'I'll have that one.' Alcibiades indicated a stewpot on the flame. 'The Twinge o' Nausea.'

He grinned at the host; a tiara from the king of Persia could not have delighted the fellow more. Alcibiades' mood was grave, however. You could see he burned with envy of Phormio, impatient for a fleet of his own. The celebrity of his person chafed upon him; he felt the spell he produced on the masses and blazed to use it. Why had he asked his cousin and me to accompany him here? 'Our friend Socrates excepted, you two alone possess the spirit to call me a hound to my face. Tell me now and don't lie: how, and where, may I make my move?'

Pericles' passing must create a vacuum, Alcibiades declared, which would stand the empire on its head. Subject states will revolt, would-be successors scurry from the woodwork. Euryptolemus cut him off, indignant. How could Alcibiades speak so coldly of his kinsman, who if the gods grant might live on another half year, or even survive as no inconsiderable number had already?

'He won't make it,' Alcibiades pronounced. 'I read it all over him. Nor am I cold, cousin, but only forethoughtful, as he was and would wish us to be. Whom do we want in his place – that truckler to the rabble, Cleon? Androcles, who couldn't mount from the gutter with a stepladder? Or Nicias, whose pious vacillation is even more malign?

Listen to me. If Athens possessed leaders of imagination, I would be the first to set myself at their service. But the worst are bullies and lick-spittles, skilled only at manipulating the mob. The best, like Phormio and Demosthenes, are warriors; they will not soil their hands with politics. What dies with Pericles is vision. But even he has not seen far enough. The Plague will end, we will survive it. What then?

'Pericles ordained as indefeasible three tenets for the prosecution of this war: the pre-eminence of the fleet, the security of the Long Walls, and the proscription of the empire's expansion while the war goes on. The first two stand sound; the third must be repealed. We have no choice but to expand, and with unprecedented vigour. Our ships must carry conquest to Sicily and Italy, then Carthage and all of North Africa. In Asia we must not content ourselves with a toehold on the coast, but advance inland and take on all comers, including the throne of Persia.'

Euryptolemus broke in with a laugh. 'How will we conquer the world, cousin, when we can't even step down from our walls to take a piss? What myriads will we employ to accomplish this masterwork?'

'The Spartans in the end,' Alcibiades replied as if this were self-evident. 'First their allies, once we have overthrown their declining generation and drawn their young men to our league.' He was serious. 'But here, friends, is the question: dare I speak in public to this effect? I am not yet twenty-five, in a nation where forty years is held the threshold of wisdom. To keep back runs counter to every impulse of my nature, but to strike prematurely may finish me before I begin. You cannot know the nights I've lain awake, tormented by this.'

Plates grew cold as the cousins examined the case. Euryptolemus spoke. This noble, though blessed with an intellect as keen as his kinsman, had been gifted with little of his good looks. Aged twenty-nine, he had already lost most of his hair, and his features, though not uncomely, did not conjoin to a union that one could call handsome. Perhaps because of this, he bore himself with a genial and felicitous modesty. It was impossible not to like the fellow, and to like him at once. He began by reproving his cousin for the lawlessness of his private life.

Alcibiades, if he wished to be taken seriously, must bring his appetites under control, particularly for drink and carnality. Such vices are unstatesmanlike. 'If you can't keep your cock on a leash, at least be discreet about where you stick it. Don't troop about the streets with courtesans while your wife languishes heartsick at home.'

Two forces are at war for Athens' soul, Euryptolemus asserted. 'The ancient simple ways which reverence the gods and heroes of old – and the new ways which make the city herself a god. We all know which side you come down on, cousin, but you must not make it so obvious. Would it kill you to display humility, to render obeisance to heaven or at least make pretence of it? Democracy is a sword which cuts two ways. It emancipates the individual, setting him free to shine as no other scheme of governance. But that blade possesses an under-edge. Its spawn is spite and envy. This is why Pericles bore himself with modesty, remote from the multitude, for fear of their jealousy.'

'He was wrong,' Alcibiades put in.

'Was he? You occupy an Athens unknown to the commons, Alcibiades, a realm whose incandescence blinds you to the real state the rest inhabit, where mixing bowls overflow not with wine, but bile and gall. I see it every day in the law courts. Envy and spite are our city's biggest businesses and they boom in hard times or flush. Let us count the avenues the state has provided for the envious man to tear down his better. He may drag him before the Council or the Assembly, into the people's courts or the Areopagus. If his victim stands for office, he may test him upon application, then audit upon expiration. If the poor fellow serves with the fleet, his enemy may haul him up before the apostoleis or the Board of Naval Affairs. He may arrest him himself or have the magistrates do it, indict straight out, sue before the arbitrators, or lay information before the king archon. Nor does he lack for charges, of which the state provides a quiverful. Let him start with dereliction, peculation, malversation; bribery, larceny, extortion; malfeasance, misfeasance, nonfeasance. Do these fail? Try tax evasion, unlawful union, depletion of patrimony. Are murder and treason insufficient? Let him snatch the shaft of impiety, which carries the death penalty, and against which the accused must defend not only himself and his actions but the very content of his soul!

'You laugh, cousin. But consider Themistocles' end, our nation's saviour, an exile in Persia. Peerless Aristides banished. Miltiades hounded to his grave, not two years after his victory at Marathon. Pericles made his name prosecuting the greatest hero our city ever produced, Cimon, who chased the Persian from the sea and set the empire upon its foundations; while he, the Olympian himself, barely escaped with his neck on half a dozen occasions. And you, cousin. What a target you present! By the gods, let me get you before a jury.' He gestured to the pack of worshippers who yet loitered, gawking from the margins of the terrace. 'I'll have these same idolaters howling for your blood.'

The kinsmen laughed, seconded by the spectators, who could not but overhear this mock tirade of Euryptolemus.

'I applaud your eloquence, cousin,' Alcibiades resumed. 'But you're mistaken. You misapprehend the character of man. No soul seeks to bemire itself in its own base fluids but to ascend on the wings of that *daimon* which animates it. Look there to the marines and infantry upon the embarkation quays. They are quickened not by bile or choler, but by heart's blood. They seek glory, no less than Theseus or Achilles.'

'Half of them are shirkers and you know it.'

'Only for want of vision by their leaders.'

'Cousin, the days of gods and heroes are over.'

'Not to me. And not to them.' Again Alcibiades indicated the troops below. 'You censure me, cousin, insisting that I must claim a vision beyond my own fame and glory, or the same for our nation. There is nothing beyond fame and glory! They are the holiest and most exalted aspirations of the soul, for they comprise the longing for immortality, for transcendence of all inhering limits, which passion animates even the immortal gods.

'You impeach me further, Euro, of squandering my time with men of brilliance and splendid horses and hounds, rather than the commons which constitute our nation. But I have observed these same men, the ordinary and the middling-born, in the presence of such horses and dogs. They swarm, as bees to honey, about the great ones. Why? Is it not because they perceive in the nobility of these champions the intimation of that selfsame quality inchoate within their own breasts? Phrynichus has admonished,

> *She is a wide bed*
> *who holds both democracy and empire,*

but he, too, stands in error. Democracy must be empire. The appetite that freedom ignites in the individual must be given an object commensurate to its greatness.'

Now it was Euro's turn to rap the table. 'And who, cousin, will light this flame?'

'I will,' declared Alcibiades.

He laughed. They both did.

'Then here is the course you must steer, cousin.' Euryptolemus leaned forward, seized it seemed by heaven's inspiration. 'If your countrymen will not attend you, mistrustful of your youth, take your case to other courts and other councils. Commence abroad, with our rivals and allies. The chancellors of foreign states will learn soon of Pericles' affliction. Who will lead Athens? they must ask. With whom must they treat to secure their nations' weal?'

Euryptolemus made his case swiftly and succinctly. Which foreign prince, hearing and seeing Alcibiades before him, could fail to recognize Athens' future? To spurn this champion for his youth would be folly, and none would grasp this more surely than the keen and the visionary. Remarking what must come, they would see the wisdom of aligning with it early. Among foreign courts Alcibiades could gain a foothold; securing foreign allegiances, he could forge coalitions. Who else but he could accomplish this? The fame of his lineage would open doors in scores of states, and his self-attained repute as a warrior, not to mention a breeder and racer of horses (a noble vice, shared by lords of all nations), would serve him in all others.

'You have split the stone, cousin!' Alcibiades declared. 'I salute you.'

The kinsmen consulted another hour, pursuing the mandates and implications of this policy. Its fundament was war. Peace was fatal to it.

'What do you say, Pommo?' Alcibiades turned at length to me. 'We haven't heard a squeak from you all night.'

When I hesitated, he clapped my shoulder. 'Politics bores our friend, Euro. He is a soldier. Tell us, then, Polemides. What does a soldier say?'

Be yourself, was all I could tell him.

'Yes.' He laughed. 'But which self?'

'Go to war. Fight out front. Win. Bring victories home to Athens. Let your enemies speak against that if they dare.'

We parted at dawn, Alcibiades fresh as if he'd slept all night. He was on his way to the marketplace, to hunt up other friends and continue his investigation. He thanked me for my candour. 'Do you need anything, Pommo? Money? A commission at arms?'

'I'd like my cousin back, if you can spare him.'

'He goes his own way, as you or I.'

I thanked him for the thought. What I needed most was sleep.

Before my door a man was waiting. He was past thirty, brown as leather and weighed down with arms like a mercenary. He grinned at me. 'You're putting me out of business, you know?' He had made his seat upon the stones, taking his breakfast of bread dipped in wine. I asked his name.

'Telamon. Of Arcadia.'

I had heard of him; he was an assassin. Curious, I invited him in. 'If you're going to slice veins for a living,' he chided, 'at least have the decency to charge for it. Else how may a poor man compete?'

I told him I was giving it up for the Prometheia. A penance.

'A noble gesture,' he observed. I liked him. I gave him what bread I had and he took it, stowing it in his pack alongside a brace of wrapped onions. He was shipping out in ten days, a brigade under Lamachus to raid the Peloponnese. He could get me on if I wanted. 'Your work lacks subtlety, I hear. Post with me, I'll instruct you.'

'Another time perhaps.'

Rising, he left a coin upon the chest. He would not hear my protests. 'I expect pay, and I offer it.'

From the doorway I watched him trek off bearing his ninety pounds of kit, then turned back to the denuded interior of my own house of death.

Perhaps something had changed. At least, I told myself, I was being offered work.

# BOOK THREE

# THE FIRST
# MODERN WAR

TEN

# THE JOYS OF SOLDIERING

I DID NOT TAKE UP ALCIBIADES' OFFER OF A COMMISSION OR FOLLOW Telamon into mercenary service. I did heed the Arcadian's advice, however, and shipped out as an armoured infantryman under Eucles to the Thracian Chersonese. That campaign concluded, discovering myself yet among the living, I enlisted upon another, equally gloryless, and another after that.

It was a new kind of war we were fighting, or so we bucks of the heavy infantry were enlightened by our elders of the Old Corps. In their day men fought battles. They armed and contended line against line, victory determined in honourable trial of arms. This was not how we did it. Our war was not just state against state, but faction against faction within states – the Few against the Many, those who had versus those who lacked.

As Athenians we sided with the democrats, or more accurately compelled all who sought our aid to become democrats, with the understanding that their democracy would be only so democratic as we permitted. Assaulting a city in this new kind of war, one contended not against heroes united in defence of their homeland, but that gang of partisans which chanced to possess the state at the moment, while one's allies were those of the exiled faction, aligned with us, the invaders, to effect their restoration.

At Mytilene I saw my first list. Our company had been assigned its exiles, those democrats of the city who had been deposed in the oligarchic revolt and now constituted a species of political auxiliary to the Athenian troops of the assault. I had never seen such men. They were neither warriors nor patriots but zealots. The one with us was named Thersander. We called him Quill. I was a sergeant then; our captain called us in to receive the list.

The list was a death warrant. It enrostered those of Quill's country-men whom, the city taken, it would be our company's chore to arrest and execute. Quill had made up the list; he would accompany us in the *syllepsis*, the roundup, to identify those upon it. You have seen such catalogues, Jason. They are written in blood. Quill's was no impartial manifest of civil foes or political opponents; his accounted neighbours and friends, comrades and kinsmen who had in their hour wreaked ruin upon him. They had slaughtered his wife and daughters. His brother had been torn from the altar and butchered before his own children's eyes. I had never known one to hate as Quill. He was no longer a man but a vessel into which hatred had been decanted. There was no negotiating with one like him, and they were all like him.

Later when the city fell, our company held eighty-two captives of the lists, Quill's and others, including six women and two boys. It was rain-ing, in sheets behind a warm west wind, so you sweated amid the drenching. We herded the prisoners into stock pens. Another Mytilenean, not Quill but a confederate, appeared with our instructions. We were to put the detainees to death.

How, I ask, are such orders to be carried out? Not philosophically but practically. Who steps forth to propose the means? Not the best, I assure you. Incinerate them, cried one of our rear rank; seal them in the barn and torch it. Another wished to butcher them like sheep. I refused the order in its entirety.

Quill's abettor confronted me. Who had bribed me? Did I know I was a traitor?

I was young; outrage overcame me. 'How will I command these?' I exclaimed, indicating my men. 'How may I call them to soldierly duty after they have committed such atrocities? They will be ruined!'

Quill appeared. These are the enemy, he cried, indicating the wretches in the sheepfold.

Kill them yourself, I told him.

He thrust the list in my face. 'I'm putting your name on it!'

My own hot temper was all that saved me as, seizing his board and scribing the mark with my own hand, this action so maddened my antagonist as to make him assault me bodily, the ensuing uproar over-throwing momentarily the impetus to mass murder. Yet let me not style myself deliverer. The poor devils were massacred next day by another company and I, demoted to private soldier, shipped off again to the North.

The years passed as if being lived by another. I glance back upon enlistments and discharges, pay vouchers and correspondence, bronze-heads extracted from my own flesh and cached as souvenirs at the bottom of my pack; I dig out trinkets and mementos, the names of men and women, lovers indeed, jotted upon the felt of my helmet caul and scratched with a blade edge into the straps of my rucksack. I remember none.

The season transited as in a single night, that species of slumber from which one awakens at intervals, fitful and feverish, and can reclaim by morning nothing save the sour smell of one's own tortured bedding. It seemed I came to myself again before Potidaea, besieging the place a second time seven years after the first. I cannot say now if it was dream or real.

For two winters after my wife's death, I felt no call to passion. This was neither virtue nor grief, only despair. Then one night I entered the whores' camp and never left. You understand the reckoning of accounts, my friend. Tot this up for me. How much in wages, and don't fail to include mustering bonuses and dividends of discharge, may a soldier accrue who remains upon campaign, retiring not even in winter except to recover from wounds, for a decade entire? A tidy sum, I'd imagine. Enough to buy a handsome little farm, with stock and hands and even a comely wife.

I fucked away every farthing. Screwed it or drank it, and in the end could not credit even my own recall that I had once harboured aspirations for myself.

Peace came, the so-called Peace of Nicias, whereunder both sides, exhausted from years of strife, contracted to retire until they could recover breath, scratching in the interval lines beyond which each vowed not to trespass. I came home. Alcibiades was thirty now, elected to the chief executive of the state, the Board of Ten Generals, the same post his guardian Pericles had held. But his star had not yet gained pre-eminence. Nicias held sway, his elder and rival, who had negotiated peace with the Spartans, or been appointed by them to do so, to deprive Alcibiades, whose enterprise they feared, of the recognition and prestige. My friend employed me, at captain's wages paid from his own purse, as a sort of private envoy to the Lacedaemonians, or those in-dividual Spartans – Xenares, Endius, Mindarus – with whom he conspired to wreck the Peace. I am no diplomat. I missed the action. I needed it.

One comes to the mercenary's calling in this way, as a criminal to crime. For war and crime are twin spawn of the same misbegotten litter. Why else does the magistrate present his perennial offer to errant youth: servitude or the army. Each inducts into the other, war and crime, and the more monstrous the felony, the deeper the criminal must plunge to reclaim himself, disremembering kin and country, forgetting even crime, so that in the end the only riddle the soldier kens is that most occult of all: why am I still living?

Peace for me was war under another name. I never stopped working. Absent licence to soldier for my country, I hired out to others. At first only to allies, but when times got tight, well . . . one's former foes proved the more eager employers. Thebes had got a taste for power, whipping Athens at Delium. War had brought into her fold Plataea, Thespiae, and half the towns of the Boeotian League; she saw no profit in buying into a Spartan peace. Corinth stood equally apart and aggrieved. The treaty had restored neither Anactorium nor Sollium; she had lost her influence in the northwest, not to mention Corcyra, whose revolt had started the war in the first place. Megara chafed to behold her port of Nisaea garrisoned by Athenian troops, and Elis and Mantinea, democracies, had lost all patience with life beneath the Spartan heel. In the north, Amphipolis and the Thraceward region defied the treaty. I worked for all of them. We all did.

Under the peace, states favoured mercenaries over popularly drafted troops. Such lives lost did not haunt the politician; their acts could be disavowed when inconvenient; if they rebelled, you held their pay; and if they were killed, you didn't pay them at all.

You have observed the mercenary's life, Jason. Of a year's campaign there totals what, ten days of actual fighting? Boil it down to moments when one stands within hazard's jaws and the tally condenses to minutes. All a man need do is survive that and he's earned another season. Indeed the mercenary holds more in common with the foe, to preserve their lives and livelihoods, than with his own officers, seeking glory. What is glory to the soldier for hire? He prefers survival.

The mercenary never calls himself by that name. If he owns armour and hires out as a heavy infantryman, he is a 'shield'. Javelineers are 'lances', archers 'bows'. A broker, called a *pilophoros* after his felt cap, will say, 'I need one hundred shields and thirty bows.'

No shield for hire tramps alone. Peril of robbery makes him seek a mate; it's easier to hire on as a pair or even a *tetras*. There are sites in each city where soldiers congregate seeking employment. In Argos a taverna named the Anthem, in Astacos a brothel called Knucklebones. In Heracleion are two hiring plazas; one beside the dry spring called Opountis, the other on the rise east of the Shrine of the Amazons, called by the locals Hyssacopolis, Pussy Town.

The countryside holds sites of custom as well. A chain of bivouacs called 'coops' runs from Sounium to Pella. 'Coop' serves as noun and verb. 'I need a dozen shields.' 'Try the Asopus, I saw a mob cooping there.' Some sites are little more than dry slopes beside streams; others – one called Tritaeia near Cleonae, another along the Peneus near Elis simply Potamou Campsis, Where the River Bends – are quite commodious, shaded copses with part-time markets, even the rude linen shelters called hourlies, where a soldier bringing a woman may obtain an interval of privacy before vacating for the next pair.

Abandoned hunting lodges are favoured sites for shields overnighting on the road. One recognizes these haunts from the surrounding slopes, logged down for firewood. An informal but remarkably efficient postal service covered the country then. Soldiers carried letters among their kit, parcels and 'sticks' thrust into their fists by wives and lovers or the odd mate encountered on the tramp. Each arrival at a coop would be encircled eagerly while he ran through his packet. If a man heard an absent mate's name called, he took the letter for him, often carrying it for half a year before at last completing delivery.

Hiring notices, called show rags, were posted at coops and brothels, even upon landmark shade trees or beside favoured springs. Learning of work, an entire coop will tramp off, electing their officers on the march. Mercenary rank is less formal than that of a state army. A captain is called by the number of men he brings. He is an 'eight' or a 'sixteen'. Officers are 'grade-men' or 'pennants', after the service sashes they mount upon their spearpoints, as guidons in assembly and dressing the line. A good officer never lacks for men eager to serve under him, nor a good man for commanders keen to sign him on. You find a crew you can count on and stick with them.

One sees the same faces in the profession. They all make the rounds. I ran into Telamon twice, on a ferry out of Patrae and at a coop on the Alpheus, before signing on with him the first fight at Trachis. Few use their real names. Nicknames and war names abound. Macedonians, 'macks', make up the main of the soldiery, hazel-eyed and orange-haired. I never served with a unit that didn't have a Big Red, a Little Red, and a gang in between.

No man unblooded or unvouched for is taken on for pay. He must serve free, and none shares food or fire till he has held his ground in a fight. Later on the rallying square, the grade-man approaches. 'When did you last draw wages?' 'Never yet, sir.' The officer takes his name and slips him a coin or two. 'Start tomorrow.' That's it. He's in.

Discipline, too, is less ceremonious among the breed for hire. At Heraclea in Trachis, the first scrape under Telamon, one of our number deserted in the assault. Astonishingly this rogue was waiting in camp when we returned, wearing an ingratiating smile and crossing towards Telamon, spouting an alibi. Without breaking stride our captain ran him through with his nine-footer, with such force that the iron shot forth, two hands' worth, from between the man's shoulder blades. In the instant the fellow lingered, impaled upon Telamon's shaft, our chief aired his edge and hacked him off at the neck. Still without a word he stripped corpse and kit, casting its contents to the whores and sutlers' boys, leaving nothing but a naked and dishonoured carcass. I chanced to be standing next to an Athenian shield we called Rabbit. He turned to me deadpan: 'Point taken.'

The rhythm of the mercenary's life is a narcotic, as the passion of the whoremonger or gambler, which careers the shield for hire, if he answers truly to that name, collaterally pursues. Its currents efface all that went before and all that will come after. First, and beyond all, fatigue. The infantryman breathes exhaustion night and day. Even in a gale at sea the soldier, returned from retching over the rail, collapses to the planks and drops off with ease, beard buried in the bilges.

Second stands boredom and third hunger. The soldier is foot-weary. He treks, ever upon the march, advancing towards some object which draws near only to be superseded by another, equally bereft of meaning. The earth endures beneath his tread, and he himself stands ready to drop upon it, if not in death then exhaustion. The soldier never sees the landscape, only the burdened back of the man trudging in column before him.

Fluids dominate the soldier's life. Water, which he must have or die. Sweat, which drips from his brow and drains in runnels down his rib cage. Wine, which he requires at march's end and battle's commence-ment. Vomit and piss. Semen. He never runs out of that. The penultimate, blood, and beyond that, tears.

The soldier lives on dreams and never tires of reciting them. He yearns for sweetheart and home, yet returns to the front with joy and never narrates his time apart.

Spear and sword, the manuals tell us, are the weapons of the infantry-man. This is erroneous. Pick and shovel are his province, hoe and mattock, lever and crowbar; these and the mortarman's hod, the forester's axe, and, beyond all, the quarryman's basket, that ubiquitous artefact the raw recruit learns to cobble on-site of reeds or faggots. And get her to set aright, my fellow, tumpline upon the brow, bowl across the shoulders with no knot to gouge the flesh, for when she is laden with rubble and stone to the measure of half your weight, you must hump her. Up that ladder, see? To where the forms of timber await to receive the fill that will become the wall that will encircle the city, whose battle-ments we will scale and tear down and set up all over again.

The soldier is a farmer. He knows how to shape the earth. He is a carpenter; he erects ramparts and palisades. A miner, he digs trenches and tunnels; a mason, he chisels a road from a sheer face of stone. The soldier is a physician who performs surgery without anaesthetic, a priest who inters the dead without psalm. He is a philosopher who plumbs the mysteries of existence, a linguist who pronounces 'pussy' in a dozen tongues. He is an architect and a demolition man, a fire brigadier and an incendiary. He is a beast who dwells in the dirt, a worm, owning a mouth and an anus and naught but appetite in between.

The soldier looks upon horrors and affects to stand indifferent to them. He steps, oblivious, over corpses in the road and flops to wolf his gruel upon stones painted black with blood. He imbibes tales that would bleach the mane of Hades and tops them with his own, laughing, then turns about and donates his last obol to a displaced woman or urchin he will never see again except cursing him from a wall or rooftop, hurling down tiles and stones to cleave his skull.

Half a dozen times with the macks of our coop we trekked through the pass at Thermopylae. Tourists, we trooped the Wall and dug for Persian bronzeheads on the hillock where the Three Hundred made their immortal stand. What would they think, these knights of yore, to behold war as we fought it? Not Hellene against barbarian in defence of sacred soil, but Greek against Greek out of partisanship and zealotry. Not army to army, man to man, but party against party, father against son, and bring the kids and Mum to sling a stone or slice a throat. What would these heroes of old think of civil conflagration in the streets of Corcyra, when the democrats surrounded four hundred *aristoi* within the temple of Hera, lured them forth with sacred oaths, then slaughtered them before their infants' eyes? Or the massacre of six hundred in the same city, when the *demos*, the people, walled their foes within a hostelry, tore off the roof, and rained death with brick and stone, that the immured wretches in despair slew themselves by driving into their throats the very arrows they were being shot down with and hanged themselves with the straps of the bedstands? What would they make of the fate later on of Melos or Scione, when the order came from Athens to slaughter all males and sell the women and children for slaves? How would they countenance their own countrymen's massacre of the men of Hysiae, or their conduct in the siege of Plataea, when the sons of Leonidas put to their captives one query only – 'What service have you performed for Sparta?' – then butchered them to the last man?

I had a woman in those years, of Samothrace originally, though when she was drunk she claimed to be from Troezen. Her name was Eunice, Fair Victory. She had been the camp wife of my mate, a captain-of-eight named Automedon who died, not of wounds, but a tooth of all things, infected. Eunice came into my bed that same night. 'You should not be with whores.' Quick as that she became my woman.

In what ways was she different from my bride Phoebe? Do you care, Jason? I'll tell you anyway.

As my dear bride was a blossom grown within the cloistered court, this Eunice was a shoot sprung upon the storm. This flower grew wild. She was the kind of woman you could leave with a comrade and she wouldn't fuck him behind your back. You'd return and they'd be laughing together, she cooking him something, and when he took his leave, he'd tug you aside. 'If you catch iron, I'll look out for her.' The supreme compliment.

Eunice was wise. When she ploughed you, her ankles set alongside your ears and her fingers clamped you hard at the ribs. You felt her greed for you and your seed, and even though you knew she'd move on to the next man with as little ceremony as she'd crossed to you, you couldn't complain. There was an integrity to it.

We were in Thrace one year under contract to Athens, raiding villages to support the fleet. The enterprise was preposterous; forty men would trek three days into the hills and come back with a single starving sheep. The wild tribes defended their flocks on horseback, with painted faces and magic symbols plastered on the flanks of their runt ponies. It was like warfare from an era antecedent to bronze, a thousand generations before Troy. To stumble back alive to camp, without even a fly for shelter, and roll onto one's woman on the steppe . . . this was not all bad.

The soldier's life is primordial; surrendered to it, he reverts to a state not just preliterate but prehistoric. That is its appeal.

I had slain my sister Meri.

My edge had opened her throat.

What remained for me but to wander, as far as war could bear me, to tramp upon the earth and bleed on it and dare it to enfold me beneath its mantle? Of course it didn't. Why? Had I become so without worth that I would live for ever?

In the second summer of the Peace our coop learned of work at good wages, rebuilding the walls of Argos and fortifying her port of Nauplia. This was Alcibiades' doing; he had double-crossed his Spartan friend Endius, leading a legation to Athens seeking to prevent this Argive alliance, making him out a fraud and liar before the people who, in rage, sealed the pact not alone with Argos but Elis and Mantinea as well.

Alcibiades was at Argos now, with four hundred carpenters and masons brought from Athens. Here was the fruit of Euryptolemus's design that his cousin work his ambition abroad. By the force of his person and persuasion, in open assembly and private discourse with the leading men, Alcibiades had brought over to Athens the three great democracies of the Peloponnese, two of whom had been allies of Sparta.

Our coop gaped at the scale of construction. From the citadel of the Larissa, as far as vision could carry, the city circuit stood compassed by scaffolding and construction inclines, derricks and roller sledges, road cutters, timber mills, factors' tents and teamsters' trains, with overall such a multitude at labour that men short of hods bore mortar on their bare backs, cupping it between their arms with fingers interlocked behind them. I located Euryptolemus, seeking a berth at wages for our coop. He clapped my shoulder, welcoming, and declared he could put us to far better use.

He signed us to train Messenian freedmen as heavy infantry, some two hundred who had been chattel at Sparta but fled to forts erected by Alcibiades and Nicias, securing their liberation. We would drill them all summer, accompanying Alcibiades to Patrae in the autumn to bring that city into alliance as well. When I remonstrated with our commander, at last securing an audience, that these Messenians would never be ready to fight by then, he only laughed. 'Who said anything about fighting?'

He would win Patrae by love.

And he did. Here is how.

Patrae, as you know, commands the western portal to the Gulf of Corinth. She was a democracy and neutral. Now, however, with the other great democracies of the Peloponnese – Elis, Mantinea, and Argos – brought into alliance with Athens, Patrae was a fruit ripe to fall.

Have you spent time in Patrae, Jason? It is a most agreeable place. Her dishes are squid cooked in its own ink and baked thrush. One dines there not in the marketplace, but at establishments called 'flags', which are private homes, many with terraces overlooking the sea. On entering, one takes a flag, a brightly coloured swatch bearing a symbol, of a dolphin or trident, say, and ties it about his shoulders. With that, he is a son of the family. That portion is his which he desires, or he may name a dish and the proprietress will produce it. At repast's end he folds his fare within his flag and leaves it on the bench.

The government of Patrae consists of two houses, the Council of Elders and the Assembly of the people. Alcibiades approached first those leading men with whom he was personally acquainted, and upon assuaging their fears of his and his nation's intentions, secured permission to address the commons. He was now thirty-two years old, twice a general of Athens, and the most spectacularly ascendant of the new breed of Greece. He spoke as follows:

'Men of Patrae, I proceed on the assumption that you, as all free Hellenes, would prefer independence and self-determination for your state, to having her affairs dictated by an alien power. Neutrality, you must agree, is no longer an option. Today each state of Greece must align with Athens or Sparta; no third alternative obtains.'

The Assembly of Patrae meets in the open air on an eminence called the Collar, overlooking the gulf. Alcibiades gestured now to these straits.

'To which element, sea or land, is your nation's future bound? This, I submit, is the decisive factor, for if land, her fate must stand with Sparta. This will produce the greatest security. But if one's hopes lie abroad through trade and commerce, one must recognize that that power which commands the sea cannot suffer another state to make use of this element to its advantage, if this works injury to herself.

'Patrae is sited on the sea, my friends, and upon a most strategic promontory. This works to your nation's benefit, making her of surpassing value to Athens as a friend, but to your peril, should you elect to make our city your foe. Do not delude yourself that this Peace will endure. War will come again. You must prepare now, determining which course yields the greater security – alliance with that naval power which needs you and must protect you, whose might opens up to your use all ports and sea-lanes of the world, shielding your merchantmen wherever their ambitions bear them and providing courts of law by which their interests may be safeguarded. Or choose to ally with a land power, Sparta and her League, which cannot defend you against seaborne assault, which will recruit your young men to fight as infantry where they are least well trained and equipped, and beneath whose hegemony you must suffer isolation and impoverishment, cut off from that intercourse of commerce which brings not alone the good things of life but the surplus of resource without which security is an illusion.'

He wanted Patrae to build long walls connecting the upper town to the port. When a Councillor resisted, narrating his fear that Athens would gobble Patrae up, Alcibiades responded, 'What you say may be true, my friend. But if she does, it will be by degrees and from the feet. Sparta will take you head-first and at one gulp.'

But his most telling argument required no articulation. This was the sight of the Messenian freedmen who, fired by their hatred of Sparta, had shaped into a crack unit. Here was what freedom and Athens could do for you, their presence said. Be like them, or face them.

Patrae did come over. With that, Alcibiades had detached from Sparta in her own backyard three powerful states and brought over a fourth from neutrality. He had fashioned a coalition whose combined armed forces rivalled that of her former master, all the while adhering to the letter of the Peace and setting not a solitary Athenian life at hazard. He would move next, or his proxies would, against a fifth state, Epidaurus, whose fall would complete that gambit by which the sixth and most crucial Spartan ally, Corinth, would find herself cut off and vulnerable as well.

Now for the first time one began to see Spartans and Spartan agents. Their cavalry appeared across Achaea and the Argolid, followed by those surrogates in scarlet of the seventy Laconian towns, the so-called Neighbours, heavy infantry drilled to such a pitch as exceeded all save the Corps of Peers itself. Mindarus arrived, the field marshal, and Endius and Cleobulus, leaders of the war party. They and their lieutenants began showing up at coops, the first time we had seen full Spartiates recruiting shields and free lances. One excelled all in the zeal of his application. This was Lysander the son of Aristocleitus, that same Lysander whose name would toll down Athenian annals, synonymous with doom.

Telamon took work from him and chided me for my reluctance. Others of our coop ran 'errands' as well. They would not recount these actions, even to me. One knew only that they were performed at night and they paid well.

With Telamon I heard Lysander address the Patraean Council.

'Men of Patrae, the speech of the Athenian general' (meaning Alcibiades, who had addressed the Assembly some days previous) 'is known to all and has been countered by ambassadors of my city, whose eloquence far outstrips my own. None the less my regard for your nation is such that, though I come before you as a soldier only, I must add my voice to these rebuttals. Make no mistake, friends. The course you elect now must bear profound consequences. I beg you resist the impulse to haste. The hare may leap into the pot, they say, but not back out once the lid is made fast.

'Let me speak to the distinction between the Athenian character and the Spartan. Perhaps you have not considered this. What kind of nation are the Spartans? We are not a seafaring people, nor is it in our nature to covet empire. Our portion of the Peloponnese we hold, content, never seeking its aggrandizement. Our alliances are defensive. Even when we strike overseas at our foes, our object is not to conquer, only to quell potential peril. Those states which border upon us we hold fast; this is true. As distance increases, however, the reins slacken.

'Your state stands at a remove from ours, men of Patrae. What do we want of you? Only that you remain free, independent, and strong. In this, we believe, resides our security, for a free state will resist incursion with all her might. Do you fear we shall harm you? On the contrary, Sparta will aid in every way to preserve your independence, so long as you do not turn such strength against us.

'Now consider the Athenians. They are a sea power. They are empire builders. Already they hold two hundred states in subjection. Patrae will make two hundred and one. This speechmaker who has come before you, this general of Athens, has dispensed honeyed words and re-assurance. You must see through these, my friends, for by just such blandishments have other states been seduced from their liberty. Ask yourselves if you will find this man so charming when he returns with warships to exact tribute of your treasury, when he drafts your young men for his fleet and imposes upon your nation Athenian codes and laws. How equitable will this so-called alliance feel when you must turn in the very coins of your purse and take "owls" of Athens in return? Your guest has promised protection under Athenian law. What does this mean, except that even the most modest private suit may no longer be settled by your own courts but be adjudicated at Athens, before Athenian juries, amid such corruption and cupidity as I pray you are never compelled to endure.

'You of the nobility are estate holders and equestrians. When war resumes, and it will – in this our Athenian friend spoke truly – who will suffer most among your countrymen? Will it be the commons, who will find work with the fleet and discover their position enhanced by war, or yourselves, whose property, which lies outside these vaunted Long Walls, will be laid waste? Whose sons will die first, whose estate be reduced and devastated?'

My mates ran other jobs for Lysander. Pay for one that autumn was thirty drachmas, a month's wages for two nights' work, but it required a man acquainted with the roads inside Lacedaemon. When Telamon informed his employer that his mate was an *anepsios*, educated at Sparta, I was sent for. Lysander had his headquarters then at an inn called the Cauldron, at Ptolis on the Mantinean frontier. We were ushered in after midnight when all other officers, and witnesses, had been dismissed.

Lysander claimed to remember me from the Upbringing, extremely unlikely as he was three age-classes ahead and in an elite training battalion. I remembered him, however. Of the four Firsts a youth could win in his commission year, in Wrestling, Chorus, Obedience, and Chastity, Lysander took three. His birth, however, was so mean, and he was seen so to curry favour with his betters, that such qualities failed to gain him the swift ascent they remarked. Peace further retarded his career. He was thirty-five or about; he should hold a lieutenant-colonelcy of infantry. Instead he was just a cavalry captain, the least prestigious element of Spartan arms. In fact nothing about him impressed me this night so much as his good looks, which were nearly as arresting as Alcibiades'. He was tall, with steel-coloured eyes and hair falling to his shoulders. That this individual would one day preside over the dismemberment of the Athenian Empire and reign as a god over the entire Hellenic world seemed in this hour impossible of conception.

Lysander detailed the prospective errand. Telamon and I were to convey to Sparta a fledgling owl in a cage, a gift from himself to Cleobulus, chief of the war party. The real chore, however, was to deliver a despatch, which for fear of discovery must be committed to memory and imparted to its addressee only. This was a plea to the Board of Magistrates to take seriously the intrigues of Alcibiades. The ephors must act, and act swiftly, for the measures set in motion by this solitary Athenian, Lysander professed, had placed the very survival of Sparta at hazard. When I balked at performing this, fearing it would work harm to my countrymen, Lysander laughed. 'Remember, you can always tender this intelligence, and all else you see and hear at Lacedaemon, to your friend' – meaning Alcibiades – 'for love or profit.' To this day I recall the text.

> . . . our peril lies neither with the knight Nicias nor the so-called popular leaders of Athens – Hyperbolus, Androcles, and the demagogues – whose vision extends no further than pandering to the mob for next year's election, but with this glory-driven aristocrat who alone possesses both strategic vision and implacable will. He employs this Peace as if it were war, seeking to advance his personal renown through the surrogateship of other states, his object to cut off our nation from her Peloponnesian allies. We must counter these conspiracies before it is too late, my friend, nor scruple at means or measures.

Lysander knew Alcibiades. From summers in boyhood, when Alcibiades and his brothers visited their xenos, guest-friend, Endius at Sparta. As a youth Lysander, as I said, had been penniless; he had secured tuition to the Upbringing only as a mothax, a 'stepbrother' or sponsoree, dues paid by Endius's father, named Alcibiades. You may reckon to what extent such subordination galled the youth's pride and fuelled the acrimony he bore lifelong towards his rival.

I ran this job and others, courier chores mostly. At Sparta one indeed felt a sea change. The war party had seized ascendancy; the young men (and, more telling, the women) clamoured for action that would restore Spartan pride. A battle was coming. You could smell it.

The army took the field twice that summer, both full call-ups under King Agis. When the second fizzled at the very gates of Argos, the Spartans turned upon their own king in fury at his fecklessness. Alcibiades leapt upon this. Rousing the allies, they took Orchomenos, securing the plain and passes north of Mantinea and cutting off Sparta from her allies beyond the gulf. Tegea and Orestheum now stood vulnerable as well. The fall of these was unthinkable to Spartan arms, as they opened the entire Eurotas valley. Yet still the ephors did not act. The knights and colonels thought their king a dunce or a coward, and no-one trusted the freed helots who now constituted a significant portion of the army. The cauldron bubbled just shy of the boil.

One night Telamon came with a job. We would run it on horseback with two Athenian shields, Rabbit and Chowder, so named for his incapacity to keep a meal down at sea. The task was to descend downvalley to Tegea, twelve miles; from there to escort in secret the commander of the Spartan regiment on-site, Anaxibius, to the fort at Tripolis, where he would receive orders from the home government. We must have him there at the second watch and back to Tegea by dawn.

Lysander did not inform us of this, but Alcibiades was at that hour at Tegea. He was there with his freed Messenians, addressing the Council.

We located the Spartan and got off. Before the party had ridden a mile, however, a runner from Lysander intercepted us. Plans had changed; we must divert to the shrine of Artemis on the Tegea–Pallantion road.

Our Spartan, Anaxibius, was a full colonel and in no way averse to employing the ash of his staff upon the tardy or slow of wit. Twice he cracked Chowder across the ribs, demanding to know who the hell had trained us and what kind of a cocked-up operation we were running.

We reached the sanctuary well into the second watch. Clearly our irascible charge would not be back by dawn. Nor, mounting the steps, could Lysander be discovered. 'By the Twins!' – Anaxibius smote the stone with the butt of his staff such a blow as nearly ruptured the drums of our ears – 'I'll flay you all for this insolence, and that bastard *mothax* in his turn.'

From behind a column emerged Lysander, alone save his squire, called Strawberry after a birthmark. He beseeched the colonel's pardon, who yet clutched his staff before him and continued to beat it upon the stone, taking in vain the names of abundant divinities. Lysander appealed to him to desist, as troops were encamped about and the racket might be taken as an alarm. 'Take your staff to me, sir, if you wish, but hear the message I am ordered to impart.'

Anaxibius at last lowered his lumber. In that instant Lysander snatched forth his own blade and, striking upon the colonel's undefended right, fetched him such a blow, backhand, as to cleave his neck to the bone and in fact nearly decapitate him. Anaxibius dropped like a sack from a wagon; fluid gushed as from an overturned pail. Our four gaped as Strawberry spun the fallen form facedown on the stone and, plunging again and again into its back the bared steel of a nine-foot spear, inflicted such wounds as could only be read as the blows of cowards and assassins.

Weapons filled my mates' hands; our squad had formed up, backs to each other, certain that our own murders were next, at the hands of other concealed confederates of Lysander. No sound came, however. No squads materialized from shadow. If indeed there was a camp about, no stir arose from it.

'What a waste.'

Lysander broke the silence, indicating the corpse of his countryman. He spat blood. He had bitten his lip through, accidentally, as one does frequently in such exigencies. 'He was a good officer.'

'For whose murder we four will be accounted.' This from Telamon, indicating himself and our party.

'Not by name,' was our employer's cool rejoinder.

Lysander knelt, examining what had been a man and was now meat.

One came by degrees to grasp his perfidy's object. The colonel's assassination would be passed off as the work of agents of Athens. We who had been dupes need neither be named nor apprehended; the act alone would suffice to ignite outrage at Sparta. The home government would shuck its sloth and rise, in time to snatch Tegea from the brink.

'Will you murder us now, Captain?' Telamon enquired.

Lysander rose, pressing at his cut lip. He had, by his demeanour, never entertained such a notion.

'Men such as yourselves, who stand apart from the fealty of statehood, are invaluable to me.'

He nodded to his squire, who accorded us our pay.

'Then we will require more than this,' spoke Telamon.

Our patron laughed. 'I'm flat broke.'

'We'll have the horses, then.'

Lysander approved this.

Rabbit had crossed to the portico; he motioned all clear. My own blood, which had run chill for all this interval, now refound its course and heat. 'Who slaughters his own, Captain,' I heard my voice address the Spartan, 'scorns God as well as man.'

Lysander's eyes met mine, as steel-black as I recalled. 'Take your man's portion, Polemidas, and leave heaven to me.'

# ELEVEN
# MANTINEA

IWOULD NOT HAVE BEEN AT MANTINEA SAVE FOR MY BROTHER. HE WAS
at Orchomenos with Alcibiades and got a message to me.

*The greatest battle in history is about to be fought. I shall try to hold it
for you, if you hurry.*

One must understand the topography of the Peloponnese to reckon
the peril to the Spartan state had she failed to carry that day. From
Mantinea the Argives and allies, had they been victorious, would have
swept down the plain to Tegea, then south to Asea and Orestheum,
from which the entire Eurotas valley lay open to the sword. Sparta's serfs
would have risen, in numbers ten times their masters'. Slaughter by hoe
and mattock would have confronted the lads and women of Sparta.
Joined by whatever remained of the Corps of Peers, the defenders would
have resisted to the last breath, perishing in a bloodbath unprecedented.

I arrived the morning of the battle, in the train with Telamon and our
Messenians, so wretched with septic fever that I must be borne on a
wagon with the infants, the pregnant camp wives, and the spare
spearshafts.

I had never seen so many troops, and of such quality. Once as lads,
Lion and I had larked after the runners in the torch race of
the Panathenaea. From the statue of Love in the Academy where the

competitors light their brands, we paced with them through the Sacred Gate, across the agora, past the Altar of the Twelve Gods, lapping the Acropolis to the Heracleum, every foot of which thronged with humanity. That was nothing beside Mantinea. The entire army of Argos stood to hand, led by their élite, the Thousand, along with the corps of Mantinea, regiment after regiment, the Cleonaeans and Orneaeans, the allies and hired troops of Arcadia, with a thousand heavy infantry of Athens, despatched in 'defensive posture', so as not to poach upon the Peace. Further, it seemed, every jack of the Argolid who could hurl a dart or sling a stone had collected, making five and six light-armed for every heavy infantryman.

We crossed with our Messenians behind the marshalling troops. I was sick and puking like a dog. I must arm, however, or never face my mates again. I was just commencing, abetted by Eunice, when Lion reined in above. He bore a courier's pennant and trailed a second mount, a mare which, he reported, had thrown her rider.

I must mount as a despatch runner. Such office, at Alcibiades' orders, would not be left this day to pages but only officers. Alcibiades was on-site not as a commander (he had failed of election this term to the Board of Generals at Athens), but only as an envoy. Such distinctions were academic, of course, as any post he held became the hub and marrow simply by his occupation of it. Here was how the battle kicked off:

There had been a false start three days prior, a full-dress advance aborted by Agis a stone's toss before contact. The Spartans had withdrawn south to Tegea. No-one knew what they were up to. Attempting to flood the plain, the allies heard. The month was Boedromion; there wasn't a course strong as an old man's piss in either river. A day passed; then another. The allies took fright that Agis would pull something truly harebrained. They came down off Mount Alesion, an impregnable position, into the throat of the plain, just north of the Pelagos wood. Word came that the Spartans were advancing from the south with every spit and jigger they could carry. That was when I arrived. The allies had formed up, two miles across, barring the plain.

Now a fresh rumour started: the Spartans had turned back. There would be no battle; our side would haul out too. The regiment above which my brother and I perched had marshalled beneath pear trees, the only crop left untorched by the Spartans because they were not ripe, and

the troops from boredom had begun gnawing the stony culls. These
made men crap like geese. By twos and threes troops fell from formation,
ostensibly to heed nature's call but in truth to get a start on packing for
decampment.

Suddenly one saw dust.

Wisps ascended from the Pelagos wood a mile away. This appeared at
first as the brush-burning in autumn, when the olive grovers rake their
piles beneath the canopy and set them alight. Now tendrils grew to
vapours, and vapours to clouds. All stir ceased within our formation.
The front of dust broadened; isolated risers conjoined. The tread of
thirty thousand could not raise such a storm; the enemy must be twice
that. Yet one saw neither a flash off a shield nor even a scout rider
cantering in the fore. Just dust, ascending in thunderheads from the
canopy of oak until the wood seemed to smoke from end to end.

Lion reined beside me; we must make to the commanders to receive
orders. He began directing me to the swiftest track. Suddenly, in-
explicably, our troops began to advance.

You have witnessed such movements in hosts of men. Soldiers in
massed formation often cannot hear even a legitimate signal, owing to
various clamours of the field. The individual finds himself stepping off
in response to the motion of others, knowing no more why he follows
than a sheep or a goose. At any event the corps began to move. 'Get to
the fore.' My brother motioned me towards the plain. 'Find out what the
hell's going on!'

I have said I am no equestrian. More, the mare was fractious; as I
sought to heel her through the milling troops she began to caper and
buck. The formation was among orchards, as I said, with branches
abounding to crack one's skull, not to say a forest of elevated spearpoints
as my mount plunged past, while my knees and ankles clamped her in a
death grip and both fists clawed into her mane. Beast and rider broke
into the clear.

From Pelagos the first columns of the foe now emerged. We learned
later that the Spartans had been startled nearly witless, issuing from the
wood, by the sudden apparition of the allied army drawn up before
them. Such was the brilliance of their discipline, however, and the order
with which they deployed from column of march to line of battle, that
it was we and not they who nearly buckled with terror.

I turned back to our side, the estate of Euctemon, whoever he was, who owned the land upon which the allied armies had marshalled. Here they came, left and right but no middle. Two corps advanced, with half a mile of daylight between. By the gods, what a mess!

Enemy regiments continued unpeeling from the wood. One discovered in aftermath the extent of the Spartan mobilization. So grave was the perceived threat engineered by Alcibiades that the foe had called up seven of eight age-classes, eight thousand Spartiates under both kings, Agis and Pleistoanax, with the full Corps of Knights and four of five ephors present as serving officers. In addition they had activated the forces of the seventy Lacedaemonian towns, twenty thousand heavy infantry, constrained to 'follow the Spartans whithersoever they shall lead', with the whole army of Tegea defending native soil, the Arcadian allies of Heraea and Maenalia, plus the freed helots, the *brasidioi*, and the 'new citizens', the *neodamodeis*. With the Argives, Mantineans, and allies arrayed in opposition, this was the mightiest massing of Greek against Greek in history.

Now I saw Alcibiades. Even at a distance one knew him by the dash with which he rode. The allied centre at last emerged, with him and other officers galloping to join the commanders in the fore.

The full body of the foe had emerged from the wood, fifteen hundred yards off. On the flat between the armies one could see materializing, as preceding all battles, boys afoot and on ponies, and even girls come to lark and goggle. Some, caught up in the moment, would dash onto the field and lose their lives; others would prove heroes, recovering the fallen; while yet more would linger to loot the corpses of the slain. One heard the cries of dogs. The wild packs can smell a battle, and even tame hounds, whipped to a pitch by that keening heard only by their race, may be driven from the field by naught but their own extinction. I galloped towards the commanders. One could see them unnerved by the foe's impeccable advance. 'Let it be now!' Alcibiades called above the approaching din. 'Let it be now!'

The foe's skirmishers led, an eighth of a mile off. Lion hauled in beside me. The first sling bullets started chewing divots at our feet; in moments stones began clattering like hail. I could not reach the commanders, scattering to their units. We must fight as cavalry now, my brother shouted. Here came our own darters and lancers, packs of them

on the scamper, and to the rear the mass of the heavy infantry, Argives, Mantineans and Athenians, Orneaeans and Cleonaeans, and the mercenary Arcadians. The plain trembled beneath their tread. They had commenced the *paean*, the same Hymn to Castor their Doric kinsmen, the Spartans, would take up in moments.

At the right of the field twined a dry course and the wreckage of a vineyard torched earlier by the foe. Over these razed walls advanced the Spartan Sciritae, eighty shields across and eight deep, whose place of honour is ever on the left. Adjacent pressed another sixteen hundred scarlet cloaks, the regiments who had fought in Thrace under Brasidas; they and the new citizens, two hundred shields more bearing the *lambda* of Lacedaemon.

On their right came the Corps of Peers. There was no mistaking the precision of their order and the brilliance of their kit. Every other nation of Greece advances to battle beneath the trumpet; only Spartans employ the pipes. These now skirled that cadenced wail which is part music and part curdling of the blood. Agis the king marched at the centre, flanked by the Three Hundred, the *agema* of Knights. The entire force, all seven regiments, strode in scarlet with their shields at march port and spears, unsheathed nine-footers, at the upright.

Across the air came 'Advance to Battle'. The beat picked up and the corps as one lifted its voice in the Hymn to Nike. The formation, shields straked solid, rolled out onto the flat of the plain. I clutched my mare's mane and kicked her like hell.

On came the line of *lambdas*. The Mantineans who must clash with them had worked themselves into a state of frenzy. Fear drove them to shout and beat their shields; out front their officers sought in vain to check the discomposure. Four hundred yards now separated the armoured infantry. The allied line kept edging right, as armies will, as each individual seeks the shelter of the shield of the man at his shoulder, so that our wing overlapped the Spartans by an eighth of a mile. An order peeled down their line; the pipers picked it up; the Sciritae went to echelon left, fanning to conform to the oncoming Mantineans. A gap opened between them and the adjacent companies. Something had got cockeyed. No reserves advanced to fill the break. The Sciritae commanders, perceiving their vulnerability, piped back to the right. Too late. A hundred yards remained. Spears lowered to the attack. With a cry the Mantineans closed ranks and fell upon the Spartan left.

Of all moments of concentrated fury in this long and bitter war, few surpassed this, as the corps of Mantinea, fighting for home and country against that race which had lorded it over them for centuries, descended upon this blood foe, while the isolated left of Sciritae and *brasidioi* set shoulder by shoulder and dug in to endure the scrum of the *othismos*.

My brother and I were on the extreme right, with the cavalry and the overlapped heavy infantry of Mantinea. The Spartan left had been cut off on both sides, to their right by the void between themselves and the Corps of Peers, to the left by the lapped wing of the Mantineans. Here is the posture a fighting force fears most – envelopment.

Slingers and javelineers of both sides, who had been passed over by the heavy troops in the advance, now flooded into the gaps, assaulting each other and the compacted infantry. They were so close to the fight, the darters, that they flung their shafts over the shoulders of their comrades, into the faces of the foe, while across, the same dish was being served hot to them. Clouds of missiles arced and ascended, plunging and vanishing within battlements of dust. The Mantinean heavy infantry swept past Lion and me, as triremes on the sea in that manoeuvre called the 'breakthrough', shooting the Spartan line and doubling back to take it from flank and rear. The enemy wing, doubled upon itself, resisted with spectacular gallantry. But the mass of the Mantineans, ten thousand against fewer than five, drove them under. The foe bellied rearward. Fusillades rained upon their shivered ranks, while the heavy armour of Mantinea heaved and rammed, thirty and forty men deep. Such a cry of joy erupted as the Mantineans, so long overawed by these masters of the Peloponnese, forecast for an instant the overthrow of Sparta entire. It seemed in that moment as if nothing could stop it.

The allies drove the Sciritae back across the dry course and into the trees, all the way to the Spartan camp where the older men and the baggage train awaited. They burned this and slaughtered all they could lay hands on.

The warrior must resist now that dislocation which in the flush of apparent victory dissevers him from self-command. I found my brother and reined beside him. Our own archers were shooting at us and the other friendly cavalry, purely from elation and the prospect of such juicy targets. 'We have to get over!' Lion shouted, meaning to the left of the field, where our Athenian troops and cavalry fought. We rallied what horsemen we could and set out.

A rack of defiles impeded our passage; light troops ranged like locusts. The field stood choked with smoke and dust. Mounting a rise, we expected to see the central corps clashing. Instead the expanse sprawled vacant, populated only by scattered wounded of Mantinea and Argos. We peered right, seeking the Spartans in flight. There was nothing.

We spun left. Already half a mile gone could be seen the rear ranks of the Corps of Peers, Agis, the Knights, and the seven regiments. They were driving the Argives as dogs drive sheep. What struck terror was the pitiless precision of the Spartan advance. Neither ravening nor keening as other armies in the rush of triumph, but in order, pressing steadily, relentlessly forward. As stalks of grain submit to the scythe, so did the allies fall before the Spartan advance. Their centre was a half mile across, victorious along its entire length.

I heard a cry at my shoulder. A rider crumpled and pitched. Sling bullets screamed past our ears. The foe's skirmishers, no longer in companies but a disordered host, rushed at us on the hinter ground. Our pack bolted; again my mount balked. Lion wheeled to my aid. We could see the mob of men and boys dashing upon us, while their bolts and missiles tore past with the sound of rending fabric.

We got to a ditch, but mounting the far wall my mare tumbled. I hit teeth-first with the beast spilling on top of me. My brother had breasted the bank and spurred on. From the brink the foe poured stones and darts. To my astonishment the mare returned. She was a warhorse! I clawed onto her back, which was lacerated in more places than my own. But the sheer bank undid us. Three boys had got within the ditch; they were slingers and too close to fire; instead they rushed and backed, bawling profanities as they sought to hamstring the mare with their sickles and foul her legs with the straps of their slings. Rarely have I experienced such terror, looking into those urchin eyes mad for my blood. My brother thundered from nowhere to preserve me, he and our pack from the right of the field. The mare flew from the trench. 'You're supposed to ride the horse, not the other way round!' Lion roared as we fled.

The far left was where our countrymen were, and the cavalry with Alcibiades. We must reach them, if only to die at their side. But the ground as if sown with dragon's teeth birthed yet more skirmishers. We were sitting ducks, up high. Damn me if I ever climb on a horse again! Suddenly the main Spartan corps reversed and countermarched. One of those implausible moments of war now eventuated. The foe broke off pursuit of the Argives and Orneaeans and came about to assist its own routed countrymen of the left. This preserved us, the erstwhile horse of that quarter, from the slingers who ravened upon our track. Massed Spartan armour swept past, interdicting our pursuers. The Corps of Peers are of course all heavy infantry; on horseback we were out of their reach. Past they surged, close enough to read the details on their unit guidons and see the men's eyes within their sockets of bronze.

On the left our Athenians had been routed too; the infantry had long fled, leaving the cavalry to range the overrun ground, defending the wounded as best they could. I saw Alcibiades' horse, dead in the dirt, and farther in a ditch his helmet.

It struck with the clarity of revelation that our nation could not survive his loss. Perhaps this distress was fatigue-spawned. Surely my bowels and belly had been void for hours. Strength had fled both arms from grappling all day with this wild beast, upon whose back the pounding had sapped the last from my hams and knees. And yet, with that lucidity that comes at the end of one's strength, this fear for our commander seemed valid utterly.

I must find him. Must preserve him. Up and down the courses I drove my unruly mare, whose name I never learned and never care to, seeking Alcibiades.

I could not find him. Only in camp, when descent of night had at last adjourned the struggle, did he emerge from the field, in infantryman's armour, which he had stripped apparently from a corpse midbattle and in which he had fought all day. He did not shed it now but ranged among the troops of Argos and the allies, the shield on his shoulder dark with blood and his eyes like snuffed tapers.

In defeat one learns who are friends to one, and by whom one is accounted friend. Past midnight Alcibiades' attendant summoned my brother and me to his tent. Only those most intimate were included – his cousin Euryptolemus, Mantitheus, Antiochus the pilot, Diotimus, Adeimantus, Thrasybulus, and a dozen others. This was the singular honour of our lives, Lion's and mine, nor did either stand uncognizant of it.

It was a most dolorous caucus. What wisdom could be culled from calamity was carved like a dry goose and shared out absent appetite.

Defeat tolled the knell for our commander's alliance. Mantinea and Elis would be compelled again into the Spartan fold, as would Patrae, whose long walls would be torn down. Orchomenos could not be held; Epidauris and Sicyon would be squeezed tighter beneath the foe's screw. The Spartans would exile or execute the last democrats and take as hostages children of all suspect families. At Argos the democracy would fall; it would only be a matter of time before she, too, toppled into the Spartan bag.

Alcibiades did not speak all evening, permitting Euryptolemus to articulate as his surrogate, as he often did, so in tune were the cousins with each other's cast of mind. Euro urged his kinsman to depart for Athens at dawn. Word of defeat would fly home; he must stand present to endure it with honour and to shore up those who had stood at his side.

Alcibiades would not leave. He must remain to take up the dead. 'The dam is down, cousin,' he accounted. 'We will not hold the flood.'

None slept that night. Retrieval parties formed up before dawn. Mules and asses, even cavalry mounts, had been rigged with the pole sleds called 'baker's boards'; wagons of the commissariat had been recruited, augmented by sledges and litters; men carried cloaks and blankets upon which a body may be borne. The Spartans sent across their priests of Apollo to sanctify the field and formalize permission to us to take up our dead. They had already reclaimed their own.

At first light the Hymn to Demeter and Kore was sung; the parties moved out by tribes. Alcibiades wore dust sandals and a white chiton without emblem of rank. He was grave but not downcast. He took up the dead in silence, working beside soldiers' squires and even slaves.

Where the Tegeans and lesser Lacedaemonians had won their victory, the bodies of the allied slain had been stripped naked. Armour and weapons were plundered; the foe had looted even the shoes.

Where the Corps of Peers had triumphed, however, no corpses had been violated. Each lay where he had fallen, intact of shield and armour. The Spartans had granted them honour to forbear this indignity. Many wept, my brother included, to behold such greatness of heart.

Midday found Alcibiades stopping with the party in which my brother and I laboured. 'Is it true, Pommo, that you dashed about the field at battle's close, seeking to preserve me?' A number had told him as much; this seemed to delight him enormously. 'I did not know you loved me so.'

I advanced some jest that we of the infantry needed him; he knew how to pay. He did not laugh at this poor joke; rather glanced soberly, first to my brother, then me. 'Of payment I know this, my friends – how to requite those whose hearts are true.'

Earlier in the forenoon, Lion and I were told later, Alcibiades had chanced to be at the extreme right of the field, that quarter where we had been when the Mantineans routed the Spartan Sciritae. He was speaking with several Mantinean officers when a captain of Spartan cavalry rode up and reined in.

It was Lysander. The rivals spoke at ease, strife forsworn beneath the truce. Lysander remarked the scale of the allied victory in this quarter. Had such prevailed across even another fifth of the field, the outcome had been catastrophe for Sparta.

'You came this close, Alcibiades,' Lysander is said to have spoken.

In response his adversary quoted the proverb 'Close captures no crowns.'

To which Lysander replied, 'God grant that be your epitaph,' and, turning, spurred away.

When the shadows began to lengthen, the Spartan Corps of Peers moved out for home. We could see them emerge round the shoulder of the wood and trek in column towards the Tegea Road. Agis strode at the fore, flanked by the Knights, with the seven regiments in order in the train. Lion pointed. There was Lysander; he had insinuated his cavalry into a role as royal guard. These trooped adjacent the fore *polemarchs*, the war leaders, and the *pythioi*, the priests of Apollo. The main body trailed, to the skirling of the pipes.

They were eight thousand, all in scarlet, spears at the slope, with squires, one to a man, trooping at their shoulders, bearing their shields, slung and burnished to a mirror's sheen. Where we stood in the dust of the field, all squatted in shadow. The victors strode in sun.

They were singing. A cadence chant, 'Haemorrhoids, Hangnails, and Hell', which to a beat bespeaks a profane disdain for death. Their spear-points were sheathed, but their helmets, bossed, flashed like gold in the sun.

A sound broke from Alcibiades. When I turned, his brow stood flushed; tears pooled in the well of his eyes. At first I apprehended this as grief, at the overthrow of all his enterprise. Examination, however, discovered this affect barren of regret. He was moved, as we all, by the splendour of the enemy's discipline and will.

'Magnificent-looking bastards, aren't they?'

# TWELVE
# A COMPANION OF THE FLEET

U PON TERMINATION OF THIS DAY'S SESSION WITH THE ASSASSIN
Polemides [my grandfather continued], *as he and I took leave of one
another, the man requested of me a service.*

*His sea chest, he declared, lay now in storage at the officers' commissary at
Munychia naval base, in the care of the porter. Would I retrieve it for him?
There were documents in it he wished to show me. More, he added, would I
keep this chest after his execution?*

*I urged the man not to get ahead of himself. Acquittal was possible, perhaps
even probable, given Socrates' conviction and the powerful association in the
public mind between the philosopher and Alcibiades. Alcibiades' repute stood
now at its ebb; this did not augur inauspiciously for any in faction of
opposition to him.*

*'Yes, of course.' Polemides smiled. 'I forgot.'*

*Passing out of the prison, I was detained at the portal by a violent thunder-
shower. As I waited on the storm's passage a boy approached, dashing from
the victualler's shop across the way and, confirming my identity, bade me bide
a few moments longer. An older man could be seen, a cripple, hobbling into
the lane from the same shop. The fellow shambled across, presenting himself
before me in the posture of a beggar. I retreated, set to step into the downpour
rather than endure the assault of this unkempt and aggressive mute. 'You don't
recognize me, do you, sir?'*

The man's voice struck me through.

'It's Eumelus of Oa, Cap'n. "Bruise". From the old Europa.'

'Bruise? By the Holy Twain, can it be you?'

This man had served with me at Abydos and Bitch's Tomb under Alcibiades, twenty years into the war and eleven prior to this day. He had been a toxotes, a marine archer, and something of a personal batman to me. A game but inexpert boxer, hence his nickname, he possessed the courage of an eagle and harboured ambitions to rise in service. At Abydos he had borne me from Europa's quarterdeck when my leg had been sheared in the action.

Bruise had remained in service to the bitter end: Aegospotami. He was captured by Lysander and sentenced to death but was reprieved to the slavers' block by the lie that his mother was Megarian and he thus not an Athenian citizen. 'Soon as they burned me, I skipped. I was home in time to watch Lysander sail in and take our surrender.'

He led me across to the victualry. The shop was his; the lad his grandson. Through his daughter-in-law, he testified, he had secured a contract under the Eleven Administrators; his mart provisioned the warders and inmates, since the refectory's shuttering in the latest crackdown. He, Bruise, had noted my passing in and out of the prison, but this day was the first, he said, that he had summoned the temerity to approach.

We spoke of vanished comrades and departed times. He remarked the case of Socrates. Bruise had been among the five hundred and one jurors; he had voted to condemn. 'A man come up to me by the Anaceum, told me if I liked my contract I'd toss the black pebble.'

Parting, my old shipmate drew me aside to confide this caution: certain unscrupulous turnkeys might approach me or others of the philosopher's party, proposing for a fee to spirit the prisoner to freedom. This was a drama he, Bruise, had witnessed no few times: the midnight horse, the dash for the frontier, the double cross. 'First peep you hear, Cap'n, come to me. I know these blackguards. I'll spring your friend myself before I'll let 'em turn the left hand upon him.' I took this intelligence seriously and thanked him from the heart.

The storm had abated; I stood upon the point of taking leave. I must enquire of my old mate if he had acquaintance of Polemides. Indeed. 'A good marine; none better.' What about Polemides' part in Alcibiades' assassination, I probed, for I knew that Bruise, as so many of the Samos fleet, revered *their old commander and upheld his memory with passion. To my surprise Bruise harboured no rancour towards the assassin.*

*'But he betrayed Alcibiades,' I pressed.*

*Bruise shrugged. 'Who didn't?'*

*At home that night, prompted perhaps by Polemides' request for retrieval of his sea chest, I mounted to the loft in search of my own. To this day sea fighters mark their coffers in the time-honoured manner, carving into the pine the stations upon which they have served and tacking beside each a coin of that province. I brought my chest into the library. When the porter delivered Polemides' next day, no other site seemed apt, so I had him set it down, side by side with my own.*

*How different were we, the assassin and myself, who had served our country, both, down thrice nine years of war? Who could tell, remarking our baggage?*

*I opened my own. At once arose the smells of campaigns, and campaigners, past. I must sit, overcome, and wept for those companions upon whom eternal night had closed, and these, philosopher and assassin, who must tread that same dark passage soon.*

*My wife, your grandmother, chanced to pass at that moment and, discovering her husband in this case, crossed to me and in kindness enquired of my state. I had made a decision, I told her – just now, this instant.*

*By all the gods I would toil for Polemides' exoneration, nor stay at any measure within the law to see him freed.*

# THIRTEEN
## THREE TIMES
## THE VICTOR'S NAME

HE GAMES OF THE OLYMPIAD FOLLOWING MANTINEA [*POLEMIDES
*resumed*] were those in which Alcibiades' teams took first, second,
and third in the four-horse. Not triumph at Troy nor the apparition of
Apollo himself in a winged chariot could have effected a grander sensation. Twice a hundred thousand ringed the hippodrome. Do you recall
the victory ode Euripides composed? How did it go? 'Son of Cleinias . . .
something something . . . this glory

> *. . . must be the height of fame,
> to hear the herald cry three times
> the selfsame victor's name.'*

I missed the race. Our coop arrived late, only ferrying from Naupactus for
the free feed. Alcibiades appeared, we heard, with all three teams at a
banquet in his honour thrown by the city of Byzantium, whose citadel
he took by storm less than a decade later. Agis the Spartan king was there
with forty of his knights. The mob abandoned him just to glimpse
Alcibiades's drivers. Ephesus, Chios, Lesbos, and Samothrace erected
pavilions in his honour. The Samians sent a barge full of hymn-chanting
virgins, which ran aground, and all the wrestlers went out, in their
garlands, to save them. The river was about a handsbreadth deep, if I recall.

Exainetos of Sicily took the crown in the *stadion* race, that Olympiad; no-one even gave the fellow a sniff. The throng had eyes for Alcibiades only or, failing him, his horses. They were battling over the turds. It's true; I saw it. No sooner would one of these champions elevate its tail than half a dozen had thrust their caps beneath it, as if this equine arsehole were a fountain disgorging nuggets of gold. They even made away with the hoofprints, cutting them out of the sand and boxing them like mason's impresses. I have never seen so many drunk, or been so myself, without spending a single iron spit. The incidence of public fornication was spectacular.

As for Alcibiades, you couldn't get within bowshot. At age thirty-four he had vaulted to the firmament, champion of champions, the cardinal celebrity not alone of Greece but of Macedonia and Thrace, Sicily, Italy, which was to say, save Persia, the most famous individual in the world.

The Games themselves were epochal in a further sense. The prior Olympiad, recall, was the one from which the Spartans had been debarred, owing to their dispute with the Elean priests of Zeus. Without the Lacedaemonians, every crown was tarnished. Now they were here. Polydorus the boxer, Sthenelaides the pentathlete, plus two teams in the four-horse, neither of which had ever been beaten except by the other. Mantinea had restored their pride. Their *mythos* was back, Alcibiades would say, and they gloried in it.

For myself the Spartans' presence bore significance in a keener sense. At every turn, it seemed, I encountered mates from the Upbringing and officers and boy-captains who had trained us. Outside the Pavilion of the Champions I ran into Phoebidas, my old commander, with his brother Gylippus, who would later scourge the forces of Athens so pitilessly before Syracuse. Endius I chanced upon as well, the boyhood friend and, some said, lover of Alcibiades. He was Captain of the Knights, in line for an ephorship with the new year.

There were many like myself, standing not in the colours of their nation, but the blistered leather of the expatriate, the shield for hire. The seasons flow so without seam into one another that a man cannot account the alterations of his person till he beholds them reflected in the aspect of a comrade unencountered in the intervening years. Here came Alcaeus, tent companion of Socrates, the merry actor of Aspasia Three. He was a trainer now. His charge Pandion had fallen that

forenoon, tethered to his stone, preferring death to second place –
Pandion of Acharnae, who had taken his ephebic oath at the shoulder
of my brother, what seemed only a summer gone. So it continued. Each
man encountered mates of his school years, whiskerless lads when last
met. How could such grey stand in this friend's beard, such scars on that
comrade's limbs? Enquiries after sister or mother, wife or babe, elicited
the same wordless reply. Soon all query ceased. Each looked into his
mate's eye and read in that glass the loss that stood, unseen by himself,
within his own.

On the third dawn Eunice shook me awake in our bivouac along the
Alpheus. 'Rise up, Sleepy-bones! And try to look the gentleman.'

Above on the bank stood Lion. I had not seen him since Mantinea,
two summers past, or replied to the fistful of his letters I yet bore within
my kit.

He was decked out, sleek and prosperous, a civilian. I clapped him
with pleasure. No more the reckless runaway of Potidaea, my brother
was a pillar of thirty years, with children in their second decade and our
father's farm, now his alone, beneath his stewardship. We hiked to town
down the traffic-clotted road.

He reproved me for yet following the trade of war.

'The money's good,' was my defence.

'Then buy me dinner.'

We both laughed.

'You couldn't prise an obol out of your arse, could you?'

Aunt Daphne had taken ill, he said. Did I know I was still her golden
youth? 'She worries about you, brother. I do too.' He wanted me to come
home with him, work the land. He would put us in co-ownership, fifty-
fifty. 'The place is more than I can manage alone, Pommo. But together
we could make her pay.'

We spent the day, my brother and I, neither capable till the instant of
parting to raise that matter which burned foremost in both our hearts.

'Have you planted their bones?'

I meant those of my wife and child, and Father's and Meri's, in the
tomb at Acharnae where they belonged.

'You're the elder, Pommo. You know it must be you.'

With that, all joy left the Games for me. I must get home. I packed
next noon to depart, which provoked a prodigious row with Eunice, for

whom it was an article of faith that one day I would 'put on gentleman's airs' and quit her. I detest such scenes with women. My kit stood already shouldered when a man-at-arms entered our camp, a squire of the Spartans, seeking me. He was Endius's man, called Forehand for his skill with the throwing axe. He wished to extend an invitation from his master to join him at table this evening. The bid included my mates and our women.

The knight's party was quartered not in the host pavilion, but on a private estate at Harpine outside Olympia town. Forehand came for us and took us over. I was then thirty-four; Endius in his mid-forties. As a boy my station had stood so far beneath his that even now I found myself addressing him as 'lord' and stationing myself on his shield side in deference. 'Relent, Pommo. We may be mates now.'

The knight was gracious to our women, even charming, permitting them to dine unsegregated beside himself and his companions, a familiarity unheard-of in Lacedaemon. 'Is it true,' Eunice's brazen tongue ventured, 'that Spartan women appear in the festivals stark naked?'

'We don't call it naked,' our host replied, 'but blessed.'

'And what if they're fat?'

'That's why they don't get fat.'

Eunice absorbed this with amusement. 'And are Spartan women indeed the most beautiful in Greece?'

'So Homer attests,' Endius replied, citing the daughters of Tyndareus – Helen of yore and Clytemnestra, and their cousin Penelope, whom Odysseus had borne away to Ithaca, his queen.

Towards the close of the meal, another Spartiate appeared. This was Lysander. He had made the leap to colonel since Mantinea – and of heavy infantry, not horse. He took the place beside Endius. When the Hymn of Thanksgiving had been sung and the party adjourned, this pair made motion to Telamon and me to linger. It was late, but there was a moon. Would we accompany them into the countryside for a breath of air? Mounts had been drawn for us; the Peers' squires would trot ahead bearing brands.

What could this be? Talk at dinner had eschewed all mention of Alcibiades, no mean exploit in this hour with his name upon the lips of all. Endius himself had spoken only two words of his friend, those in response to an observation by our captain Telamon that the most magnificent of the pavilions erected in the victor's honour was that of Argos, which, since Mantinea, had made herself a democracy a second time, and among whose men of influence Alcibiades numbered scores of allies and friends. Could he be exploiting this occasion politically? 'Nothing he does,' remarked Endius, 'is absent politics.'

We had advanced several miles along the Alpheus. The countryside sprawled, rich in olives and barley. Endius observed that these lands, specifically the estate we now overlooked, were the property of Anacreon of Elis, his wife's kinsman, who stood gravely in his, Endius's, debt. At a nod the Spartans' squires drew up. Our party reined in on the bluff above the river.

'What my comrade and I speak now,' the knight began, 'comes neither from the kings nor the magistrates of Lacedaemon, but alone ourselves, as private individuals. Will you attend and repeat nothing?'

The hair stood up on my neck.

'We'll ride back on shoe leather,' I replied, dismounting. Telamon's hand drew me up.

'These gentlemen wish to speak of business, Pommo. I for one am in business.' He rapped my knee to cool me. It obliged nothing to give ear to a proposition of employment.

'Would you call yourself a patriot?' Endius resumed, addressing me.

I would return to Athens with the dawn, if that was what he meant.

'I mean would you defend your city against her foes? Would you count your life as nothing, if expending it preserved your country's freedom?'

Trusting the gods, I replied, I would hope to save both.

He smiled, glancing to Telamon. My mate held silent. Lysander spoke, addressing me.

'You have said you would sacrifice your life against the enemy which threatened your country. I believe you and honour this, as any would. Now let us pursue the supposition. Were a great pestilence to advance upon your nation, a famine, say, or affliction . . .'

'Say it straight out, friend.'

'. . . would you strike as boldly? Say that with a single blow you might preserve . . .'

'Do you take me for a murderer, Lysander?'

Endius broke in with heat. 'Who slays a tyrant is no murderer but patriot. A deliverer of his country, as Harmodius and Aristogeiton!'

'Gentlemen, gentlemen.' Telamon raised a hand. 'We speak of commerce, not passion.'

Endius ignored this, continuing to me with fire. 'Would you not name him saviour, who cleansed his homeland of this scourge?'

'Endius!'

This from Lysander, sternly.

With effort Endius brought himself under control. 'Let us speak straight then. No more fencing. You have eyes, Polemidas; you are not stupid. Your country's enemy is not Sparta. Her real foe lies twined within her own bosom. Not ourselves, but that thrice-crowned serpent whose ambition, fuelled to fever pitch, would by its excesses destroy her.'

'Do you fear him so much, Endius?'

'I fear and hate him. And love him too, as you.'

He turned away. For long moments none spoke.

'What would be this patriot's portion,' my mate broke in, 'who purged the breast of Athens of such a viper?'

'All you see.'

This from Lysander, indicating the olive groves and fields of barley. Telamon whistled.

'A noteworthy incentive. But how long would this saviour live to enjoy it?'

'Beneath our aegis, all his years.'

'Since when does Sparta,' I enquired of both Peers, 'trouble herself so with the well-being of an enemy?'

'Enough!' Endius barked. 'Will you kill him?'

'I'd sooner you both, and for half the price.'

The Peer's knees dug so hard that his mount began to fret. Lysander must reach across and seize the bridle.

'Relent, my friend,' he addressed Endius. 'We will not convert our comrades here tonight. Perhaps they are correct. If Athens is indeed our nation's foe, then our role, yours and mine, must be to succour all by whose agency she may be brought low.' He smiled, looking me in the face. 'May heaven prosper our friend who wears the triple crown.'

Telamon and I dismounted. Endius wheeled above us on his balking mount. 'Hear this now; I will speak a prophecy. One day Athens will lie broken, her fleet sunk, Long Walls razed, widows and orphans wailing in the streets. All this shall come about by the instrument of one man . . .'

I burned to cut him off with something sharp, but at his words my blood ran chill; I could summon no rejoinder.

'What crime is it, brothers,' Endius continued, 'which the gods abominate beyond all? Not murder. Not treason. Pride! To quench this, Zeus himself looses his bolts of heaven.' He wheeled above us, elevating his palm. 'Mark this testament, which I pronounce this night in your hearing.'

The knight drove in his heels; man and mount spurred off. Lysander lingered, motioning to the squires, who sprang onto the backs of the beasts which had borne Telamon and me to this promontory. Before our vantage the groves and fields sprawled silver beneath the moon.

'Enjoy the prospect, comrades,' Lysander spoke. 'Perhaps on this account we shall do business at another hour.'

# FOURTEEN
# A PROSPECTUS OF CONQUEST

AFTER THE GAMES WE TREKKED HOME TO ATHENS, MY BROTHER AND I, employing the four days to reacquaint ourselves. I had wages due and sent Eunice ahead on the ferry, via Patrae and the Isthmus; she would be safe travelling with Telamon and Chowder. Others of our coop had set themselves to try the city as well. There would be work with the new fleet for Sicily.

Home again my brother and I at last disinterred from their unquiet berth the bones of our father and sister, and I those of wife and child, and set them to rest in the tomb of our ancestors at Acharnae. Perhaps now they would find peace. For myself, standing upon the earth that had borne the sons and daughters of our family time out of mind, I was stricken with such grief that I could not keep my feet even for the interval of the rite but sank to a knee, overcome.

Tell me, Jason, what is this power by which our native soil possesses us and holds us captive? We think we have seized it but it has taken us. It belongs not to us, but we to it.

I had spent few seasons on the farm as a boy. My aunt took me into the city at four; by ten I was abroad in the Upbringing. I never really knew my father's father or his cousins and brothers. I made their acquaintance now, largely by standing, with Lion, up to my ears in their debt.

You have run a farm, Jason. None who hasn't knows the meaning of poverty. In war at least one's wages pass one night in one's fist before scattering to the wind. The farmer doesn't get even that. Before a seed is in the earth, the husbandman has mortgaged his crop, so that even if his harvest bears a bounty and he loads for market with prime figs and pears, the profit may not even wave how-do-you-do before it is whisked away by the counting clerk, the tax collector, and his own cranky kin. To say that a man owns a farm would be preposterous, were it not so cruel. He carries it, like an ox or an iron anchor, on his back.

The soldier thinks he knows fear. Tell that to the farmer. I have dropped off at battle's eve and snoozed sound as stone; now on my landsman's cot I tossed, sleepless as Cerberus. The farmer greets the dawn with one query only: what calamity has struck overnight? I never knew how many ways a sheep could run ill, or a spring turn sour.

Something is always breaking on a farm. You start mending at dawn and don't stop till midnight. Troy herself never suffered such assaults. Fungus infiltrates the farm, as mould, blight, mildew, rust, and dry rot; one duels canker and palsy, ague, colic, distemper. Every creeping thing is the enemy. On the tramp I swatted insects and never thought of them more; now they haunted my nightmares. Termites and carpenter ants, hornets and wasps, locusts, mites, aphids and grain beetles, moths, mites, weevils and blowflies; the corers and borers, burrowers and devourers. God alone may testify to the creatures which infest the innards of the farmer's livestock; canker and cutworms, leeches and tapeworms; into how many dungholes must one plunge to the elbow? The earth itself may not be relied upon, but each morn another retaining wall has toppled, another runoff ditch caved in. Every task costs money on the land, and the landsman never has money. The farmer's cash is sweat, the only commodity he possesses in unlimited bulk. Rain is the farmer's nemesis, too much or too little, and sun and wind and fire and time. Hired hands put out work only on payday, and if you're mad enough to invest in a slave or two, you import only their troubles. Calf-deep in sheep shit, my brother and I exchange this wordless query: how in hell's name did the old man do it? How could one man alone wring profit from this dirt when the team of us, yoked, is vanquished utterly? The farmer is ancient at forty. He endures season to season through the offices of one ally only: his dog.

Tireless, ever faithful, the landsman's Number One (all secondaries comprising a useless pack of curs) bounds to his heel at cock's crow and toils there daylong, unshirking, ever cheerful, craving no wages save the sound of his master's voice and a quick pat and ruffle at labour's end. Lord of all beasts, night sentry, bulwark of the line, the farm could not survive without him.

The land of course is bliss for a child, for whom each chore is a lark and every creature a playmate. A woman, too, comes into her own on a farm. Eunice revelled in it. Lion's Theonoe was a city girl; the country bored her. But her children thrived, inflicting on Eunice that ache only a childless woman knows. I must take her to wife soon if I meant to remain; she would not stand the tramp more.

That autumn a message came from Euryptolemus. There would be a fleet to invade Sicily; Alcibiades would hold command. I could name my appointment, as could my brother. The mustering bonus would be three months' pay, with officers' double wages for the duration.

Eunice would not remain in the room when Lion and I debated this.

Not long thereafter, Alcibiades appeared before our clan to make a presentation. He rode out to Weather Hill at Acharnae, my grand-father's ancient tile-roofed farmhouse. Above thirty of our kinsmen assembled – old wealth primarily, but with a salting of the younger bloods as well. Alcibiades addressed the gathering after dinner. He wanted money for the fleet. Not an assessment of the *eisphora*, the war tax, for which all citizens had been levied hitherto, but additional capital ventured uncompelled. Specifically he sought private sponsors, individuals to endow warships in their own names or as syndicates. He desired them to build these vessels from the keel up, bear all costs of commission and shakedown, then donate the completed craft to the fleet, with funding for a year for officers and crew. This was for Sicily, for the great invasion.

One must here note a distinguishing characteristic of Alcibiades' political style. This was his temerity to advance a cause, absent all office. Though he had been four times elected to the Board of Generals, the prestige he brought this night was neither backed by state authority nor issued in an official capacity. He came before us entirely on his own.

As to this Sicilian enterprise: it chanced, as you know, that Athens at that time had a treaty of mutual defence with the city of Egesta; representatives of this state had recently appealed to the Assembly, seeking assistance in a dispute with their neighbours, the Selinuntines, who, aided now by the might of Syracuse, held them besieged. Alcibiades and others who favoured war had seized upon this pretext; in no time the measure was ratified by the people. Funds were appropriated for an expedition; three generals, Alcibiades, Nicias, and Lamachus, appointed. Opponents, however, including Nicias himself, intrigued successfully to cap expenditures, hoping to sap the venture before it began. Alcibiades took his case to the people, meaning those with money, the great families and the private political associations. By the evening he appeared before our family, he had made presentations to at least three score such gatherings and had four more scheduled for the next four nights. In all Alcibiades put his pitch, it was estimated, to over two hundred clans and brotherhoods; it took the better part of autumn and winter. Men joked of these nocturnal canvassings that at least they kept him out of the brothels.

This was serious business, however, and Alcibiades approached it in deadly earnest. Prior to his evening with the men of our family, he had taken the time to seek out each in private, on the land or in town, wher-ever he could catch the man at ease and speak with him informally and apart. This was to soften him up. Further each potential benefactor had received at his home a prospectus, and Alcibiades brought more, updated, which he distributed upon the actual evening. Worthy of note was that to two of my uncles, whose resources were too slender to foot such a monumental contribution, were proffered not brochures of the fleet, but more modest briefs soliciting donations to the cavalry. I recall my grandfather's astonishment, not to say indignation, that Alcibiades had acquired such intelligence of our family's most privileged holdings. What must he know of the city's loftier *eupatridai*, the true old-money rich?

The evening broke frosty and clear. Braziers had been set up on my grandfather's south terrace, which had for the occasion been cloistered on three sides by woollen blinds, open on the fourth towards Decelea. Alcibiades arrived early, accompanied by his comrades Menestheus and Pythiades, with the naval architect Aristophon to answer technical questions. It was lost on no-one that both Alcibiades' colleagues were recipients of fleet prizes of valour, Menestheus as a ship's master at Mytilene, Pythiades as a squadron commander at Cos, and that the pair were men of mature years and oligarchic inclination, recruited no doubt to offset their principal's youth and notoriety as a champion of the commons. The meal and hymn concluded, and all dining vessels cleared, Alcibiades saluted his hosts and thanked them for their attendance and hospitality.

'Let us plunge right in and, as the Spartans, keep it short and sweet. Though, as you gentlemen know, I have been elected to the Board of Generals and share command of the expeditionary fleet, I come before this college tonight in no capacity other than private citizen. I address you, friends, in my own name only. One may reprove this, calling it prideful or presumptuous. This is what our enemies the Spartans would say, who act, when they do, alone by procedure and through channels. This is why our polity is superior to theirs and why they never have, and never shall, excel us. For our way provides that any citizen may place an issue before any other or aggregation of others, seeking by reason and persuasion to build a constituency for his cause. This is democracy in its best sense. Not the grandstanding of the demagogue to the mob, but the cool and measured appeal to the judicious and the prudent, in the interest of all.

'I am aware, gentlemen, that a number of you are sceptical of my motives and hold me personally in less than high regard. Permit me to address this at once and, I hope, persuade you that those qualities of my person which may cause you distress will prove in the present circumstance not liabilities but assets to our cause as individuals and to our city as a whole.

'Some of you disapprove my ambition, of which I make no secret. It smacks of outrage; you fear its consequence. Others have been scandalized by instances of my personal deportment. If I may say, I've been scandalized myself! This is no more than youth, gentlemen, and excess of spirit. When someone purchases a colt he wishes to race, he looks not for docility, but fire. He seeks a horse that will run. Let his trainers school the beast. This is what I ask of you gentlemen tonight. Take me in hand. Harness my rashness to your temperance. This balance is how great teams are made and mighty races won.

'Sicily is a mighty race. Her lands are vast, richer than all the Peloponnese and in arable acreage greater than Greece entire. Barley grows in Sicily, and wheat and rye and oats. Olives thrive, and fruit of all kinds. Sicily has water and timber and horses; who holds her has no need of Black Sea grain. And Sicily possesses mineral wealth, gold and silver, iron and copper and tin. Her cities, fifty in number, are the equal of Greek *poleis* in resource and treasure.

'More tempting, Sicily squats on the threshold of Italy. I need not detail the wealth of that unexploited land. I see none disputes this, gentlemen. Good. Yet your unspoken question stands clear: what's in it for me?

'All of you have sons, some with sons of their own. Each heir dilutes your patrimony, as holdings must be divided. What may we leave our successors? Where will they find their portion? You, my friends, are of the fifty-measure and equestrian classes; you are estate holders and knights. Let me put a question to you. Which is easier: to build up a landholding from dirt and stone, or to conquer one whole and entire, a founded property already in possession of cleared and planted fields, with water and fences and pastureland and even crofters who know and work the land? When we take Sicily, to whose sons will the choicest of these prizes go? Whom but those who have funded the arms by which they have been mastered?

'You are thinking: war is no mean undertaking, Alcibiades. It brings in its train evils unnumberable; its outcome may as well be calamity as conquest. You frame this question as well: Sicily is strong, her fifty cities will not simply roll over and quit. In answer I wish she had more cities, for the more, the more divided, and more easily subdued. We must think of these cities as islands. That is what they are. Each apart and self-interested, jealous of all others. We will take these cities as we took the islands of our empire: ally with the strongest against the weakest, conquer the main, then turn upon the stubborn. Leave one or two independent, that we may point to them in proof that none has been coerced into our alliance.

'Many of you have held command with the fleet. You understand sea power. You question the feasibility of its projection over so many leagues, so far from friendly harbours and resupply. I answer, friends, that were a fleet unnecessary, I should seek pretext to commission her anyway. Let me tell you why. Against a prize the size of Sicily, brute force will not suffice, but diplomacy and audacity, and above all the sudden and dramatic presentation of overwhelming might. For that, nothing may rival a fleet. Hear me, gentlemen.

'Land forces, no matter how numerous, present to the eye a spectacle bedraggled and ill defined. When they marshal upon the field, their numbers are often obscured by planted crops or hidden by defiles and mountains. A thousand infantry occupy a space little greater than this estate. An army even of fifty thousand is often dwarfed by the landscape or masked by the dust of its own tread; despite its numbers it looks puny and undaunting.

'Ah, but a fleet! Her spectacle sprawls unbroken across the main, brilliant with sails spread and oar banks extended. An army in the field looks like a mob, an armada like God's wrath. And recall: the foe never gets the chance to see our fleet eclipsed in scale by the vastness of the ocean. He beholds us only within the confines of his own harbour, which we fill end-to-end with fighting ships and men, daunting and overawing him.

'There is another telling aspect to a show of naval might. This is its temerity. A fleet carries with it the audacity of its enterprise. The stay-at-home foe is stricken by its sudden apparition. The enemy beholding a navy advancing upon him out of the aether is struck with dread, as Priam himself when Achilles' black ships beached upon the plain of Troy.

'A fleet minimizes risk and casualties. Employing the theatre of its spectacle, we overawe one city and another, rolling them up within our bag. Rhegium, Messana, Camarina, Catana, Naxos, and the native Sicels have all taken our cause in the past; played right, they will again. Our advance acquires a momentum of its own, indistinguishable in the foe's eyes from fate. He cannot prevail, he sees, and enrolls himself beneath our banner of his own will. Yes, yes, you say, all this sounds brilliant on paper, Alcibiades. But who will make it happen?

'Here I must set delicacy aside and speak straight and blunt. There are those who are jealous of me, of my private celebrity. I understand this, friends. I ask you, however, to consider that I now place this fame at your disposal, to be yoked to your ends. What I achieve by my private exertions redounds to Athens' glory as well as my own. Recall Olympia; the leading men of Sicily stood present in the stadium when my horses took the triple. They erected pavilions in honour of my victory and clamoured about me, seeking my friendship. Will they not be favourably disposed when I and my fellow commanders, backed by this mighty armada, address them as I do you tonight, not with arrogance, threatening the destruction of their homes and enslavement of their families, but seeking their alliance, bidding them join us? Immodest as it sounds, I ask: who else in Athens may command such attention?

'Two more points, gentlemen, and I will finish.

'First, to those who protest that our nation now stands at peace, that we have a treaty with the Spartans, and that this Sicilian venture, though technically not in violation, will in the event plunge us back into full-scale war. I answer with a question: what kind of peace is it when the nations of Greece are in fact fighting on more fronts now than they did under formal declaration? What peace is it when the third part of our young men elect to serve as mercenaries for these very states? War will come again, this is certain. What remains for us to decide is when. Will it resume at the hour of our enemies' choosing, when they have elevated their forces to the peak of readiness? Or will it come at our election, when our cause stands most likely to prevail?

'Now to the nub. To others, gentlemen, I may confine my appeal to considerations of profit and risk, and these are not inconsequential. But to you who perceive with the eyes of wisdom, I may speak to deeper designs.

'Our nation is great. But greatness begets obligation. It must prove worthy of itself or it falls. You have all seen what this war, prosecuted piecemeal and without vigour, and this so-called Peace have done to our young men's spirit. Those fresh to maturity crave action, while veterans turn sour and sullen. They are going bad – let us call it by its name. Sicily is the antidote. A call to brilliance which will summon ourselves and our youth back from their depletion and despair. Pericles was in error to set us on the defensive. This is not Athens. It is not our style. We are dying by inches, shackled by this ignoble Peace, declining not for lack of goods, but want of glory.

'Athens is a sword rusting in her sheath. We may not sit still, we Athenians. Idleness is fatal to us. What I hate most about this Peace is the toll it has taken on our nation's soul. It will finish us, my friends, as surely as defeat in war. Athens is not a draft mule, but a mighty racehorse; she must be harnessed not to a plough, but to a chariot – and a chariot of war.

'Lastly this, gentlemen. To those who mistrust me and fear my ambition. When this fleet takes station before Syracuse, you will not discover me shrinking from the foe. My ram will be the first to seek and strike the enemy. Perhaps I will be slain. Then you will be quit of me. My pride will no longer vex you. But hear this . . .

'The fleet will remain.

'Long after my bones are dust beneath the earth, you will have her. Athens will have her. She will be yours, to make use of as you wish.

'Consider this proposal, my friends. Think it over. The spoils of our enterprise will be shared by all, even those who remain safe behind. But glory and honour are his who early sets his name upon the rolls. Join me, brothers and countrymen. Launch from our harbours this mighty armada and let the world stand back in wonder.'

# FIFTEEN
# A LECTURE FROM NICIAS

THE DEBATE THAT SUCCEEDED ALCIBIADES' DEPARTURE FROM MY grandfather's halls replicated in heat and animation, no doubt, that which transpired within every other cell or association to which he had spoken or subsequently did speak.

Beyond the merit of our guest's presentation, whether one agreed with him or not, what could not but strike each listener was the force of his personality. Many of the clan's elders had had occasion to view Alcibiades only in Assembly. They had never had the chance to examine him close up, across their own board, where they might look him in the face, see the intelligence in his eyes, the expressiveness of his hands, the resolve in his voice. In person he was a force. His belief in the enterprise he championed was so genuine, and delivered with such conviction, that even those chary of its wisdom or in out-and-out opposition were called upon to summon all their stoniness of heart to resist the persuasiveness with which he represented it. The beauty of his person easily won over those previously ill-disposed, and disarmed even those who abhorred his character and conduct.

Even his lisp worked in Alcibiades' favour. It was a flaw; it made him human. It took the curse off his otherwise godlike self-presentation and made one, despite all misgivings, like the fellow. Though I have here rendered his speech as if it unspooled seamlessly and without interruption, in actual moment its impact was augmented by a certain charming foible.

Alcibiades had the habit, when memory failed to summon the word or phrase he sought, of pausing, sometimes for moments, his head tilted to one side, until the precise idiom presented itself. There was to this an attractive lack of artifice, an ingenuousness and authenticity. It was winning.

Within our clan, reaction split dramatically. My uncle Haemon, a diehard of 'the Good and True', scorned our guest's representation of the expedition as honourable and himself as a patriot. 'He is a panderer to the mob, plain and simple, and this Sicilian stunt seeks to pass off audacity of action and scale of ambition for justice, to contrive a simulacrum of honour. It is not honour but *thrasytes*, boldness, alone.'

More spoke, opinion divided. My grandfather frowned, volunteering nothing. Pressed at last by his son, my father's brother Ion, he rejected Alcibiades, declaring, 'His skirt is too long.'

This was greeted with howls from the younger men. 'Go back to your snooze, Grandfather,' my cousin Callicles hooted.

The patriarch responded. 'Traditional generations hemmed their garments higher, to honour their origins as tillers of the soil, whose dress must not trail in the dirt and muck. But the new generation, born of the city, knows nothing of the land, so they cut their skirts to drag about, immodest and unseemly. What I fear has nothing to do with groves or vines, Callicles, but the virtues which cultivation of the land imparts: modesty, patience, reverence for the gods, of which this Alcibiades knows little and cares less. He is a product of the city and evinces all its vices: vanity, arrogance, impatience, and immodesty before heaven.'

Callicles responded with heat. 'I will give you more virtues of the country, old man. Narrow-mindedness, misanthropy, skinflintedness, insularity. Good riddance to these! The virtues of the city are boldness, imagination, vision, and inclusiveness.'

'The man of the land,' Grandfather rejoined, 'is in the business of peace, he of the city in the service of war.'

'This service has done your purse no harm, Grandfather. Nor any here beneath this roof.'

A general uproar ensued.

'Gentlemen, gentlemen.' My uncle Ion restored order. It was he of all assembled who most embodied that sagacity which country men call 'dirt wisdom' – the down-to-earth common sense of middle years. What did he think, his kinsmen enquired, not alone of our guest's proposal but of the man himself?

'I fear him. But I fear more dismissing him. As I watched him address us tonight I could not but imagine, as he suggested, how he would appear in halls like these in Sicily, braving these foreign nobles and soliciting their alliance. Sicily is rich, yes, but she is also rude. Her princes are like ours a hundred years ago. They may be awed less by the might of Athens than by her aggressiveness and audacity – qualities which they fear, admire, and envy, and which our guest personifies more than any other. He is Athens, or that portion which indeed may over-awe and win these foreign knights.

'That point made by the captain Pythiades is also well taken, that Syracuse – whose conquest, all concur, holds the key to Sicily – is a democracy. We have witnessed our young champion's appeal to the mob. Perhaps this, too, may work in the expedition's favour. And yet . . .'

'And yet nothing,' put in our youthful firebrand Callicles. He spoke of his service, this winter past, on the Naval Resources Board. Among his duties was to treat with the brokers who represented the foreign sailors – the islanders of Samos, Chios, Lesbos, and the other maritime nations who served for pay in the Athenian fleet. He knew these men, Callicles said.

'They are neither pirates nor grog-besotted salts, but responsible pro-fessionals, possessed in abundance of the spirit of adventure and harbouring keen hopes of advancement. They know their skills' worth and hire it out cannily. Yet these foreigners serve in our fleet not for money alone, which they could get anywhere, but for a far more potent intangible.

'They are in love with Athens.'

Observe them, Callicles submitted, on any holiday. They parade in the festivals, pack the benches of the dance and chorus. In their off-hours they congregate in the Lyceum and the Leocorium, the marketplace and the Academy, and the groves and enclaves where the philosophers and their students assemble. You have seen them, cousins. They roost in the margins, attending spellbound to Protagoras of

Abdera, Hippias of Elis, Gorgias of Leontini, Prodicus of Cos, and the scores of sophists and rhetoricians who set up shop in the open air to vend their wares of wisdom. They cluster about Socrates. But before all, they are taken with the theatre.

'On the morn of a competition one discovers them by hundreds in the forecourt, seeking shade beneath the statues of the generals, or trooping from the plane grove of the Amazoneum with their sweethearts and their picnic baskets, with their woollen sea blankets over their shoulders, employing as theatre cushions the very pillows upon which they sit at oars.

'I have seen them in the gymnasia, those which admit foreigners. The Hebrew sailors endure the pain of those copper clamps called "mushroom caps" which stretch the circumcised flesh of their members back over the exposed foreskin, so that, naked, they may look like Greeks. Like Athenians. That is how smitten they are with our nation. Open the rolls of citizenship and the lines of applicants will lap the agora thrice over.

'But here is my point, gentlemen. In any overseas port I am approached twenty times a day by foreign seamen, crack mariners beseeching me to use my influence to gain them a berth. Many offer to serve without pay. They wish only to learn under an Athenian captain, to further their skills and advance their aspirations.

'These foreigners, I believe, will be drawn powerfully to serve under a commander like Alcibiades. The better and more ambitious they are, the more they will wish to sail with him, because they believe he will bring them victory, and because they are just like him. He is who they dream of becoming. He knows it and knows how to exploit it.

'Remember, these sailors all know each other. They frequent the same taverns and brothels; they know every officer in every fleet and which seamen sail with him. I make no brief for the man Alcibiades. But the chance of serving under him will draw to this force, I believe, the élite mariners of the world. I leave it to you to evaluate their impact, upon Sicily and our foes of the Peloponnese.'

Many of the wealthy, that winter, made warranty to lay keels. Yet as happens with men, when spring came they discovered excuses for delay. Alcibiades and his circle pressed forward on their own. Euryptolemus and Thrasybulus commissioned *Atalanta* and *Aphrodisia*; others *Vigilant*,

*Equipoise*, and *Redoubtable*. Alcibiades commenced construction on *Antiope* and *Olympia*; these in addition to four he had already donated. Could he afford such an outlay? Perhaps not, but the start drew others who had hung back. The sight of these vessels rising on their timbered ways in the shipyards of Munychia and Telegoneia, the daylong thump of adzes and chisels hewing their beams, the stink of pitch and oakum being paddled into the seams of their mortise-and-tenon hulls, and the mob of *technitai* and *architectones*, carpenters and shipwrights employed upon them, created a momentum of its own, magnetic and irresistible. Soon an expanse of shoreline a mile long at the Cantharus and twice that along the Sounium Road stood chockablock with hulls under construction, not to mention those simultaneously arising on timber sites in Macedonia and the Chersonese, while the waterfront boomed with joiners' shops and chandleries, sailmakers' lofts and foundries, blacksmiths, armourers, rope weavers, and mast and spar factors. Pennants and ensigns painted the lanes with colour; beneath their plumage drayage wagons lumbered night and day, bearing the matériel of construction.

The fever had caught. The city could talk of nothing but Sicily. In the marketplace, clay models of the island were snatched up by the hundred; men and boys scratched outlines in the dirt and extolled her wonders in the barbershop and the saddlery. It was as if we had conquered already and had no more to dispute but division of the spoils.

The aristocrat Nicias addressed the Assembly one blistering forenoon, when the sun-blasted Pnyx stood packed to the rearmost station.

'Athenians, I see your hearts are set upon this venture. Today departing for this congress, I could not locate my attendant; he was discovered at last among the grooms, blathering ecstatically of Sicily. What else? It is your nature, men of Athens, to count as yours already that which you have set your hopes upon and, your minds made up, you will suffer no-one to quarrel counter to your whim. You will shout him down, as if he sought by his speech to take from you that which you already possessed instead of counselling you for your own good in regard to that which you may never get and the pursuit of which may bring you to ruin.

'I see before me, too, in the foremost row, that young man and his confederates whose ambition has inflamed your hearts to this folly. He is smiling, this proud breeder of horses and corrupter of the public morals, because he knows I speak the truth. I hate to see that smile, my friends, however comely. And do not you, gentlemen, chancing to find yourselves beside this buck's henchmen, permit yourselves to be intimidated by their bluster, or feel shamed if they call you coward for demurring to underwrite this expedition. Yes, his friends heckle me now. Let them. But if these hotbloods will not attend seriously to my words, I pray that you, their elders and betters, will.

'I see there also, in that shaded precinct he favours, Socrates the philosopher, to whose counsel alone our youthful champion attends. We all know where you stand, sir. You have spoken out, resisting this Sicilian adventure as unjust, to bear war to a people who harbour no intent of bringing it to us. Speak up, my friend, if I say false. Your famous *daimon*, that voice which warns you of peril or folly, has proscribed this escapade, has it not? Yet I see none heeds your grey hairs or mine.

'Let me speak, then, men of Athens, not in opposition to this enterprise, for I perceive that your course is set and nothing may deflect you from it, but only to set before you from experience's locker, as they say, those concerns which must be addressed if we wish to pull off this spectacular undertaking and not make fools of ourselves into the bargain.'

Nicias spoke of the hazards of venturing far from home and resupply, across such distant and treacherous seas, at such a remove that in winter even a fast despatch ship might require four months for the passage. In all previous overseas campaigns we had had the bulwark of allied harbours as forward bases and friendly territories from which to secure supplies. Not in Sicily. We would stand there at the ends of the earth, with not a crust to gnaw but that which we bore with us. He warned, too, that in taking on this new enemy we left another on our doorstep, the Spartans and their allies, who had very nearly laid us low before and who, though forbearing now under the Peace, would resume operations with vigour once we committed ourselves to this western front and, should we suffer a reversal there, would take fresh courage and, reinforced by new allies similarly emboldened, redouble their efforts to finish us off.

He spoke of the foreign merchants, mechanics, and sailors who manned the docks and shipyards and no minor portion of the benches of the fleet. With what confidence could we rely upon these who were not of our blood but without whom we could not hope to prevail? Were we not placing ourselves upon the same perilous perch occupied by our enemies, the Spartans, who must fight with one eye on the foe and the other on their own serfs? In war even one's own countrymen may not always be relied upon. How much less those who serve only for pay?

'Today as I walked to the Assembly I observed numerous construction sites of houses and shops going up. This is well. But do not put from your memory, Athenians, that these very properties are those abandoned and even torched by their owners during the Plague. Have you forgotten, friends? Is your recall so fleeting of those hours when our survival hung by a whisker and no resource we possessed, neither of wealth nor power nor entreaties of the gods, proved of avail to lift this siege of heaven? Peace, which I negotiated, has brought its blessings. We may open the city's gates, ride again to our estates, repair them and replant. Children are born who have not inhaled the stink of the enemy's incendiaries or witnessed their mothers' corpses carted away in the night. You have stumbled ashore upon safe haven, my countrymen. Yet what is your first thought? The bones of your own fathers have barely found rest within their tombs and now you propose to plant your own beside them. Can you not enjoy the quiet life? Am I so old, that I find comfort in a fireside at close of day and take joy to watch my children at play within the court?

'But this is not your nature, men of Athens. Nothing is more unendurable to you than peace. Each moment at leisure is to you an interval squandered and a chance for gain cast away. The farmer has learned that fields must lie fallow, and fruit bears only in its season. But you have repudiated these quaint premises. You inhabit another realm, a fictive country which you call the future. You dream of what will be and disdain what is. You define yourselves not as who you are, but as who you may become, and hasten over oceans to this shore you can never reach. That which you possess today you count as nothing, valuing only what you gain tomorrow. Yet as soon as your hands seize this treasure, you disown it and press on for what is new. I do not wonder that you esteem this young man, this chariot racer, for he lives further beyond his means even than yourselves.

'What want of character, my friends, compels you to seek war when you have peace? Are not our own troubles sufficient? Must we sail off pursuing others? I beg you, friends, to reject this injudiciousness. And I call upon you, President of the Assembly, to put the matter again to a vote.'

A number spoke following Nicias, the majority expressing views in favour of the expedition. When Alcibiades at last arose, summoned by acclamation, he confined his brief to essentials.

'I thank our schoolmaster' – he bowed toward Nicias – 'for his astute and salutary sermon. Clearly our character as Athenians is riddled with imperfections. We have fallen far short of the standard to which we all aspire. But if I may speak frankly, we must be who we are.'

Tumultuous acclamation saluted this. My own position was at the *epotis*, the 'ear' of the Pnyx; I could see Nicias, among the citizens, smile darkly and shake his head.

'In fact,' Alcibiades continued, 'we can be nothing else, neither as individuals nor as a nation.'

Additional clamour ascended. When Alcibiades resumed, he refuted Nicias's contentions smartly and point by point, each counterstroke mounting to this summation.

'And as to the restlessness of our nature, Athenians, in my view this is not imperfection of character, but evidence of vigour and enterprise. Our fathers did not drive back the Persian by propping their feet at the fire, or gain their empire watching their children play in the yard. Nicias says that fruits bear in their season. I say the season is now. To our friend's assertion that security is best derived from a posture of precaution and defence, that may be true for other nations, but not for us. For an active people to change her ways is fatal. It is in our nature to venture far and boldly. This, and not in defence, is where our security resides.

'Nicias speaks of foreign oarsmen: he reproves us that our fleet cannot sail without them, and cites this as a liability. It is proof, he says, that our native resources are insufficient. To me it demonstrates the opposite. In fact nothing could display with more telling measure the depth of our vitality and the magnetism of our *mythos*. Why do these foreigners come to us and no other nation in Hellas? Because they know that here and only here they may be free.

'And as for the derogation implicit in his assessment of these newcomers as our inferiors, I say he knows them not, and does them and us a disservice. Consider the hazard these men have undertaken, my friends, these whom Nicias devalues and demeans. They have put behind home and family, native soil and sky; the very gods of their race they have abjured, to venture across oceans to this stranger's land where they may enjoy neither protection of law nor participation in the political process, where they are exempted and excluded, nameless, voiceless, ballotless. Yet still they come, and no force under heaven may stop them. Why? Because they know that life at the ends of the earth in Athens is better than life at the centre of the universe at home. Nicias is mistaken, my friends. These foreigners may not be the brick and stone of our nation, but they are the mortar. And they will stick.'

Deafening applause seconded this. Nor was it lost upon the orator's allies, and his foes, that report of his words would peal at once and echo nightlong among the foreign sailors and craftsmen, by whom he would now more than ever be acclaimed patron and champion.

Alcibiades stood, calling for order. When the tumult at last subsided, he turned, absent all rancour or vaunting, and summoned his rival to the rostrum.

'Nicias, you have been appointed senior commander, which your record of service demands and which I honour without reservation. I esteem your wisdom and, not less, your proven luck. I have no wish to supplant you, sir, but to enlist you wholeheartedly in your country's cause. Help us. Don't tell us why we will fail but how we may succeed.

'I summon you now, sir, not as rival, but as compatriot, to come forward again. The reservations you have voiced are not without merit. Tell us, then, what we need to succeed. Give us hard numbers. Let us hear the stern truth. And I make you this pledge: if Athens will not grant what you believe the expedition needs to prevail, I myself will mount the stand beside you in opposition to it.

'But if she will grant you what you say we require, then I call upon you in like spirit to accede to your countrymen's decree. Do not shirk the command with which she has honoured you, but seize it with vigour. We need you, Nicias. Tell us what we must have to make you feel confident of success.'

Nicias accepted his antagonist's challenge. Mounting at once to the box, he proceeded to detail a seemingly interminable list of supplies and armament, warcraft and matériel, everything from spare masts and sail to parched barley and the bakers and ovens to make it into bread. He demanded overwhelming superiority of sea forces, one hundred men-of-war at a minimum, plus heavy infantrymen in numbers greater than any force the enemy could raise against us, reinforced by an equal number of light-armed troops, archers and slingers to neutralize the enemy's cavalry, since over these leagues of ocean we could not transport our own.

In addition the expedition would require ironworkers and masons, sappers and siege engineers, despatch craft and troop transports. Alcibiades had asked for hard figures and Nicias gave them. A hundred talents to hire supply ships, two hundred for dumps and magazines along the way, another two hundred to purchase horses for the cavalry on-site, and if the Sicel tribesmen refused us this aid, then the same amount to fund raids to take them by force. Of course this figure did not include the infantry or their attendants, or the seamen or maintenance of the warships. That would be a thousand talents, with another thousand in reserve. This figure, it was understood, covered just the summer; for winter the sum would double, and if the expedition had not achieved success in the first year, Athens must mount another and send it to the aid of the first. On and on Nicias's necessities mounted. Clearly he anticipated that such massive outlay, set before his hearers in this bald and brutal form, would act as cold water in the face of a dreamer.

But Alcibiades' grasp of his countrymen's character was shrewder than his opponent's. Far from being daunted by Nicias's demands, the citizens declared them excellent and embraced them with animation. The grander the expedition, the more certain they became that it could not fail. As Nicias completed his table of requisition, he perceived, as did every citizen of the Assembly, that he had been outgeneralled by Alcibiades, whose stock with the people mounted higher with each instant his rival sought to bring him low. Now all Athens felt that not only would she soon possess a fleet of insuperable capacity but in Alcibiades a general of spirit and cunning who could not fail to lead it to glory. At one stroke Alcibiades not only had got everything he wanted but, despite his station as junior commander, had seized control of the expedition and made it his own.

# SIXTEEN
## A SOLDIER'S DREAM

T HE FARM SURVIVED, THANKS LESS TO MY BROTHER'S EXERTIONS AND
my own than to the abundantly donated counsel and assistance
of various uncles and elders, not to say their liberal advances in equipment, skilled labour, and cash. We had not realized, Lion and I, how
sorely missed we had been and how bereft our family, as so many
others, in the aftercourse of plague and war. Nothing is so irreplaceable
as youth, and none so dear as the prodigal. They could not do enough
for us, our senior kinsmen, and wished only to see sons and more
sons. My aunt made the trek from the city just to satisfy herself
that we were well; stationed beneath the sunshade on her hired
carriage's bench, she looked on Lion and me, bare-backed and dirty
as dogs, digging a trench for a runoff channel. 'Now I can die
content.'

I failed to present Eunice that day, nor, calling upon Aunt in town
later that month, did I include my mistress. Thus began another of those
beastly rows, between myself and her, which endure nightlong and leave
one lacerated to the quick.

'What do I lack, Pommo, that you won't take me past your aunt's
door? Is my skin not soft enough? Perhaps you fault the shapeliness of
my calves. Well, these lines would not show in my face, my friend, or
sinew in my shanks, had I not slogged at your side through hell and
damnation, you ungrateful hound! I am not a citizen, is that it? Then by

God, make me one! Pull strings. Engage your fancy friends who make white black and turn it back again!'

Fury boiled from her, long-censored and suppressed.

'I'll tell you why you won't present me to your aunt. Because she seeks a bride for you even now, as she found your virgin Phoebe years ago. Someone proper, of proper Athenian family, with whom you may have children whose names may be set upon the rolls, not alien brats such as a foreign bitch like me would drop, who may not vote or sacrifice or claim their education when you fall in war.'

She discovered me one noon in reflection beside the family tomb; now the fancy took her, that I craved my dead bride and not her. I was ashamed of her, Eunice declared. She was not suitable. She did not fit.

One night she bolted from our bed in a state.

'You will put me aside now.'

I was exhausted and wanted none of this. 'What are you talking about?'

'You will be a gentleman. You will set me aside.'

I ordered her back to sleep. She struck me, hard, with the flat of her hand. 'There are too many in this bed, Pommo. I cannot sleep beside the ghost of your bride. One of us must go!'

From my lips I heard: 'Then go.'

The woman struck me in fury. 'I will tell you something: she is in the grave, your child bride. Your sister, too, is dead. While I live.'

I punched her full in the face, as hard as I would a man. She crashed to the wall and dropped. I felt horror to have struck her, a woman, but at the same time I blamed her entire. Only she could drive me to such extremity.

'You feel shame to be with me.' Eunice spat the blood from her lips. 'You hold in contempt the life we have led and wish to dismiss it as if it never happened. Well, it happened, Pommo. It happened. I have been your wife in fact if not in law, and you have been my husband. You are my husband.'

She began to sob. I knelt beside her, proffering comfort with words but in my heart wishing only to be gone, or have her so.

'What will become of me? Will I bear a child at last, or continue to abort myself as you command?'

She begged me to take her out of Athens, apart from family

expectations and mobilization for war. There were places we had seen in our travels, safe places. Let us go! We have all we need with just our hands and hearts . . .

Though I knelt so close that her knee rose between mine and her hands set upon my forearm, my heart held isolated and apart, with leagues of silence dissevering.

'You will put me aside, Pommo. I read it in your eyes. But it is not me you part from, only yourself. What I have set before you, no woman will again. Go, then. I won't stop you. But I will make this prophecy, and it will prove true.

'You will eat,' she declared, 'but ever go hungry. You will drink and still be dry. You will fuck and find no pleasure. You will stand before the fork, but it will make no difference which pass you take. All will bear you nowhere, till you come to yourself and come home to me.'

Jason, my friend. I have had greased bronzeheads shot into my guts and, worse, pulled out. I have had walls of stone collapse on top of me. But never had any blow hammered me to the heart like the words of this woman.

It would make a better story to say that she walked out then, or I. In fact we stayed together another eleven months. She bore a son and was with child again when I signed as a lieutenant of marines on the *Pandora* under Menestheus, the Titan squadron commanded by Chaemedemus, the Thunderbolt division under Alcibiades.

The farm had failed that winter. Lion's wife Theonoe made her divorce. With notes overdue and children yet to support, my brother could not turn down three months' mustering bonus and a year, at least, of officer's pay. He shipped as a platoon commander under Lamachus. Telamon took a unit of fifty, Arcadian mercenaries like himself. The farm my brother and I let to our uncles; I assigned half my wages to Eunice and made over the bonus to my grandfather, a start on the debt we owed for his, and all our family's, aid.

I could not make my living on the land. That was only a soldier's dream. Where else was there to go, for me or any of us, except back to war?

# SEVENTEEN
## A DOCUMENT
## OF THE ADMIRALTY

L ET ME SHOW YOU SOMETHING, MY GRANDSON. IT IS THE FLEET ORDER of Sail for Sicily, or more precisely one of the hundreds of copies drawn up by the demosioi, the secretaries of the Admiralty staff. Feel the paper; it is neither reed nor pulp, but linen. It is woven.

This was a document made to last. It was conceived of as epochal, an artefact of glory which each officer would pass to his heirs for generations. I now cede mine to you, my child, but not for the reasons its creators envisioned, such are the unknowable ways of God.

The Office of the War Archon was responsible for the production of this instrument, a duplicate of which was distributed to every trierarch of the fleet, as well as all pilots and captains of marines, fleet patrons and syndicate officers, the Board of Generals, the hundred members of the Board of Naval Construction, and the Curators of the Yards, as well as the chief executives and corporate officers of the private construction firms, shipbuilders, suppliers, sailmakers, and armament manufacturers who had built and provisioned the fleet. I worked on this document, myself and six other officers, night and day for seven months.

Regard the underlay. It is a pilot's chart of the Piraeus, the Grand Harbour and the Cantharus, extending from the fort and naval establishment of Eetioneia to the Emporium and the Still Harbour to Acte, with soundings indicated for flood and ebb, sitings for all channel markers from the

*Diazeugma to the Ephebium, including distances mole-to-mole and angles of triangulation among each of the four beacons and twenty-seven benches, so that a ship's master could, by striking azimuths to the various guidons, determine his position within a boat-length at any point of the harbour. This degree of precision was ordained by Nicias and Alcibiades, in concord for once, that each of the fleet's three hundred and sixty-four primary vessels could site herself upon her assigned station and the whole colossal departure come off with an order and symmetry both grand to the eye and pleasing to the gods.*

*Upon the facing sheet are indicated the priests' and magistrates' stations. The squares along the fairway are the stationary barges erected for the King Archon, the Chief Priests of the Ten Tribes, and the Priestesses of Athena Poliachos, Protectress of the City, as well as the chaplains and sanctuary guardians of Agraulus, Enyalius, Ares, Zeus, Thallo, Auxo, and Hegemone. Each demarch had his own barge as well, plus privately funded viewing stands in excess of two hundred, which stretched for three miles opposite the Sounium Road. The Choma jetty was reserved to the Council members, likewise garlanded and mounted upon the tribal steps from which they looked out, across the water, upon the Temple of Aphrodite Mistress of Navigation, whose precincts held the delegations of women, the wives and mothers of the trierarchs, in white, bearing wands of yew and hyacinth. At the head of the bay stood the altar of Poseidon, upon which a bull was sacrificed to the sea.*

*Sorrowful age has ravaged my sight; the document in your hand is but a blur. Yet still I see, ship for ship, that magnificent armada as she passed before my vision half a century gone.*

*First in ceremonial escort rowed the state galleys, Paralus and Salaminia, the fastest ships in the world. Their sails, as all the fleet, rode reefed upon the topstay awaiting the trumpeted order 'Make sail!' Upon this command, each line loosed in succession, the topmen riding the fabric down, unfurling it with their feet as they plunged, so that like a pennant suddenly sprung to the breeze, the sails snapped and filled with an audible concussion. Cheers rose from the thousands massed upon the shore as each fresh sail, emblazoned with some design honouring its namesake deity or heroine, filled and drew. These were all ceremonial sails, woven for this day alone and superfluous to the point of absurdity, as all vessels made way entirely under oars. Yet they did look grand! It was remarked that the sigh of relief of the Admiralty staff would have sufficed alone to get the ships under way, so trepidatious had they stood of the ill omen of dead or contrary winds.*

*Lamachus's division moved out first, though he himself and his flagship,* Hegemonia, *had embarked days prior with his squadron to secure the cape and alert our Corcyrean allies to the fleet's departure. Now: the fast corvettes, called 'cutthroats', in columns of two, sixteen in all, then the fifty-oared galleys, thirty-six, flanking the cargo, troop, and horse transports which advanced in a mass in the centre. These, numbering a hundred and sixty-seven, took an hour to clear the reviewing stands.*

Next came the men-of-war, the triremes, in formation by squadron, ten and twelve across and four deep, with each commander on the left in the post of honour. First one-hundred-seventy-four-oared Procne, Autocles' ship, Lamachus's vice-admiral. Her squadronmates were Pompe, Ajax, Ptolemais, Gorgon, and Grampus, whose sail was crimson and bore the image of its guardian beast; then Circe, Thrush, Hippolyta, Theama, Ram and Relentless.

Under her crimson sail with griffin emblem came Pyrpnous, Fire-Breather, Pythiades' ship, the hero of Cos. Then Indomitable, Dynamis, Thraseia, Amphitrite, Euxinaia, Achilleia, Centaura, and the triplets Tisiphone, Megaera and Alecto.

The Nereid squadron under Aristogenes: Thetis, Pytho, Panope, Galatea, Balte, Alcyone, Euploia, Sea Eagle, Invincible, Endeavour and Aianateia. Then Two-in-Hand, Epitome, Vigilant, Equipoise, Redoubtable and Medusa.

Nicias' flagship, Trident, led the Oceanus division, her sail of purple and gold and her forepeak triple-pronged in sheathed bronze. Flanking her advanced Tethys, Doris, Eurynome, Zephyr West Wind, Aias and Antigonis, then Mentor and Bay of Marathon, the sister ships Styx and Acheron, funded by Crito, Socrates' devotee. Next Strife, Castalia, Scylla, Cecropis with its blazon half-woman, half-dragon, and Aphrodisia, whose figurehead, bare-breasted, had been crafted by Phidias himself.

Then Typho, Medea, Hellhound, Anthesteria, Tauropolis, Clytemnestra, Fear and Discord; Paean, Indefatigable and Dauntless. Last Syntaxis, Hippothontis, Eleusis, Hecate, Merciless, Ostracon and Arete.

Now the Thunderbolt division, forty-one ships, under Alcibiades. His helmsman was Antiochus, wing commanders Chaemedemus, Menestheus and Adeimantus. At the fore rode the flagship, Artemisia, then Atalanta and

Parthenos, *the Virgin*, trailed by the Amazons, Antiope, Hippolyta and Penthesilea, with Iris, Aigle, Valour and Europa.

Next Leaina, *Lioness*, flanked by Hysteria, Reckless, Olympia, Fury, Sophia, Danae, Rhea, Psyche and Euphranousa. Then Palladium, Semele, Althaea, Nightingale and Leopard. Hebe, Devastator, Daphne, Erebus, *the three Fates*, Clotho, Lachesis and Atropos. Last Pandora, Swift, Terror, Penelope, Owl, Corsair, Necropolis and Calypso.

*This was the mightiest armada ever launched beneath the banner of a single city. So densely lapped rose the sails of the second and third divisions that their mass cut off the wind of the first. What open water remained stood so thick with small craft that one could have trod from Eetion to Munychia and never got one's feet wet. There must have been a thousand boys' 'itty-bits', pressing so densely about the warships that the oars in their sweep overturned no small number. The boys cheered even as they foundered, clinging to the keels of their overturned pots.*

*You are impatient, my grandson. You wish me to get to the notorious affair of the Herms. Here is how I learned of it:*

*The date was twenty-one days before departure. I had been up all night at Naval Affairs, racing not only to complete this document but to pack up the office, which was being relocated to quarters in the Choma mews, at the harbour. With two other officers, my friend Orestiades, captain of the Resolute, and the younger Pericles, son of the great Pericles and the courtesan Aspasia, I emerged to the dawn from our basement space. It was the morning after Gleaning Day, the early barley harvest, when the widows and orphans had had their hours to scavenge and the stubbled fields, picked clean, had been set ablaze outside the city and across on Euboea. The haze, drifting down the channel and mingling with the sea fog, cast the city in an eerie pall. We had just started towards the marketplace when a press of women hastened past on the Street of the Weavers. They were wailing and uttering cries of distress.*

*We turned the corner into Council Square. More throngs clamoured in disorder. Two slaves dashed past. Pericles seized one and demanded to know what was going on. 'They've knocked all the cocks off, sir!'*

*'By Heracles, speak plain and clear.'*

*'The Herms, Captain. The whole city's prickless!'*

*During the night a pack or packs of vandals, identities unknown, had rampaged through a number of quarters, defacing the stone statues of Hermes* that stood with their erect phalluses as good-luck pieces before private residences and government buildings. The criminals had batted these knobs off and even smashed the statues' faces.

Who could have committed such an outrage? No sentence short of death could requite such an act of desecration! Here was a violation not alone of clan or tribe but of the commonwealth itself, of the divinity who shields all voyagers and sustains the very polity of our nation! Already the crowds – stricken with terror at the vengeance of heaven which such a stroke of impiety was certain to draw down, not to mention the evil luck it would pronounce upon the fleet – hissed with the names of notorious malefactors. Troops of vigilantes dashed off. The wheel and rack were readied. The square seethed in mob fury.

I recall the look of consternation upon the face of my comrade, the younger Pericles. Of his family, so devastated by plague and war, none remained save himself to link Alcibiades to the elder Pericles. For this reason, and the young man's native gifts, Alcibiades had clasped him close, more as an older brother than a twice-removed cousin; Pericles esteemed his elder without reservation.

'This is Androcles' work,' the young man declared at once. 'He or the Philaidae in league with Anytus and his ilk.' He directed our attention to certain men who circulated, inflaming the mob's passion. Surely these were provocateurs, recruited to foment this unrest. 'They will accuse Alcibiades. I must find him and inform him at once.'

Charges were lodged against Alcibiades that morning. Witnesses were produced, slaves and freedmen, the former put to the torture, the latter granted immunity. On the wheel no few named the object their tormentors sought. In the Assembly Pythonicus, Androcles, Thessalus, and Anytus called for the penalty of death.

Alcibiades came forward, dismissing these accusations as a ham-fisted attempt by his enemies to frame him for a crime only a madman would commit. How witless did his foes imagine him to be, that on the eve of his most passionately sought triumph he would sabotage his own cause in this preposterous manner?

Alcibiades denied all charges and demanded to be tried at once. This hysteria must be put behind him before the fleet sailed. But his enemies, reinforced now by Procles, Euthydemus, Hagnon, and Myrtilus, brought forward fresh indictments, including profanation of the Mysteries. The accusers produced slaves and attendants who, under grants of immunity, described evenings in private homes when Alcibiades and others of his circle had donned mock-sacral garments and, prancing about in unholy caricature of priests and mystae, had amused themselves by presiding over sham initiations in disreverence of divine Demeter. These offences were cited not merely as outrages against the gods, meriting death on that account alone, but as evidence of their perpetrators' contempt for the democracy itself. They were the acts of a would-be tyrant, who set himself above all law.

Nor was Alcibiades the only man so charged, but scores and even hundreds, of all parties, fell under the informer's suit. For the scale of the desecration was so vast, the people believed, as to have been perpetrated only by a coalition, or coalitions in collusion with others of like minds, with intent to overthrow the state.

Rounds of arrests began. An informer of one faction would come forward, naming fifty or seventy or even a hundred. At once a second stooge materialized, as spokesman for the accused faction, to denounce those who had denounced his own.

In terror the people threw them all in jail. Arrests went on for days, enacted not by officials observing due process, but by armed posses snatching their victims off the street and even from their own homes. The agora stood vacant; none dared enter for fear of arrest. Appeals to the courts went unheeded; the magistrates were terrified of being hauled off themselves. Such was the chaos in the Assembly that sessions were not merely adjourned in disorder but suspended entirely. Nor did this reign of terror abate with time but, fuelled by its own excesses, heightened and intensified until it had set the state at the very threshold of anarchy.

What had driven the city mad?

In my view it was Sicily – the people's fear of this epochal enterprise, and fear of its author and his equally monumental pride. Remember, my grandson, that Alcibiades possessed no dearth of enemies. Like a lightning rod, his ambition drew the mistrust and hatred of both democrats and oligarchs. The aristocrats feared him as a traitor to his class. He had sold out his kind, they believed, to pursue his ambition as champion of the masses. In the nobles' view, the Sicilian expedition boded nothing less than their own extinction. Should Alcibiades return victorious – which he doubtless would, backed by this insuperable fleet – what would be his first act upon setting foot ashore? With the mob's blessing he would set himself up as tyrant. Nor would he tarry long to make his second move, the gentry believed, namely to strip them of their *power or put them to death. Such were Alcibiades' enemies of the nobility.*

*Of the commons his foes were equally virulent – those halfpenny rogues who had ridden to fame on the backs of the multitude, before he had snatched this constituency from them. Hyperbolus, the arch-demagogue, whom Alcibiades had conspired successfully to exile; Androcles, his successor, who nursed a bitter grudge to requite his friend; Cleonymus, that most arrant of wretches; Thydippus, Cleophon, and the great thug Archedemus. What characterized these villains was beastlike cunning and shamelessness. No outrage was beneath them. They knew how to play to the people's baser motives and would stay at nothing to achieve their ends.*

*Which brings us back to the mad stunt of defacing the statues of Hermes. Who could do such a thing? Both extremes possessed equal incentive – and equal want of scruple. And why would the people react with such hysteria?*

*In Polemides' account of the Sicilian disaster he relates a tactic employed by the enemy when harrying the mass of our army in its retreat. The foe would launch his attacks not along the entire column, but concentrated upon one point of the rear guard. His object was to incite a panic in one sector which would be communicated, as occurs so frequently in large bodies of men, to the rest.*

*A city can panic too. A polity may go to pieces.*

*The evil of panic is this: that even the brave man is powerless to stand against it, but is either overrun where he stands or swept up in flight, indistinguishable from the coward.*

*I had an acquaintance in those years named Bias, a ship's executive officer, thrice-decorated, whom all knew to be blameless of wrongdoing. He was arrested none the less and sentenced to death. In desperation he resorted to the following gambit: he confessed to crimes he had not committed and, granted immunity, promised to name the names of his co-conspirators. He then cited only those who had already been denounced by others, or had fled the city and were safe. It worked; he was released. But one of the men he had named, Epicles the son of Automedon, had not yet got clear; he was arrested and executed. Grief-stricken, Epicles' brother Polites marched to Bias's house and, hauling him forth to the street, slew him in broad daylight, daring any to bring charges.*

*Such extremities, multiplied a thousandfold, had now seized the city. Suppose your friend tugs you aside and asks as a friend, 'Tell the truth: do you have information about the guilty parties?' If you do and confess, your friend* may inform against you, under pressures you cannot know. So you tell the truth as it were a lie, or a lie as it were the truth, and he performs the same. Thus friend becomes dissevered from friend, even brother from brother, for in the atmosphere of terror and mistrust, one could set faith not even in one's own kin.

In the end, after all stool pigeons had sung and informers wriggled clear of the rack, it came to light that one political club of a hundred members had carried out the mischief. In my opinion it was damn stupidity. They struck out as children in spite, owning no notion of the evils their heedlessness would unleash.

Recall the insight of Euryptolemus, reported by our client Polemides, from that evening at the harbour tavern, Fair Wind. Two currents were at war for Athens' soul, he professed: the ancient ways, which revere the gods, and the modern, which make the city itself a god.

It was the ancient ways which now rebelled. These cracked-pate young aristocrats had defaced the city's divinities by night, and this struck the fear of God into the masses. That bulwark which understays any society, the simple God-fearing soul of its people, quailed and broke before this affront to heaven. Now their audacity to mount this spectacular overseas enterprise became, to them, that pride which calls down the wrath of Olympus. Their nerve failed. They recalled the Plague and the death ships coming home with the ashes of their sons. Staring at the shattered statues of Hermes, who escorts men to the underworld, they felt dread of hell and terror of the Almighty. The Sicily fleet seemed now an armada of doom. They recoiled before the scale of their own ambition and, inflamed by those with motive to profit thereby, struck out at its author.

Numbers had now been executed. Scores more mouldered in prison; hundreds had fled the city entire. Yet Alcibiades' enemies dared not arrest him, such was his backing with the fleet and the army, the foreign sailors and the allies. Instead they sniped with rumour and defamation. An indictment for treason was being prepared, they said. Reports were published that Alcibiades stood in league with Sparta to conduct the fleet to destruction. His foes calumniated the memory of his father and grandfathers, citing the Lacedaemonian derivation of their names, and Alcibiades' own, and blackening even their heroic deaths in battle against the Persians by recalling that these actions had been fought in alliance with the warriors of Sparta. Not even the memory of Alcibiades' Lacedaemonian nurse Amycla was spared. Even as a babe, his foes testified, Alcibiades had 'suckled at the breast of Sparta'.

My comrade the younger Pericles, in concern for his kinsman, went seeking him one morning.

'It was still early, that hour when shadows are long and the market vendors have not yet set up their stalls, when we came upon him, Orestiades and I, in the Lyceum. The square was deserted; he was with Socrates, the pair obscured in the early mist, beneath the plane tree that grows out of the hillside above the fountain. So locked were they two in converse that my companion and I drew up at a distance, not wishing to intrude.

'Alcibiades stood before the philosopher in a posture of abjection. I had never seen him so chastened or contrite. His head hung; tears streamed down his face. Socrates had one hand placed in kindness upon the younger man's shoulder. He was speaking to him quietly but with force. At once Alcibiades dropped upon one knee and buried his face in his master's cloak. Even at a distance my mate and I could see his shoulders shudder as sobs wrenched from his breast. We withdrew at once, neither wishing to be seen nor to let our friend know that he had been.'

Despite his insistence upon being tried without delay, Alcibiades' enemies conspired to have the arraignment postponed. They knew if they gave their rival the chance to speak before a jury, he would sway the people to his side. His enemies wanted Alcibiades gone, at sea with the fleet, so they could try him in absentia, where he could not speak in his own defence.

Throughout this ordeal Alcibiades maintained his rounds of exercise and attendance upon the fleet. I was present one morning at the expeditionary offices, housed temporarily in a dockside warehouse, when Alcibiades arrived. He was alone save his trainer; they had come straight from the gymnasium, their flesh still mottled with the dust of the wrestling pit. Alcibiades was clearly distraught.

'What more do the people want of me? I have donated all I own to the city, my fortune to the last obol, and now they defame even the memory of my fathers!' He was desperate to have his day in court. Let the demos convict him now and wake to their folly when he was dead.

'I can't take this any more. I can't take it!'

His hair was tangled and matted with sweat. He paced barefoot and barechested, appearing, one could not but envisage, as Achilles in his tent before Troy, storming in rage at his maltreatment at the hands of Agamemnon. At one point his shoulder brushed a stack of crockery, sending several vessels *crashing to the floor. 'Let them charge this to my account as well!'*

*To deflect Alcibiades' attention onto less doleful matter, an officer presented several documents of the Admiralty which required Alcibiades' approval and which confirmed the readiness of the fleet to sail. This sight seemed only to aggravate the man's distress.*

*'Who is to blame for this?' He wrung his fingers through his hair. 'None but myself. No-one but me.'*

*A number of ship's captains had entered through the wharfside portals and now collected about their commander, attesting their loyalty. Tears stood in Alcibiades' eyes; for a moment it seemed he would be overcome. Then, regarding the dismay upon his colleagues' faces, he was struck by the comic aspect and burst into a laugh.*

*'Cheer up, my friends; our enemies have stabbed me only with the pen. I bleed ink, not blood.'*

*He strode onto the wharf, followed by the officers, and dived from its planks into the bay. A cheer arose; hands hauled him dripping forth. A cloak was set about his shoulders. The men surrounded him.*

*'To hell with these jackals,' a captain named Eurylochus spat. 'Let the sea wash their lies from our backs.'*

*Another trierarch, Patrocles, seconded this with passion. Forget the trial, he urged Alcibiades, embark now with the fleet. 'God made no anodyne like victory.'*

*Alcibiades drew up, clearly aware of the resonance of this man's name and its forebear of glory, the beloved companion of Achilles.*

*'Patrocles, my friend. Is your name an omen? Will my wrath, like Achilles', be the cause of your death and my own?'*

*The moment hung like a sword from a strand. Then, from the men as one: 'Sicily!'*

*Alcibiades regarded them. 'Shall we sail, brothers, with enemies at our backs?'*

*'Sicily!' his mates resounded, more ardent.*

*There beyond his shoulder the vessels of the fleet awaited in their slips or rode to anchor, line after line filling the harbour, while he whose will and ambition had summoned this armada into existence and elevated it to its pitch of readiness drew up gravely, weighing in his heart this decision which necessity and his own fate had forced upon him and his country.*

*'Sicily!' the officers cried, and again: 'Sicily!'*

# BOOK FOUR

# SICILY

# EIGHTEEN
## A DISLOCATION OF RECALL

BEFORE SICILY [*POLEMIDES RESUMED*] I HAD NEVER FOUGHT AS A marine. The sea fighter's skills were new to me. I knew nothing of two-and-ones or concentrics, the breakthrough or the cutback; I had never thrown a javelin from a kneeling position or dashed forward along a trireme deck, that my weight and my comrades' decline the drive of the ram and cause her to rip the foe more lethally beneath the waterline.

I have had a nightmare here in prison, the same repeated eve upon eve. In the dream I am in Sicily, the Great Harbour of Syracuse. Of our hundred and forty-four warships, the Athenian and Corcyrean fleets combined, under fifty remain, fit to fight. These have fled to the strand beneath the Olympieum and are thrown up in disorder behind the palisade. Syracusan and Corinthian warships drive at us; the axes of their marines assault the towers bearing the massive drop-weight 'dolphins', while their archers sling ironheads upon us in the water.

Out in the harbour our ships are burning and going down. Along the shore the enemy infantry waits. Where I am, on the palisade, the foe keeps coming. Ram and back water, ram and back water. These sons of whores are good. Even after ten hours, their blades bite in unison. I am flung rearward into the backwash. The surface is choked with arrow-shafts, marine javelins, and shivered oars. My strength fails. A ship passes over. I'm going down for good when I wake in terror.

It has been my experience that in certain instances of battle or other moments of extreme peril, reality as it is normally experienced becomes supplanted by a dreamlike state in which events seem to unfold with a stately deliberateness, a retardation almost leisurely, and we ourselves stand apart as if observers of our own peril. A sense of wonder pervades all; one becomes vividly, preternaturally aware, not alone of danger but of beauty as well. He sees, and keenly appreciates, such subtleties as the play of light upon water, even such surface incarnadined with the blood of comrades dearly loved, or his own. One is able to observe to oneself, 'I am going to die now,' and absorb this with equanimity.

My brother was fascinated by this phenomenon of dislocation. Its stem, he maintained, was fear. Fear so overpowering that it drives the animating spirit from the flesh, as in death. In those moments, Lion believed, we actually were dead. The element of soul had fled; it must find its vessel of flesh and reinhabit it. Sometimes, Lion professed, the soul did not wish to. It was happier whereto it had vacated. This was battle madness, *mania maches*; the lost soul, the 'thousand-yard stare'.

Lion believed that ambition, too, could drive the soul from the body, as could passionate love, greed, or possession by wine and drugs. He warranted that certain forms of government, or misgovernment, could deprive entire populations of their soul. But I drift apart from our tale.

You must bear with me, my friend, if recollection of those days passes before the inward eye as flotsam and marine debris, untethered to the moorings of time. This is how Sicily stands, or drifts, within my recall – as neither dream nor reality but some third state, recaptured only in snatches, as a battle glimpsed through smoke upon the water.

I remember the eve of Alcibiades' recall. This was at Catana in Sicily, three months gone from Athens. Lion and I had embarked in posts not directly under our commander, but he had ordered us and others of long-standing acquaintance seconded to his party. He wanted men he trusted. And he wished to present the most concerted corps of companions when he opened negotiations with the Sicilian cities.

Naxos came over at once; Catana after a little persuasion. Messana lacked only a nudge. He took a deputation of four ships to Camarina, which, though Dorian, had been Athens' ally in the past and which, our commander's agents now claimed, was ripe to fall. She sealed her gates, however, refusing even to let us land. Alcibiades ordered the tiny flotilla back to Catana. When it got there, the state galley *Salaminia* was wait-ing, with the orders revoking his command.

I was in Alcibiades' party when *Salaminia*'s master approached, accompanied by two summoners of the Assembly. These were both men of Scambonidae, Alcibiades' home district, known to him, so as not to provoke his defiance. All were unarmed. The officers presented their papers and commanded him to accompany them to Athens, to stand trial for impiety, profanation, and treason. All expressed regret at the unfortunate nature of their errand. If Alcibiades wished, he need not return a prisoner aboard *Salaminia* but follow in his own ship. However, he must embark at once, no later than morning.

That night one spoke of nothing but the prospect of a coup. Nicias and Lamachus called out the marines, myself and Lion among them; we were posted eight to a vessel and by companies at arms up and down the strand.

Years later I served aboard *Calliope* with the younger Pericles. Alcibiades' executive officer Antiochus had been his mentor in naval warfare. Antiochus had told him, Pericles recounted, that Alcibiades, anticipating his recall for trial, had for months been orchestrating a campaign via post and through allies at home whose object was to have the charges against him reframed and the indictment of profanation, the only one he truly feared because of the passionate outrage it evoked among the people, dropped. This goal, letters received two days previous confirmed, had been effected. Such was the news Alcibiades had been hoping for. Against these reduced charges he was certain he could prevail, defending himself in person before the Assembly. Now on the strand at Catana, however, the summoners informed him, apparently in ignorance of the consequences, that the profanation charges had in fact not been dropped. Alcibiades had been double-crossed, and with brilliance, too late in the game to reply with a counter.

Among Alcibiades' counsellors, Mantitheus, Antiochus, and his cousin also named Alcibiades lobbied most vehemently for a coup, dissent voiced by Euryptolemus and Adeimantus. Those who championed this supreme stroke urged Alcibiades to seize command of the expedition here and now, imprisoning or if necessary putting to death all who refused to take his side. Nor did these radicals stop there. They proposed abandoning the Sicilian campaign where it stood and setting sail with the entire fleet for Athens, where Alcibiades, backed by army and navy, would declare himself master of the state.

It was Alcibiades himself who repudiated this. 'I would not take Athens as a mistress,' he asserted, 'but a bride.'

Many have derided this quip as facile and disingenuous, contending that Alcibiades only acceded to the summoners' decree because he believed he had in place at Athens sufficient cohorts to carry his case; or that his agents had already suborned ample in authority to effect his exoneration. I don't believe this. I think he meant exactly what he said. I allege this not in defence of the man, to characterize him as chivalrous or honour-compassed (though he was both), for consider: such a statement bespeaks an arrogance both supreme and breathtaking.

That was how he felt, I believe. Athens was in his view not nation to be served, but consort to be won; to gain her by means other than her own freely offered affection would be to dishonour her and himself. He craved not love nor power but both, each fed by and founded upon the other.

I had conjured none of this then, as the deputies served their summons beside the beached Artemisia. All, I account, however, comprised Alcibiades' reflection. I regarded him. His expression was informed neither by rage nor vindictiveness, though he came subsequently to act with both in abundance. What I perceived was sorrow. I believe he stood in that instant apart from himself and his fate, as a man at the peak of peril will be lifted and granted vision of the full field. Like a master gamesman, Alcibiades perceived move and countermove four and five turns ahead, all boding evil, yet could discern no masterstroke by which he or his city could escape this end.

'What will you do?' Euryptolemus asked his cousin.

Alcibiades stared gravely, straight ahead.

'Not sail home to be murdered, that much is certain.'

# NINETEEN
# A CHRONICLER OF STRIFE

ALCIBIADES FLED AT THURII. TO ARGOS FIRST, MEN SAID, THEN ELIS when that became too hot, one jump ahead of the state agents and fee hunters. My brother was among the military posse, led by the crew of the *Salaminia*, that chased him around Italy's boot.

> . . . *these vaunted élite of the state galley are a pretty confection, brother. Though of the cult of Ajax and thus kinsmen of their prey, they hunt him as if he were a rabid dog. At Padras he was rumoured to be fled to an inn; our search party torched the site in darkness, nearly incinerating a dozen innocents, nor tarried to proffer reparation, but another rumour of our quarry's whereabouts drove us on a further wild-goose chase. These buggers play for keeps, Pommo. They put one poor lad to the cheese grater, though the boy was no older than twelve. Next up was a sprat fisher. These heirs of Eurysaces took him two miles out and, heaving first one of his sons, then the other into the drink to drown, at last chucked the skipper himself. Such feats these agents of the state perform with a dry eye and a wisecrack.*
>
> *Clearly they fear the consequences of returning home without their charge; yet it is more than this, Pommo. Why do they hate him so? His own kinsmen! They own a zealotry more void of pity than the partisans we used to see in the islands. This very note must be smuggled out. If*

*these birds get a look at it, they will stretch my hide, and yours, upon the nearest door.*

Alcibiades was not the only commander ordered home for trial. Mantitheus, too, was indicted, trierarch of the *Penelope*, as was Antiochus, the ablest pilot in Greece, Adeimantus, and Alcibiades' cousin also named Alcibiades. Six other officers were summoned as well.

From my cousin Simon at Athens:

. . . Salaminia *returned. No Alcibiades. He legged it in Italy, on hearing the Assembly had condemned him to death in absentia, though you probably have this news already. 'I will let Athens know,' he is said to have pronounced, 'that I am very much alive.'*

Winter came. With Alcibiades and his companions gone, the fleet had lost not only its boldest and most enterprising officers but those most passionately devoted to the expedition. Nicias and Lamachus now shared command. At once all initiative fled. Instead of advancing with vigour against the cities of Sicily, cutting Syracuse off from her natural allies, Nicias made one halfhearted pass at cowing her directly, then ordered the fleet to retire for winter to Catana. I languished there two months before *Pandora* was despatched, mercifully, to Iapygia, seeking horses for the cavalry. Lion was there too, with Medusa.

Iapygia, as you know, is the heel of Italy's boot. It blows like hell up there, wild gales the non-Greek natives call *nocapelli*, bald heads. You get all the news, though; every vessel puts in at Caras, and the crews, flush with gossip, are glad of a toasty hearth to spill it in. Lion and I learned of our absconded commander from the master of a Tyrrhenian coaster who had it from a boatswain of Corinth who had run Conon's blockade of the gulf. This Corinthian had accompanied his captain to Sparta; he had passed two evenings in the Hyacinthieum and even been permitted upon the porticoes of the *apella*, the Assembly, where foreigners are occasionally licensed to attend upon the debate within.

Alcibiades had fled neither to Italy nor to the moon, imparted our informant. He was at Sparta. 'And not on the gibbet either. But free and in his glory, the cynosure of all Lacedaemon!'

This intelligence was greeted with hooting disbelief by the mariners who packed the public room.

'This same perfumed coxcomb,' our captain continued, unperturbed, 'who in the Assembly of Athens swathed himself in purple and trailed his robe astern in the dust, this same profligate and libertine, I say, in short this consummate Athenian, now in Sparta has recast himself and hatched a new Alcibiades, unrecognizable to all who knew him hitherto.

'This new Alcibiades garments himself in plain Spartan scarlet, tramps about with soles unshod, curls cascading to his shoulders in the Lacedaemonian style. He takes his meals in the common mess, bathes in the frigid Eurotas, and lays himself down each night upon a bed of reeds. He dines on black broth and takes wine only in moderation. Of speech he is as parsimonious as if words were gold and he a miser. At break of day one may discover him afield and asweat, training upon the running course. Forenoon finds him in the gymnasium or upon the athletic grounds, into whose games he plunges with a passion exceeding even that of his most ardent and accomplished hosts. In short the man has become more spartan than the Spartans, and they idolize him for it. Boys trail him about, Peers compete to call him comrade, and women . . . well, the laws of Lycurgus promote polyandry, as you know, so that even men's wives may dote openly upon this paragon of whom all declare,

> . . . here is not a second Achilles,
> but the man, the very man himself.'

The seamen responded with an anthem of knuckle raps on the bench-tops. Later Lion and I interrogated the Tyrrhenian aside in a more sober vein. What had his friend reported of Alcibiades' intentions? Clearly our erstwhile commander had not decamped to Sparta to play at ball or train on the track.

'That square of sail I trimmed from my fable, mates. I doubted it would prompt a smile.'

'Spill it now, friend.'

'He works against you, brothers, and with all his bowels. That avidity with which he in past paid court to Athens, with matching

gall he now plots her ruin. You know what stay-at-homes the
Lacedaemonians are and how tardy to act. Well, Alcibiades gave them
an earful of Athenian fire, enough to rouse even those boneheads from
their slumber.

'The Spartans had held the fate of Sicily as not affecting their
interests. Alcibiades apprised them otherwise. Who, he enquired, would
know better the expedition's object than himself, its author? This he
declared to be neither Sicily, Italy, nor Carthage, but these, conquered,
to serve as stepping-stones to an assault upon the Peloponnese, whose
ultimate aim was the conquest of Sparta herself. In terms most passionate he exhorted his hosts to despatch at once to Syracuse all aid they
could spare and proffered divers other counsels to bring evil upon his
countrymen.'

We returned to Catana with the spring. The place was gloomier,
even, than I remembered. Curfew had been instituted. Wages came late,
and in chits not coin; there were brawls every payday. Simon reports
Alcibiades' odour at home:

> . . . the Assembly has gone so far as to enact a motion of imprecation;
> the Eumolpid priests have placed a curse upon him. How Homeric! So
> many turned out, it sparked a riot. This is no joke, Pommo. Alcibiades
> will doubtless seek to bring the Spartan army against you, or at least
> have them despatch a crack general. Win fast, cousin. Or better, get
> home.

On the second of Munychion the army moved out for Syracuse. Lion
brought his new woman Berenice. We held all in common, including
correspondence. When I finished reading aloud cousin Simon's letter,
Berenice asked if she might have it. 'For Lion's *historia*.'

My brother was compiling a chronicle of the war.

'Why the hell shouldn't I? I know my alphas and betas as well as the
next moron. Besides, here is a tale worth telling, one whose publication
cannot fail to produce fortune and renown and relieve its author ever
after of squandering his hours with such as yourself.'

I declared this a noble ambition.

'Attend my logic, Pommo. These verses of Homer:

> . . . into the manslaughter advanced Peleus's
> peerless son, god-born Achilles, and in their
> ranks he broke the enemy before him . . .

Or this:

> . . . these he left in numbers upon the field,
> a feast for dogs and crows . . .

'Now I put this to you, brother. Who would you and I be, upon that thousand-years-gone field? Not Achilles, that's certain! We'd be the luckless bastards mown down beneath his blade. And our obituary? One louse-ridden line, lumped with fifty other nameless ciphers. Yet these are the men, don't you see, whose story cries out most to be told. Our story! By the gods, we are heroes too. And is not the paying public comprised precisely of such as we? Other gentlemen of the armoured infantry. They will eat up my narrative, which I will recite to unceasing citation within the salons and auditoria of our nation. I may even set it to music and accompany myself on the lyre.'

A number of mates had clustered with their women. And who, our comrade Chowder enquired, will play Achilles to your Homer?

Why, Alcibiades of course!

'The *Iliad*,' Lion re-edified his adherents, 'narrates the tale of the wrath of Achilles

> and the destruction in its train which wreaked
> havoc upon the Achaeans, hurling in their hosts to
> hell stout souls of heroes . . .

'Consider, friends. Wronged by his king and commander, Achilles sheathes his blade and retires to his tent. This prayer he makes: that his countrymen discover, by the sufferings they must now endure, how far the best of them he is, and bemoan bitterly that they have let him be so ignobly used.

'Is not Alcibiades' equation identical, my friends, excepting only this: our modern Achilles has gone one better than his counterpart. Not only had he retired from contending at our side, depriving us of his skills and counsel, but now he yokes himself to the cause of our enemy, applying his full rage and resourcefulness in their interest, against us.'

Lion's listeners began to squirm.

'It gets worse, brothers. For this enemy, Sparta, has never wanted in valour or skill in warfare. All she lacks is that which our contemporary Achilles may provide her: vision and audacity. Alcibiades will rouse this enemy to initiatives she would never have undertaken absent his urgings and provide her with masterstrokes of strategy she could never have advanced upon her own.'

'Enough, Lion!' Chowder elevated his palms.

'Ah, friends, you fail yet to perceive the genius of my construct. For my epic, unlike Homer's, discovers its significance not among divinely spawned champions and their destinies, but here in the dirt with us sons of mortals who must endure them. Upon us, the grimy heroes of my tale, falls the necessity to gift it with significance. Alcibiades will serve our story, not we his. This is how modern war differs from mythic.'

To my cousin, that summer:

> . . . we are in action at last, if you can call building a wall action. The army took the heights, called Epipolae, overlooking the city. A few hundred killed, mostly theirs. This is what it is like. We start our wall. The Syracusans commence a counterwall at right angles to cut ours off. They march out in mass and erect a stockade. Behind this they bring the counterwall out, then build another stockade and continue. They are scared pissless and work feverishly.

Several days later:

> . . . the picked companies attacked their wall at noon, when the sun's heat renders all insensate. Tore it down. They built a second, across the marsh called Feverside adjacent the harbour. Our marines were called up in support of about two thousand heavy infantry. We marched into the swamp carrying doors and boards to lay over the muck. At one point our lads were planting their own bodies, upon which we trod and fought from. At the height of this nastiness, the fleet, which had been held back up north, sailed into the harbour. That did it. The Syracusans ran for cover. Lamachus was killed, however. Now Nicias holds sole command.

*The Syracusans are beaten, though. It is only a matter of raising our
wall, harbour to sea, and completing the investment of the city. That
done, Syracuse is cooked.*

The architect in charge was Callimachus son of Callicrates, who had
built the third Long Wall for Pericles. He had six plants producing
bricks and twenty forges fabricating fittings. Nicias had taken the point
called Plemmyrium, renamed the Rock for its want of water, across the
harbour mouth from the city. Syracuse was now blockaded by sea. The
enemy no longer ventured out to fight.

*. . . the broken ground east of the city had been, before we arrived, a
pleasant suburb of temples and promenades. There was a boys' school,
residential blocks, a games field. Now it's all rubble. Every house, wall,
and road has been demolished. The stones are now part of the wall. All
trees have been felled for timber for forms, inclines, and stockades; not
a blade of grass remains for miles. The only edifice spared is a mill for
the bakers' ovens. The army and its followers are a hundred thousand.
The tent city is big as Syracuse; it has not lanes but boulevards. Latrines
are numbered; otherwise one loses one's way taking a crap.*

*Across the plain, piles of stone are set along the line where the wall
will advance. Before these are spiked ditches, with palisades on top. At
night the two and a half miles from harbour to sea are lit solid with bonfires and torches. It is spectacular. This of course does not account the
fleet, at anchor in the harbour or visible running drills at sea. It is
literally one city besieging another.*

Lion and I trekked down to visit Telamon, whose Arcadians were
stationed at the southern end of the wall, a pretty park area called the
Olympieum. The mercenary commended his comrade's literary under-
takings but with a wry amusement that exasperated the aspiring
historian. Lion wanted Telamon's views. Our mentor regarded him as if
he had gone barmy.

Lion offered pay. This turned the trick. The topic was heroism. Was
the valour of men in mass as worthy of note as that of the solitary
champion?

'We have a proverb in my country,' Telamon declared:

*Heroism makes good song but poor soup.*

This means steer wide of champions. Passion is their coin. Lion has chosen his hero well in Alcibiades, for this creature breathes passion and arouses it. He will end badly.'

Lion pressed our mate to elaborate.

'In Arcadia we build no cities; this is how we like it. The city is the spawning ground of passion and the hero. Who is more consummately a man of the city than Alcibiades?'

'Are you saying, Telamon, that heroism has no place for you, a professional soldier?'

'Heroes are recognized by their tombs.'

At this I protested. Telamon himself was a hero!

'You confound prudence with valour, Pommo. If I fight up front, it's because I find it safer. And if I fight to win, well . . . the dead line up before no paymaster.'

Telamon had said all he wished; he stood to depart. Lion pressed. 'What about pay, my friend? Surely you feel passion for this.'

'I use money but never permit money to use me. To serve for pay sets a man at a remove from the object of his or his commander's desire. This is money's proper use; it renders service in its name a virtue. Love of country or glory, on the other hand, unites one to the object of one's desire. This makes it a vice. The patriot and the fool serve without pay.'

'The patriot because he loves his country,' proposed Lion.

'Because he loves himself. For what is a man's country but the multi-plied reflection of himself, and what is this but vanity? Again your choice of champion is surpassing, my friend, for who of all men loves himself more than Alcibiades? And who more personifies love of country?'

'And is love of country a vice?'

'Less a vice than a folly. But then all love is folly, if by love one means that which one clasps to one's heart, rendering no distinction between it and oneself.'

'Then Alcibiades by your measure is a slave to Athens?'

'None surpasses him in abjection.'

'Even as he works with might and main against her?'

'Same coin, obverse side.'

'Then we ourselves,' Lion suggested, indicating the soldiers and marines attending within the tent, 'are fools and slaves?'

'You serve that which you value.'

'And what do you serve, Telamon? Other than money.'

Indignation informed Lion's tone. He was offended. Telamon smiled. 'I serve the gods,' he declared.

'Wait . . .'

'The gods, I said. Them I serve.'

And he exited.

Construction continued on the wall. The expedition had ceased to be war, if it ever had been. It had become public works. There was a defect to this. Men ceasing to act as warriors cease to be warriors.

By midsummer it began to show. Soldiers now paid others to stand their watches and bought their way out of labour on the wall. They hired Sicels, the non-Greek natives, or employed camp followers, setting themselves at idleness. Even sailors began enlisting surrogates. When their officers sought to check this, the men voted them out and replaced them with commanders who knew, like the cub of the marble fox,

*from which tit flowed milk and which water.*

Inaction spawned discontent and discontent bred insurrection. Men dozed brazenly on watch; they lounged about the barbers' tents and packed the closets of the whores' camp, presenting themselves in every quarter except the drill field. Discipline could not be enforced by the newly minted officers, who owed their very station to their men's contempt for them. Malingering grew epidemic. Soldiers went absent without leave and on return did not deign even to offer excuse. At night units no longer stuck together, but individuals scattered to their own, with no object nobler than hunting trouble. Theft grew rampant. Vigilantism rose in response. A man would open another's guts over a stolen shoe or jealousy of a woman or boy.

Where was Nicias, our commander? Ill in his tent, with nephritis. His sixty-second birthday had come and gone. The men laughed at him and the seers and soothsayers who winged about his tent like gulls above the refuse dump.

That current of enterprise which properly conducted by wise and effective officers produces a disciplined army now, turned from its proper course, flowed into more malignant channels. Those who had bought themselves out of work turned this leisure to commerce, in women and contraband and even legitimate matériel. Who would stop them? They were businessmen and traders, who knew how to hold out a palm and how to grease one. Good men, witnessing this corruption and observing their commanders impotent to impede it, lost all incentive to keep their own order. Soldiers' kits looked like trash. Hygiene went to hell. There were more men down sick than at work on the wall. Even I succumbed to this swell of misfeasance. My protests had long since got me demoted to private soldier. I took to hunting. I had dogs and beaters, a regular racket going. I fled camp ten days at a time and was never missed. *Pandora*'s marines had scattered, some back to the ship, thinking sea duty easier than hod-humping, others ducking work in obscure wards of the camp. With Lion I vacated as well, to the Olympieum, adjacent Telamon's Arcadians.

One evening we took a ramble up the heights called Epipolae. Lion brooded, seeking the deficiency that had turned the army so sour. Telamon was taking a piss and didn't even look up.

'No Alcibiades, no empire.'

Night fell; that fort called the Circle was lit up beneath cressets. We walked, looking out over the city and harbour. 'Nicias has had his career,' Telamon continued. 'He's like an old ploughhorse who wishes only to get back to the barn.'

The mercenary gestured to the ant colony that sprawled beneath us, harbour to sea. 'Look at this hell. Why would any man cross an ocean to besiege a nation no threat to his own? Fear won't make him, nor even greed. Only one force will call him. A dream! That dream is gone. It defected with your friend Alcibiades.'

We were on the wrong side, Telamon declared. We were going to lose. Lion and I laughed. How could we lose? Syracuse is cut off. The native cities flock to our side. No armies are coming to preserve the Syracusans, and they certainly can't save themselves. Who will teach them?

'The Spartans,' testified Telamon, as if it were patent. 'Once Alcibiades despatches them, schoolmasters to their fellow Dorians of Syracuse.'

# TWENTY
# SCHOOLMASTERS OF WAR

AMONG THE WAYS THE SPARTANS DIFFER FROM OTHER PEOPLES IS THIS. When an ally in distress applies to them for aid, they alone despatch neither troops nor treasure but a solitary commander, a general. This officer alone, assuming charge of the beleaguered forces, is sufficient, they feel, to turn affairs about and produce victory.

This as the world knows is what happened at Syracuse. The general's name was Gylippus. I knew this man from my schooling at Sparta. A true story:

When he was a boy, Gylippus was an exceptionally fast runner. At ten he won the boys' Hyacinthiad over the Long Course, a cross-country trial in excess of ten miles. The ordeal of the event is as follows: each entrant must fill his cheeks with water, preserving this unswallowed, then produce it entire at race's end into a receptacle, a bronze of Apollo Crabwise holding out his cupped hands. If you swallow, you're out. Almost all do. Sometimes one simply trips and gulps his cargo by reflex.

Gylippus had contrived a ruse. Beyond sight of the judges, he swallowed and raced all out. He had secreted a portion of water in a hollow stone about a mile from the finish. Beating the other boys to this, he was able to fill his mouth again and hold it to the pole. In this way he won at ten and again at eleven. But one night, sleeping beside his elder brother Phoebidas, he boasted of his secret. Phoebidas determined to teach a lesson. At next year's race he dashed out to the stone and overturned it. When Gylippus reached the site, in the lead, he found no means of refilling his cheek – and the other boys were bearing down fast from behind.

Gylippus sprinted to the finish, first again. Now the judges commanded him to fill the god's hands, that is to spit, deliver his water. Gylippus obeyed. He had bitten his tongue through, filling his mouth with blood.

In his twenties Gylippus, serving as a brigade commander under Brasidas in Thrace, not only distinguished himself repeatedly for personal valour but achieved signal successes commanding inferior troops, helot conscripts without adequate armour and with minimal training. He seemed to possess an affinity for these roughshod rogues and a genius for whipping them into crack troops. This faculty held no small bearing, it is certain, upon his election by the ephors as commander for Syracuse.

This same Gylippus, now a *polemarch*, a war leader, of thirty-six years, holder of three prizes of valour including Mantinea, arrived in Sicily with only four ships, two secretaries, one junior lieutenant, and a handful of freed helots serving as marines. Within twelve months he had overturned all. Commencing with the Syracusan Admiralty, which prior to his arrival had bedazzled with a peacock's array of robes of rank, he banned all colours but white and burned the offending rags in public, inaugurating the Festival of Naked Poseidon, Gymnopotideia in Doric. To roust his cohorts from the sack, he instituted a predawn sacrifice and required attendance by all commanders. Headgear at sea he prohibited, partly to efface all distinctions of vanity but primarily to make his men dark and vigorous from the sun.

The Little Harbour, whose shipyards had lain open to Athenian depredation, Gylippus fortified with seawalls and palisades. Behind these he set his charges to work. Naval architects and shipwrights had heretofore been deemed artisans, among the meaner orders. Gylippus overturned this, granting to these trades brooches of honour and acclaiming them *poleos soteres*, Saviours of the City. Prior to his reformations, lads under eighteen might not inscribe their names upon the citizen rolls, while those past sixty, regardless of skill or vigour, suffered mandatory retirement. Gylippus repealed these ordinances, attracting to his corps of shipbuilders the brightest youths as prentices and the most practised elders as masters. By winter's end the navy of Syracuse possessed nearly as many warcraft as her besiegers, and her commanders had acquired such temerity as to challenge the invaders ship for ship at sea.

Gylippus likewise refashioned the army. He made trials to discover which men craved most neither riches nor power but honour. These he appointed captains. All who had secured their stations through wealth or influence must reapply, with no eye on them save Gylippus's and his new commanders'. The army itself he reorganized into companies mobilized not by tribe, but by precinct within the city. He set side by side those wards which bore a natural rivalry, offering prizes for competitions between them. In this way the battalion of the Geloan quarter roused itself to excellence against their adversaries of the Andethusia. Then he pitted these as allies against others. By such exercises each unit gained confidence in itself and the army as a whole developed faith in each division.

Discovering weapons and armour to be lacking, Gylippus ordered all who possessed shield and breastplate to present themselves in the central square. The rich, showing off, produced armour gilded to its most dazzling. When these had been erected in prideful display, Gylippus set his own plain *panoplia* alongside. All excess was stripped and sold, proceeds applied to acquire arms for the commons.

To raise revenue, Gylippus employed the following stratagem. Fearing that direct levy might turn the aristocratic element against him, he induced the Assembly instead to require each citizen to come forward on a specific day and render a public accounting of his wealth. Now each could behold with his own eyes the extent of treasure his fellows had hoarded. At once the privileged felt shame not to have contributed more, while the humble who had served with honour were esteemed as better men than the rich. Contributions flooded in. The cavalry grew flush with mounts, while the vaults overflowed with treasure.

Exploiting the linguistic bonds of the Doric Spartans and Syracusans, Gylippus enlisted words, too, to the cause. Armoured infantrymen he now called *homoioi*, Peers or Equals. Regiments were designated *lochoi*, divisions *morai*. Among other Spartan usages he compelled each member of a military unit to discontinue the practice of dining at home or with friends and to take his meals in the common mess with his

company. In this way unit esprit was fostered, and all felt themselves
equal and united.

Gylippus outlawed drunkenness and declared it a whipping offence to
neglect the marching condition of one's feet. He made it a crime for a
man to have a potbelly or appear at large with stooped shoulders. He
introduced anthems of ridicule, the same as at Sparta, and recruited the
city's children to swarm upon any slovenly fellow, rebuking him in song.
These and other reforms Gylippus instituted. But supreme among all
stood his own presence, the fact that he had come in person to share his
comrades' peril and to donate all to preserve their freedom.

One morning in late winter as Gylippus marshalled his battalions and
we hastened to position to engage them, I noted Lion jotting notes.
'Have you noticed,' he remarked, 'with what discipline the Syracusans
take their stations now that Gylippus has forged them in his image?'

I looked. Of the allies about us – Athenians, Argives, and Corcyreans
– many knelt or squatted. Breastplates sprawled on the earth; shields
canted, splayed flat or even perched upon by their owners. Squires
served double- and triple-duty, their fellows hired out as labourers long
since. Directly across, every Syracusan stood in full *panoplia*, shield
against knee, squire at his left, taking the weight of helmet and cuirass
in the Spartan manner.

They beat us that day. By late summer their counterwall had cut our
wall off. With this all hope of investing Syracuse was lost. In a night
attack Gylippus took Labdalum, that fort and storehouse on Epipolae
which held not only our siege gear but our paymaster's cash. He fortified
Euryalus, the Heights' lone avenue of vulnerability, and continued his
crosswall to fortify the elevation entire. Even at sea, where the skill of our
mariners stood pre-eminent, Gylippus set his new navy on the offensive.
The ingenuity of his commanders now served him. Recognizing that the
fight would come not in the open sea, but in the confines of the Great
Harbour, he had the prows and catheads of his triremes reinforced and
built out triple-wide, to ram head-on instead of from the flank as the
skilled Athenians preferred. We learned a new word from him, *boukepha-
los*, oxhead. With these brutes he pounded our lighter, hollow-rammed
ships, chasing us back behind both breakwaters to the inner harbour. Now
it was we who were sinking pilings for half-moons and manning the dredging barge to plant 'hedgehogs' and 'dolphins'.

By autumn's close Gylippus's dreadnoughts had sunk or disabled forty-three of our ships and his troops had driven us off Epipolae entire, save the Circle fort at Syce. His own fleet had suffered terribly, more than seventy vessels crippled or sunk, but these losses he made up swiftly, bringing in fresh timber through the Little Harbour and overland, protected now by the counterwall.

Gylippus was blockading us now, and his fist screwed the press tight. The Syracusans could afford to lose two men for every one of ours, two ships, two walls, and every day their position grew stronger as more Sicilian cities, smelling blood, defected from the invaders to their compatriots. Nicias ordered the upper walls abandoned. We lost lines of assault across city and harbour and, more telling, the baker's mill, which had supplied our bread. Sutlers and camp followers, and many of our women, melted away. We crouched, hemmed like rats south of Feverside, the marsh at the gut of the harbour. And when in another night attack Gylippus's troops drove us from the Olympieum, he threatened this wretched toehold as well.

My old ship, the *Pandora*, had passed all summer fending the enemy off Plemmyrium, the foe's attacks so unremitting that the ship could not be dragged up and dried out. When at last she beached for refitting, I went aboard to visit an old snoozing spot, fore of the catheads. Setting my heel on the king-beam, I felt the timber give like a sponge.

Our ships were rotting.

The paymaster's reserve had run out; wages fell three months, then four, in arrears. Foreign sailors began to desert, while the attendants and slaves who replaced them slid over the side at their first taste of the lash. Nicias' infirmity worsened. Morale was at rock-bottom. Mercenary officers could no longer hold their men. Telamon had lost a fifth, gone over to the foe.

At the start of the second winter came this letter from Simon. He reports Lion's wife remarried, to a good man, a war cripple. Our cousin has encountered Eunice, harbouring deep bitterness towards me, and my children, who are well.

> . . . *numerous reports of Gylippus and his mischief. Athens has only herself to blame. What did they expect Alcibiades to do, thank them for their death warrant?*

*We at home are in our friend's debt as well. In addition to sending Gylippus to you, he has convinced the Spartans to redouble their efforts against us. King Agis is before our walls with his whole army, and they are not going home. They have fortified Decelea, another stroke urged by Alcibiades. Twenty thousand slaves have hotfooted it there already. Three hundred go over every night, skilled craftsmen sorely missed. Wheat and barley no longer come in overland via Euboea. All must go by sea round Sounium. A loaf costs a morning's wages. As for me, the pawnshop has taken my last dandy's cloak. The Meleager has dropped me from the roll of Knights. Can't reprove them, as I no longer possess a horse. Ah, but fortune has smiled . . .*

*A second fleet outfits under the hero Demosthenes, embarking at once to your aid. Parting with my last duck to bribe the recruitment officer, I have been accepted in a cavalry unit without mounts. These we shall acquire in Sicily, or so our commanders assure us. Therefore brace up, cousins. I ride (or walk) to your rescue!*

By the time this letter arrived, four months after its posting, the fleet under Demosthenes had reached Corcyra. Another ten days and the first corvettes appeared. Seven more and here came the armada – seventy-six vessels, ten thousand men, armour and money and supplies. Gylippus's defenders withdrew to Lardbottom and Pedagogue's Frock, their third and fourth counterwalls; their fleet fell back behind Ortygia to the Little Harbour.

The fortunes of war had reversed again. As these fresh ships of Athens streamed into the Great Harbour, brothers and mates swept towards one another with joy. Arriving marines leapt from the vessels' decks, embracing companions hip-deep in the sea. Others onshore stripped naked and swam to the ships, mounting the oar ports hand over hand. Lion and I found Simon, on the strand with his horseless cavalry, both of us weeping as we clasped him to our breasts.

How long it had been! Two bitter winters since the expedition sailed from home so full of hope, two summers of dilation and demoralization since its men had seen beloved friends and brothers, heard from their lips news of home, or pressed them in the flesh to their bosoms. Nor had these, our reinforcements, come an hour too soon.

Each man of the first expedition, soon as he had made certain of friends and kinsmen, must seek with his own eyes Demosthenes. Our new co-commander came ashore on foot, mounting to the strand with his helmet under his arm and his cloak trailing in the sea. On the palisades, the troops whooped themselves hoarse. There he stands, brothers! His flesh is not sallow like Nicias' with illness and care, but sun-burnished with vigour and resolve. Nor does he make at once to erect an altar seeking counsel of the gods, but strides to assess the issue with his own eyes and reason. Demosthenes, men! Now at last we have a winner, who triumphed in Aetolia and Acarnania and the Gulf, defeated and captured the Spartans at Sphacteria!

Demosthenes' first order was to get the men paid. He marched forty thousand past the tables in an afternoon, making good all arrears in newly minted owls and virgins. That night his speech was terser than a Spartan's.

'Men, I've looked this hellhole over and I don't like it. We came here to pound these bastards. It's time we started.' This was acclaimed with a riot of spearshafts clashing upon shields; the army roared its resolution and approval.

Three nights later a force of five thousand retook the Olympieum. The succeeding dawn an assault by ten thousand cleared the Syracusans from the bay. The fleet recaptured the Rock and reblockaded the city; another night attack took back a mile of our old wall.

Casualties were massive. Four days' losses exceeded the total for the year, yet they must be borne so long as their produce was victory. Nor would Demosthenes permit momentum to flag. He harvested armour from the dead and wounded, converting auxiliary troops and even cooks to heavy infantry. My cousin's horse unit was among those reconfigured. Simon had never fought on foot in armour. It is not a skill one acquires in a night. Nor would he or his mates of the mounted troopers be granted the luxury of breaking-in on some soft or easy target.

The next assault must be against only one place, Epipolae. The Heights must be retaken; without them no assault on the city could prevail.

# TWENTY-ONE
# DISASTER ON EPIPOLAE

TEN THOUSAND WENT UP AT THE SECOND WATCH OF THE NIGHT, heavy infantry and marines carrying four days' rations (for we were meant to take the counterwall and hold it), with ten thousand missile troops in support. That left no force at all, except the sailors and the general crowd, to defend the perimeter against a counterattack aimed at the fleet. The game, Demosthenes believed, was worth the gamble. He massed all he had and threw it at Gylippus.

I felt confident the assault would succeed; what struck terror was concern for my cousin. He was no soldier, and anything could happen up on those rocks, particularly in the dark and in a unit of dismounted cavalry untrained in armoured assault and in no shape to tackle that hill. Worse, Simon's commanding officer Apsephion, a moron we both knew from Acharnae, had, seeking to play the hero, succeeded in getting his boys slotted in where the action would be hottest – the western approach via Euryalus, the Park Way, where the slope was most exposed and the enemy position most heavily fortified.

They would be in the third wave, my cousin's horseless cavalry, under the general Menander. Lion and I were in the first, the left wing, behind the Argive and Messenian heavy infantry, eleven hundred in all, with four hundred light troops, darters of Thurii and Metapontum, in support. The centre, once it re-formed up top, would be all-Athenian, the tribal regiments of Leontis and Aegeis, both crack units with their own peltasts and incendiaries. On their left were the mercenary troops, including Telamon's Arcadians, supported by two hundred Corcyrean marines serving as javelineers, then another picked Athenian regiment, the Erechtheis. Linking this to our wing were four hundred Andrian, Naxian, and Etruscan marines armoured as hoplites, my own among them, with a hundred Cretan archers and fifty darters of the Messapian tribe of Iapygia. The heavy units would assault the walls, with the missile troops immediately to the rear, firing overhead to clear the ramparts.

Topside, the troops' name for Epipolae, is several hundred feet up, crumbly white limestone with scrub oak and fireweed, sheer on three sides except the west, where it is steep but climbable. There is a race-track called the Polyduceum at this end, the last flat space of any scale, and upon this the assault troops marshalled during the first watch of the night. A light-armed force of two hundred rangers had already started up the Heights. It was their job to rope the face and secure the precipice.

The night was hot and dark as a tomb. The troops had been awake all day, keyed-up and impatient; few had slept for fear the previous night. Each man carried fifty pounds in shield, helmet, and breastplate and another forty of ironmongery and kit, for our orders were to take the counterwall and rebuild our own. We had all our masons and carpenters with us. Now massing on the marshalling ground, men sheeted sweat, flaked out at all postures, pillowing their heads on shields, stones, and each other's sprawling limbs. Many discarded helmets, for the heat and vision in the dark; others shed breastplates and greaves. The god Fear had made his entrance. Across the field one descried men evacuating bowels and emptying bladders. 'It's starting to smell like a battle,' Lion observed.

Our cousin Simon appeared. He had spotted us passing and got leave to call. He was decked in full *panoplia*, including helmet with horsehair crest. 'What happens now?'

'We wait.'

I introduced him round; he knew Chowder from Athens and Splinter, another of our mates, from Phegae near Marathon. 'What do you call this?' the latter enquired, indicating Simon's top-brush.

'Affectation,' prompted Chowder. They teased Simon, laughing from nerves.

'Is it hot,' Simon spoke, 'or just terror?'

'Both.'

I unballasted his helmet for him.

'Are you scared, Pommo?'

'Petrified.'

Among Lion's notes is this observation:

*When soldiers seek to name the object of their terror, they rarely cite its true source but some unrelated or even ludicrous corollary.*

My cousin had become obsessed with the dread that Lion or I would be slain tonight and not he. This would be infamous, he portrayed, as he deserved it and not we. He was already making vows to change his ways.

'No-one's dying,' my brother assured him.

'Right,' seconded Chowder. 'We're all immortal.'

When the call came down, I tugged our cousin apart. 'It'll be hot Topside; you'll be sweating. Don't take wine, understand? Only water. Eat every chance you get or you'll cramp. And don't be ashamed to crap yourself. We'll all be scraping mud off our thighs by sunrise.' We could hear the guidon bearers passing the word to assemble; all must form up and dress the line. 'You'll be fine, Simon. So will we. We'll take our wine later, with victory.'

The signal came. We went up in column. Even at this hour heat radiated off the west-facing stone, which had been baking all afternoon. There were three tracks, each wide enough for one man; switchbacks turned so tight you could reach up with your capped spearpoint and tap the shields of the column snaking ahead across the face. We could hear shouts and fighting two hundred feet above; word came to advance at the double, as if we could. Up we went, clinging to the roped face, humping full kit plus tool packs and gear bags, shortsword and dagger, nine-footer in the right fist, oxhide skirt beneath the shield to deflect ironheads, plus leathers and battle pack with bread, wine, and water-skin. Sweat slathered; one cooked inside one's carapace.

By the time our unit reached the top the rangers and lead units had driven the enemy from the Labdalum fort. We surged onto the flat, remarshalling. 'Party hats off!' our captain bawled. We chucked the cornel plugs that protected our mates from getting stabbed accidentally, exposing the spearpoints' steel.

The table on top of the Heights measured three miles east to west and just under two at the waist. We must cross it the long way and cross it fast. 'Dress the line!' 'Take your water now.' Of *Pandora's* original sixteen marines we had lost nine to disease and action over two years, added ten from depleted units and lost six of those. Our current eleven had been subsumed under an Etruscan platoon whose captain, though past fifty, was a fire-eater with wrists thick as anchor ropes and hams like an ox. He could lift a mule, they said, though I never saw him do it. 'She'll be raining iron soon, lads. Keep the ranks tight, arsehole to belly button, and you might live to chase pussy another day.'

The line stepped off at slung shields. We had dreaded the Labdalum fort, but it had fallen with barely a fight. The front surged forward. Terrain was raw, ascending, broken with dry courses and defiles. In a way it was worse than cleared fields of fire. Branches caught the bowl of your shield; brush snarled your stride; it was impossible to advance on line. Squads first, then entire platoons faltered to regroup; gaps opened, filled by units from the wing or rear. We saw flames ahead and heard cries.

A whistle cut the darkness. Three Athenian rangers materialized, identified themselves by the password, 'Athena Protectress', and were conducted to Demosthenes' post of march, somewhere off to our right. Our Etruscan dashed off to find it. Men gulped water and dumped rations. Here he came back. The first manned defensive position lay a quarter mile ahead: a stone outwork with a palisade. Forms and timbers had been laid for construction of the wall; the enemy had torched them – that was the blaze we saw – but the wood had gone up too fast, tinder-dry in the heat, and the rest our lads had broken apart. Still the foe was there. He was waiting. The rangers were hard characters, faces blackened, wearing *pilos* caps and armed only with rabbit-stickers and the Lacedaemonian sickle, the *xyele*. They were tired now and scared; they wanted wine. Who didn't?

Lion and I set our two files at six and five, with the pair of us up front. It was so hot, sweat coursed from beneath armour with an audible flush; you could hear it sluice onto the limestone, like a dog pissing. When we wrung our undercaps, the liquid gushed as from a sponge. A marine made to ditch his helmet. Our Etruscan cuffed him. 'Do you want your brains bashed in?'

Lion would not let our men loosen their breastplates or rest except on one knee. Wine they could have; we all needed it. Fear was on us now. You could hear it, like a comber at the base of a cliff, as the skins passed hand-to-hand and each ranker gulped the liquid courage which is never enough and, with that breathless overhaste all soldiers know, ran through his prayers and superstitions, fingered the charms pended within his shield's bowl and chanted his magic phrases. 'Whatever happens, don't break apart. Shield-to-shield all the way to the top.' Lion tugged our eleven about him. 'Who runs, better see me dead first.' He meant he would kill that man himself when he got back.

The word came: step off.

I could hear my brother hyperventilating beside me.

'You little lion.'

'Take it to hell.'

The ranks pushed off in silence. The slope was wide now, broken by patches of scrub spruce and fennel. The formation achieved a pace, maintaining the line. Our tread crunched on coals. Where was the foe? We had gone a hundred yards. One fifty. Suddenly a crock of flaming naphtha peeled out of the dark and shattered, slinging fire. 'There they are!' an enemy voice cried ahead.

With a shout the line bellied forward, elevating shields to high port. Fire flared underfoot, embers and brands of the foe's blazes. The hair of one's legs caught and sizzled; already terror made each man edge right, to the shelter of his mate's shield. 'Upfield!' Lion bellowed. Advance straight!

Now each crouched and fanned at the trapezius, seating the nasal and cheek pieces of his helmet against the sweat stain at the upper rim of his shield, eye slits alone exposed for vision, or such purblind daze as the infantryman calls by that name, and locked bronze to bronze, bracing to receive the onslaught that must come, and soon. We could hear the first projectiles ringing off *aspides* fore and aft. Each man's left shoulder set into the concavity at the upper rim of the shield. Simultaneously his right fist, clutching his nine-footer at the upright, seized as well the hempen grip cord at the right of the inner bowl and, using the shaft of his spear as a brace, secured it by its two iron collars to the outboard edge of the shield, locking it against the concussion to come. Every sinew from heel to crown tensed within the swinging, lengthening stride.

Now came the storm of rock and bullets. 'On, boys! They're only pebbles!' 'Courage, men! Strong knees!'

As a trekker on the crestline plants his soles and leans, shoulders drawn, into a hailstorm, so the attackers' ranks waded against the gale of stone and lead.

'Who'll be a brave man?'

'Who'll strike the foe first?'

Ahead in the fire-flare: archers.

'Toothpicks!'

Ironheads drummed into the bronze facings of the shields, ricocheted off the upright spears above. The *aspides* of the front ranks filled like quill cushions with the enemy's shafts, which ripped through the bronze to bury in the oak chassis beneath, thick as a kitchen cutting board and as impenetrable. One heard the rebounds clatter at one's feet and the misses screaming overhead. 'Keep moving!' Lion bawled. All were shouting now, as men called upon heaven and advanced into the rain of death.

Here came moonrise.

We could see the rampart ahead.

'Javelins!'

The marine at my shoulder cried once and dropped. Now descended the fusillade of sheathed ash. There was no wind, so the shafts came on warhead-foremost, no deflection. Lion went down beneath a thunderous strike. 'I'm all right!' He hauled to his feet beside me. A second hit. I fell. 'Get up, you son of a whore!'

The line is everything.

Terror must not break it; one must not flee.

The line is everything.

Fury must not break it; one must not dash forward.

The line is everything. If it holds we live; if it breaks we die.

'I hate this! I hate this!' Lion was roaring. The enemy broke before we hit them. Our line poured over. Men were cheering.

'Shut up! Break up the fires!'

The Etruscan rallied our mob into a perimeter against counterattack.

Exhaustion hit like a mawl. You could hear helmets clatter against the limestone and the crash of shield and kit as they fell.

'On your feet! Facing out! Stay in ranks!'

We had taken the first fort. The second took two more hours, and nearly broke our backs with heat and fatigue. Of six fallen in our platoon, only two were lost to wounds. The others were groin and hamstring pulls, broken bones, mishaps of weariness and thirst, plunges into defiles in the dark. We were all cramping terribly. All construction gear had long since been dumped; we would send parties for it later.

Rumours peeled along the line. Our companies attacking from the Circle fort had been routed; Gylippus had led another five thousand from the city; he held the counterwall, the final position we must seize and occupy. True or not, this report fired the troops with vigour. Nail that bastard and Syracuse is taken. We slugged water and wine and strapped up to move.

This second bastion was not yet Chalk Hill, not the linked series of redoubts the foe had built last autumn when he drove us off the Heights, but a new one, higher-walled and at the peak of a steeper slope. The enemy had thousands here; it must be stormed. He had cleared fields of fire to two hundred yards and spiked this expanse with bales of faggots, doused with pitch. Mounds of thorn had been piled on both flanks to channel attackers into the missile troops' killing zone. These our incendiaries set ablaze. A yellow moon burned through the haze. The order came to hold till the obstacles burned down. But the troops could not contain themselves, from fever for the fight, fear of Gylippus's reinforcements, or apprehension spawned by their own blood-sapping fatigue. The ranks piled unordered into the inferno, using shields to plough apart the blazing packets, while the enemy concentrated fire on the avenues down which the Athenians, Argives, and allies now advanced.

Our brigade was second from the front. The first hundred hit the wall. Its face was stone, bristling with stakes. From the crown the enemy rolled boulders. We turtled up, shields across backs, tearing at the stones with our bare hands. The light troops raced up behind. You could hear their shafts and sling bullets shrieking overhead. A boulder from above hit me square in the spine, pounding me into the spiked wall. The stones were knitted too tight to tear. 'Climb!' all were shouting. A body fell on me. Some whore's son drilled by our archers. I tried to mount, keeping him on my shielded back. The bugger came to life! I felt fingers claw my sockets and heard the scrape of a blade seeking my throat. I jammed the flange of my helmet down, sealing the seam against the cuirass, and rose with the strength of terror. He went limp, shot by his own from above.

'Climb!' Lion was screaming beside me. I saw, or felt, his stumpy form clamber up the face. Shame seized me. I mounted beside him. The defenders were dumping flaming pitch on us. Up we went. They backed before their own blaze. Our javelineers poured volleys into the enemy on top of the wall. As I hit the crest, a man rose before me swinging a gut-cutter; I lowered and butted him. We plunged entwined. He had no helmet; I bashed in his skull with my bronze. I heard cheering. The second companies surged past, spewing sweat and spit as they fell on the backs of the fleeing foe. I sank to all fours on the smoking stone.

'Lion!'

'Here, brother!'

We pushed our helmets back, enough to confirm each other's survival, and collapsed from relief and exhaustion.

The moon stood full up now. The men rallied, surging over this second fort. 'Get up, get up!' We must not yield to fatigue, not while the counterwall stood and Gylippus had time to fortify it with more troops. The men had been climbing and fighting four hours. The night had not cooled one iota. The troops' tongues hung like dogs.

We heard Argive accents. A colonel of the élite Thousand burst from the darkness. He was closing up the line. 'One more rock to take!'

The call came for officers. Lion was puking and cramping, so I went. Demosthenes was there. His brigade had started up before ours, against the fort at Labdalum; either he or we were completely out of order. His lieutenants directed the men to eat, but who could choke down bread absent wine or water?

The troops are spent, sir, one captain reported. The third wave is still behind us, mounting from Euryalus; should he hold here and let them take the advance?

Demosthenes stared as if the man had gone mad.

'The moon is up. We take this shithole now.'

A colonel said he didn't know if his men could do it.

'The men don't tell you what can be done,' Demosthenes roared. 'You tell them!'

The commander could see his officers were reeling. They had all drunk too much wine, and though fear and exertion had sweated most out, yet the grape's fire had taken a toll on the blood, like a two-day drunk, bringing on that state of bone-weariness that no measure of will may overcome.

'Gather, cousins.' Demosthenes mustered the officers like a father his sons. 'I know the men are exhausted. Can you think I don't feel it too? But we must seize the Chalk Fort. No other outcome is acceptable.

'If we fail tonight, Gylippus will drive us off the Heights tomorrow. Then we're back where we started, and worse because the enemy will believe nothing beyond his power. But the Chalk Fort taken this night turns all in our favour. The counterwall will fall; the city will be invested. Brace up, men. We can't give the foe time. Finish him now and get this trick over!'

But Gylippus did not wait for our attack. Putting the counterwall at his back, he led his troops straight for the marshalling Athenians. We heard their *paean* and raced back to our places. Lion already had our marines moving. I fell in and swam forward.

The enemy was massed in uncountable numbers. Our ranks closed; the armies crashed together. A mêlée ensued that could be given the name of battle by its scale only. No-one could swing a sword, such was the press of bodies. The nine-foot spear was useless. You dropped it where you stood, fighting instead with the shield as a weapon, struggling simply to take your man's feet out or stick him Spartan-style with the short thrust and draw. Any part of the body that bore armour became a weapon. You fought with your knees, driving them into your man's testicles, with elbows fired at the throat and temple, and heels against those fallen on the earth. In the mêlée a man seized the rim of the enemy's shield and pulled it down with all his weight. You clawed at a man's eyes, spit in his face if you could summon spit, and bit at him with your teeth. We could feel the foe falling back. Our reinforcements poured from behind, driving by their weight the mass of contention forward. The moon rose behind. The enemy broke and ran.

For what happened then, blame must be laid upon our officers, myself included. We could not restrain the men; they bolted in a mass, ravening upon the foe like beasts. The spring of their fury lay no doubt in two years' woe and frustration under Nicias. I believe the men feared as well that their endurance was at its end; they had been fighting five hours without food or water; they must finish the enemy now, before strength failed.

You have witnessed the rout, Jason. Performed properly, the cavalry run down the fleeing foe, disabling him with the sabre or slaying him outright with the lance. Allied with the horse troopers, the swiftest of the infantry overhaul the enemy in his flight, bringing him down from behind with the thrust of the nine-foot spear. The wounded he spikes where they lie. Here on the Heights, however, we had no cavalry and by this stage no nine-footers; all had long since been slung or shivered. Instead our troops fell in disorder upon the stampeding foe, hacking at him with the sword. This is no way to kill a man. The edge-on wound is not reliably fatal or even disabling, and, more ruinous, it rouses its object to such desperation as to goad even the coward to turn and fight, when, taken down as he ought, with a penetration wound or missile weapon, this same fellow would continue to present his back and be slain with ease. The second axiom of the broken field, drummed into the raw recruit's skull, is never to take the foe one-on-one, but always by pairs, and from opposing quarters.

Both precepts went by the board in the fatigue-spawned extremity. Out front our infantry could be seen slashing at the foes' hamstrings and necks, then, as these rearmost fell, rampaging on to the next lot, leaving the outstripped foe wounded but still able to fight or, if he was clever, faking it entire, and now, as the next rank overran him, alive and unharmed among our own troops. The line broke down across the entire field. Topography enlarged the dislocation. Chalk Hill, to which the enemy now fled, was a good half mile away, over ragged and broken ground. Our men, spent, broke apart while the foe in flight was able to use the fells and declines to make his escape.

None the less the Athenian advance encountered scant opposition; cries of triumph rose as our troops, disordered as they were, rolled on towards the redoubts that ringed the chalky rise commanding the counterwall. The moon was over our shoulders as we advanced; ahead you could see the enemy debouching in masses from half a dozen portals, shields and helmets gleaming in the light. They were smart. Gylippus was smart. He had chosen not to hold his men behind the battlements, upon which our disarrayed troops would press, regaining order simply by their own compaction. Instead the Spartan elected to meet us in the open, throwing his massed, rested troops against our disordered, exhausted ones.

The world knows how spectacularly this succeeded. Lion and I had caught up with Chowder and Splinter and the orphans of other units who had attached themselves to us. Our side continued to overrun the foe; the Argive Thousand on our left was mowing down the Syracusan division arrayed against them. We could see the Chalk Fort, a hundred yards ahead. 'It is fallen!' I heard an Argive officer cry.

At that instant the man on my right toppled into me. I caught him and held him up, for a man in armour on the ground is as good as dead. I turned right and there was the enemy, rolling us up from the flank.

We learned later that this was the Cadmus division, Boeotian volunteers, and the Thermopylae regiment of Thespiae, two thousand in all, whom Hegesander had stationed before that redoubt called the Ravelin. Where all others broke, these held. Like a great rock upon which the ocean wave crashes and bursts, these stood and turned all.

I was on the earth, toppled before their rush. It was impossible to rise in fifty pounds of armour. A man, one of ours, was trying to burrow under me, so my flesh and not his would take an enemy spear. The Boeotians passed over, plunging the butt spikes of their nine-footers. I heard the burrower take it; the sound of his skull pierced, cranial fore-ships staving and the soup gushing from within. I took one blade outside my hip and another two whiskers from my globes. The foe passed over. I rolled free. Lion hauled me clear.

In routs escape is rarely demanding if one keeps one's head. You simply dump what weight you must, bucking your nerve with the certainty that you're willing to run harder and longer to preserve your life than the foe is to take it. Here on the Heights all such usage was overturned. It was dark. There were no roads. Moonshadow cast all into chaos. You couldn't hold where you were; you had been overrun. To advance was suicide, while to flee only hurled you among the very troops by whom you had just been routed.

We had to get round. But now a fresh hazard confounded us: the enemy our troops had outstripped in the advance. These were on their feet now, rallying into bands of butchers. They ranged the killing ground, slitting the throat of every downed Athenian. I was with Lion, Chowder, Splinter, and about a dozen others. We had migrated somehow to the extreme right of the field. The bluffs dropped sheer, two hundred feet. Chowder peered down with Lion.

'Shall we try it?'

'After you.'

We tracked the brink, seeking a descent. From a rise Lion and I squinted. In the distance: a battle.

Stripping helmets, we could hear the *paean* – their Dorians or ours, who could tell? – and that anthem all soldiers know, the toll and rumble of the *othismos* as the massed formations compact and clash. 'I'd as soon give this a miss,' observed Splinter.

Lion asked what had become of his taste for glory.

'I lost it hours ago, with the contents of my bowels.'

We skidded down the slope towards the battle. At the bottom men transited like phantoms. We heard Attic accents.

'Athenians?'

'Move up!' an officer shouted. 'We're forming beyond that rise!'

We tagged the troops, but lost them in a defile. There was fog in the low places, the light had gone strange. The moon in your eyes, you were blind; behind you, you trod in ink. Emerging from a fell, we saw a mass of several hundred infantry, their officers dressing their line. We dashed in, seeking one to report to. A trooper waved us down the line. A man spoke, addressing a comrade. Syracusan dialect.

These weren't our troops.

We were among the enemy.

A Syracusan tugged at my shoulder; handsome chap, a six-footer. He was asking me something. Lion's blade sliced his throat. He dropped like a pig, gushing fluid.

We ran for our lives. I called to Lion to take over. I was unstrung; my thoughts would not obey me. 'How did those sheepfuckers get there?!'

We drew up in a ravine, out of our wits with terror and clutching each other like children. 'Are we turned round? How did they get on that side of us?' We tried to orient ourselves by the moon, but in the defile you couldn't tell which direction its light came from. Sounds! Men advancing in a body, from where we had just come. 'It's them!'

Three rangers scrambled over the crest. We unloaded everything at them.

'Athenians!' they shouted in fright.

We demanded the watchword.

They had forgot. So had we.

'By Zeus, are you Athenians?!'

'Yes, yes! Stop shooting!'

They were our countrymen. In a minute their main body scrambled over the rise, about a platoon; we located their lieutenant. Lion told of the enemy we had blundered into, immediately north.

'That's west.'

'It can't be. Look at the moon.'

'It's west, I tell you!'

'Then where's the fight?'

'It's over. We've lost.'

'Never!'

We bolted, seeking the battle. More men ahead. We formed fast, fearing the enemy. 'Athena Protectress,' their point pair called. The password! We countersigned. They hurried towards us. 'By the gods,' our youngest advanced with relief, 'what the hell's going on?' Their point plunged a nine-footer into his guts. More fell on us from the flank. We bowled through in terror.

We could not tell if they were the enemy, discovering our watchword, or our own mistaking us for the foe. One imperative drove us: to reach our own lines. It didn't matter if we were eviscerated one moment later, we must reunite with our countrymen. We were out of our minds with this necessity.

Forms ghosted past in the darkness, fleeing and advancing in all directions. They kept silent as we, each in dread of the other. A new fear had seized me. I was terrified that I would encounter my cousin and each, taking the other for the enemy, would slay the other.

When men passed I called out, 'Simon!'

'Shut up!' Lion barked.

I couldn't.

'Simon! Is that you?'

'Have you lost your mind?'

At last we got out onto the flat. A breast-bursting slog of a mile carried us to the Labdalum fort, the first one that the rangers and shock troops had taken, what seemed like a lifetime past, this night. There were mobs everywhere: dead and wounded being borne rearward; masons and carpenters just now mounting the switchbacks of Euryalus; and scores of remnants like us, bunching up in terror and disorder. Troops streamed by, fleeing. Battling each other to get down the cliff face.

'What has happened?'

'Lost! All lost!'

'Hold up!' Lion advanced into the stream. 'Rally, brothers! Summon your courage!'

The sight of our countrymen in flight filled me with such shame that fortitude, or some simulacrum, reanimated. I took my place beside Lion.

'Have you found your head, Pommo?'

'Yes.'

'You scared the wits out of me.'

Men fled past us. We caught a few, shamed as we, and formed them into a front. I recognized one, Rabbit, who had fought as a shield with Telamon. When I clutched his arm, I saw he was in tears.

'I killed a man,' he cried.

'What?'

'Our own. One of ours.'

He was unhinged and begged me to cut his throat. 'God help me, I couldn't see . . . I thought he was theirs.'

'Forget it, it's the dark. Make your stand.'

He bared his steel and set its point beneath his jaw.

'Form up!' I shouted at him. 'Rabbit! Take your place!'

He grasped the hilt with both fists and jammed the blade up into his brain.

'Rabbit!'

He dropped like a cut puppet. Men gaped in horror. We could hear the enemy's *paean*.

'Hold!' Lion bawled to our comrades. 'Hold where you stand.'

'Why?' cried one.

They ran.

We ran too.

# TWENTY-TWO
# THE AVERTED
# FACE OF HEAVEN

YOU HAVE HEARD RECOUNTED NUMBERLESS TIMES, JASON, THE chronicle of the lunar eclipse which occurred a month succeeding the calamity on Epipolae, and the terror into which it plunged the fleet and army, coming as it did in the instant their vessels made ready to embark for safety. Men have censured Nicias as commander and indicted the troops themselves for yielding to such dread, superstition-spawned, at the hour of their deliverance, when they had at last set their purpose to abandon Syracuse and sail for home.

Of those who condemn us I say only: they weren't there. They weren't there to feel the dread that breathed in that hour, when the moon hid her face and its benediction from men's sight. I consider myself a man of practical usage, yet I, too, stood stricken at my post, staring skyward in consternation. I, too, turned about, unnerved and unmanned by this prodigy of heaven.

Nine thousand had been lost since Epipolae. In the panic at the cliffs, men had leapt and fallen by hundreds. I went out that first dawn with Lion, seeking our cousin. Thousands were still missing. Many who had made it down off the Heights had lost their way seeking camp. Now with first light the Syracusan horse were making mince of them. At the base of the cliffs, dead and dying lay strewn for acres. They were all ours. Some had tumbled in the panic as thousands bunched up at the brink and each, in terror to reach safety, had dislodged another, spilling him in turn onto those picking their way down the switchbacks below. Many in despair had leapt of their own will, stripping armour and casting themselves to fate.

At the top of the cliffs prize parties of the foe now collected. They called down, taunting. 'You are so clever, Athenians, did you think you could fly?' Take a good look, the enemy vaunted, slinging severed limbs and even heads down onto the mounds of our slain. 'This is the only way you will leave Sicily!'

Again in camp Telamon awaited us. He had found Simon, alive and unwounded, tending the sick. I dropped where I stood and slept the day round. Only four remained of our sixteen marines; it took five platoons to make one new one. I passed the day beside *Pandora*, writing widow letters. Her foreships had rotted through; she lay careened on the site the soldiers called Dog Beach, awaiting timbers.

The camp had become one sprawling mudhole, stinking to heaven. Our tents were pitched in the swamp where Gylippus's troops had driven us, fifty thousand kennelled in a bog narrower than the agora in Athens. Every step sank into sucking ooze. My bed was a door on a flat of muck, which I shared with Lion and Splinter, taking turns as one does shipboard. The men called these bunks 'rafts'. You had to watch your raft or someone would steal it.

Foreign sailors began slipping the cable. It was impossible to hold them; they simply waited for dark, then swam for it. Some even took their oars. Victualry ceased, and refuse removal; there were no armourers, cooks, or nurses. Line troops must be assigned details customarily performed by drudges; twice in ten days altercations flared into near mutinies. The one thing the troops had was money. But what could you buy? Not a dry patch to lay your head or a clean divot to empty your bowels upon. You could not buy water; the foe had dammed the streams that fed the camp and poisoned the solitary spring. Hundreds sickened, swelling wards already packed with the thousands of casualties of Epipolae, who worsened daily in this hellish miasma.

A phrase swept the camp: 'hoisting the *akation*'. You know this, Jason: the foresail of a trireme, the only one borne into battle, run up at life-and-death, to flee. Not a man did not burn to hoist the *akation*. Epipolae had turned Demosthenes against the whole expedition. In his eyes

Sicily was a quagmire; we must get our boys out now, or failing that, withdraw to a part of the island where the country could be overrun, supplies obtained, and the wounded and sick given proper care.

Now of all people Nicias acquired resolution. He refused to retreat without orders from the Assembly at Athens. One night I took supper with my cousin and the physician Pallas. This doctor's family was the Euctemonidae of Cephisia; he was related to Nicias and had tended him here for kidney disease, which ravaged him yet. The medic had had enough and spilled his tale straight.

'If Nicias takes us home wanting victory, how will the demos express its gratitude? He knows, believe me. Those same officers who squall loudest now for withdrawal will, safe in Athens, turn upon him to hide their shame. Our commander will be impeached for cowardice or treason or taking bribes of the enemy; his accusers' mouthpieces will inflame the multitude, who will howl for his head, as for Alcibiades'. Say what you will, Nicias is a man of honour. He would sooner meet death here as a soldier than be butchered at home like a dog.'

Days passed and the army did not move.

Gylippus returned from the Sicilian cities, having recruited a second army more numerous than the first. A camp of ten thousand arose on the Olympieum and another twice the size on Ortygia. The foe had lost all fear. He manned his benches in broad daylight and passed to and fro before our palisade, daring us to launch and face him.

At last Nicias saw the wisdom of withdrawal. Word was passed; the army would be taken aboard this night. Across the camp, the mood was elation. Far from feeling shame at packing up, the men felt chastened and restored to grace. Humility and piety, however tardily rediscovered, had delivered them from the ruin heaven had prepared, witness all the turns of evil that had plagued the expedition, from the banishment of Alcibiades on. What derangement, men asked now, had made us tear him from us? Could any believe that, Alcibiades in command, our force would stand in such straits? Syracuse would have fallen two years ago. The army would be halfway up Italy's boot; the fleet would have reduced Carthage and be rounding on Iberia. But the gods had not ordained this, such was apparent. Perhaps heaven scourged us for our pride in mounting an enterprise of such moment, or for bearing strife to a country which had borne none to us. Perhaps the immortals bore malice towards

Nicias for his luck, or Alcibiades for his ambition. It was all moot now. All that mattered was we were going home.

All that mattered until the moon disappeared.

No night is so dark as that, orb-illumined, plunged into the ink of lightlessness. No place may be so black as the starless sea, nor men more prone to dread than those in peril of their lives. So evil were the omens, when at last the diviners had taken them, that the first victim and the second and third were cast aside; the seers slaughtered beast after beast seeking any that would bleed propitiously.

Thrice nine days the fleet must abide, so the portents read.

For thrice nine days no ship may sail.

### TWENTY-THREE
## UPON THE WALL
## OF SHIPS

GYLIPPUS STRUCK ON THE TWENTY-SECOND DAY. HE CAME AGAINST the ramparts with thirty thousand and with seventy-six vessels on the fleet in the bay. The walls held; the ships didn't.

Our squadron leaders *Clotho, Lachesis* and *Atropos* all went down. Of twelve in our reconstituted company of marines save Lion and myself, five were killed and four disabled. In all, forty ships were lost, including sixteen driven aground at the salt marsh called the Horns, where Gylippus's men penned the crews between seawalls and slaughtered them to the last man. The captured vessels were now in service against us. Eurymedon's *Ariadne* was lost off Dascon. The foe nailed the general's corpse to the prow and paraded before our palisade, vowing to make us all envy the dead.

Here was an overthrow as monumental as the calamity on Epipolae. Men's hearts broke. They could not believe they had been routed, again so utterly, or what was yet more patent: that worse would come, and soon.

The enemy was erecting a wall of ships across the harbour mouth. Word came that we would make a run for it, all or nothing. The upper walls of the camp were abandoned and a new crosswall thrown up, tangent to shore. Our estate had shrunk to a rectangle of mire, less than a mile at its base, penned on all landward sides. Sixty thousand, including ninety-five hundred wounded, and a hundred and ten ships packed every stinking foot. The last slaves and camp followers were kicked out, even though they, who had proved so steadfast, entreated to stay. Bread remained for five days only; it must be spared for the troops and the wounded.

No footing remained to plant the dead. Burial parties stacked the corpses in squares, layering ship's timbers between, that faces might be visible for identification. The lanes between these barrows filled with brothers and comrades, seeking their own. Men returned from these errands struck through with such woe that they could neither sleep nor eat, and no threat or blandishment could make them obey an order. So unwholesome had the hospital site become, so grisly and dispiriting, that physicians bade their charges scatter where they would among the camp. Corpses of men slain at sea collected like booms of logs, choking the strand, while those not borne onto our palisade by tide and swell were driven there by vessels of the foe, herding them with boat hooks and boarding pikes.

We must break out or die. All who could fight were taken aboard. The date was the sixth of Boedromion, the feast of the Boedromia, when Theseus defeated the Amazons. A hundred and fifteen triremes put out; twenty-two were left dry; we had no more oars. No attempt was made to render the ships seaworthy. We would worry about that later. Nicias delivered a speech, a good one, and Demosthenes made one too. Absent was the customary shirking of battle or the prayer for late-hour reprieve. Every man stood to his place before dawn, and none wanted rousing. The troops of the army, under nine thousand, defended both extremities of the camp, one the seawall fronting Feverside, beyond whose expanse massed the Syracusan Temenites division under Hermocrates, forty thousand who had been a mob twelve months previous and were now crack troops. The west, the bluff called Bad News, was held by a palisade of rock and wood. Four thousand of ours faced twenty of the foe.

Twenty-seven thousand Athenians and allies embarked, eleven thousand fighting men, sixteen thousand at oars. The ships shoved off in darkness so profound the helmsmen could not make out vessels starboard or port but must steer by sound, the bow officer's tapstone and the chirp of the fog whistle. Here was an hour like no other. Each man would fight today, victory or death, to see children again, wife and country. None spoke or even sighed. That which each could do, he would or die.

The ships advanced in column to their assembly marks, then formed in line abreast, twenty-five across and four deep, with a squadron of ten in reserve. *Pandora's* place was in the first rank, sixth from the left, the division under Demosthenes. The enemy's wall of ships lay east, a mile and a half. We could not see them, even their lamps, with the dark and the mist.

The waiting began. That interminable interval as the line dressed and all vessels were brought on station. Corvettes shuttled, completing count and relaying instructions. It is always cold on the water; men's teeth chattered in the dark. At their benches the sailors choked down a meal of bread, oil, and barley. Topside marines huddled in their cloaks, packed against the sidescreens saying nothing. For the twentieth time their orders were repeated. No bread for us; it had been forgotten.

At last, at the cloaked lantern, the line moved off. There was no sound, no orders, nothing at all save the squeal of oar looms against their pins and leathers, the *choonk* of their blades as they bit, and the gliss of the surface spooling past along the hull. You could hear the tap of the cadence stones, light and clear, and the unisoned expulsion of breath as the oarsmen set their blades and pulled. *Pandora* drove forward by surges.

The sky began to lighten. Our ships could be made out now. The spectacle they presented could not have appeared in more inglorious contrast to that golden aspect with which they had set off from home, so few seasons past and with such expectations. Paintless and unadorned, displaying ensigns only to differentiate themselves from the foe, the warships ploughed low in the water as scows, burdened above decks with such a load of men-at-arms that they looked less like warcraft than ferries. Hides and skins bedecked their carapaces, topside to deflect incendiary bolts and along the waterline to shield the hold oarsmen at their banks. Cloaked in this motley, the vessels appeared as some species of derelict, limping ragged upon the foe.

Like the others, *Pandora's* masts had been unstepped and left ashore. Prow- and sternpeaks had been cut down, replaced by platforms defended by sidescreens, with drop-planks at intervals as boarding ramps. The helmsman worked behind a bunker of timber and hides.

'Make her ugly!' *Pandora's* captain Boros, her sixth since Athens, had urged his crew, labouring alongside them through the night. '*Pandora* must be a box of evil for the foe.'

Forward where her sail locker had been (my old snoozing spot), the foreships had been reinforced with timbers salvaged from our own ruined hulks. Triple-wide rams had been rigged to counter this innovation of the Corinthians. These outrigs stood vacant now, but on closing with the foe, marines would mount to each, armed with grapnels. The mass of *epibatai*, my squad and Lion's, held now aft of amidships, so their weight would keep the prow high and the oxhead clear of the water's drag. On the forepeak squatted the first of three fire-pots, from which darts and brands would be lit. A second stood beside me now, amidships, and a third by the steersman's bunker aft.

From my place inboard of the outrigger I could see into the foreships. Already *Pandora* was taking water in such quantities that the footboards of the hold oarsmen were awash. Scupper lads bailed on the beat, sling-ing the bilge past their comrades' ears out of the hide-sheathed ports through which the oars projected. Above the oarsmen's heads, new decks had been framed to support the mob of infantry, archers and javelineers who now crouched topside, numbers retching already.

We could see the enemy now. His rampart of ships rose like a wall; the harbour had become a lake. Palisades had been erected, plaited with hides to retard incendiary missiles and notched with embrasures from which the enemy would loose his own artillery. Before this the foe had spiked the surface with spars and timbers. A gap had been left of about a furlong. Beyond this in the open sea we could see his warships, above forty, pulling hard in column. They would come to line abreast, three and four deep, to bottle any Athenian breakout. Enemy small craft by the hundred filled out the field of obstacle, while upon both quarters further squadrons launched from shore. The foe held nine-tenths of the harbour perimeter. Gylippus's army waited at the margins of the swell. God help the ship and crew falling within their killing zone.

The line had been advancing at two-and-one, resting each bank by turns. Now, a half mile out, the boatswain piped 'At the triple' and *Pandora* shot forward on the swell. On the forepeak Boros bellowed through his megaphone to skippers port and starboard, as each singled out the vessel he would attack. He scampered back with a little kick-step of joy. 'Dolphins, lads! Racing the cutwater!' With a laugh he bolted aft to the steersman's post. Now came the *prostates*, the bow officer, a midshipman named Milo who had been caught in the grass with his lover and nicknamed Rhodopygos, Rosy Cheeks. He was an anxious sort, always dreading the worst, and now crabbed forward at the crouch, bearing above his crown an oak plank heavy as himself.

'Expecting rain, junior?' Lion called.

Rhodopygos frog-hopped back and forth, peeping over the prow to assess our distance from the enemy. At his signal we would press forward in a body, to launch our own missiles, while our weight would drop the ram at the deadliest instant. That was the plan anyway. In the end as ever chaos prevailed.

Three hundred yards out, clouds of enemy small craft swarmed at us out of the vapour. Darts and firebrands began clattering on the deck. Rosy Cheeks took a spike through the foot; in an instant we were all at the outrigger, unloading everything we had. Dead ahead rose the wall of ships. We would not make it. Two of the foreline converged on us, one a triple with a forepeak of a bare-breasted female, the other a converted galley beamy as a barge. The mob on her deck must have made a hundred. *Pandora* swung bows-on to meet her; the trireme lanced in on us from the flank. On our prow marines were slinging pinwheels onto the triple; arcs of smoke shot across the fast-foreshortening gap. The men launched javelins from their knees, then dropped prone behind the sidescreens as the enemy's volleys rainbowed in return. Both sides were hurling the rope-handled jars of smoking sulphur the Syracusans call 'scorpions' and Athenians 'hello-theres'. Already all three craft were afire.

Now came the collision. The ships crunched together, *Pandora* and the converted freighter. But the angle was askew, and both vessels, fore-ships locked, began to slew sideways along each other's hull. Our marines flung grapnels across the interval; the foe replied with a fusillade of darts and stones. The enemy had stripped rails and drawn hides across all objects of purchase. Grapnels were bouncing like beans. What heads caught, the enemy bashed free with mawls or hacked through with axes. One luckless bastard had been hooked through the calf and now hung, pinned against the mast step, while three of our marines hauled on the line with all their strength. Moments later Two

Tits punched broadside into *Pandora*'s belly, and, instants beyond, our own *Dauntless* reamed her up the arse.

The enemy bore stones, great boulders of thirty and forty pounds which he had stacked as ammunition along his prow and rails. He had his most cyclopean men forward; these now elevated their projectiles and heaved them into our sidescreens, staving them to splinters.

A titan of the foe led their wave. Six and a half feet and naked from the waist up, this ox strode onto our prow unarmed save one massive boulder, a sixty-pounder, which he wielded before him, bowling our marines from their feet. A youth named Elpenor opened the man's fore-arm to the bone; the brute turned with a bellow and drove his stone, crushing the marine's skull, then wheeled and stove in another's face. With thighs like oaks he was kicking men over the side.

This was no time for heroics. I seized two others, Meton Armbreaker and Adrastus, whom they called Towhead, and hauled them to the monster's rear. We took him three-on-one, putting one spike through his liver and a second into his haunch. Towhead hacked through the hamstring with a boarding pike. The savage dropped to one knee, roar-ing. He never looked back to see who had unstrung him, just raised the great stone and flung it with all his strength into the bilges. It plunged through the undecked oarsmen's compartment, shearing off a second-banker at the knee, then crashed through the keelson timbers, shivering the hull like a shot. Up boiled the sea. *Pandora* was sinking.

It is impossible to reconstruct in afterthought the sequence of events, the sequence of sequences, transpiring so rapidly and amid such chaos, when one's faculties are deranged by rage and terror, fear for one's men and oneself. At one point a marine of the foe had me by the beard and was pounding the crown of my helmet edge-on with his shield with such fury that I felt the bone of my skull begin to rupture. I seized his testicles with all my strength and wrung free, the mass of my tangled whiskers coming off in his fist. I tumbled over the rail into the gallery of the outrigger. Lion, behind the man, decapitated him with a two-hand swipe, left-handed; helmet and skull pinwheeled onto my belly, gushing fluids, and bounded through the posts into the sea.

There is this aspect to fighting on the water: a man has no place to run. Somehow the mass of our company succeeded in capturing the galley, if such a term may be applied to the occupation of a pack of blazing tinder fast on its way to the bottom, achieving this triumph primarily because the scow was sinking from the stern and we advancing from the bow had the advantage of fighting downhill. We ploughed the enemy into the sea behind a wall of shields. An ancillary battle, grisly as the main, now commenced in the gutter between the burning hulks, as oarsmen of *Pandora* and Twin Tits, forced to abandon ship, grappled hand-to-hand, each seeking to drown the other. Axe and boarding pike had supplanted spear and javelin as weapons of favour. The shivered oar served as well. Marines hacked and stabbed and clubbed the foe in the water even as the decks on which they stood subsided beneath them. By this time the Athenian third and fourth waves had reached the enemy's rampart and were attacking it in escalade, like land troops assaulting a fortress. We were taken off the freighter onto *Dauntless*. In moments we, too, were on the wall.

My cousin narrated for me later how this spectacle had appeared from the vantage of shore. The wounded had pleaded with their physicians to bear them down to the sea. Each man's fate hung on battle's outcome; they could not bear to loiter in ignorance. The soldiers, too, had pressed down to the water's edge, even wading into the sea, as did the Syracusans along their shore, straining across the smoke-obscured main for any index of victory or defeat.

In the offing, my cousin said, the wall of ships could not be made out, only the smoke, black at the base and grey as it rose, ascending in thunderheads so dense it seemed the entire firmament was ablaze. In quarters about the harbour battles were being fought of such scale and savagery that, taken apart from this holocaust, would have been called epochal, yet which, accounted here within the context of such numbers of men and vessels in conflict, appeared as sideshows or afterwords. Of ships fighting in open water, my cousin reported, tactics and manoeuvre had long since been abandoned. Instead vessels grappled one to another and slugged it out, belly-to-belly. The surface of the harbour seemed sown with islands and archipelagoes of ships, four, six, and even ten fused, while the men on deck fought it out hand-to-hand, do or die.

About the ships in uncountable numbers swarmed the small craft of the Syracusans, dinghies and coracles, catboats and even rafts, manned by every urchin and pensioner who could hurl a firepot or bash a sailor's brains with bat or brick. You could tell which ships were Athenian by the clouds of mosquito boats about them, piking at the steersmen's blades, slinging missiles or driving into the banks, seeking to foul the oars.

As the tide of battle alternated, the consternation produced upon the men witnessing from shore became excruciating. Directly one beheld comrades embracing in elation, my cousin recounted, as the warcraft of their nation drove the foe in flight. Now the men's gaze bent to another quadrant where the opposite state prevailed. Despair at once repossessed their hearts; with dreadful dirges the spectators bewailed their doom, crying to heaven those lamentations as men are wont to make in such hours.

As if this audience did not suffice, a supplemental took station in the summit seats. These were the wives and daughters of the Syracusans, looking on from the city battlements which directly overstood the arena, so proximate that the ladies' cries could be heard by their champions below. Whose ship boldly struck at an Athenian was requited with acclamation resounding, while he, beleaguered, who sought to withdraw retreated into cataracts of scorn.

On the wall of ships, our side was winning.

The enemy had strung together above two hundred vessels, merchantmen and barges, scows and galleys as well as men-of-war, the line bound by rope and timber so that their front presented a solid rampart broadside to the attackers. Against this the ships of Athens hurled themselves. The fight differed from all others in my experience in this particular: nowhere upon the field could one discover vessel or man holding back. So possessed was each side by the passion to prevail, the Athenians to escape extinction, the Syracusans and their allies to wreak vengeance upon those who had made war to enslave them and, more so, to wrest the deathless renown of driving them down to ruin, that none gave thought to saving his skin but each sought to outdo the other in skill and valour. Midway through the forenoon I fell, hamstrung by that hyperextension called a 'bonebreaker', plummeting from the deck of a barge into its belly, which was awash chest-deep and into whose depths I sank like a stone. Chowder hauled me topside, where we discovered a pocket of haven, and he went to work on my leg. 'Look there, Pommo' – my mate pointed down the line of strife – 'have you ever seen the like of it?'

I stared. As far as sight could carry, the sea stood curtained with smoke and paved with warcraft. Immediately left, a battleship had rammed one of the vessels in the wall; all three of her banks were backing water furiously, to extract and ram again, while across the breach screamed storms of stones, darts, and brands of such density that the air appeared solid with steel and flame. As the Athenian's ram sucked free, rending the foe's guts, a second battleship materialized, hurtling upon the same vessel. Her ram took the enemy's stern, lifting her entire aftersection clear. Men topside spilled like pegs. As the struck ship hung impaled, her elevated weight forcing the ramming vessel's prow into the sea, while yet denser fusillades screamed between the antagonists, the first ship, having backed clear to a boat-length, rammed the same ship anew. To the opposite hand, three Athenian galleys had grapnelled to vessels in the wall. So intervolved were the marines of both sides that there were more Syracusans on the decks of the Athenian ships and the contrary upon the Syracusan. Out beyond the attackers, three more cruisers of Athens passed with murderous slowness, archers unleashing broadsides of tow and pitch over their own and into the enemy. As one vessel in the wall caught, flame leapt to its consort, borne by the wind or men who pitched or hurled or shot it. By sun's zenith a dozen breaches had been punched in the palisade. At one point, Lion told me later, he saw three battleships of Athens pass abreast through the wall, led by Demosthenes' *Implacable*, making signal 'Follow me.'

We had won. And yet . . .

The enemy still held both jaws of the vice, the city promontory of Ortygia and Plemmyrium, the Rock, the southern mandible of the harbour mouth, between which the wall of ships extended. He had fifty thousand at one end, twenty at the other, and they kept pouring out onto the wall. Where the line of ships had been breached, the foe's small craft flooded in and sealed the rupture. Flea boats ferried replacements across the breaks, while others hauled themselves over the timber and chain bindings which yet anchored the embattled wall. Morning had gone; we were slaughtering the enemy in such numbers that he could not, it was certain, hold out much longer.

There is an error in densely packed fighting committed by those lacking experience of war, even brave men, as the Syracusans and their allies were, and this is called in Sparta 'downstreaming' or 'rat-holing'. A man duelling in this fashion will stand against the individual facing him, receive or deliver a blow or several, and then, he and his antagonist unhurt, roll or shift laterally to the next of the enemy, to commence a second bashing match and in turn sideslip again. Fear makes him do this. He seeks a closet of refuge, a 'rat hole' amid the slaughter. In Sparta boys are beaten who evince this habit. They are schooled instead to fight 'upfield', to seize one man and battle him alone until one or the other falls. This the Lacedaemonians call *monopale*, 'singling up'. The Syracusans had not learned this art, for all Gylippus's direction. Now on the wall of ships the superior experience of the Athenians began to tell. It came to this: fighting topside, twenty against twenty, forty on forty, a *parataxis*, pitched battle, in miniature. Or brawling belowdecks man upon man, in water thigh- and hip-deep, the walls, often afire, pinning friend and foe in the cylinder of slaughter. The Athenians had the hang of it. And they possessed a further advantage. Defenders on the sea must of necessity kill men, never an easy business. But attackers need only destroy things. The marines of Athens went after the wall with fire and the axe. Ship after ship had its belly gutted, hull torched; along the rampart hulks settled, sizzling, to the waterline.

I had found Lion and Telamon. Reunited, we were hacking through a jacket of timbers, eight logs bound with belts of iron, that yoked one section of enemy line to another. Too exhausted to stand, Lion and I straddled the timber, bashing with blades blunt as butter knives. Here came the foe. Flea boats bearing slingers hauled upon us from another smoking hulk. There were ten in our party. Telamon, Lion, and Chowder were the only ones I knew; the others had collected by ones and twos; I never learned their names. One with a red beard trumpeted to a cruiser, calling for fire. As he shouted, a bullet tore his throat out; he dropped like a gunny of rocks. The shooter vaunted, already reloaded with his sling whistling overhead. I heard an alarm from behind. Somehow another score of enemy had got onto the hulk we had just crossed from. Two more slinger boats closed from seaward. We had no helmets; all shields had been ditched. We were sitting ducks. Lead bullets screamed past. Telamon yelled go; we hit the drink. An hour later we were on another hulk, hacking through another sheaf of timbers, each man with only a *pilos* cap and whatever rags still clung to his body.

The enemy kept coming. They flooded in hundreds from Ortygia and the Rock. There was no end to them. They were strong and rested, they had food in their bellies and fresh legs beneath them. They were not slashed or beaten or concussed. The shafts of their weapons had not been shivered by blows daylong struck and fended. They did not bear bone-weary, as we did, the third and fourth shield of the hour, snatched from the discards of comrades dead and dying. They breathed with lungs unchoked by smoke and unseared by fire; their guts held fresh water; they could still sweat.

Yet with all this, our men would still have prevailed if not for wind and tide. The sun had transited now, dropping hard towards shore; now the breeze got up. The tide turned in evil conjunction. There is a channel called the Race, abutting the isle of Ortygia, through which the current, compressed by the configuration of shoreline and sea bottom, streams at tide's turn with unwonted velocity. Now the foe opened a break in his ships' wall. The race shot through, driving our vessels back. Worse, twenty warships of the Corinthians now appeared, rounding the point from the north. Driven by the stiffening breeze and emboldened by this impetus of heaven, they fell upon the vessels of Athens engaged at sea, including *Implacable*, putting them to flight.

Our oarsmen could not drive into this rising gale. Broken with exhaustion, rowers 'caught crabs', fouling their mates' oars. The wind struck their slewed surfaces and began to head them. The tidal race heightened their way. Those vessels which managed to come bows-on to the gust, which they must merely to hold position, discovered themselves vulnerable to attack from the flank, by the inrushing Corinthians with their fresh crews and by those others of the Syracusans now rallying behind the cry that the gods had answered their prayers, by sending this gale to rout the foe. I was on the cruiser *Aristeia* now, the fifth or sixth ship of the day, when her commander turned to ram one of the oncoming Corinthians. Our ship was literally moving backwards, so stout was the gale. The Corinthian slipped her with ease, put her helm over, and wheeled, outboard banks pulling while inboard backed, to ram us amidships. The cruiser fled stern-first, backing water amid fresh broadsides of missiles. The Corinthian, hampered herself by the wind as it struck her now from abeam, managed only a glancing blow upon *Aristeia*'s prow, but this was sufficient to open a tear broad enough for a man and boy to pass through abreast. The sea flooded in. A mile still remained to shore.

The oarsmen pulled with the desperation of men who know they have been vanquished and that their conquerors, falling on them, will grant no quarter. They could hear Gylippus's men along the foreshore, ravening for blood. Men groaned in despair; limbs quaked as if palsied. The ship fled into the shadows thrown by Epipolae, across the dark water which now extended hundreds of yards out from the shore. It was cold, like the morning.

*Aristeia* ran afoul at the Athenian palisade. Earlier vessels, jamming up in flight, had beaten the stakes from alignment, or ripped out their own bellies rushing upon them. Marines and sailors now ganged the surface by hundreds, labouring to restore the front. I glimpsed Lion and Chowder, striving in this chore. Why did they have to be so noble? With a cry I plunged in to aid them. I had no weapon, shoes, nothing. My flesh had been wrung to enervation. So had everyone's. We could feel death, not alone in the cold and dark but in our bones.

I could see the battleships of Corinth and Syracuse sweeping down upon our rampart like great winged creatures of prey. They advanced as in a dream. By the gods, they were beautiful! Divers strove in the water beside me, seeking to rig to a float of timbers the chain that yoked two submerged hedgehogs. The weight kept dragging the float under; the men struggled to hurl its monkey fist to the marines astraddle the platform, but the strength of their arms failed; the rope flopped to the surface with a slapping sound, again and again short of the mark. Two ships of the foe had centred on our gap; they were closing so fast the first ironheads flung by their *toxotai* were already ripping the water at our elbows. More men thrashed to our aid from shore. After ungodly exertions, the chain was at the last seated in its notch and drawn taut.

With titanic impact the foremost battleship flung herself upon the palisade. I saw Chowder, fouled among the lines. A pike drove through the gristle of his neck. Diving for our lives, Lion and I could hear the rampart's submerged stakes, massive as trees, plunge into the foe's guts and the hedgehog's spikes rend her belly. Still the Corinthian's oarsmen heaved, seeking to tear a breach through which her sisters would pour, bringing fire to those vessels of Athens battered and broken behind the barricade.

The maddest mêlée of the day now ensued. Athenians like ants swarmed upon the impaled dreadnought. The dead made a carpet upon the sea. Our men hauled themselves bare-handed up the shafts of the enemy's oars, hacking at her bankers through the hide-defended ports, while the foe's marines piked in return from topside and their archers rained fire point-blank. Pitch bolts which the enemy's bowmen had flung into the beached craft of Athens, our men now plucked still blazing and slung again upon the assailants. The Corinthian was going down now, adding her hulk to the fragile bastion which yet preserved us. Out beyond the stakes another dozen men-of-war had drawn up broadside, deep in shadow, archers launching their tow shafts upon us while their oarsmen sang the *paean* in triumph and joy.

I found Lion in the wash of bodies. Chowder was dead, Splinter slain earlier with an axe. The waves, barely enough to topple an infant, buffeted us to our knees; we must crab in on hips and elbows, shuddering with such violence as to no longer command our own limbs.

Our cousin Simon hauled us from the soup. He got wine into us, clasping me in his cloaked embrace; others swathed Lion, abrading his flesh to restore the warmth of blood. Despair rang from every quarter, such chagrin more acute among those unable this day to fight, the army and the wounded who could only look on without striking a blow. I glanced up the strand and thought, This is what hell must look like.

Above us a knot of seamen laboured to resuscitate a comrade. No hope. At last the final man yielded and pitched. Night was on us. Across the darkening field the warships of the foe quartered, piking the last of our seamen bereft upon the swell and calling that we would not tarry long to join them. Beside Lion and my cousin, the clutch of sailors peered hollow-eyed on this tableau.

'Did you see him out there?' one uttered in awe and dread. 'He was on the ships, fighting for the enemy.'

'He was there when they broke us, leading them.'

'No-one could stand before him.'

What nonsense was this? Would these morons claim to have descried Poseidon, or Zeus himself, among the champions of the foe?

'Who the hell are you talking about?' I demanded. 'What phantom do you madmen think you saw?'

The sailor turned as if I were the madman.

'Alcibiades,' he declared.

# TWENTY-FOUR
# THE ISSUE OF DEFEAT

LATER, IN THE QUARRIES, ONE OF OUR NUMBER ENQUIRED OF A
Syracusan warden if Alcibiades had in fact been present at the battle of the harbour.

The keeper laughed in his face. 'You can concoct handier fictions
than that, Athenians. Or can you still not believe you could be beaten
other than by one of your own?'

There is a crime in Sicily which the non-Greek natives call
*demortificare*. It means to occasion someone to experience shame or,
equally blameworthy, to be aware of such distress and take no action to
relieve it. Among the Syracusans, who have embraced the concept as
their own, this is an offence graver than murder, which they regard as an
act of passion or honour and thus sanctioned or at least condoned by the
gods. *Demortificare* is different. I once witnessed a boy, one of our
laundry urchins, beaten half-senseless by his father for permitting his
female cousin to sit alone at a dance.

The Syracusans hated us for a thousand causes, but beyond all for
having surrendered to them. It was Lion who remarked this, in the
branding kennels, compiling observations for his *historia*, which he kept
now in his head and recited aloud to keep his mates from cracking. 'The
Syracusans can absolve us for bringing war upon them. They may abide
even the despoliation of their city and the slaughter of their sons. But
they will never forgive us for our shame.'

You are a gentleman, Jason, but you are also a warrior. And you call yourself a philosopher. I believe you are. Do you know why I sought you out to aid me in my defence? Not because I believed you could help. None can; my grave is dug. Rather I imposed on you out of self-interest. I wanted to meet you. I have admired you since Potidaea. Will it surprise you to learn that I have followed your career, as much as one may at the remove at which I found myself from the city of my birth? I know of the death, or murder, of your two dear sons at the hands of the Thirty. I know the ruin brought upon the family of your second wife. I am aware of the peril in which you placed yourself and your kin, defending the younger Pericles before the Assembly; I have read your speech and admire it greatly. To own to honour lifelong is no mean feat.

Yet I flatter myself that I share with a man such as yourself, if not qualities of honour, then of perception. Here is my crime, and to account it I haul all Greece into the dock beside me: to save my skin I abandoned my fellows, both on the field and within my heart. But let us plumb this unbosoming. I abandoned not only my brothers but myself. To save myself, I abandoned myself.

All vice springs from the flesh; your master Socrates teaches as much, does he not? As Agathon sets in the speech of Palamedes before Troy, himself on trial for his life:

> . . . to the extent to which a man unites his self-conception to his flesh,
> to that measure will he be a villain. To the extent he unites it with his
> soul, he will be divine.

But who among us has done that? Your master indeed. Men hate him for this, because to acknowledge his nobility is to concede their own baseness, and this they can never do. They hate him as fire hates water, as evil hates good.

We who have abandoned our countrymen and our own nobler natures, we whom long and brutal war has compelled to such abjuration, is there one, other than ourselves, who may be called our object? One whom we have individually and collectively abandoned?

Who else but Alcibiades? Not once but three times did Athens spurn him, when he knelt before her proffering all he owned. And what made Athens hate him more? Just this: that he repudiated her abandonment.

Compelled by his own proud nature, in which he confuted himself and his native land, Alcibiades demonstrated this truth of the soul: that which we cast out returns to revenge itself.

How apt that Athens reviles these twain as few others: the most measured of men, your master, and the most reckless, his friend. And they hate both for the same reason. Because each – one bearing the lamp of wisdom, the other the brand of glory – illumined that glass in whose reflection his countrymen might see their own self-forsaken souls.

But I have strayed afield. Let us return to the Great Harbour, to defeat and its issue . . .

With Chowder's death and Splinter's, *Pandora* had lost all her original marines except myself and Lion. Of our fourteen after Iapygia had fallen to wounds Meton called Armbreaker, Teres called Skull, Adrastus called Towhead, Colophon Redbeard, and Memnonides; to disease Hagnon called the Small, Stratus, Maron, and Diagoras; deserted Theodectes and Milon the pentathlete. If the measure of an officer be the number of his command he restores to home alive, this roster speaks with its own eloquence. I may say in defence only this: none did better. Of sixty thousand free citizens, subject-state volunteers, and conscripts inclusive of both fleets, fewer than a thousand made it home, and these on their own and only after appalling trials.

The fault I own as mine, for my men. The tuition in obedience I had received as a boy, reinforced by the code acquired in the mercenary service, was too severe, too Spartan if you will, to be imposed upon Athenians, particularly the unpropertied roughnecks who constituted the bulk of the latter-day fleet marine force. Courage and initiative they owned in abundance. They were born to debate and disputation, abashed by no authority established over them, brash and spirited and untamable as cats. Invincible when events ran their way, they could not summon the self-command to rally when the sky began to rain shit, nor was I, or Lion, capable of inspiriting it in them. They personified that type of warrior who beneath a commander of vision and audacity may roll resistlessly from success to success. Compelled, however, to endure adversity over a sustained interval – not alone defeat but simply delay and inaction – the restless enterprise that made them great would turn upon itself and, like a caged rat, commence to gnaw its vitals. From Lion's observations:

*A soldier must not own too much of imagination. In victory it overheats his ambition; in defeat it inflames his fears. A brave man possessed of imagination will not be brave long.*

The soldiers and sailors of Athens had won so often that they did not know how to lose. Overthrow unmanned them, as a sudden blow will a boxer who has seldom been hit. I never saw men lose weapons and armour as these. Restless, easily bored, our citizen campaigners possessed not the patience of the warrior and did not care to acquire it. The virtue of obedience, in Sparta so highly prized as to be worshipped as a god, was to Athenians the same as want of vision or deficiency of daring. In victory they disdained their officers; in defeat they mutinied openly. One could not pound it into their skulls that obedience and command are reverse and obverse. Those generals of quality who by luck arose to command held up to their men the very virtues – forbearance, stead-fastness, endurance – which to these youths were worthless as piss and imposed punishments which could not be enforced in a democratic camp. The best one may say to honour these dead is that they perished when the fight might yet bear the name of honour.

Two nights after the defeat in the Great Harbour, the army packed up and pulled out, all forty thousand who could trek, seeking any part of the island where survival could be fought for. The sick and wounded would be left to die.

My cousin would not desert them. I confronted him as the army massed to move out. The night was pitch, yet one could see the shades of the maimed and mutilated, hobbling and even crawling to the for-mation of their fellows, pleading to be taken with them. Please, one without legs would implore, I can be drawn! Pull me like a sack! Men would promise gold when they got home, all their fathers owned. Others appealed in the name of the gods or of filial piety, of boyhood bonds, oaths sworn, trials endured in common.

The order came to move out. The sick pressed their treasure upon the able – bear me only a mile, friend! – while the well forced all they had into the fists of the disowned. Here, mate, buy your life if you can. The distress of those pleading for deliverance was exceeded only by the agony of their comrades, possessed of no option but to deny them. I begged Simon to depart with us. What good could he accomplish, holding here to die? The failing ringed him about, imploring him to heed. Go – and take me with you! Others importuned Lion and Telamon, who, with kind hearts steeled, sought to deflect them. Suddenly a youth lurched from the press. This was the petty officer of the *Pandora* called Rosy Cheeks, who had taken a spike through the foot. He clutched at my cloak. 'Friend, I can hobble. I beg you, lend me your arm!' In two years of campaign I had not yielded to terror or rage. Now my belly failed. I flung the beggar off me, cursing him and all the sick. Why don't you die, the mob of you, and get it over with! I pleaded with Simon not to cast his life away on these who were already dead. He responded by requiring my blessing. I called him a fool who deserved to die. He struck me in the face. 'Give me your blessing.'

'Take it to hell.'

My brother caught me from behind. We embraced our cousin, weeping.

'See my boy gets his schooling and my lass her dowry.' Simon pressed into my palm his rings and an ivory charm he had won for a solo at the Apaturia. 'For Road's Turn,' he said, meaning Acharnae, his tomb.

The track beyond the palisade ran across the marsh held by the enemy throughout the sea fight. It had been vacated. The men took cheer and accelerated the pace. 'He's afraid of us,' someone proposed, meaning Gylippus. The Syracusans were behind their city walls, celebrating. You could hear their cymbals and drums. We were missing a hell of a party.

We must link with the Sicels inland, then drive to Catana, twenty miles north. The way round, for we dared not skirt Epipolae, climbed stony slopes from the harbour. The army was to advance in a hollow square with the noncombatants in the centre, but great flocks of camp wives pressed out, seeking their men. Lion's Berenice and her sister Herse trekked beside us; it went with excruciating slowness. The formation extended on both sides of the road; every time it came to a wall the mob bunched to a standstill.

Near dawn enemy scouts overhauled us. We could hear them, on horseback, calling to each other in the fog. By night their whole army would be on us. The women must get out now. Lion parted from Berenice on the move, pressing into her kit the packet of his notes and all the cash he had. Others groped godspeed. A few got in a farewell fuck. You saw them, grappling in the dirt or humping each other against trees.

There was a holm oak beside the track. Someone had hung a *kypridion*, fillets of wool bound with the passion knot, the sign of Bridal Aphrodite, which the women tack for luck above the lintels of newly-weds. Who could have set such invocation upon this tree of blood, whose bloom produces the scarlet pigment that colours the war cloak of Sparta and Syracuse? Death was our bride now. I fell in step beside Lion.

At noon the column reached the first river. The Syracusans had either dammed it or diverted its course; it was dry. We learned this, miles back in the column, from enemy cavalry, who called across as they fired the underbrush on our flanks. They shouted, too, that our camp had been taken. The wounded and those attending had been slaughtered to the last man. I sank in grief on the roadside and must have remained unmoving for a term because we again, Lion and I, became separated from our company, the third or fourth so far in the retreat. 'Get up!' My brother tugged me. 'Pommo! We must keep with the column!'

The track ran through underbrush. Enemy cavalry had fired this to windward and now the passage clotted with smoke. 'This is why Gylippus opened the gate!' a trooper at our shoulders snorted. 'Why attack us behind our walls when he can let our brilliant officers lead us into this waste where thirst will drive us mad!'

At last a rider came down the line. Our men were digging wells in the dry riverbed, seeking the underground flow. 'What's the holdup?' an infantryman shouted. 'Attack upstream! That's where the enemy is – and the water!'

The rider relayed the generals' decision: that the brush was too dense, we might march into even worse.

'I haven't drained a drop of piss in two days, mate. How much worse does it get?'

Cavalry hit when we reached the plain. There were not many yet, as their main raced ahead to fortify the way against us. The column pressed on, in that infuriating spread-and-compress repetition of large bodies on the move. We came to a farm with a springhouse. The site had been assaulted by the thousands before us. None the less men fought over the oozing clay, which they held in wads above their lips and squeezed like pomegranates for the juice.

The column reached the second river at nightfall. The wells produced muddy soup. Each got a cup. We moved on.

Men were melting by twos and threes into the brush, taking their chances on their own. Telamon fell in beside us. Time to fold the flag. Would we join him? Athens, Lion replied, is our country.

'With respect, friends. Screw your country.'

We laughed. He took our hands. He was no man for long farewells.

Two dawns later the column came to a great plateau. A pair of ravines cut through at the southwest; there was no way round; the enemy held the heights. We must force it or never see Catana. Lion and I were incorporated into a company under a captain whose name we never learned, a garrulous fellow whose men clearly loved him. We got to the base of the track just past noon. Men were going up and dying. That was all there was to it. Our company was shunted beneath a hastily cobbled palisade. We would go up next.

Behind us stretched the column. Syracusan cavalry made rushes at a hundred points; you saw nothing for miles but their dust ascending from the scrub. The earth at our feet was cracked clay; I observed that we must get water or die. Lion indicated the 'beaten zone' beyond our palisade, where the foe's missiles and stones rained.

'Step out there and solve your problems.'

Three times our company went up the hill. The pass narrowed to a single wagon-width; the enemy had sealed it with a wall. Behind it he was massed twenty across and a hundred deep; thousands more blanketed the cliffsides. They sent stones and javelins, even landslides upon us. By the afternoon they had it worked out; they let the attackers advance to the wall, where the facing rocks compacted them into a body; then they opened fire. Each assault company bore it in turn; when enough had gone down, or simply cracked, the unit fell back and another went up in rotation. The track had acquired a name, Blood River, though this was a misnomer, as all fluid soaked at once into the desiccated earth. Exposed on the uptrack, we pressed ourselves like lizards against sheltering rocks or crouched beneath makeshift palisades, burrowing into these clefts, while the foe's stones and darts crashed upon us. You could see the shields of the fallen, great piles dragged back by their comrades repulsed in subsequent assaults or toppled or slid down-slope on their own. Their oaken chassis had been bashed to splinters by the stones and boulders of the foe, signia and blazons effaced beneath a paste of dust and blood.

The track up had become a calf-deep furrow, riven to powder by the soles and knees of the assault troops as they mounted, marinated by their piss and sweat, then reground by their backs and heels as their corpses were passed down by others who mounted to take their place. The companies assaulted the hill all day. Next day the same. We had learned to shiver the enemy's javelins where they struck, for each time we fell back the foe retrieved them to fling upon us afresh. The lances slung downhill terrified the men, not just the impact but the sound, and the stones and boulders were worse.

A cavalry captain galloped up, calling for volunteers. Gylippus had got in the rear of the column with five thousand; he was throwing up another wall to pen us for the slaughter. Lion and I leapt to it. Anything to quit this hellish ravine.

In the rear, our ten thousand assaulted Gylippus's five. By nightfall the foe fell back, depleted of missiles and stones. The company ahead of ours took the wall. They tore through the abandoned kits of the foe but could find no water. These companies must rejoin the main body. Ours and two others were ordered to remain, to bury the dead and set up a night perimeter. We flopped down on the wall, dirty as death, and watched the units trudge back. From our vantage we could see the enemy cavalry, the dust of more squadrons than could be counted, and across the plain additional plumes, columns of infantry converging from the north and east – a hundred thousand, two hundred thousand, massing for the kill.

Thirst tormented the army. Men cursed Nicias and Demosthenes, and Alcibiades too; him more than them, for he had abandoned us. I hated him too, for my cousin and all the dead, but most for not being here to preserve us.

Twice Nicias passed on horseback. One must give the man credit. Though racked with disease, he displayed tireless resolution, passing up and down the line absent all care for his own affliction. I heard him, an hour past dark of the fifth day, surrounded by two thousand:

'Brothers and comrades, I must speak with haste. I know we have no water and this goes hard with us and the beasts which bear our armour. But we will turn about tonight and march back to the sea. There are rivers along the track to Helorus of greater volume than the enemy may dam.

'Be of steadfast hearts, my friends, fortifying your resolve with this knowledge: that the forty thousand of our army is not only a formidable force but a city in itself, greater than any in Sicily save Syracuse. We may go anywhere, drive out the inhabitants and establish ourselves in their places. We may find food and water. We may build ships and get home. Remember this and be not downcast. As for the reversals you have suffered, do not let them make you lose heart. Fortune cannot hold herself indifferent for ever; even the sternest of immortals must be moved by our plight. For those decisions which have brought us to this pass, I take responsibility. You are not to blame. Never has your fighting spirit shown itself wanting, but your exertions have been set at naught by the gods' perversity and our own ill generalship.'

Lion studied the men as they listened. He was struck, he said later, by the intelligence of their faces; they recalled to him the countenances one beheld in the theatre on the morn of a competition. Now they seemed, my brother observed, to assess Nicias as they would an actor and to class him of the leaden and the second-rate. Nicias, his hearers' expressions betrayed, is pious; he is valiant, even noble. But one thing he is not: he is not Alcibiades. Neither, for all his craft and courage, is Demosthenes. Desperate as the army's pass now was, could any doubt that, Alcibiades in command, he could not overturn it? Nicias was right about one thing: we were an army, redoubtable even now as any on earth. Yet we were broken and we knew it. I hated Alcibiades the more. There was none to replace him. As Nicias spoke, men's hearts cracked, apprehending this.

'Lastly, my friends, remember that you are Athenians and Argives and Ionians, the sons of heroes and heroes yourselves. You have won great glory in this war and, fortune willing, will claim more. Remember your fathers and the trials they have undergone with courage. Hold fast, brothers. With heaven's aid and our own exertions, we will endure to see again our homes and families whom we love.'

Orders came to light a multitude of fires. The army stoked them and packed out. By dawn the column had reached the Helorine Road, right back where we started. We would flee south this time, pick a river, and track it inland, to scribe the circle and try for Catana again.

All day long and all the next the Syracusan cavalry made rushes on the column. We had no horses or archers; we could do nothing but endure. The enemy attacked in squadrons of fifty and a hundred; we would form up at the double, so spent we could barely move, while the foe loosed volleys upon us. At first our youngest made rushes upon them, slashing at the horses' legs or seeking to drive their bellies through with the nine-footer. But a man on foot is an easy target. Two or three horsemen would converge; if our man fell the foe's cavalry trampled him or slung point-blank to open his guts. Others of ours must dash to the rescue. With each rush by the enemy, another two or three fell. A broken arm, gashed thigh, a concussion. Men must bear others. The strong carried the weak, and when they failed, others carried them. An officer recruited the asses of the train for makeshift cavalry. But these were too spent and terror-stricken to be managed. We passed one mule, gutted; our men crazed with thirst licked its blood.

The column was in open country now, without shelter from the sun. One's skin ceased to sweat, only burned. Among soldiers on the march is this term, 'sun stupid'. The column laboured in fever, a procession of the doomed. The senses spawned mirages. A man would cry aloud the names of his children; his comrades, too abashed to chide him for it, trudged on in mortification. At last one, unable to endure longer, would bark at the first to shut up, and he, roused as from a dream, would not even know he had cried aloud. One tried to start a song, something crude to cheer the march. It failed before the second verse. Thirst hammered the column. One gnawed twigs and set pebbles beneath the tongue. 'Here they come!' Another attack, another siege of terror leaving one yet more exhausted and in the aftermath, another three wounded, another three who must be borne.

Now one longed no more for Alcibiades for his leadership. Now one hated him for his absence. It was he who had sent this scourge upon us, out of his own pride and from the foe's embrace; he who, set upon that balance point between his country and himself, chose his own survival and directed hell on us, his brothers. God preserve me, a man cried to heaven, to see him paid out! Let me live, if only long enough to deal him death.

Two days later, mad with thirst, the column reached the Assinarus. We were at the rear and heard the story later.

The enemy had not dammed this river. Instead he was drawn up on the far side, two thousand across and ten deep, with five thousand cavalry on the flanks, funnelling our column as it approached towards the massed armour and missile troops of their comrades. The Syracusan archers and slingers had been drawn up in the fore, on the opposite bank, less than a hundred feet away. They began firing while our troops were still two hundred feet from the river. Nicias and the commanders sought to hold our men back. But the soldiers stampeded into the river, even as the enemy poured volley after volley upon them. Men were shot through and dying, yet still battling one another for drink. Thousands fell in the water; thousands more, fleeing, were run down or rounded up for slaves. Behind us, Demosthenes' division had been overrun by fifty thousand, the columns we had spotted from the summit of Gylippus's wall. Our force was tatters. Forty thousand had set out; under six remained.

Nicias surrendered next morning. Two nights later we were in the quarries.

Here is how they branded us. They had chutes, four of them, like a farmer's for sheep. We were driven forward in lines. At the end was a stanchion. This captured your skull. At my station the man with the brand was instructing a prentice. 'Not like an ox, boy! This is man skin, not cowhide. Kiss the flesh . . . just a sweetheart's kiss, like that!'

I remember rising to my feet, seeking a reflecting surface to behold my new slave self who bore the *koppa* brand. This was not necessary. One glance at your mates told all.

In the quarries men clung to the frailest vessels of hope. Many reasoned that because the Syracusans had not put us to death, they must eventually make us work or sell us. Others held out the hope of ransom. Lion made it his task to dash such expectations, the harbouring of which, he felt, served only to demoralize us further. We must make up our minds to die like men. Those we had abandoned at the Great Harbour, he recalled to us, had already done so.

There were sixty-eight hundred in the quarries, all Athenians, Argives, and free allies. Fifteen thousand had been killed on the roads; perhaps five thousand had been rounded up by private soldiers and hidden from their officers for slaves. Of the remaining thirteen thousand – mercenaries, mechanics, camp followers – great numbers had been slaughtered; the rest had been sold.

The quarries were limestone defined by that cleft – the infamous *spelaion*, the cavern – which split the cliffside; the rest exposed, varying in depth from thirty feet to above a hundred. The site was immediately outside the city, abutting the sector of Temenites. Our captors let us down by ladders, then pulled the ladders up. When a man died he could not be buried, and the corpses collected in piles, emitting an un-endurable stench. Those summoned by their captors for punishment, or fun, would be hauled out feet-first, elbows pressed tight for protection to their skulls, which banged into the stone at each heave on the tackle.

Rations were a pint of grain a day, uncooked slop, and a half-pint of water, both lowered in vats contrived to be too cumbersome for a man or even two to receive without spilling, and roped down at sites of such precipitousness as to make those who received them risk their necks from a fall. Our captors routinely urinated in our water; we plucked turds from our dinner every day.

The warders called us 'ponies', for the horse brand on our brows. Their officers took a census the first day by unit; we must count out eight times each day subsequent. All must be on our feet before dawn and not sit till dark. A man caught would be stoned or roped topside for a 'pony ride'. Those who returned alive from these sessions did not remain so for long.

The Syracusans moved to crush our spirits by eliminating officers. Those whose identities they had obtained were hoisted to the pit rim, there to endure within earshot of their men below sieges of barbarity as long as two and three days. Beneath this torture, the names of other officers were extracted and these hauled up to undergo like atrocities. The dead were pitched back over the brink. Any who attempted to honour them by burial were shot down or stoned. This ordeal continued until no commander above the rank of subaltern remained.

This was not the finish, however. By some misintelligence, or inspired by malice alone, our captors pronounced their conviction that three officers remained yet unsurrendered. The foe commanded that this trio be produced. It went without saying that, absent immediate compliance, the enemy would commence butchering at random.

At once three stepped forward. These were Pythodorus the son of Lycophron of Anaphlystus, Nicagoras the son of Mnesicles of Pallene, and Philon the son of Philoxenos of Oa. Their monument, the Three

Officers, stands at Athens now, on the slope opposite the Eleusinium. As the Syracusans bound and hauled these up feet-first, none of whom had held rank beyond squad commander, our men unprompted commenced the Hymn to Victory.

> *Goddess, born of bitter labour,*
> *Joy-bringer, Truth-revealer,*
> *Long-sought Nike, our voices*
> *We lift in song to thee.*

> *Sternest of immortals,*
> *Yet clement to the brave,*
> *For him who endures*
> *Thou effaceth all evil.*

So fierce was the emotion produced by these stanzas that it seemed to fill the great bowl like a liquid, echoing stone-amplified about the quarry face.

> *Thunderer's fickle daughter,*
> *Enter we thy precincts of agon.*
> *To thee, Brightling, or to Death*
> *Do we our souls consign.*

In Sicily summer's end produces days of blistering heat, succeeded by nights of bitter cold. We were permitted no bedding or fire; the site was open to the elements. Many bore wounds of battle, others suffered with disease; now under sharpening exposure these failed. That state called *aphydatosis* set in, in which the organs, for want of liquid, cease to function. The brain cooks in its skull. One cannot draw piss. Vision fails; limbs go racked by palsy.

Tours were conducted from the city, children in school uniforms attended by their pedagogues, to look upon those who had sailed to enslave them and been brought low by the valour of their fathers. Captives would be hauled forth and the children would break their teeth out with hammers. In the quarries men were melting away by scores every night. Yet such is the nature of existence that any site, hell itself, becomes with time home. The men had got to know the place. One knoll became the Pnyx; a hollow the *theatron*. There was an agora and a Lyceum, an Acropolis and an Academy. The day was given shape by this fanciful geography, as men assembled in 'the marketplace' and passed on to 'the wrestling schools'. To pass the time they taught one another. One skilled in smithing would impart the principles of his practice; others shared instruction of joinery, mathematics, music. Lion taught boxing. He could not demonstrate; this would draw attention from the sentinels. So he lectured beneath his breath to students under the pitiless sun.

They caught one teacher, a choirmaster, and cut his tongue out. That put a crimp in our college. But the despair which succeeded could not be endured. Lion resumed. He taught gymnastics and isometrics, con-centration exercises and endurance drills. He lectured on the humours of the blood and that saturation of the tissue that must be sustained over time for the athlete to build the stamina for the Games. This is what road drills are about, and rowing, and the Long Course. Its landscape, he taught, is what trainers call the precinct of pain.

'I was taught as a boy that a goddess resides there, silent, in that sanctuary at the pinnacle of pain. This goddess's name is Victory. Look around you, cousins. We reside in that precinct now. And she is with us, this goddess. Even here, my friends, we may give ourselves to her and be lifted by her wings.'

Someone informed. We never knew who. The Syracusans roped Lion topside and tortured him three days. What they did to him I will never repeat, except to say that it was not as evil as what they performed later.

They dumped him back down. I held him all night, while others kept him warm with their bodies. Five days later he began teaching again. No-one would come. 'I will instruct the air, then!' And he did. I took station before him, the only act of my life in which I truly take pride. Others stood too, knowing they were signing his death warrant and their own.

The Syracusans hauled Lion topside again. When they dumped him again, I was certain he was dead. I held him against the cold, swathed in every rag our mates could muster. Sometime after midnight he stirred. 'What a thing of trouble this body is. It will be a relief to let it go.'

He slept an hour, then came to with a start.

'You must carry on my *historia*, Pommo. You're the only one I trust.'

I fell asleep, cradling him. When I woke he was cold.

Once when we were boys our pack had played bowl hockey on that field called the Aspis which runs outside the walls adjacent the sanctuary of Athena Tritogeneia. Do you know the place, Jason? There is a downgrade on the Carriage Road where the carters allow their wagons to gather way, building momentum for the ascent west of the gate. I was nine then, as were my mates, but Lion, only six, had beseeched us so passionately as to be permitted to join our game. Suddenly a ball, kicked loose, bounded for the freighters' track. Lion took after it. I spotted his dash from across the field. He was not oblivious, as another boy might be, sprinting into the path of a wagoner's cart whose massive oak wheels rumbled in their unchecked rush. He was simply without fear. I flew across the turf, tackling him at the terminal instant. Amid the carter's curses I hauled my brother to his feet and slapped him bloody, adding my own invective, coarser than the wagoner's, for scaring me so to death. When Father interrogated the lad that night on the origin of his blackened eye, he would give up nothing. I received a thrashing none the less and a second next evening when from my brother's innocent lips sprang a brilliant replication of my tirade of the previous day.

Here in the quarries, however, I could not preserve him from his own valour.

I buried him, such as one could, in the deepest precinct, where the goddess dwelt. All speech is superfluous to his elegy, save a plain recital of his deeds. He was, excepting none, the bravest soldier and finest man I ever knew.

Next morning my name was called. They hauled me up by the tackle. Death still held terror for me, I am ashamed to confess. Yet what grieved me most was that I would not survive to pay out Alcibiades. 'God preserve me, let me cry out no names.'

The swing arm hauled me over the quarry's lip. Men's teeth littered the ground by hundreds. It was hot. Flies swarmed in masses above patches on the earth, blood doubtless, or fragments of flesh, fingers, and toes. I could see benches, upon which several men were strapped, disembowelled yet still alive. Rude tables sat beside these, upon which implements were spread as at a dentist's or physician's. I recognized cleavers and bonebreakers. The uses of the other tools I could not surmise. Across a space stood a colony of execution posts. All were vacant at the moment, their sides and the limestone at their bases black and swarming with flies. Behind this stood tents and a circle of stone where the guards took their meals. There was a miniature slaughter area to the side, for pullets and doves for their eating. The adjacency of these charnel tracks for men and fowl struck me as ludicrous. I laughed aloud.

A guard walloped me across the kidneys. He shoved me forward. Others demanded my name. I must repeat it over and over while they scoured the roll. 'Polemides the son of Nicolaus of Acharnae, yes?'

Yes.

'Son of Nicolaus?'

Yes.

'Of Acharnae?'

Yes.

'This is the man. I will take him.'

A new voice spoke these last. I turned towards it and discovered a sturdy youth with a strawberry blemish, a brace of javelins across his back and a Lacedaemonian *xyele* at his hip. He was a warrior's squire of the Spartans. He came round before me, extending a wooden bowl in which slopped a base of wine and a heel of barley. 'Don't drink it straight or you'll pass out. Soak it with the bread.'

My wrists were unbound, pins hammered from my shackles.

'Who are you?' I prayed of the youth.

'Eat your bread,' he commanded.

I peered into his face, which I had seen before, I was certain, but could not remember. For his part the youth measured me, absent compassion, assessing what strength I yet possessed and what demands might be made upon it.

'I serve the *polemarch* Lysander of Sparta,' he pronounced. 'By God's clemency are you spared and commanded to accompany me by sea to Lacedaemon.'

# BOOK FIVE

# ALCIBIADES
# IN SPARTA

## TWENTY-FIVE
# THE SOLDIER IN WINTER

IT WAS HALF A YEAR BEFORE I REACHED LACEDAEMON. MY HEALTH broke down on the crossing to Rhegium and again on the trek from Cyllene; I must be settled on a sharecroft of Endius's *kleros*, his estate, at the north end of the Eurotas valley. I did not see Sparta herself till spring.

All winter I lay abed, with my fare in my fist as the Lacedaemonians say. The skin stretched thin as paper across my breast. A skeleton stared back from the glass. From Sicily my legs bore twenty-seven unhealed wounds – punctures, undercuts, and peel-backs including two of three fingers'-breadth above both Achilles tendons. Ribs were cracked in a dozen places, the crown of my skull so contused that when the hair was shaved to be scourged with lye, the flesh showed purple and peeled in layers like an onion. I must eat and sleep. My benefactors, an elder couple of the land, settled me in the room that had been their son's and left me to my rest. Days I lay in the sun of the south-facing court, evenings before the fire, bundled in the borderless mantle of the countryman. There was an antique hound of the farm, Kicker by name; as strength returned I ventured at his side, forked on my staff like a fossil, upon the winter hills.

Nights were long and I dreamt often. I felt old, ancient as Cronos. Shades passed before my vision, my own among them; I saw father and sister, Lion and Simon and my wife and babe; with them I held converse nightlong of such profundity as must reform my soul for ever, yet when I woke these had dispelled, gossamer as smoke. I retained nothing. Shadow and sun were one to me, as visions intruded at their will and not the widest daylight could dispel them. I saw again the wounded in the Great Harbour and the dying as the troop trekked out. Again I trudged in column to the Assinarus. A hundred nights I woke in terror, only to confront this fresh indictment: that of my own survival. By what grant did I endure above the earth when so many better than I had been banished beneath it? The panel parted one midnight; Alcibiades arose before me. So vivid stood his apparition, down to the wolf's-fang brooch he had won at Potidaea, that I was certain he inhabited the chamber in the flesh. He and not Lysander, I was informed, had been the agent of my preservation. I did not thank but reviled him. 'Why did you save me? Why me and not my brother?'

'Your brother wouldn't have come.'

The truth of this lanced me to the quick. I sought to lunge at my tormentor, to throttle his witness at its source; but my limbs would not obey me. Such grief wrung my heart as to strangle all speech and stir.

'I needed one at my side,' Alcibiades pronounced, 'who had passed through the same portal I had.'

In daylight I could countenance my cowardice and even extenuate it. At night I sweated, as on trial. I saw myself in Phreatto at Piraeus, where one accused of murder overseas must make his defence standing offshore in a boat, as the laws of ritual pollution forbid his feet, defiled with bloodguilt, to tread the earth of Attica. In dreams I sought to sacrifice, but always the priests debarred my offering. Nightlong I slaughtered victims and read damnation in their entrails. I had not lost fear of heaven, rather become possessed by it, or more accurately that no-man's-land through which mortals and immortals pass and commingle and where, as Craterus testifies, the living and the dead, the unborn and the soon-to-die

*share song and society at the same table.*

Alone memory of my children seemed to vouchsafe salvation. I clung to the vision of their faces as one shipwrecked to a spar. I had no right to. What endowment had I bequeathed them, not even my name? War had called and I had gone. Now I was sick of war. The farm on which I recuperated was what they call a 'freeholding'; the freedman and his wife grew pears. I watched them with their graftlings and their winter boxes. With what poignancy such homely tasks wrung my heart! I longed to be woken no more by the trumpet but by the lark, to hear again the peal of children's laughter. Let another take my place at muster, let him sing out 'Aye' as the mark tolls down the line. Of my thirty-eight years, nineteen had passed in war. It was enough.

Yet each night's board enlarged my debt to Sparta and to Lysander. Could I run? Where? My breath could barely snuff a candle; it took the strength of both arms to turn in bed. Lysander would find me, or his agents, those who for a price track their prey to the gates of hell. I would become one of those myself before settled in my homeland again, though I did not know it then.

That spring I saw Alcibiades speak. This was in open-air assembly before the kings and ephors and the Corps of Peers. Gylippus had returned from Syracuse in glory; the scale of the calamity to Athens had been accounted. My country and her allies had lost twenty-nine thousand fighting men, two hundred prime ships of war, with merchantmen and transports too numerous to tally. The toll in talents of gold was four thousand, bankrupting the treasury of the state. More devastating to the spirit of the people was that the expedition had been lost in its entirety, every ship and man, every scrap of sail and armour.

Alcibiades began:

'Men of Sparta, you have commanded my counsel on matters today before this body and I must comply although the occasion brings me no joy. My countrymen have suffered a calamitous overthrow. Men I knew and loved have perished and much of their ordeal must be placed at my threshold. The counsel I gave you has helped bring about their ruin.'

The Spartan acropolis, the High City, is so scanty of elevation that it is called by the children the Knee-High City. The site, however, possesses extraordinary acoustics and is in its unassuming way august. The Corps of Peers, near eight thousand, had assembled in a body, with deputations present from a number of foreign nations, including Athens herself. Another ten to fifteen thousand Spartans of lesser citizenship status, and even boys and women, attended as well, along the slopes towards the playing fields and Artemis Orthia, the speakers' words relayed by heralds.

It had been two winters since I had seen Alcibiades. I was struck with undiminished force by the beauty of his person. His years approached forty; strands of silver shone within the burnished copper of his curls. These served, however, not to diminish his comeliness, but to enhance the gravity of his self-presentation. A becoming modesty was another gift of the plain Spartan dress. One glanced about at the warriors and athletes who compassed the speaker, attending in sober propriety. No nation rivals the Spartan for beauty. The simplicity of their diet, the rigour of their regimen, even the air and water of their unspoiled country, combine to render them supreme physical specimens. Within thirty paces could be counted a dozen of peerless athleticism, perfect in feature and symmetry. Yet to turn from these to Alcibiades was to look from moon to sun, by so much did his gifts excel theirs.

'I am grateful to you, Spartans. When you granted me sanctuary, an exile from my own country under sentence of death, I made this pledge to myself and to you: that I would speak the truth, neither more nor less, and leave it to heaven whether you would heed. I entertained no illusion that you bore affection for me, or that my presence was tolerated except as it might serve your interests.

'As to the injury my counsel might bring upon my country, I exculpated myself by the notion that she was no longer mine; that the Athens I loved had been supplanted by another, to which I owed no allegiance, and that against this Athens I might without demurral direct my energies. But I had left out an element from my equation. That nation I abetted you and your allies in bringing to harm is no bloodless abstraction, but constituted of real men who bleed real blood and die real deaths. It is a stern vocation you place upon me, men of Sparta, commanding my counsel again to direct destruction upon my countrymen. Yet my lot I have cast with you. So be it. That which I proffer now is the best my reason can devise.

'First, don't be too quick to rejoice at this calamity which has overtaken your enemy. The she-bear is never more dangerous than when penned and gored. Athens has lost a fleet, yes. Two, if you wish. But the naval might she retains is still the greatest in Greece, and her character is such as to impel her to resuscitate this power at once and by all means.

'Now at your request, I will come to what you must do to defeat your enemy. But first, knowing your taste for concision, I beg indulgence of a digression. For the course I propose is unprecedented, and your first response will be to repudiate it. But consider, Spartans. The way of life you follow now was once without antecedent as well.

'When your ancestor Lycurgus introduced his laws, so remote in antiquity that none can say whether he was man or god, no other state had seen or even contemplated their like. Who had heard of such things: to ban money and make possession of it punishable by death; to efface all distinction by wealth or birth and declare all men Peers and Equals; to proscribe venture abroad and debar foreign custom from infecting the homeland; to forbid the practising of all trades other than war; and countless other reforms down to forbidding your women to wear makeup or your carpenters to hew the beams of your houses square. All these measures Lycurgus instituted and you embraced, to forge your nation into an unvanquishable engine of unity. This was without precedent, my friends. But it was a response consentient to the times. Your ancestors perceived its genius and took it up. And it succeeded.

'Similarly when the threat of Persia arose in our grandfathers' time, your kings Cleomenes and Leonidas had the vision to adopt new methods for a new kind of war. They compelled the disunited cities of Greece into a coalition to resist the external foe. More, you included the helots in your scheme, arming them and permitting them to fight at your side in numbers far exceeding your own. That prospered too. Now, if you wish to defeat Athens and end this war, you must summon the wisdom to take up another revolution.

'First, you must sanction empire and embrace money. You must become conversant with the use of both and no longer despise them.'

At these words the assembly revolted. Howls of outrage compelled Alcibiades to bite his tongue. Voices cried that empire degrades, foreign ways debase, and cupidity corrupts all; commerce turns citizen against citizen and avarice makes men seek wealth instead of virtue. Protests resounded about the speaker with such an uproar that for an instant it seemed he might be in physical danger. At length the tumult subsided, quelled by the magistrates and proctors.

'Money is not evil of itself, men of Sparta,' Alcibiades resumed, 'but like sword and spear, whose use you understand and do not contemn, it is as good or bad as the uses to which it is put. In war money is a weapon. But since you revolt with such passion against its introduction, let me propose this: use it only overseas. Don't permit it at home. But use it you must and for this, the second alteration I counsel:

'You must embrace power by sea. You must have a navy. Not a bath-tub armada of allies and amateurs as you possess today, but a first-rate fleet capable of challenging Athens upon that element she calls her own. I do not suggest, Peers and gentlemen, that you renounce shield and spear and mount to the oarsman's bench. You would sooner cut off your right arms. But you may learn to fight as knights upon the sea. You may be officers; you may command.'

Indignation greeted this, though characterized less by cries of outrage than murmurs of disquiet, whose text was that sea power degrades the polity, elevating the meanest and emboldening them to strike for equality with their betters. Have a navy and you have democracy – and this the commonwealth of the Spartans would never countenance. Alcibiades waited again, till this clamour had abated.

'Already subject states of Athens have applied to you, men of Sparta, entreating your aid in throwing off the imperial yoke. Now is the time, while Athens reels beneath this Syracusan calamity. But how may you abet these would-be rebels, who are island states and cities of Asia Minor? Your army cannot swim there. You must have a navy. Remember, too, that every subject state of Athens you draw into revolt will add her call to others, for each, fearing reprisal if her insurrection fails, seeks allies to share her peril. Each state detached depletes Athens' tribute and impoverishes her treasury. The infallible maxim remains: so long as Athens commands the sea, she cannot be overthrown. The converse, however, is equally self-apparent. Defeat her fleet and you defeat Athens.

'Now I arrive at the third and final point, and this you will find hate-ful tenfold beyond the first two. Therefore shout me down. But admit as you do so the inevitability of what I propose. For without the implementation of this third point the first two stand moot.

'You must treat with the barbarian.

'You must ally yourself with Persia.'

To my astonishment, and Alcibiades' as well judging by his expression, this final proposition did not provoke the anticipated storm of outrage. Reaction stood divided, it seemed, between shock and quiescence, even acquiescence, for all must admit, if not publicly, that this policy had been in effect for years, though clandestinely convoked and ham-fistedly implemented.

'Only the Persian possesses wealth of a scale to buy and man the ships that will defeat Athens. You must swallow hard, Spartans, and seek his alliance, not as you do now, with contempt and aversion, but sincerely and earnestly. You must find officers who can pull this off, without being outwitted by the barbarian (for the cunning of his courtiers is celebrated) and without estranging your Hellenic allies, who call you, as you yourselves proclaim, the liberators of Greece.'

A conjoining with the Mede, Alcibiades at once qualified his counsel, did not mean crawling into bed in Persian pyjamas. It signified only a confederation of convenience, to be exploited so long as it served Spartan interests and renounced the instant it ceased to.

'Hateful as this counsel may ring to you sons of Leonidas whose heroism preserved Greece from the Median yoke, it possesses the inevitability of history. Persia has the gold. The Great King fears Athens. His treasure will purchase the fleet that will bring victory. All that is wanting is your will to command it.'

Alcibiades drew up. He did not glance to the envoys of Athens, though plainly he was aware of the enormity he had just pronounced, that is, to define that course which, enacted by his hearers, must bring upon his nation vanquishment and prostration. A species of awe transfixed his listeners. What Alcibiades had proposed was treason of such breathtaking scale that, like tragedy on the stage, its very pronouncement evoked terror and pity. Never had I feared heaven as in that moment. I strained towards Alcibiades, to discover on his face any token of such awe or dread. There was none. The exile occupied a promontory upon which none but himself dared tread. 'You have commanded my counsel, men of Sparta, and I have given it.'

Two further exchanges recall that day. The first took place immediately succeeding Alcibiades' speech. He had stepped down and was withdrawing among the crowd when his way was interdicted by the knight Callicratidas, who later would distinguish himself so singularly in the cause which he now condemned. Conceding the utility of that course proposed by Alcibiades, he demanded of his compatriots if victory at all costs was their aim.

'What will have become of us, brothers, when we, emulating this programme of infamy, mount victorious to the Athenian Acropolis? What kind of men will we have become, who place ourselves in league with tyrants to enslave free men? Our guest here has taught himself to dress like us, train like us, speak like us. But the chameleon, they say, may turn every colour but white.' He faced about towards his antagonist. 'What is this new nation into which you wish to turn us, Alcibiades? I will name it in a single word: Athens!'

Cries of endorsement seconded this. Callicratidas continued to Alcibiades: 'Will we, embracing your counsel, turn ourselves into money-grubbing, pine-pulling Athenians? Will our boast be that we in our turn enslave all Greece? And who will rule this pseudo-Athens you propose – this democracy . . .'

He gestured with contempt to Lysander, Endius, and a number of their fellows with whom, clearly, Alcibiades had allied himself. These held in silence, leaving it to their confederate to rejoin.

'I understand and expected such from you, Callicratidas. Were I you, I might reply the same. But understand this. What I have set forth I do not for my own gain – how can it profit me? – but as one who counsels a friend for his own good. I hate the course I have placed before you. But it cries out with a god's voice and that god is Necessity. You will embrace it willingly, with wisdom and forethought, or unwillingly, compelled by events. But you will do it. You must or perish.'

The second exchange came moments later; I chanced to overhear it as I attempted to approach Lysander, with whom I still had gained no intercourse, as he was making his way out through the crush. The ephor Antalcidas, an elder of sixty who had distinguished himself in battle at both Mantinea and Amphipolis, had closed beside the younger man and tugged him apart in debate.

'. . . I wish with all my heart, old uncle,' Lysander was saying, employing that deferential and affectionate epithet proper for addressing one's senior, 'that options held as clear-cut as in our grandfathers' day. But this is not Thermopylae and we are not Leonidas. Lacedaemon today is like a ship driven before a storm; she may not turn back and cannot stand still. Her only chance is to beat onward, crowding on all sail.'

'And does all sail,' Antalcidas replied, 'mean treating with despots, debasing our honour with deception and duplicity?'

'Where the skin of the lion will not stretch, it must be pieced out with the skin of the fox.'

'God preserve us, Lysander, when men like you ascend to dominance in Lacedaemon. You and that villain of Athens whose name, accursed, I abhor to utter. A pair spawned in hell, to rule these hell-spawned times!'

'Times have changed,' Lysander replied coolly, 'and what has compelled them if not God's will? Tell me, old man. Do mortals not honour heaven by altering with the alteration of the times and profane her by adhering mindlessly to antique ways?'

'Lysander, you elevate blasphemy to a new acme.'

'What would you have us do, Antalcidas? Cluster on the salt shore chanting hymns of glories gone, while the future speeds past us more swiftly than a racing man-of-war?'

The elder now espied Alcibiades, crossing to Lysander's shoulder. His glance swung from one to the other, as if fixing as the foe these twain together, representative of their generation and not their several states.

'I give thanks to the Almighty, Lysander, that I will not live to see that Sparta over which you and men like you come to rule.'

# TWENTY-SIX
## AMONG THE SONS
## OF LEONIDAS

ALCIBIADES WAS ABSENT MUCH OF THAT SUMMER, IN IONIA AND THE islands, working as an agent of Sparta. As earlier during the Peace his enterprise had brought into alliance with Athens such great states as Argos, Elis, and Mantinea, now he enlisted such powers on the counter hand. He incited Chios, Erythrae, and Clazomenae to revolt from Athens, then sailed to Miletus and brought her over too. He then produced the prime prize: alliance for Sparta with the king of Persia. He induced Teos to tear down her walls, and Lebedos and Aerae to revolt. He did this alone, backed by one Spartan commander and only five ships. He directed the Chians to widen the rising to Lesbos, where they incited to insurrection the great states of Mytilene and Methymna, while Spartan land forces moved to secure Clazomenae and capture Cyme. And Alcibiades had conquered another sovereign province. This was the heart of Timaea, wife of the Spartan king Agis. She was his lover, every chambermaid and urchin of Lacedaemon told, and carried his child as well.

As for myself, recovery came laboured and tardy. As late as summer I could not hike the slopes at Therai, let alone sprint them. Soldiers say a man dies when more of them he loves reside beneath the earth than above it. That was my story. Yet breath is a resistless river, and dawn a reveille sore to ignore.

Alcibiades had drawn a berth for me before he left: imparting a chest with full kit, a *phoinikis* cloak, and ten minae in gold, an enormous sum, all I could have saved from Sicily had the expedition succeeded. I was lodged in the guest barracks at Limnai, a room of my own, and enjoyed the status of *xenos*, guest-friend, the same as an ambassador. Meals I might take at Endius's mess, the Amphyction. I could train in the gymnasia or hunt if invited. Sacrifices I might offer at any temple save those proscribed to non-Dorians. In addition I was granted privileges to both Endius's and his brother Sphrodias' estates. This meant I could help myself to horses or dogs, as Peers do, even claim a helot as my attendant. I might take water from any spring or public well. The only rights denied were those to bear arms or take fire. My benefactor's final instructions were to keep my mouth shut till he returned.

It was Alcibiades indeed who had compelled Lysander's intercession for me; this I learned from old friends, mates of the Upbringing with whom I now re-established acquaintance and through whose eyes and confidences I assimilated afresh the state of the Lacedaemonians.

The city had changed much in the years since I had seen it. I was invited on a hunt. The yeoman of snares was a Messenian serf they called Radish. As he and his seconds staked the trail, our host, a Peer named Amphiarius, called to him to speed it up. 'I'm going as fast as I can,' replied the fellow, without a breath of 'sir' or 'my lord'. A decade earlier such insolence would have left its utterer *ekpodon*, 'out from underfoot'. Now it was let go with a shrug and a jest.

The effect of the *neodamodeis*, the 'new citizens' who had earned their freedom serving under arms, and the *brasidioi*, who had done likewise beneath the great general Brasidas, was everywhere. No vassal, however lowly, regarded his abasement as irremediable. 'Hope is a dangerous drink,' my saviour Lysander had addressed the ephorate in a speech so notorious it had actually been written down and circulated, unheard-of in Lacedaemon. 'War has unstoppered the flask, and nothing may seal it again.'

Lysander and Endius had set themselves up as patrons of the unfranchised, or at least recognized the inevitability of integrating these into the polity. Neither was an altruist, and certainly no democrat, but like Alcibiades a realist. The pair had been reconciled to him, I was informed, or embraced the wisdom of mutual exploitation. It was Endius who had procured his friend's admission within Laconian borders and Lysander, as *polemarch*, who stood surety for him now.

'All great states,' the transcription of Lysander's address read, 'found themselves upon an outrage of nature, from which springs both their vigour and their vulnerability. Athens' derangement is democracy. To the good, this species of licence unleashes enterprise in the citizenry unknown in more closely governed states, and these energies may propel the nation to unprecedented prosperity. Its mischief is the envy it looses in the body politic. Democracy devours its young. The higher a man ascends, the more fervidly do his fellows work to procure his downfall, so that when an individual of legitimate greatness does arise, the state may make use of him a moment only before the mob lashes his limbs to the stake and fires the brands at his feet.

'As to Lacedaemon, our aberration is the servitude we have imposed upon our helots. Our bondsmen's sweat produces, we imagine, that might by which we knuckle them under. But who rules whom? We lie down upon a carpet of those who would eat us raw in the night and wonder that we toss in our slumber. And our army, for all its vaunted invincibility, ventures afield timorously and tardily, trepidant to turn its back on the kitchen cleavers it leaves behind at home. On campaign we face our pickets inboard, more in fear of those who serve us than of the enemy. Our unemancipated masses are the sword by which we thrive or perish, and we must seize this or be slain by it.'

Lysander wanted a navy. He wanted expansion and inclusion. But the ancient constitution would not permit purchase to enact reforms. Nothing could change. Nothing would. Yet it must, and these young men knew it.

Here was the further unsettling phenomenon – the political clubs or 'oil-and-dusters' as they were called after their spawning grounds, the wrestling schools. Such hives of ferment had never existed. Now they were rife and dominated all.

Part of the genius of the ancient laws, by which the Spartan polity had maintained herself intact over six centuries, was the leavening of youth with age throughout all institutions. There were veterans everywhere; no club or clique escaped supervision by its elders. The oil-and-dusters were tearing this apart. They were young men's clubs and they were impatient. They sided with the future, and their leaders were

Lysander and Endius, Chalcideus and Mindarus. Gylippus, too, was a member of 'the Ring', as the hero Brasidas before him. In short this camp comprised the most brilliant and ambitious Spartiates irrespective of fortune or birth.

Endius was far the wealthiest. His estate in the north valley produced such exceptional wine as to be called *meliades*, honey-sweet, and sufficient surplus of barley, figs, and cheeses that Endius could sponsor no fewer than four score defrocked Gentleman-Rankers whose fortunes had fallen so far as to no longer support their membership in a mess. Endius advanced their dues, restoring their station as Spartiates. In addition he stood guarantor for a number of *mothakes*, Peers' bastard sons, funding their tuition to the Upbringing. These stood now as loyal to Endius as to the commonwealth. Accounting the helots by whom he was considered patron, it was said that Endius commanded a private army second only to the king's.

Championing Alcibiades had elevated his influence further. Each success his friend produced overseas redounded to Endius' credit at home. His horse property at Kranioi was a hundred and ten acres; on this site he had set up a headquarters in exile for his companion. There, on the eve of Alcibiades' decampment to work his mischief in the East, I found myself called to attend upon him and a number of his comrades, Peers of Sparta and those Athenians who had been banished with him. A boys' equestrian competition was just finishing as I arrived; the companions, Alcibiades and Endius foremost, made a show of the awards presentation, to the delight of all. Sacrifice and feasting followed, at which no syllable of care was uttered. At last past midnight the party settled in Alcibiades' hermitage. I was summoned to the bench beside him.

'Tell me of Sicily,' he commanded.

The room was his office. Every surface sprawled with transcripts of Assembly proceedings, law-court records, and administrative warrants of Athens, Argos, Thebes, Corinth; the eye took in fleet documents, construction vouchers, Orders of Sail, court-martial transcripts, decoded *skytalai*, every species of military and political intelligence imaginable, while the floor-to-ceiling cubby holes superabounded with the personal correspondence which, by a glance at its addressees, flowed to every city of Greece, the islands of the Aegean, Ionia, and mainland Asia.

'You have heard it all already.'

'Not from you.'

I told him. It took all night. Endius and the others drifted in and out, or curled in corners, snoring. Alcibiades did not stir. He listened with unwavering attention, interrupting only to command further exposition when I appeared ripe to move on, to his mind prematurely, from a topic or event.

He wanted to hear it all and hear the worst. A name arising, he pressed for particulars of the man's fate. No detail was too inconsequential. A joke the fellow had made, his woman, the way he died. Alcibiades cared nothing for topography or strategy. The contour of Epipolae, deployment of the fleet, these he passed over. No emotion showed. Only his eyes altered during the sternest parts; they and the muscles beneath the jaw, which all soldiers have witnessed working involuntarily in a man under torture.

'Are you tired, Pommo? Shall we take up later?'

'No, let's finish it.'

'I'm bored to tears,' Endius broke in.

'Then go to bed.'

'How many times must we hear this?'

'Until I've heard it enough.'

Alcibiades made me recount instances of individual sacrifice or intrepidity, not only of Athenians but of allies and even slaves. At each his secretaries noted name, patronymic, and home district; I was queried again and again to be certain.

'Either stop pacing, Endius, or go to sleep!'

Near dawn I finished. Alcibiades had not budged all night. 'That's all of it,' I said, and rose.

I walked out to the paddock alone. The estate was just coming awake. I watched the grooms advancing to their chores, the ring being sprinkled and raked, riding mounts taken out to their exercise. I could feel Alcibiades emerge behind me, in shadow, yet turned neither to speak nor acknowledge his presence.

'I have never felt anyone,' he remarked, 'hate me as you.'

'Don't flatter yourself. Many hate you more.'

He chuckled. 'You came here to kill me. Why haven't you?'

'I don't know. Failure of nerve possibly.'

I turned back. I have never seen anything like the look that stood then upon his face.

He appeared as a man utterly alone beneath heaven. One who may confide in no-one, not even the gods, least of all the gods. His own death, one could see, accounted nothing to him. Rather he was held, like an agonist in a trial, by that perverse genius which licensed him to perceive with a clarity beyond all others of his generation the dictates of necessity and granted him in the service of this gift the powers of passion and persuasion to articulate its imperatives. Yet his own countrymen would not heed him to their weal, but only his enemies, and they, the more advantage they derived, hated him the more.

Every other captain of war held some rank or office, spoke or commanded in the name of some authority. Only Alcibiades stood alone, owning neither station nor commission nor even the garment on his back. Here he stood, stateless and accursed, outcast among his worst enemies, yet still he more than any, Spartan or Athenian, manipulated the course of the war by his will and enterprise alone.

Later among the pavilions of the Persian, I found myself seized on occasion by an unnameable panic. This was the discovery of myself at too distant a remove from all I knew. How might my benefactor have deflated such distress? What frontier could be more remote than that upon which he already stood? What greater crimes might he commit? How much more alone could he get? And yet he burned. Not, as his enemies professed, for wealth or glory. Not even, I believe, for re-demption. Rather he was locked in battle with fate or heaven, that ruinous genius which set at naught all his endeavours and brought to those to whom he wished only advantage destruction and evil.

'Will you ever absolve me for preserving your life, Pommo?'

My glance fell on the shoulder clasp which held his cloak. It was the wolf's tooth of Potidaea. I experienced that species of encounter called by the Spartans a 'revenant', when one feels that he relives an event, as it had happened before. 'Why did you save me,' I heard my voice ask, 'and not my brother?'

'Your brother would not have come.'

He uttered this absent malice, as an observation, plain and true.

'And why bring me here?'

'I needed one at my side who had passed through the same portal I had.'

This was the phrase, precisely, which his apparition had spoken in my fever dream. Did I inform him? Why?

'And what portal is that – to hell?'

He did not answer. Rather, with an expression at once rueful and ironic, reached to the fang clasp and detached it. It read: 'For Valour.' He pinned it to my cloak.

'There is another reason I had you reprieved.'

The sky had lightened beyond Mount Parnon. Towards this he turned. I waited.

'When I am slain, I want it to be by one who truly hates me.'

He turned back, meeting my glance with absolute directness. 'Do you reckon how long we have been fighting this war, Pommo? We were children when it began. Babes of that day are grown men now.'

He asked if I was sick of war.

'With all my heart.'

Across the fields one could see the helot groundsmen departing to work.

'Lysander will summon you soon. What he instructs, you must perform.'

'Why?'

'For my sake.'

I felt his hand upon my shoulder, sturdy as a friend's. 'Don't condemn yourself so cruelly, Pommo. Sometimes it's harder to live than to die. Besides, you had no choice. Heaven made you for this purpose, as me for mine.' He released my shoulder with a laugh. 'Haven't you learned yet, my friend? We are in this, you and I, to the bitter end.'

It was the afternoon of a brilliant day in the Spartan month of Karneius when Lysander sent for me. The city was decked for the Festival of Apollo; all training under arms had been suspended. I came to him beside the ball field they call the Islet. 'You have served as a marine,' Lysander plunged in, skipping the small talk. 'You will serve again.'

'You mean not as assassin?'

'Don't try to be clever with me, you whore's son. Were the casting vote mine you'd be rotting in the quarries still. And don't think your friend has sprung you out of affection. He'll make a run for it soon. That's why you're here; he thinks you'll stand by him.'

'Will I?'

'You look upon heaven at my pleasure only, and take no breath unlicensed by me.'

Lysander was not a physically powerful man. He stood only half a head taller than myself, possessed of shoulders of no greater breadth, yet I make no shame to say he scared me witless. 'If you're so certain he'll betray you,' I enquired, 'why not kill him now?'

'He's of use to me, as I him. For the present we are thick as brothers.'

At his side Strawberry motioned; we were being observed. Lysander led off, beneath the acacias that front the Running Course and the little bronze of the god Laughter. We passed down the Amyclaian Way to the Ribbon, that straight track where the girls train, barefoot in their singlets. 'Stop here.' Lysander indicated a site beneath thorn trees with grass for his horse to crop. 'You must understand what will happen.

'Sparta will ally herself with Persia. The price will be the Greek cities of Asia. We will sell them out to Darius in return for gold and a fleet to finish Athens. Alcibiades will produce this for us. No Spartan, myself and Endius included, could pull it off. That accomplished, Alcibiades will betray us. He must and will. He will move heaven and earth to get home and redeem himself in his countrymen's eyes.

'Now the tricky part. Three forces will seek his destruction. His countrymen who hate him, his enemies in the Spartan camp, and whatever far-seeing Persians recognize the double cross he has in store for them.'

Lysander turned towards me.

'You will keep him alive, Polemidas,' he said, employing my Laconian name. 'You and the marines I will hire and you will train.'

'You mean until you yourself require his slaughter.'

The Spartan drew up at this. It was clear that neither I nor my hollow righteousness arrested his interest. Yet the question itself bore consideration. For a moment his stony mien relented and, discovering in me not so much a fellow in whom he might confide as a proxy standing in for some wider constituency, met my eye an instant, with regret.

'It will not be myself who requires our friend's extinction, Polemidas, but that solitary god to which he himself proffers worship.'

'And what god is that?'

'Necessity.'

A T THIS POINT IN THE RECOUNTING OF POLEMIDES' TALE [GRAND-
father interjected], *a fortuitous turn transpired.* My detectives, Myron
and Lado, *appeared at my study one evening, beside themselves.*

'Sir, we have found her! The woman!'

What woman?

'Eunice! The woman of your client, the assassin.'

*This was indeed news, as I had from Polemides believed her dead.* She is
here, Myron insisted, *with her children, and has agreed – for a sum – to
speak.*

*An interview was arranged and conducted at my town house in the
Piraeus. Little came of it, however, beyond the discovery, achieved serendipitously when she misspoke herself, that she, Eunice, knew and was known by
that Colophon the son of Hestiodorus who had brought the charges of murder
against Polemides.* More, Eunice confirmed, *she had herself witnessed the
killing, which took place at a* kapeleion, *a rough tavern, at Samos during the
twenty-third year of the war.* Though I pressed vigorously, *she would speak no
more on either subject and in fact made off in such haste as not even to collect
her fee. Nor had she, or an agent, returned to claim it.*

*Of this I informed Polemides at our interview next day at the prison. He
reacted without surprise to this report of the presence in Athens of the mother
of his children.* 'Nothing about her surprises me.' Did he wish to see his son
and daughter? Perhaps I could prevail upon Eunice, *compensate her if*

necessary, to effect a reunion. The prisoner's response abashed me. 'Did you actually see the children? Did she state categorically that she had them?' When I replied in the negative, he grunted and broke the matter off. The best I could deduce, more from the man's evasions than his attestations, was that boy and girl had last been in his custody, flown from their mother's. This had been within the year apparently, at Acharnae, on Polemides' family estate, Road's Turn. I pressed the query. If indeed I could locate the children, would their appearance be welcome?

'Let them not see me in this place.'

There was no window in the cell but an opening in the roof through which a rectangle of sunlight fell upon the northern wall. Polemides turned away to this spot, which he could reach shackled as he was, then faced back towards me. At once I recalled seeing him, years past. In much the same posture, with the identical expression, he had stood in armour in the bows of a longboat as its bumpers touched at Samos and he stepped off onto the dock, which that forenoon teemed with sailors and soldiers in the thousands, seething with anticipation. Three marines followed Polemides, one fore and two aft. Shielded by these advanced onto the quay Alcibiades. 'You were his body-guard, Polemides,' I remarked this unexpected recall. 'I remember you. On the quay at Samos, the day he came back.'

The prisoner did not react, held, I felt, by reflection upon his children, now nearly grown no doubt, and whatever disquietude preoccupied him on their account. I, however, struck by this recollected vision, felt myself piped back to that site and that forenoon.

The fleet lay at Samos then. The war was in its twenty-first year. The time was seven, perhaps eight months subsequent to the conversations in Sparta which our narrator had last recounted.

Let me recite briefly events in the interval.

Alcibiades, as our client related, had indeed sailed from Lacedaemon to Ionia, he and the Spartan Chalcideus, now fleet admiral of the Peloponnesian navy. This force was then a ragtag regatta of outdated triremes and pentecounters contributed by Sparta's allies, primarily Corinth, Elis and Zacynthus, with a few galleys built at Gythieum and Epidauris Limera and crewed by volunteers, mostly fishermen and those wishing to avoid the call-up. There was not a Peer in the lot.

None the less within two months Alcibiades and Chalcideus brought into revolt against Athens not only Chios, with her squadrons of warships (who herself brought over Anaia, Lebedos and Aerae), but Erythrae, Miletus, Lesbos, Teos and Clazomenae as well as Ephesus, with her great harbour, later Lysander's bastion. By these coups Alcibiades had deprived Athens of a third of the tribute of her empire, critically needed in the wake of Syracuse. Worse, these strongholds, now in enemy hands, threatened the grain routes from the Pontus, without whose produce Athens could not survive.

If these colours were not grim enough, reports now came that Alcibiades had made contact with the Persian governor Tissaphernes and brought him under his spell. Tissaphernes was satrap of Lydia and Caria under Darius the King. In addition to limitless treasure, he commanded the war fleet of Phoenicia, two hundred and thirty triremes (when Athens could man little above a hundred) crewed by Sidonians and Tyrians, the finest sailors of the East. Should Alcibiades incite his patron to bring these up on the Spartan side, the sequence of Athens' doom would be ordained.

The lone report which stirred promise involved Alcibiades as well. This was the gossip that he had seduced and impregnated the lady Timaea, wife of the Spartan king, Agis. Nor did this gentlewoman, reports testified, exert care to conceal the affair. While in public she called the babe in her womb Leotychidas, in private she named him Alcibiades.

She was out of her head in love with the man.

Why did this inspirit us at home? Because it held out hope that Alcibiades could not keep from his old tricks and would fall inevitably by his own hand, beneath the rage of Agis and the party of hard-line Spartans.

This of course is exactly what happened. Within five months he had added sentence of death, pronounced from Sparta, to that same distinction already worn of Athens.

This time he fled to Persia, the court of Tissaphernes at Sardis, where he again reconstituted himself, no longer in the coarsecloth cloak of Lacedaemon but the purple robes of a dandy of the court. Tissaphernes had fallen so beneath his bewitchment, it was told, that he made Alcibiades his tutor in all things and even named his favourite paradise (as the Persians call their deer parks) in his honour, calling it Alkibideion.

At home, Athens lay bankrupt and bereft. All of able body had been called up for the fleet. Only elders and ephebes remained to man the walls. That masculine eros which is the pith and marrow of a nation stood absent. The streets ached for it. The beds of wives lay barren of it.

The polity possessed no champion. Its depleted soil produced only shoots of evil, stunted and malformed. Their posturings upon the political stage disclosed what hollow caricatures they were and made the people lament the more of their bereavement, shorn by plague and war of the bloom of two generations. Reared in such impoverishment, the young grew wild, absent respect for law or decency.

Civility had fled. Age ducked its duties; youth dodged the call-up. Of theatre, the comic poets displayed the most vitality, and that only to excoriate those buffoons who dared set themselves up as statesmen. The few of quality who might have served well held back, abandoning the field to those whose greed for prominence was exceeded only by their want of scruple in its pursuit.

Now the people remembered Alcibiades and longed for him.

In memory they revisited the stages of the war, descrying in each his vision and vigour. As a youth none surpassed him in valour. Come to command, he had harried the foe as no other, compelling them to set their very survival upon one day's battle at Mantinea. His enterprise alone had called into being the greatest armada in history. Him in command, we would not have lost in Sicily. In command now, we wouldn't be losing in the East. Even the evils he had brought upon the state by his counsel to her foes were cited not as criminal or treasonous, but as evidence of his generalship and audacity, which capacities the city needed desperately and could discover nowhere. Further citation sprang from the roster of the fleet, whose most able commanders – Thrasybulus, Theramenes, Conon and Thrasyllus – were either intimates of Alcibiades or officers he had sponsored from their debut. Impute what vice you may to his conduct or motive, the demos declared, in statesman's terms he appeared a titan among midgets. In the barbers' shops and wrestling schools, the commons recalled that Alcibiades had not taken up with the enemy of his own. We ourselves had driven him to it! In our folly we had franchised the knaves and conspirators, jealous of Alcibiades' gifts, to deprive the state of the champion she needed most!

My wife and I attended a comedy by Eupolis in which appeared a player garbed in extravagant style and meant to represent Alcibiades. The playwright had intended to hold this peacock up to ridicule; instead the audience erupted, chanting his name. On the street the actor was mobbed and borne home in triumph.

On walls throughout the city appeared in scrawl, Anakaleson: 'Bring him home.'

It took another year, my grandson, but at last he was recalled, by the men of the Samos fleet, if not yet by the Assembly of Athens – promising Tissaphernes' gold and alliance with Persia.

This was the moment I recollected to Polemides, when the longboat's bumpers touched the timbers of the quay at Samos and, compassed by twenty thousand sailors, soldiers, and marines of Athens, Alcibiades made his way to that elevated platform called the Load-out, where the drivers back their wagons in to receive the sardiners' catch, and around which now congregated the throngs of the armoured divisions and ships' companies, mounting every rooftop and pergola, even the masts of the ships, their spars and warpeaks, beneath the Hill of the Dolphins, to await with hope and trepidation what the repatriated renegade would say.

# TWENTY-EIGHT
# THE HILL OF
# THE DOLPHINS

TWICE HE BEGAN AND TWICE HIS VOICE MISCARRIED, SO OVERCOME was he by the sight which now enlarged before him. When he failed a third time, a cry burst from those pressed in ranks to the immediate fore. 'Again! Again!' men called, this summons reinforced at once by the thousands packing the bowl, the roar of men approving what they see. When the tumult had subsided, Alcibiades recommenced, so softly at first that the heralds, stationed at intervals to relay his words to those higher on the slope, must turn laterally and address their compatriots beside and even below.

'I am not . . .' Alcibiades began, and, when his voice once more faltered, the heralds picked up that portion and relayed it.

'I am not . . .'

'. . . not the man I was . . .'

'. . . not the man I was . . .'

'. . . moments ago, mounting this platform.'

Again the heralds flung the phrase up the amphitheatre. At last Alcibiades found his voice and, gesturing his seconds to mount farther, resumed.

'I had meant to cast myself in the role of saviour. To present myself before you as one who brings with him, for your deliverance, alliance with that nation whose treasure and naval might will bring the victory which, unaided, you have thus far been unable to achieve. I had planned to address you as a commander and to wring from you a pledge of fidelity for the effort we must *now make. But the sight of you . . .' Again his voice failed. '. . . the sight of you, my countrymen, breaks my heart. I am struck through with shame. It is not you who must pledge, but I. Not you who must serve, but I. That Athens which exiled me . . .'*

*Once more he must re-collect himself, a hand upon the platform stanchion, to recapture his self-command.*

*'That Athens which exiled me . . . that Athens I no longer recall. You are my Athens. You and this.' He gestured to the fleet and the sea and sky. 'To you and to this I pledge my allegiance.'*

*A cheer that was half sob and half cry of approbation ascended from the centred ranks to the outer peripheries. Intended or not, Alcibiades had set in words that grief and affliction that the men, too, felt for their nation, which to them as to their recalled leader seemed remote as Oceanus and dissevered not just from these, her sons, but from her own misplaced and misremembered soul.*

*'If I have offended the gods, and I have, before you I entreat now their pardon. By their clemency, and to you who have honoured me with your faith, I vow that no constraint of heaven or earth, nor the armies of hell itself, will stay me from spending for you and for our country all I possess. My blood, my life, all that I am and own, I pledge to you.'*

*He stepped back and receded into the press of officers upon the platform.*

*The amphitheatre rang with fire and approbation.*

*Thrasybulus now spoke, followed by the generals Diomedon and Leon. Individuals among the nautai and infantry addressed the assembly as well. The blood of all was still up from the coup and countercoup which had racked Samos itself just days past, in mirrored requital of the overthrows of state at home. At Athens, all knew, the democracy had been deposed. Acts of terror and assassination had cowed the demos, and that government styling itself the Four Hundred stood in command of the Assembly and the people, having proscribed from political participation all but themselves. Rumours of outrages inflamed the fleet, of violations inflicted upon free citizens, lawless arrests and executions, properties confiscated, the constitution of Cleisthenes and Solon overturned. The men on Samos feared for their families at home and for the nation herself which these tyrants, fresh reports testified, plotted to sell out to the foe to drive a deal to save their own skins.*

*Now in the flush of Alcibiades' reaccession, the men cried for action and blood. Sail on Athens! Butcher the autocrats! Restore the democracy!*

Men of the infantry began to pound their thighs and stamp their soles; sailors on the ships beat their decks and timbers; on the quays the marines' stomping feet made the harbour resound; and even the boys and women set up such a racket of yip-yipping ululation that none could be heard who sought to quell them. Two of the taxiarchs arose; the men cried them down. Diomedon boomed in his great voice and even Thrasybulus, though the men, who loved him, let him speak, could not stanch their frenzy. Infantrymen rose and advanced upon the stacked arms. A press swelled towards the ships, as if on the instant of embarkation. As one they clamoured for Alcibiades. Lead us! Take us home!

The folly of this course, self-apparent to the cooler heads of command, yet held such passionate appeal for the men that no commander could dissuade them or dared try. Now Alcibiades must confront this derangement, not out of a base of the men's trust earned over time, of shared victories and attained respect, but on the instant and on his own.

'If we sail, men, we will easily overturn our enemies at home and establish a government obedient to our whims and gratifying to our vanity.'

The men cheered and rallied. He signed for silence and bade them ring him in.

'But what mischief will we have left behind here in the Aegean? Let us consider this, brothers, and if we find the course you champion wise, not another hour shall expire before we sail, you and I, to depose the usurpers.'

More salutes and cries of acclamation.

Alcibiades called the Assembly to order. This was the phrase he used, and it had the effect intended. He commanded each individual to impose upon his ungoverned heart that self-dominion which differentiates free men from slaves and recall himself to what he was – a man of reason, capable of reflection and deliberation. Now, he directed, let us as an exercise place ourselves in the position of our enemies.

'Imagine we are Mindarus, Spartan commander at Miletus, learning of our resolve to sail for home. Recall, friends, that spies among us will report to him before nightfall all we debate here this day . . .'

Coolly and rationally Alcibiades instructed the men on those opportunities the fleet's withdrawal would present to the foe and how the enemy must and would pounce upon them. He addressed his hearers not as a general his troops, but as an officer in counsel with brother officers or a statesman in discourse before the ekklesia.

The Aegean undefended, the Spartans will seize the Hellespont, and with that cut off all grain for us and for Athens. The enemy holds Lampsacus and Cyzicus. Byzantium has revolted to him. He will overthrow Ionia and seize every strategic choke point on the straits. We must turn about from home at once, merely to preserve from starvation the very prize we have just won. And what will await us here on our return? Not an enemy as at present, on the sea where we hold advantage, but dug in on land, from which fortifications we must then dislodge him. He enquired of the men if they were ready to fight Spartans on land, on their own terms. And what base will we employ? The first place the enemy will seize will be Samos, the very stones and timbers upon which we now stand.

Now he presented the most ruinous consequence of withdrawal: its effect upon the Persian. How will he, our benefactor upon whom all depends, respond to this unadvertised decampment? Will he perceive us as reliable allies in whom he may place trust? Tissaphernes will drop us, as an eagle an asp, and re-ally himself with Sparta. He must, if only from fear of their new power, no longer checked by us, that they may turn upon and overrun him.

'Remember this, brothers. Athens is ours any time we choose to take her. But Athens is not her bricks and stones, or even the land itself. We are Athens. This is Athens. The enemy lies there,' he proclaimed, gesturing to the east and south, the occupied cities of Ionia and the Lacedaemonian bastion at Miletus. 'I came to fight Spartans and Peloponnesians, not my own country-men. And by the gods, I will make you fight them too!'

A murmur of self-chastisement swept the host, who at last perceived not only their own folly, in contrast to the sense of their new commander, but his dexterity in deflecting them from this course of calamity. Already in the first hour of his recall he had preserved the state. More, the men now reckoned, he had displayed such iron temerity to face them down, single-handed, as no other would or could. One felt a sea change as the men came to themselves at last, perceiving the sureness of their principal's hand and the slenderness of the margin by which he had steered them from ruin.

'But if your hearts remain set on this course, brothers, sail for home now. But look first there, to that arm of the breakwater the Samians call the Hook. For I will station my ship at its shoulder, and this I swear by Nike and Athena Protectress, that I will strike as thunder the first vessel that seeks to pass me outbound, and the next and the next after that, until you slay me upon the site. He will sail for Athens, he that will, over my cold corpse.'

Such a shout greeted this as eclipsed even the tumult that had preceded it. At once Thrasybulus stepped to the fore, dismissing the assembly, ordering the men to disperse to their duties and all trierarchs and squadron commanders to report to fleet command.

This headquarters was situated in what had been the old Customs House, which filled now with the swarming officers, above four hundred counting ship's masters, infantry commanders, and captains of marines. The overflow including Thrasybulus, Thrasyllus, Alcibiades, and the taxiarchs settled after some confusion in the hall adjacent, employed formerly for storage of contraband and now serving as collection site for spare masts and sail, hull girdles and sundry hanging and wooden gear of the fleet. A number of commanders spoke, addressing the requirements of the hour. Protomachus set as paramount the need for cash; the men must be paid; they are demoralized and have been for months. Lysias professed the imperative for further training; Erasinides spoke of the ships and their seaworthiness. Others clamoured to follow; it seemed the deficiencies of vessels and men must mount to infinity, each more pressing than the next. Alcibiades shifted upon his feet, a move so subtle as barely to merit notice. At once all hubbub stilled. The officers, gone silent as one, turned unprompted towards him who, though technically holding a third only of the tripartite command, the congress now acknowledged by its deferral as supreme commander.

'I approve all you say, gentlemen. The fleet's needs are many and urgent. One, however, must take precedence. This item the men need before all, and we must get it for them without fail and without delay.'

Alcibiades drew up, as a poet or actor upon the stage, drawing by his silence his hearers more raptly to attend.

'We must get the men a victory.'

# BOOK SIX

# VICTORY
# AT SEA

# TWENTY-NINE
# THE INTERSECTION OF NECESSITY AND FREE WILL

Sidescreens up, it is no easy matter to sight over the prow of a hurtling man-of-war. Spray blasts over the forepeak; the catheads sling seas with each belly and bounce; the craft's gunwales ride so tight to the waterline, her trim so precarious, that the marine topside who rises even to move half a yard is pelted with oaths, as his displaced weight, even for that reckless instant, destabilizes the entire ship. The oarsmen's backs are to the target; they can't see either. The top-bankers' eyes dart to the marines on deck, athwartships through the step-down, to guess at impact.

At Cyzicus Alcibiades' flagship was *Antiope*, taken over after *Resolute* went down off Teos. The top-bank oarsman beside me was an Acharnian called Charcoal, whom I knew from a chorus of the Lenaea when we were boys. A renowned gourmand, this fellow; he was instructing me on eels, the proper way to prepare them for the grill. The ship hurtled towards that stretch of shore called the Plantations, upon which two score Spartan triremes had been driven in flight, their seamen and marines, above eight thousand, hastening to form the vessels into a rampart, as *Antiope* and two squadrons of sixteen bore down upon them. Such a delicacy must not be profaned with excess spice and seasoning, Charcoal proclaimed as he heaved on the beat; a simple basil and oil marinade will reveal the flesh's intrinsic sweetness. That was the word he used: intrinsic. We were among the breakers now. Marines braced on their knees topside, slinging the salt-sticky javelins raked from the surface following the sea fight. 'I'll write it down for you,' Charcoal bawled, meaning the grilling instructions, when a Magnesian ironhead took him square at the base of the ear, driving through and out the sheath of the neck. His oar fell and so did he.

There was a seawall shielding the planters' estates, and from the top of this the defenders unleashed a fire of ungodly concentration as the ships drove onto the muck flat beneath. The foe hurled stones and javelins and the wicked double-edged darts the Boeotians call 'nut-cutters' and the Spartans 'hatpins'. I felt two rake the backs of my thighs and was seized with fury, diced by these utensils. A fist hauled me to my feet. 'What are you doing – rat-holing?'

It was Alcibiades.

He rushed forward onto the prow, flanked by the others of our party, Timarchus, Macon and Xenocles, whose office it was with me to protect him. Marines in armour rode both catheads and the wales at the cut-water, even the rams themselves. The trumpet blared 'Back water!'; oarsmen set into the straps of their footboards and heaved forward on the beat. Marines were pouring over the prow and both gunwales. Alcibiades had sprung to the strand, shouting for grapnels.

The Lacedaemonians were above us, supported by the Persian Pharnabazus' infantry and mobs of Magnesian mercenaries, whom one recognizes by their beards, jet as ink, which they wear parted and netted. Furious fire poured from the foe. We wore only felt caps; you had to, or you couldn't pick out the flung ash as it shrieked towards your man, to deflect it. The Athenians foundered, fighting uphill in the sand. Now the Spartans made their rush. The lines crashed along the length of the strand. I heard Macon at my shoulder screaming profanity. Where was Alcibiades?

He had burst through on his own. We could see him, churning up-slope into the no-man's-land between the Spartan rush and their beached ships. One cannot know the meaning of rage until one has served to protect such a man from his own fire for victory. Alcibiades wore no helmet and bore only his shield and a marine axe. He reached the first ship and sank a grapnel. Two of the foe fought to rip it free; he stove in the first's skull with his shield, hamstrung the second with his axe. He hammered the iron into the timbers of the enemy prow. We of the lifeguard must now emulate him. There is a terrible skill to defending the flung javelin, particularly when one must set one's own flesh as shield before another. I have never cursed any as our commander; I spat at him and slung stones; so did the others. He never saw a thing.

Three and a half years later, before Byzantium, I attended a night-long drinking bout. Someone had put the query 'How does one lead free men?' 'By being better than they,' Alcibiades responded at once.

The symposiasts laughed at this, even Thrasybulus and Theramenes, our generals.

'By being better,' Alcibiades continued, 'and thus commanding their emulation.' He was drunk, but on him it accounted nothing, save to liberate those holdings nearest to his heart. 'When I was not yet twenty, I served in the infantry. Among my mates was Socrates the son of Sophroniscus. In a fight the enemy had routed us and were swarming upon our position. I was terrified and loading up to flee. Yet when I beheld him, my friend with grey in his beard, plant his feet on the earth and seat his shoulder within the great bowl of his shield, a species of eros, life-will, arose within me like a tide. I discovered myself compelled, absent all prudence, to stand beside him.

'A commander's role is to model arete, excellence, before his men. One need not thrash them to greatness; only hold it out before them. They will be compelled by their own nature to emulate it.'

Along the length of the strand Athenians bore cable and iron upon the foe. Alcibiades dragged the first ship off, and another and another. Mindarus's troops held as only the Spartan-commanded can, in the face of Athenian reinforcements under Theramenes and more, including cavalry, driven on by Thrasybulus, the Brick. Alcibiades fell three times, seeking the Spartan commander. At last Mindarus's own wounds took him down. When the enemy broke and fled, Alcibiades ravened upon their backs and every other followed, and when he dropped they dashed to his side and lifted him, in terror that some fatal dart had found their champion. But it was exhaustion only. And I, too, who had so few seasons past pledged to bear hell's bane to this man, could no longer recall his crimes, even my own brother's murder. All were eclipsed in that flame which he bore for our country and by which he conducted her to triumph.

I cite a moment from the sea fight earlier that day, not to panegyrize him, for all testimony is superfluous in that cause, but as exemplar of this beast, this form of courage he evinced which one glimpses in a lifetime as frequently as a griffin or a centaur.

The sea trap had been sprung: Alcibiades' forty triremes emerging as he had planned out of the squall line had lured the enemy's sixty to pursue, thinking ours the whole of the Athenian force. These crews of Athens, the Samos fleet, were so good that when they fled, or even pretended, they maintained such order that the helmsmen must cry across to row more sloppily and make better feint of terror. Antiochus was Alcibiades' helmsman. At his signal the lines came-about employing the Samian *anastrophe*, or 'countermarch', where the ships do not put about simultaneously, making rearmost foremost, but wheel in sequence of line-ahead, as chariots round the turning post. Alcibiades ordered this, the more demanding manoeuvre, to unnerve the enemy, to let him know he had been suckered and must pay.

Now Thrasybulus's triples fell on the Spartans from astern. From concealment behind the promontory they emerged in four columns of twelve, pulling, as the shanty goes, with every shaft including the skipper's wooden dick. They cut Mindarus off from the harbour. From the shoulder of the squall Theramenes' thirty-six materialized, blocking all flight to the north. Alcibiades was shouting for Mindarus's ensign and vowing a talent to the lookout who found it for him.

The Spartans fled for the shore two thousand yards distant. Alcibiades' division pursued from the flank, picking a line to overhaul the foremost vessel. This was a squadron commander's and she, sighting *Antiope*'s admiral's ensign, made to make it a fight. At two hundred yards the foe wheeled to port, executed a cutback around two of her own ships whose oars had fouled, and came back at us. Antiochus slipped her rush, passing with such swiftness across her bows that her helm, hard over seeking to strike, put her onto her sisters, each furiously backing water to clear. Antiochus holed two almost at leisure, but striking the third amidships as she fled, *Antiope*'s ram became embedded; the momentum of the fleeing craft levered us against her flank-to-flank, snapping oars like kindling. As the ships crunched together, Spartan marines let fly with everything they had. Our men plunged for cover as the fusillade swept *Antiope*'s deck. I heard a bellow of rage and glanced up. Alone and exposed stood Alcibiades amid the storm of steel, scouring the sea for his rival in flight. 'Mindarus!' he cried. 'Mindarus!'

There is a causeway on the Macestos plain, just a farm dike, to which the Spartans had fled from the rout on the strand. There in the dusk their infantry were making a stand of spectacular stubbornness, supported by Pharnabazus' satrapal guard, which had dashed up from Dascylium. The clash funnelled to a neck a wagon-width wide, while round this the fight slogged on in the muck, flax fields which the foe had flooded to impede the Athenian advance. Horses of both sides sank to their barrels; cavalrymen slugged it out on mounts dying and already dead, which beasts remained upright, marooned in the mire.

Alcibiades galloped upon this impasse, fresh from the shore. Ahead squatted the bottleneck. Three squadrons of our cavalry and above a thousand infantry hung up where embankments conjoined. A furlong ahead could be seen enemy horse advancing, with clouds of light troops and militia, farmers wielding pitchforks and muckrakes, driven by their masters' whips. If we couldn't break through we'd be overrun. You could get round by dikes east and west but there was no time, and if even a dozen of the foe beat the party to a juncture, there would be no breaking through.

Alcibiades rode a mare named Mustard, which had been Agasicles', Thrasybulus's adjutant, who had been slain by the ships. A horse, un-coerced by its rider, knows how to make its way through mire. Alcibiades slung the beast's bridle and, taking about forty cavalry and two hundred infantry, set off through the slough. Mustard cut a thousand yards off the go-round, mounting muck-slathered up a dikeway in the foe's rear. From there Alcibiades led the assault on the Spartan infantry, slaying their commander, Amompharetus the son of Polydamos, a knight and victor at Nemea. If you go even now to the Eurysacium at Athens you will see, on the left as you enter, a matchless bronze of a warhorse, no taller than a man's hand, with this dedication:

*I led, Victory followed.*

That afternoon Mindarus was slain, the Spartans' peerless general. Of the foe's total ninety ships, fifty-eight were sunk and twenty-nine captured. His brigades of Lacedaemon and the Peloponnese were routed on the plain of the Macestos by Thrasybulus and Alcibiades, along with the mercenaries and Persian cavalry supporting them. Next night found Alcibiades master of Cyzicus, calling in the carters to load up contributions in cash, and within twenty days before Perinthus and Selymbria as well, raising more money, and fortifying Chrysopolis to bind the straits and exact a tenth from all passing, to fund the fleet. This despatch, intercepted, from the remnant Spartans to their home:

*Ships sunk, Mindarus slain, men starving. We know not what to do.*

I need not recite for you, Jason, the litany of Alcibiades' victories. You were there. You won your prize of valour at Abydos and earned it too. Did you know I forwarded the text of your commendation? That was one of my duties in those days. I see you flush; I'll embarrass you no further, though I recall the citation, word for word.

To the young soldiers and sailors of the fleet, they for whom these victories under Thrasybulus and Alcibiades were all they had known, such bounty seemed no more than the merited produce of their pre-eminence, their birthright as Athenians. But for those of our generation, who had cut our teeth on plague and calamity, the experience of such ascendancy, each conquest succeeding so swiftly upon its predecessor, arose as if within a dream. No *pharmakon* like victory, the proverb says. And though we who bore the scars of Syracuse could not bring ourselves to trust them at first, when the wins kept coming, Bitch's Tomb, Abydos, Methymna, Fool's Cap Bay, Clazomenae, the Hollows, Chios and Nine-Mile Cove, then second Chios and Erythrae, both on the same day, at last we, too, began to believe, as the youths from the start, that this run was neither fluke nor fortune but that at last conjoined upon one field Athens possessed such ships, crews, and commanders as to render her, barring the sons of Earth themselves ascending from Tartarus, invincible.

History was being made. A blind man could see it. Honouring Lion's wish of the quarries, I set about enlarging his chronicle, or at least preserving within my sea chest such documents as I imagined one day in retirement editing and publishing in my brother's name. I went so far as to record notes and even sketch terrain. Only later did I grasp that a recounting of actions or tactics was not what interested me, or anyone.

What held us all was not what our commander did, but how he did it. It was clear that he manipulated some force to which others commanded no access. Though he possessed on occasion superiority of might, he never needed it to best the foe. He was always clement to the vanquished, nor was it in him to pursue vengeance against those who had worked him harm. He acted thus, not out of sentiment or altruism, but because he reckoned such actions ignoble and inelegant. Here, a communication to Tissaphernes, whom he called friend despite the notorious arrest at Sardis and after the Persian had bid ten thousand darics for his head.

> . . . it is not possession of force which produces victory, but its apparition. A commander of ability manipulates not armies but perceptions.

From the succeeding paragraph:

> . . . the function of disciplined movement in battle is to produce in the mind of the friend the conviction that he cannot lose and the mind of the foe that he cannot win. Order is indispensable for these considerations beyond all others.

Alcibiades was an abominable speller. When he worked late, he got worse and would shake awake anyone to hand. 'Brick, sit up. How do you spell *epiteichismos?*' His bane was inversion of letters; his secretaries teased that he even wrote with a lisp. Thus many half-composed missives found their way to trash and from there to my chest.

In this note, addressed to his great enemy Anytus at Athens, but intended for circulation among the political clubs beneath his sway, Alcibiades seeks to allay the fears of those who had brought the indictments which led to his exile – fears, that is, that he, returning at the head of an all-conquering fleet, would exact vengeance upon them.

> . . . my enemies accuse me of seeking to impose my will upon events, either for glory or fortune or, those who admit me a patriot, for the weal

*of my country. This is erroneous. I do not believe in personal will, and haven't since I was a boy. What I have tried to do is to follow the dictates of Necessity. This is the solitary god I revere and in my opinion the only god that exists. Man's predicament is that he dwells at the intersection of Necessity and free will. What distinguishes statesmen, as Themistocles and Pericles, is their gift to perceive Necessity's dictates in advance of others – as Themistocles saw that Athens must become a sea power and Pericles that naval supremacy prefigures empire. That course of individual or nation aligned with Necessity must prove irresistible. The trick is that each moment contains three or four necessities. Necessity moreover is like a board game. As one option closes, a new necessity obtains. What has disfigured my career is that I have perceived Necessity but been unable to persuade my countrymen to act upon its dictates. My hope with you now, sir, is that we may act as mature men of politics . . .*

From Thrasybulus to his fellow general Theramenes, the latter impatient at his star's overshadowing beside the sun of Alcibiades.

*. . . I have found it of great utility to regard him less as a man and more a force of nature. My concern alone is for Athens. I brought him back from exile, and placed my neck on the block thereby, the way one confronting an insuperable enemy at sea calls down a great storm, or facing the foe on land enlists a mighty earthquake.*

From the same letter:

*. . . remember, my friend, that Alcibiades himself does not comprehend his gift and is ruled by it as much as ruling. His immodesty, however galling you may find it, is to him objectivity. He is superior. Why conceal it? To a mind such as his this course would be hypocrisy, and he is nothing if not the most frank of men.*

Another:

*. . . though his enemies style him a great double-crosser, in fact he is incapable of duplicity, and of all he has ever done, he has warned foe and friend long in advance.*

The men loved Thrasybulus and feared and respected Theramenes, but Alcibiades they clasped to their hearts with a fierce solicitousness, as a magical child. Had he eaten? Had he slept? Fifty times a day sailors and marines approached me to enquire of their general's well-being, as if he were a sorcerer's lamp whose flame they feared would by heaven's jealousy be snuffed. The security party's charge now turned upon its head, shielding our commander no longer from harm but the excessive affection of his own men and the relentless importunities of those trucklers and petition-pleaders who dogged his circuit day and night.

Then there were the women. They descended in clouds, not alone *hetairai*, courtesans, and *pornai*, common whores, but free women, maids and widows, sisters presented by their own brothers. More than once I must chase a lad pimping his mother. Her response? 'How 'bout you, then, mate?' Buck lieutenants screwed themselves witless, just on their commander's castoffs.

As for Alcibiades himself, the allure of the debauch had abated. He didn't need fornication; he had victory. He had changed. A becoming modesty settled about his shoulders like the plain marine's cloak he wore, albeit clasped at the throat with a brooch of gold. He had become a new Alcibiades and he liked it. I never saw a man so revel in the triumphs of his comrades, absent envy, even and especially those who might be called his rivals, Thrasybulus and Theramenes. When a villa was vacated for him on Pennon Point at Sestos, he declined, not wishing to displace its occupants, and continued to bunk in the tent beside his ship, refusing even a floor till the carpenters framed it on their own while he was absent with the fleet. He became if not cheap, then frugal. Every spit went for the men, and every moment.

Correspondence. He posted a hundred letters a day. Entire watches were consumed with this, amid rotating shifts of secretaries, often through night and morn and into the next night. This was the grind of coalition-building, the day-by-day extension of influence and persuasion. 'How can you stand this?' I asked him once. 'Stand what?' he replied. He loved it. To him these letters were not chores but men; it was a symphony to him and at last he held the conductor's stand.

There were other missives, the main in truth, whose lines he dictated late or scrawled in his own hand. These were the widow letters, the commendations of the maimed and fallen – ten, twenty, thirty a day. He directed these personally to the recipient himself if he was still alive, but often, as well, he had the rolls despatched to father or mother or wife without the honoured man's knowledge. Can you imagine, Jason, the pride and relief such communications brought to those at home sick with fear for husbands and sons? I have met no few in subsequent seasons; they hold these artefacts yet in vaults, extracted with reverence, to be read aloud to children and grandchildren of the valour of their fathers.

When he wished to honour a man of the fleet, he despatched meat or wine with his compliments to that officer's mess. He distinguished others by inclusion at his table. But to those he wished most to esteem, he sent not boons but trials. He singled them out for the most perilous duties, for in these, he said, he sent out lieutenants and got back captains. 'Nothing he does,' as Endius had remarked, 'is absent politics.'

He led not by edict but example. Rather than direct the commanders to intensify their training, he took his own wing to sea and commenced. Those drills he wished the fleet to master, his own squadrons practised first. That mark he meant them to exceed, he drove his own ships to surpass. He did not command the fleet to embark before dawn; the captains simply arose to discover his ships gone, already at their exercise.

To his friend Adeimantus, a squadron commander:

*. . . if force must be employed with a subordinate, take care that it be minimal. If I command you, 'Pick up that bowl,' and set a swordpoint to your back, you will obey but no part will own the action. You will exculpate yourself, accounting, 'He made me do it, I had no choice.' But if I only suggest and you comply, then you must own your compliance and, owning it, stand by it.*

Later, when he took Byzantium, the tenor of the siege was, if such a word may be applied, cheerful. The men set to with a will, absent malingering and disgruntlement, and even the foe, in capitulation, appeared not downcast but sanguine, optimistic of the future.

*The proper manner of investing a city is to present to the foe a choice of alternatives so constellated as to compel him to elect surrender or alliance, not as imposed upon him by force, but of his own will. A decision made in this way may not be disowned later, when we need our new ally to stand by us in future peril.*

In the planning before Cyzicus, when Theramenes had presented to the commanders the brilliant scheme of bait-and-wheel, so that in his scenario the foe was cut off on all sides, Alcibiades approved it with this alteration: the leaving to the enemy of an avenue of egress. 'Not that he get away, but that he know he played the coward. And we not only destroy his forces on that day but break his spirit to face us again.'

In like manner he applied discipline to the fleet. He never ordered a man beaten but only banished from his mates' company. Such correction, he believed, spared the offender's spirit while spurring him to return with renewed vigour and will. If a man committed the same offence twice, he was exiled to the rear with the baggage and the cowards. By this measure and others Alcibiades made such posts pillories of shame.

I had participated in several actions with the younger Pericles, a squadron commander then and already pre-eminent among the corps. He was thrallbound by his commander. 'It's mediocrity, do you see, Pommo? Alcibiades has debarred it altogether. One would rather die than fall short of the mark. Remember the night we made a hash of the soundings off Elaeus? I was making my report, trying to put the best face on it. He didn't utter a syllable. Just gave me a look. By the gods, I would sooner be flogged through the fleet than stand in its path again. It was a look that said, "I expected so much of you, Pericles, and you have let me down."'

Corollary to the principle of minimal force was that of minimal supervision. When Alcibiades issued a combat assignment, he imparted the objective only, leaving the means to the officer himself. The more daunting the chore, the more informally he commanded it. I never saw him issue an order from behind a desk.

*Always assign a man more than he believes himself capable of. Make him rise to the occasion. In this way you compel him to discover fresh resources, both in himself and others of his command, thus enlarging the capacity of each, while binding all beneath the exigencies of risk and glory.*

Another to Adeimantus:

*As we seek to make our enemies own their defeats at our hands, so we
must make our friends own their victories. The less you give a man, and
have him succeed, the more he draws his achievement to his heart.
Remember we may elevate the fleet in two ways only. By acquiring
better men or making those we have better. Even were the former
practicable I would disdain it, for a hired man may hire out to another
master but a man who makes himself master stays loyal for ever.*

There was an oarsman of the *Mnemosyne* named Lysicles, who could
not swim. His mates had exhausted all remedies. Alcibiades, learning of
this, walked the man out into the sea one evening, some fifty yards from
the fellow's vessel anchored offshore. Such a sight was extraordinary to
say the least; hundreds congregated, looking on. Alcibiades spoke to the
man quietly for a number of moments. At once the fellow screwed his
eyes shut and plunged into the foam. When he made it, the entire
strand erupted.

What had Alcibiades said to the man?

'He told me I could do it, and made me believe him.'

When *Panegyris* and *Atalanta* were mauled at Nine-Mile Cove and
their trierarchs blaming themselves had made their spirits disconsolate,
he called the pair to his tent and, stripping before them, commanded
them to regard the many wounds upon his body. 'I'd rather have a man
who has closed with the foe and bears the scars than all the bronze-and-
brightwork of the regatta. I can find unscathed captains anywhere. But
where will I get brave men like you and your crews?'

This to the younger Pericles and his officers, when they had made
plea for additional vessels:

*Never forget, gentlemen, that you command Athenians and that those
elements which make our countrymen great are intangible. Daring and
intelligence, adaptability and esprit. Put these in the bank for me and I
will get you all the ships you need.*

As he chastened men with banishment from himself, so he rewarded
them with access. He loved to have his officers about him, particularly

late at night as he worked. 'Bear in mind, my friends, that access to your person is a mighty incentive to those in station beneath you. A smile, a kind word, a nickname spoken with affection. Recall how we as boys gloried in the moments at our father's knee, or how even now an invitation to dine with our commanders makes light of many a long pull into a hard wind. Don't hoard your person, gentlemen. Money cannot buy the prize of your attention, and the men know it.'

He schooled his captains to think in terms of squadrons and wings, never single ships, and to bear in mind ever the fleet as a whole, which squadrons were where and how quickly they could be brought up, how swiftly one's own may withdraw to their aid. He would react with fury to the report of vessels advancing out of formation. The phrase 'in support of' permeated his orders. To any scheme his first question was 'Who sails in support?'

In the advance he demanded ships 'blade-to-blade', that each draw courage from her mates' proximity. At sea he maintained signal traffic night and day, to link all vessels as a unit. Casualties he refused to segregate, but the wounded must be borne home with their shipmates, no matter if the deck sprawl with litters and blood trail onto the oarsmen's backs. Each must know he would never be abandoned, but his mates would bear him off. 'None fears death more than the sea fighter, for the infantryman, falling, cedes his bones to the earth from which they may be recovered, but the sailor to the barren and pitiless main.'

This to the younger Pericles, when he heard he had lost his temper with one of his oarsmen:

> The infantryman may fight without his captain and take to flight without him. But the sailor advances to battle yoked to his commander, with naught dissevering him from hell but his faith in you and a thumb's-breadth of pine.

Alcibiades drilled the fleet tirelessly in self-presentation, to make few look like many and many like few. He practised the exploitation of headlands and promontories to conceal our presence and numbers. He accustomed the men to launching in all weathers, for storms and squalls not only offered concealment but magnified the theatre of terror with which to overawe the foe. In the great victory at Cyzicus he obscured the fleet in a downpour he had anticipated for months, intelligence of the terrain having determined that at that hour at that season such weather could be counted upon.

Before he came, the men had tended to break up by specialties, marines and infantry disdaining the *nautai*, topside oarsmen despising holdsmen, and cavalry styling themselves superior to all. Alcibiades effaced these distinctions not with chastisement, but with glory. Later, when Thrasyllus came out from Athens with a thousand heavy infantry and five thousand sailors trained as javelineers, but suffered defeat at Ephesus, Alcibiades' men would not let them enter the camp; they who had never been beaten disdaining their countrymen who had let the enemy erect a trophy to their shame. Alcibiades broke this up by pitting them side by side against main-force Spartans. Victory again effaced all distinctions.

He sought to keep fresh those squadrons not on campaign or pillage by employing them to bewitch the civil populace. The report of Athenian men-of-war, even two or three anchoring in a cove, would draw the locals from miles. Far from spurning these gawkers, Alcibiades ordered them haled aboard. Let them see what battleship and battle crew look like. Lads he sought especially to beguile, for their youth makes them seek heroes and models of emulation. They will tell us everything. Intelligence of tides, currents, and weather he prized above silver. Fishermen, whom the Spartans despised, he ordained favourites. No dinner lacked at least one of these characters, debriefed later for quirks of tide and channel, storm and season.

*Under fire I cannot read the chart, but a pilot at my shoulder who says steer there where the rip runs.*

Often he led raids himself, materializing from the darkness to strike a harbour with axe and brand, or sailing in in broad daylight, compelling the populace to fear him more than the garrison who occupied them. He loved to snatch from their beds mayors and magistrates. These he often interrogated in person, restoring them to home with gifts, his object to abash them with the might of the fleet,

*for one snatched in the night will behold all he sees with eyes widened by terror and magnify reports of the invincibility of his captors.*

He sought not to drill the fleet to dull uniformity, but to enliven it with individuality and self-enterprise.

> . . . each wing, and squadron within a wing, must be encouraged to forward its own identity, some skill or talent at which it exceeds all and in which it may take pride. Let one wing carry double complement of marines; let them train with the grapnel and the flying outrigger. Let another build out its catheads Corinthian-style and call itself Hammerhead or Ram. When sailors from different divisions meet in a tavern, I want insults to fly. I want fistfights. The more the better, for in their aftercourse the men are bound yet more tightly together.

Here is how he went about acquiring cavalry.

From raiding to support the fleet he had become acquainted with Thrace, their hordes of horsemen and the spirit of their savage princes – two in particular, Seuthes the son of Maisades, and Medocus, lords of the Odrysians. Thrasybulus and Theramenes pressed him to pay court to these. The army could acquire cavalry nowhere else. But Alcibiades understood the hearts of these wild knights. One may not approach them giftless, nor may the friendship offering be less than spectacular or presented in any manner other than the grand.

Now Alcibiades had two trierarchs he favoured, brothers, Damon and Nestorides, of his home district, Scambonidae. They were the youngest of the fleet, the one twenty-three, the other a year younger. Do you recall the scandal at Athens, Jason, of the chorus of boys? This was ten years earlier, before Syracuse. Alcibiades' uncle Axiochus had sponsored a chorus of beardless lads at the Panathenaea; in the celebration of their victory Alcibiades had contrived to have the youths overnight at his estate rather than return home with their fathers. Lubricating his charges with their first noseful of the grape, he then produced a cohort of glamorous (and full-grown) hetairai.

He got the boys laid.

This touched off a terrific hubbub. Suit was brought for outrage, hybris. That was when Meletus issued his famous indictment, 'Cite not the whores but the whoremaster!' Alcibiades of course had judged the prize worth the hazard. He recognized in these lads the flower of the city, commanders and generals of the future. He sought by orchestration of this passage to manhood, the most indelible of their young lives, to bind them to him with chains of adamant.

Now the brothers, Damon and Nestorides, had arrived from Athens. Alcibiades had brought them out as armoured infantry, they being far too callow to be given command at sea without causing a mutiny among the senior captains. Here is how he got them ships. He despatched the lads first as marines, in a series of reconnaissances of the Spartan ship-works at Abydos. They went in, ten nights in all, mapping the yard and its approaches. They reported four vessels under repair, nearly sea-worthy. 'Bring one back,' Alcibiades pledged, 'and you'll command her.'

A rainy night, the boys landed with thirty men, Antiochus lying off-shore with four fast triremes. They towed off not one ship but two, naming them *Panther* and *Lynx*. These kits became holy terrors. They pitched their hulls black and painted cat's eyes on their prows. They ran the night missions that struck every other skipper with dread. It was these, lads not yet twenty-four, who severed the chain at Abydos, laying the harbour open to the raid that burned half the wharf district, assassinated a score of mayors and administrators, and kidnapped out of his mistress's bed Pharnabazus' secretary and all his notes. But their chief *athlon*, the exploit that brought the fleet its cavalry, was the carrying off of the three hundred women.

These were two slave parties, a hundred and fifty in each, whose movements the lads had detected and whom Alcibiades had ordered held under observation up and down the coast beneath Mount Coppias. The women were captives, Odrysian Thracians, digging irrigation works. He sent the brothers in at dusk with twelve ships. The lasses ran out to them, into the sea, shrieking with joy, while their Persian masters lobbed ironheads at the raiders, then fled like the wind up the Caicos Valley. The 'Cat's Eyes' brought the maidens back to Sestos, thinking Alcibiades meant to sell them to the whoremasters. Instead the commander had them bathed and oiled, with orders to the fleet that they be treated as gentlewomen.

Here was the gift for the Thracian princes.

He sent the lads first, to inform the savage nobles that Alcibiades wished to meet with them and appointing time and place. He himself took the women in four galleys escorted by a dozen men-of-war, the girls themselves garlanded as brides, to efface all shame of captivity and render them legitimate consorts for the princes to bestow upon their favourites, to the wild strand of Salmydessos, where he presented them to Medocus, Bisanthes and Seuthes, the great princes of the plains.

By the twin gods, those whores' sons knew how to say thanks. They set up Antiochus and the lads with brides on the spot, brooking no protest, and brought down five hundred horses out of the hills, a gift for Alcibiades and the cavalry. Have you ever seen five hundred horses, Jason? It is a sight. We of the support party wished only to corral the beasts and make our exit before these savages changed their minds.

Except now comes the bolt. Alcibiades turns the princes down. He will not accept the horses. Worse, he informs Seuthes, the prince has insulted him by offering these animals instead of what he knows his guest really wants. The hour is deep past midnight. A hundred bonfires blaze; our ships wait, shored on the strand with tribesmen cavorting all over, men and women drunk as coots, while an army a thousand times our party swells out of sight across the plain. More ominous yet, our host lord Seuthes is a mad buck, blind soused, as all habitually in that country; they don't trust decisions unless they make them drunk. And, as all Thracians, recipient of boons, he is honourbound to outdo them in generosity first; if he cannot come up with a better gift than he has received, what looms but a bloodbath? Alcibiades repeats that the prince has offered offence by his present and turns to us, the two score of his escort, commanding that we launch and begone.

Seuthes won't let us. He orders the horses brought forward and commences haranguing his guests, and his own tribesmen, on the magnificent qualities of these beasts, which all know the Athenians need desperately, possessing few cavalry of their own and at the mercy of Pharnabazus' Royal Persian Horse every time they advance inland out of sight of their ships. The prince has worked himself into a lather of incendiary dudgeon. What kind of a man, he demands of Alcibiades, what kind of commander turns down wealth like this, if not for his own use and glory, then for that of the gallant warriors entrusted to his charge?

Alcibiades weaves to his feet, as drunk as his host, and proclaims that he would in fact be the wealthiest man in the East if the prince will give him what he wishes instead of the horses. And what is that? the buck demands.

'Your friendship.'

At one breath Alcibiades is sober, so cold and composed you realize he has not misplaced his wits for an instant, and the look on his face snaps-to every bandit round the blaze. If I take these horses now, he declares, I sail with a splendid gift but I myself remain poor. If on the other hand I leave the horses with you, their masters, and depart with your friendship – and now he crosses before Seuthes, who has gone as sober as he – then I count among my wealth not only these valiant mounts, for I may call upon them from my friend any time I wish, but mighty warriors to fight from upon their backs. For my friend will not send me his horses and leave me to face my enemies empty-handed.

Now, Seuthes is no fool. He knows this man across from him has planned it all from the instant he first saw the women. He recognizes the genius of it and recognizes that Alcibiades knew before and knows now that he would recognize it. He wants this genius, does Seuthes, and knows he's got a mentor now if he'll make him his friend, to counsel and instruct him in the acquisition of it. The prince embraces Alcibiades. Ten thousand tribesmen whoop. Our party goes limp with relief.

And he did come with his horses, Prince Seuthes. Not five hundred but two thousand, when the fleet and army took Chalcedon and Byzantium, bottled up the straits, and drove the Spartans to their blackest ebb of the war. But I have got ahead of myself and overshot a tale, and a turning point, which must be recounted.

Passing down the straits, a month after the great victory at Cyzicus, the flag party was met by a despatch cutter from Samos. The night was moonlit and she signalled by flare; the vessels hove-to in midchannel. The state galley *Paralus*, the cutter reported, had this day arrived from Athens with news that a Spartan legation had approached the Assembly, seeking peace. A great cheer erupted from the men, clamouring to learn the terms proposed, which were an armistice in place, each side to withdraw from the other's territories, repatriating all prisoners. Another cheer, and a cry from the crews that they would soon go home.

'The Spartans are at Athens now?' Alcibiades called across to the cutter.

'Aye, sir.'

'Who leads the embassy?'

'Endius, sir.'

Fresh cheers arose.

'The Lacedaemonians have singled you out for honour, Alcibiades. Why else send Endius, your friend?' This from Antiochus, Alcibiades' helmsman and among the exiles who had shared his seasons at Sparta. 'It shows they see you, even technically an exile, as foremost among the Athenians.'

Thrasybulus's *Endeavour* had come up to leeward and now hove-to within earshot. Her steersman called across. Did this indeed mean we could go home? Alcibiades made no answer, only held motionless in the moonshadow of the sternpeak.

'Here is no offer of peace,' he spoke soberly to the officers on the quarterdeck and the stern oarsmen close beneath at their benches, 'but a ploy to sever you and me from the people of Athens and ruin us all.'

He turned to his quartermaster: 'Make signal to all, continue to Samos, and to Thrasybulus, follow us alone.'

Then to Antiochus at the helm: 'Take us in now, there, to Achilleum.'

# THIRTY

# BESIDE THE TOMB
# OF ACHILLES

THE PLAIN OF THE SCAMANDER SPRAWLS AS SERE AND WIND-SCORED today as it did a thousand years past, when Troy fell beneath Achilles' spear. On the strand where Homer's Achaeans beached their undecked fifties, Athenians and Samians now made shore in their bronze-rammed two-hundreds. That freshwater spring around which Diomedes pursued Sarpedon still flows cold and sweet. Our parties had overnighted on the site a dozen times, transiting in and out of the Hellespont, but never till this eve had our commander directed us inland to the mounds.

There are eighteen in all, seven great ones for the nations of the Achaeans, Mycenaeans, Thessalians, Argives, Lacedaemonians, Arcadians and Phocians and eleven lesser for the individual heroes, and the final pair, conjoined, Patrocles and Achilles.

It is chill this night. The wind bends the sickle grass on the tombs' untended slopes; sheep have carved stairsteps in the faces. We purchase a goat of some boys, enquire which mound is Achilles'. They stare. 'Who?'

Upon this plain, Alcibiades has observed, men of the West carried war to men of the East and drove them under.

Our commander dreams of accomplishing it again.

Ally with Sparta and turn on Persia.

'As long as I have been with the fleet,' he states now, as he has heretofore, 'we have believed we must bring Persia to our side in order to
defeat the Spartans. We must ask: is this a phantom? I believe it is.
Persia will never align herself with Athens; our ambitions at sea conflict
with hers; she can never let us win this war. And though we thrash her
satraps' armies up and down the coast, the wealth of the Eastern empire
replenishes all. Persian gold makes her Spartan allies unkillable; we
destroy one fleet, they build another. We cannot patrol every cove of
Asia and Europe.'

Thrasybulus protests, sick of war and eager to accept this offer of
armistice. 'The enemy honours you, Alcibiades. All it takes is you to
clasp his hand and peace is ours.'

'My friend, the Spartans' intent is not to honour me, but by this wile
to make our countrymen fear my ambition. They slant their favour
towards me to inflame Athens' fears that I, returning with the victories
this fleet has won, will set myself up as tyrant. If they win – that is, incite
the *demos* to displace me – that is Sparta's victory. This is her design, not
peace.'

We must have more victories, he declared. 'More, and more after
that, until our forces possess the Aegean absolutely, the straits and every
city on them, with the grain routes clamped tight in our grip. Till then
we cannot go home.'

It took scant imagination for those about the fire to conjure the
bastions of Selymbria, Byzantium and Chalcedon, each formidable as
Syracuse, and the trials we must endure to take them. Thrasybulus slung
his lees into the embers. 'You mean you can't go home, Alcibiades. I
can.' He rose, unsteady on his shoring timbers.

'Sit down, Brick.'

'I will not. Nor take your orders.' He was drunk, but plain-spoken and
fit to have his say. 'You may not go home, my friend, till you garb yourself in such mantle of glory that none dare fart within a furlong. But I
can go. We all can, who are sick of this war and want no more of it.'

'None may go. You least of all, Brick.'

The men looked on, torn between their commanders. Alcibiades saw
it.

'Friends, if your eyes cannot perceive Necessity's dictates, I beg you to
trust mine. Have I led you anywhere but to victory? The Spartans dangle

peace before your noses and you snap at it like winter foxes. Peace to them means respite to rebuild for war. And us? Since when do we, or any victor, quit the field owning less than at contest's commencement, when that and more stand plump for the taking? Look around you, friends. The gods have led us to this plain, where Greek vanquished Trojan, to direct us to their will and our destiny. Will we die in our beds, praising peace, that phantom with which our enemies swindled us, who could not defeat us in fair fight upon the sea? I despise peace if it means failing our destiny, and I call upon the blood of these heroes to witness.'

He stood, addressing Thrasybulus. 'You accuse me, my friend, of hunting glory at the price of devotion to our nation. But no such contradiction obtains. Athens' destiny is glory. She was born to it, as we her sons. Do not devalue yourselves, brothers, accounting our worth as meaner than these heroes' whose shades eavesdrop upon us now. They were men like us, no more. We have won victories equal to and greater than theirs, and will win more.'

'Those you call us to emulate, Alcibiades,' the younger Pericles spoke, 'are dead.'

'Never!'

'Sir, we encamp beside their tombs.'

'They can never die! They are more alive than we, not in occupation of fields of Elysia, where Homer tells us

*not pain nor grief may follow,*

but here, this night and every, within ourselves. We cannot draw a breath absent their exemption, or close our eyes save to see their heritance before us. They constitute our being, more than bone or blood, and make us who we are.

'Yes, I would stand among them, and bring you with me, all. Not in death or afterlife, but in the flesh and in triumph. You command me to look, Brick, to these about the fire. I am looking. But I don't see chastened men, or meek. I see that valiant quick to which invincible battalions may be drawn; a corps of kinsmen who may say when death comes, as it must to all, that they have left no drop within the bowl. We clash tonight as brothers. What could be better? To gather on this site among brave and brilliant friends! And who grander to stand among than these of yore? But one may not enter their company for the price of an iron spit. The toll is everlasting glory, won for that which one loves, at the risk of all he loves. I for one will pay that fare gladly. Let us dine with these, brothers, who brought fire to the East and claimed it for their own.'

Thrasybulus stood across, remarking the embers, which his mate and fellow commander had kindled to the blaze.

'You scare the breath out of me, Alcibiades.'

# THIRTY-ONE
# THE INTREPIDITY
# OF THE GODS

I WAS IN ATHENS [GRANDFATHER NOW NARRATED] WHEN ALCIBIADES TOOK
Chalcedon Selymbria and Byzantium, as he said he must and would.

The first he surrounded with a wall from sea to sea, and when the Persian
Pharnabazus came against him with his troops and cavalry while simultaneously Hippocrates, the Spartan garrison commander, rushed upon him
from the city, Alcibiades divided his forces and defeated them both, slaying
Hippocrates. At Selymbria he had mounted the walls himself with an advance
party, confederates within having colluded to betray the place, when, one
among them failing of nerve, the others must give the signal prematurely.
Alcibiades found himself cut off, supported by only a handful, with defenders
swarming to overwhelm him. He had the trumpet sounded and, commanding
silence, ordered the inhabitants to surrender their arms and receive clemency,
this mandate issued with such authority as to make the foe believe that his
army had already taken the city (which was nearly true, as his Thracians,
massed in their thousands, clamoured to sack the place entire), that the
citizens consented to submit the state if he would only call off his dogs. And
he kept his pledge, maltreating no-one, only requiring that the city return to
alliance with Athens and hold open the straits in her name.

He took Byzantium by the following stratagem. Having circumvallated the
city and blockaded it also by sea, he made public that other urgent concerns
must call him away and, embarking with a great show all beneath the city

walls, he sailed and marched off, returning that night in darkness to overwhelm the slackened and unsuspecting guard.

He had now achieved all he had said he would, secured the Hellespont and
beaten every force pitched against him. He had covered himself with such
glory, as Thrasybulus had professed, that he might at last come home.

I was in Athens then, recovering from my wounds of Abydos. Twice the
sawbones carved timbers off my peg and each time suppuration assaulted the
unexcised tissue. My wife nearly came undone with the fright of it. It was not
so hard on me. I was a hero. Those who had procured Alcibiades' banishment
and those who had by their acquiescence abetted it now sought to ally themselves with me and every other officer associated with his triumphs and those
he, Thrasybulus and Theramenes continued to send home like so many
bouquets. Soon they, the commanders, would come home too. Athens burned
for them as a bride for her beloved.

Our client Polemides, it turned out, appeared briefly at Athens as well,
which episode must be related, as its consequence affected if not the course of
the war, then a direction she might have taken had events transpired otherwise.

Polemides resumed his tale on the twenty-eighth of Hecatombaion,
Athena's Day, by coincidence the date his own son – named Nicolaus after his
father – appeared at my door, beseeching me to take him with me to the prison.
But this chronicle must hold a moment. Let us return to the Hellespont . . .
and Polemides' narration:


NEWS OF ENDIUS' PEACE MISSION [POLEMIDES RESUMED] HAD REACHED
the straits two days before Alcibiades' ships returned from their
detour to the tombs. Many celebrated, believing the war over. I had
caroused pretty freely myself, when a summons interrupted the spree. I
was instructed, by Mantitheus in Alcibiades' name, to pack my kit,
informing no-one, and report to him at his command post, late, after the
secretaries had departed.

I recall the night as well for another reason, an encounter with Damon,
the young Cat's Eye. I must put a point here, that is, my own retirement
from service to Alcibiades personally. I had begged off; I couldn't take the
pimping. I now served the younger Pericles on the Calliope.

It was like this. Many competed to provide their commanders with
feminine flesh. Certain officers had become professional procurers,

importing from as far as Egypt. Any beauty stumbled on in the field would be tossed in a bag and presented at his superior's threshold. Sometimes our commander needed two or three a night, just to get to sleep. That was his business. But I could no longer station myself at his doorstep, fending spurned mistresses and aspiring suicides. He laughed when I proffered my resignation. 'I'm astonished you lasted so long, Pommo. You must love me more than I thought.'

This night, returning after the secretaries, I encountered the Cat's Eye, Damon. He had a girl with him, his fiancée, he said. He wished to show her off to Alcibiades. Would I let him in first? I glimpsed enough of the maid's face to see she was a beauty, though no comelier than any of scores who had worn a groove in the courtyard heretofore. Damon and the girl went in. I waited. My turn came.

The place was cleared out, not even junior officers or marines present.

'An embassy was despatched to Endius this morning on the *Paralus*,' Alcibiades began, 'to convey the generals' official response to the Spartan proposal of peace. You'll be unofficial. From me only.'

I would carry no papers, Alcibiades informed me, register at no frontiers, and impart my intelligence to no-one save Endius himself. Interrogated upon my task, I might give any story so long as it was false. Alcibiades asked if I knew why he sent me and none other. 'Because Endius will believe you. You need do nothing, Pommo, only be yourself. A soldier on a soldier's errand.'

It came down to this: if Alcibiades could deliver Athens, could Endius deliver Sparta – to end the war and fight as allies in the conquest of Persia?

He laughed. 'You don't even blink, Pommo!'

'I have known you a long time.'

'Good. Then listen closely. After Cyzicus, when we slew Mindarus, I had expected the Spartans to send Endius out in his place, or Lysander, who are far their ablest commanders. That they have made Endius peace envoy means his party has fallen. Lysander will abandon him, if he hasn't already.

'You need waste no time convincing Endius of the wisdom of the course I propose; he has grasped it for years. His reaction, however, will still be suspicion. He will think I seek to command this coalition. Tell him I yield to him, or whomever he appoints in his stead, and if he laughs, which he will, and says he knows I scheme already to displace whatever luckless son of a whore sails across my bows, laugh back and tell him he's right. But that will be then, and such whore's son will have had time to prepare.

'Tell him the ephors have outsmarted themselves electing him as envoy; now I may not come home until I have swept my country's enemies from the sea. He will know this. The point is that then will be too late. If he can bring his country over, it must be soon, or the *demos* at Athens, inflamed by the victories I will bring them, will make such demands as Sparta may never accede to.

'If Endius asks you of Persia and her vulnerability, tell him what you have seen with your own eyes. No Persian fleet may stand up to Athens' navy, and no land force to Sparta's army. Darius ails. Succession struggles will tear the empire apart.

'That being said, Endius will assume that simultaneous to this embassy to himself I also despatch ambassadors to the court of Persia re-proposing alliance with them, as I know his countrymen have messengers on the track now to the Great King. Say only that I must play my hand as he his, but Necessity casts the final ballot; someone must trust someone some time. God willing, it will be he and me.

'Find out what you can of the parties at Lacedaemon, but do not press him on this. He will know what can be done, nor do we need to. Enquire, however, of the feasibility of recruiting Lysander, or even Agis. I welcome either or both. Endius will realize of course that such an alliance between our cities will produce further war between us if it succeeds. Tell him I would rather fight that war then than this war now, which can only destroy us both and leave our mutual enemies triumphant by default.'

What if Endius required me to return with him to Lacedaemon to repeat this overture to others of his party?

'Do so. My needs are for the most and best intelligence you can acquire. No sight-seeing now. If you are spotted at either city, our foes will know you come from me and to whom I have sent you. The audacity of the stroke gives it a chance. The faintest glimmer, premature, dooms it.'

He issued me money and passwords, assigning a ship to bear me as far as Paros, from which I must proceed on my own. I drew up upon departure. 'Are you serious about this, Alcibiades? Or am I putting my neck on the block for some ruse or gambit?'

As ever when he laughed, his face regained the flush of youth.

'When we return home, Pommo, which we shall in due course, Athens will hand herself to me on a plate. We will stand then upon the utmost promontory of peril, as expectations of such an order will be released as to make their disappointment a calamity surpassing even Syracuse. Do you know why I call the men and the fleet the Monster? Because they must be fed, tomorrow and the next day, and if they are not, they devour you and me and then themselves.'

He pronounced this lightly, as a gambler long since wagering home and treasure sets without qualm his own life upon the cast. I perceived then, and believe now, that his intrepidity was of an order not of men, but of gods.

'Defeating the enemy is child's play alongside feeding this monster, which itself is nothing alongside the demos of Athens, the Supreme Monster, particularly inflamed as she will be upon our return in glory. Do you understand, my friend? We must place before this monster an enterprise worthy of her appetite.'

He laughed, bright as a boy. 'This is how destiny works. As this, tonight at the intersection of Necessity and free will.'

I heard a rustle from the chamber and, turning, glimpsed in shadow a female form advance and recede.

'Now go, old friend,

> *. . . nor let dawn o'ertake you,*
> *untossed upon the winding main.'*

Passing that tavern calling itself Conger Eel, I descried young Damon, alone, drunk and getting drunker. I asked where his girl was.

'I am an imbecile,' he declared. 'And merit an imbecile's deserts.'

THAT GIRL WAS TIMANDRA, IN WHOSE GARMENTS ALCIBIADES' CORPSE was wrapped so few years later, in Phrygia, there being no other swathings with which to devise a shroud.

She was twenty-four, then on the straits. She entered his keep and no woman displaced her. She was what he needed; he knew it and she, at once. Those parasites who could not be chased even by armoured marines, this slip of a lass scattered with but a glance. Other than his wife while she lived, I never heard Alcibiades defend a woman save in jest or irony. Now his eyes darkened with such wrath at the least affront to this girl that captains of a thousand approached on tiptoe, lashes lowered as boys. She was like the dove of Trapezus, mated with an eagle, who became an eagle herself.

Much has been made of Alcibiades' lawlessness in his private life, by which his traducers meant that he would fuck an eel if it would hold still long enough. You have met Eunice, Jason. She is no eel, but he took her to his bed one night, or she went of her own, at Samos a year prior to Timandra's advent. This was her way of striking at me, when blows would not suffice, for lack of attendance upon her and her children, of which laxity I was surely culpable. I could not fault her, who was help-less as all women before the tempests of her heart, but must confront him who ought to know better, which prospect engendered no small apprehension, I confess, even in one like myself who, if possessed of no grander accomplishment, at least may say he feared no man face-to-face. Not that I thought my commander would invoke authority against me, as he would never bend to such, but that upon the passion of the instant he might aim a blow. Such a prodigy was he as athlete and antagonist that I possessed, I felt, only a middling chance, myself armed and he empty-handed. Of course nothing of the sort fell out. When I called him to account, on a moment alone beside the hulk works, his response was of such grave rue that my anger failed at once, replaced, as you may believe or not, by sorrow on his account. For his incapacity to govern his appetites was the single failing that made him feel mortal.

'She told me she was no longer your woman, that you had cast her into the street. Her pretext for entry to me was want of money.' He met my eye. 'I knew it was a fraud and went ahead anyway, such a dog am I.' Then, dropping his hands: 'Here, flatten me where we stand, Pommo, and I'll make no matter of it.'

What was I supposed to do, strike our fleet commander, there beside the strip yards?

'You don't even remember her name, do you?'

'My dear, I don't remember any of their names.'

Two evenings later I was training on the seawall when Mantitheus passed in a racing eight, working with ephebes fresh from home. 'Got a clean set of spruces?' he called across, meaning the forest-green dress cloak of the fleet marine force. 'The pleasure of our company has been requested. And bring your gentleman's manners!'

This was how my second wife was introduced to me, or I to her to put it exactly. She was the daughter of our Samian host of that evening, by name Aurore, whom I loved at once and with all my heart, though her time as my bride was barely a year before heaven took her, such has been my fortune. I never learned what Alcibiades told her father of me, or how it was communicated. But upon the instant of this gentleman's welcoming Mantitheus and myself at his threshold, it was as if I were a prince anointed.

This was how Alcibiades made up his transgression, do you see? It was the malformation of his destiny, and our own, that he must make up so many.

Timandra could not change him, but she took him in hand. They did not share the same room on the straits; she would not abide it, absent marriage, nor would she consent to such union, though he appealed for it strenuously. He must come to her bed and return to his own, unless she permitted. Nor did she install her lodgings adjacent his, to spy on him, but in the opposite wing, and as offices as well as quarters. She had means of her own which she managed, but her primary vocation upon entering his domain was to facilitate his practice, not of affairs of war, which were and must be his, but of matters of his well-being and efficient functioning.

Once, ambassadors of the Persians, Mithridates and Arnapes, called upon Alcibiades at his villa on Dog's Head Point and, being welcomed by Timandra in flawless Aramaic, took her for either the general's interpreter or his lover and brushed past her, seeking his offices. She had the marines jerk them up at swordpoint, and when the envoys expressed outrage and demanded her credentials, she told them:

'Gentlemen, it has been my observation among those whom men call great, that these may be addressed in only two ways – either to serve or to contest. In neither of these estates may the great man discover one to whom he may in safety unburden his heart. This is the service I afford our commander, and you, who have had abundant acquaintance of the great, may judge its worth.' She smiled. 'Yet I have acted in over-haste to detain you thereby by force. Consider yourselves free, gentlemen, to pass as you wish.'

The envoys tendered that obeisance the Persians call *ayana*, proper to a prince or minister. 'Summon us when you wish, lady, but please accept, until we find more material means of expressing it, our regrets at this infraction.'

From girlhood this Timandra had been pursued by suitors, offering, through her mother the courtesan Phrasicleia, worlds and universes to possess her, much as men had courted Alcibiades in his youth. Perhaps this was a bond between them, an understanding. One would say, observing them in public, that they conducted themselves as chastely as brother and sister; yet it was clear that each was passionately devoted to the other.

Timandra domesticated Alcibiades, if such a word may be applied, and lent order to the often chaotic practice of his genius, managed as it was entirely in his head. But the sword of her advent had an under-edge, which was that the apparition of this female, wielding such influence at the epicentre of a coalition of war, contributed to an atmosphere about Alcibiades that smacked of royalty. What was she anyway? A queen? An imperial gatekeeper?

Yet it must be said that someone had to shield him from the siege of distraction which drew him apart from the business of the fleet. For Thrasybulus and Theramenes, though of equal rank, never experienced such inundation of celebrity. They might walk abroad unmolested by the throngs of petitioners, supplicants, and arse-lickers whose importunities tormented their counterpart without cease.

But to return to my embassy to Endius. It took a month to reach Athens by the required route; by then the Spartan mission was gone, repudiated by Cleonymus and the demagogues. I set off at once to overhaul them, but they had crossed the Isthmus; I must enter the Peloponnese on my own, at last catching up at the border fort of Karyai.

Endius listened gravely to my recitation of Alcibiades' message, rejoining nothing. Next dawn Forehand appeared, bearing a message for Alcibiades in Endius's hand, whose despatch, the squire stated in distress, was an act of either extraordinary devotion or plain recklessness. Fearing for his master should the letter be intercepted, Forehand refused to depart. I broke the seal. I myself destroyed the letter, committing its contents to memory, to shield this Peer of Lacedaemon whom I had always respected but for whom, till that day, I had felt scant affection.

> *Endius to Alcibiades, greetings.*
> *I despatch these contents, my friend, knowing that their discovery may purchase my death. You are right; I may not contest the wisdom of the course you propose. I cannot help however. Not that our party has been overthrown; its agenda holds sway. But I myself have been displaced. Lysander now dominates. I can no longer control him.*
>
> *Hear what I tell you. Lysander has made himself mentor to young Agesilaus, King Agis's brother, who will himself be king. Through the youngster he has made Agis his patron, who hates you and you know why. Agis will welcome your head or your liver, but no other part.*
>
> *Lysander intrigues tirelessly for appointment as fleet admiral. He believes he can handle the Persian, unlike our other navarchs who could*

neither dissimulate their contempt for the barbarian nor their despising of themselves for grovelling for his gold.

You know this yourself of Lysander's character. To him a lie and the truth are one; he employs which will effect his ends. Justice in his view is a topic of the salon, personal pride a luxury the warrior may not afford. He despises as fools those of our country who will not bend the knee to the Persian, as he himself has before Agis and others, each prostration advancing himself and his influence. Lysander is by no means evil but by all means effective. He sees human nature for what it is, unlike yourself, who cannot resist sounding it for that which it may become. For what you must brave in him, you may reprove only yourself, as he has studied in your academy and disremembered nothing. All Spartan commanders are as children beside him, as they understand the fight and nothing more. Lysander understands the rest. He grasps the workings of the Athenian democracy, specifically the fickleness of the demos. He believes you capable of vanquishing all, save your own countrymen. They will destroy you, he contends, as every other of excellence before you. In other words, he does not fear you. He wants a fight. He believes he can win.

Lysander possesses all your virtues of war and diplomacy and one other. He is cruel. He will order assassination, torture, and murder wholesale, which are but tools to him, as perjury, bribery, subornation. He will not scruple to apply terror even to his own allies. Like Polycrates the tyrant, he believes his friends will be more grateful when he gives back what he has taken than if he had never taken it at all. Victory is his solitary standard.

Lastly, he believes he knows you. He understands your character. He has studied you, all the time you were in our country, knowing one day he would face you. Do not expect a fair fight. He will demur and dilate, absent all pride as a warrior, then appear from nowhere and overwhelm you.

It will come as cold comfort but I believe the course you outline, of Greek alliance against Persia, is one Lysander himself would champion were it politic at the moment.

I offer this page from his brief: do not undervalue cruelty or the employment of main force. Your style is to eschew coercion, which to you demeans coercer and coerced and backfires in the long run. But, my friend, everything backfires in the long run.

Be of stringent care. You may have met your match in this fellow.

The war for the Hellespont continued; Alcibiades' victories mounted. Lysander failed, for that year and the next, to achieve his posting as fleet admiral.

As for myself, I served at sea with the younger Pericles and in shore units, primarily under Thrasybulus. I paid court, by post and in person when action bore me south to Samos, to my heart's joy, Aurore. With time, acquaintance deepened as well with her father and brothers, for whom I came to feel such fondness and regard as I had known before only with Lion and my own father.

I returned to Alcibiades' squadrons in time for the capitulation of Byzantium. This was the sternest fighting of the Hellespontine War, against frontline Spartan troops, Peers and *perioikoi* of Selassia and Pellana, reinforced by Arcadian mercenaries and Boeotian heavy infantry of the Cadmus regiment, the same who had hurled us back on Epipolae. At one point a thousand Thracian cavalry under Bisanthes made a rush upon the Spartans, whose numbers had been cut to below four hundred, fighting before the walls all night. The Spartans carved them up, horse and all.

When at last the enemy gave way, overwhelmed by our numbers and the desertion of their Byzantine allies, it took all of Alcibiades' force, in person and shield in hand, to hold the Thracian princes from butchering them to the last man. He had to order our troops to drive the Spartans into the sea, as if to drown them, before the blood-mad tribesmen, who fear water more than you or I fear hell, would give back.

Our ships could not be beached that night, but rode to anchor, bearing the enemy dead and wounded. I assisted a physician of the foe, whom my tongue in error addressed as 'Simon' more than once.

The strait lay choked in the morning, with smoking timbers and bodies drifting in the eddies where the outbound current abuts the in. Alcibiades ordered the channel swept and bonfires lighted on both shores, Byzantium on the European, Chalcedon the Asian. Athens held them both now and with them the Hellespont.

At last Alcibiades commanded the Aegean.

At last he could go home.

# BOOK SEVEN

# FEEDING
# THE MONSTER

## THIRTY-THREE
# THE BLESSINGS OF PEACE

I MUST INSERT THIS CHAPTER ON MY OWN, MY GRANDSON, AS IT BEARS
powerfully upon our client's fate, though he himself elected not to confide
these matters as part of his history, deeming them too personal. They concern
the Samian maiden Aurore daughter of Telecles, a privileged introduction to
whom, you recall, was Alcibiades' way of requiting to our client his own in-
discretion with Eunice.

Polemides took the girl to wife.

This was close after Byzantium, in the flush of victory, and before Alcibiades'
return to Athens. As with the bride of his youth, Phoebe, Polemides passed over
this matter with reticence. That which I gleaned came from the testimony of
others and, largely, correspondence discovered thereafter in Polemides' chest.

Here, a formal decree from the Archon's office at Athens, granting
Athenian citizenship to the bride Aurore (as all Samians were accorded,
several years later, for their steadfast service to our cause). Another parcel,
from his great-aunt Daphne at Athens, contained apparently a golden hair
clip, once Polemides' mother's, as a wedding gift for his bride.

In this letter to his aunt Polemides recounts incidents of the wedding,
describing with pride his new father- and brothers-in-law, both officers of the
fleet, with whom already he feels a bond as friends as well as kinsmen.

   . . . lastly, my dear, I wish you could have seen her who has, heaven
   alone knows why, consented to be my wife. A match for me twice

over in intellect, possessed of a beauty both chaste and passionate, and of such strength of character as to make my own pride as a warrior seem like a boy's idle conceit. I experience in her presence such hopes as I have not permitted my heart to entertain since the passing of my own Phoebe, that is, the wish for children, life at home, a family. I thought I would never feel these again; to you only, and her, may I own such a confidence. To bring innocents into such a world as this seemed not only irresponsible but wicked. Yet with but a glance at this dear girl's face, before I had heard her voice or spoken to her a word, such despair as I have borne so long fell away as if it had never existed. Hope is indeed eternal, as the poets say.

*From station with the fleet, to his bride at Samos:*

. . . before you, it seemed the next milestone I would cross would be my own death, which I anticipated at any moment, marvelling that it had not found me sooner. All I thought and did arose from this resolution, simply to be a good soldier till the end. I was an old man, dead already. Now with the miracle of your apparition, I am young again. Even my crimes are washed clean. I am reborn in your love and the simple prospect of a life with you, apart from war.

*Aurore becomes pregnant. This from her to him with the fleet:*

It's a good thing you can't see me, my love. I'm porky as a piglet. Haven't seen my toes in a month. I waddle about, clutching at walls to keep from toppling. Father has moved my bed downstairs, fearing my clumsiness. I gobble desserts and double portions. What fun! All about wish to be pregnant too, even the little girls, with pillows on their bellies. The whole farm has caught the contagion. My joy – our joy – has spilled over onto them . . .

*Another from the young bride:*

. . . where are you, my love? It tortures me, not to know where your ship sails, though, if I knew, my torment would be equally excruciating. You must preserve yourself! Be a coward. If they make you fight, run away! I know you won't, but I wish it. Please be careful. Don't volunteer for anything!

*From the same letter:*

. . . you must now remark your life as mine, for if you fall, I perish with you.

*And this:*

Grant women rule and this war would end tomorrow. Madness! Why, when all good things flow from peace, must men seek war?

*Again from her:*

. . . life seemed so complicated to me. I felt like a beast who rushes this way and that within its cage, yet discovers only more bars and walls. At once with you, my love, all is simple. Just to live, and love, and be loved by you! Who needs heaven, when we have such joy now?

*Polemides responds:*

It daunts me, my love, that I must now prove worthy of you. How shall I ever?

*He takes steps to dissever himself from Eunice. He signs over half his pay to her and her children, makes application for citizenship for her and them, citing his years of service and the hardships Eunice and the children have borne at his side. He arranges transport for them to Athens and applies to his uncles and elder kinsmen to look to their care until his return.*
*This from his bride:*

. . . I have learned from my father and brothers that a man's conduct at war may not be accounted by the measures of peace, certainly not one such as yourself whose youth and manhood have been spent in service far from home and constant peril of his life. That existence which you have made before we met is yours; I may not judge it. I wish only that I might help, if that were possible without causing by our happiness unhappiness in those we wish to aid. Know that those children of the woman Eunice, yours or not, will receive support from our resources, my own and ours, yours and mine, and my father's.

*Polemides dreams of re-establishing his father's farm, Road's Turn, at Acharnae, and settling there with his bride and child. Peace, or victory which will drive the Spartans from Attica, is everything to him now. He writes to his aunt, seeking to bring her, too, back to the land, and to those crofters who served during his father's term. He even prices seed and orders, at a bargain, an iron ploughshare from a merchantman's inventory at Methymna. He ships this implement aboard the freighter* Eudia, *whose passage homeward is escorted by the fleet of Alcibiades, with Polemides again aboard the flagship* Antiope, *as her supreme commander returns to Athens in glory.*

<br />

# THIRTY-FOUR
# STRATEGOS AUTOKRATOR

ALCIBIADES HAD WISHED TO RETURN AT BREAK OF WINTER, BUT elections at Athens were delayed; he must abide abroad, raiding the Spartan shipyards at Gytheium and killing time at other such offices. At last reports came. They could not have been better. Alcibiades had been elected again to the Board of Generals; as was Thrasybulus, who had brought him home from Persia; Adeimantus, his mate and fellow exile; and Aristocrates, who had championed his recall before the Assembly. The other generals were either neutrals or men of independent virtue. Cleophon, leader of the radical democrats and Alcibiades' most bitter foe, had been supplanted, replaced by Archedemus, a thug but an amenable one, and a solicitor of Critias, Socrates' close friend.

Thrasyllus was at Athens already with the main of the fleet, whose crews would back their commander in anything. Yet still Alcibiades, whose sentence of death had not yet been rescinded, harboured apprehensions of the people's disposition. It was his cousin Euryptolemus's device, communicated by post from Athens, that the warships' arrival, only a flag squadron of twenty, be preceded by grain galleys (twenty-seven waited at Samos then, with another fourteen due out of the Pontus) and that these be known vessels of prominent houses, particularly those who had suffered most from Spartan depredations, and laden for the city, to recall to her that bounty set at her table by the son she had scorned. This was only good manners, Euro's letter noted, as one would be rude to appear for a feast empty-handed.

So the galleys went ahead. These made port at Piraeus two days prior to the squadron, accompanied by a fast courier with instructions to return, reporting the vessels' reception. But the arrival of the merchant-men precipitated such elation in the port, with the news that Alcibiades' ships followed, that the people would not let the cutter re-embark until a proper reception could be mustered to accompany her. Meanwhile the squadron, advancing unapprised of what awaited, began to fear. Beating round Cape Sounium into a fierce westerly, the lead vessels descrying a score of triremes bearing down out of the sun so that their ensigns could not be made out, the younger Pericles, officer of the van, had brought the formation to line abreast to defend itself when it was realized that the advancing vessels bore not hazard but welcome, garlanded, and laden with parties of kinsmen and notables.

Still Alcibiades feared treachery. Beneath his cloak he wore not the light ceremonial cuirass, but a bronze breastplate of battle. Directions were rehearsed to the marine party to remain about him at alert. The ships, which had been advancing in two columns, deployed to singles approaching the harbour entrance at Eetoniea. *Antiope* lay off, seventh in column, that she might put about at once in the event of duplicity. We could see the ramparts now. Reflections flared, as from spearpoints and armour of massed infantry. The flagship bore sidescreens 'at the step', primed for deployment. But as the vessels drew abreast of the bastion, the men could see the flares were not of missiles or armour, but of ladies' vanities and children's sundazzlers. Clouds of wreaths descended. Youths launched sweetmeats upon the breeze, suspended from the spruce spinners that old men whittle wharfside, which can soar for miles on the updraughts. These now came winging overhead, clattering against the hull and splashing amid the oar sweep.

Small craft swarmed, hailing the heroes. It seemed the entire city had taken holiday. The ships came parallel to the Choma now, where the trierarchs of the fleet for Syracuse had assembled so gravely before the *apostoleis* to receive the blessing and the Council's order to launch. Such a mob now swarmed upon the mole as to hide it entire. *Atalanta* advanced to our starboard, obscuring the vantage. Amid the throng, glimpsed through the rigging of our squadronmate's stern, ascended the figure of Euryptolemus, bald dome reflecting. With one hand this noble embraced himself, as if to fix his self-command; the other, with exuberant welcome, waved his straw sun hat.

'Can that be you, cousin?' Alcibiades spoke in a whisper, and, bending towards the apparition, permitted his arm to respond. Ahead rose the pediment of the Bendidium and, beneath, the raked beaching ground of Thracian Artemis. *Kratiste* and *Alcippe* already executed reversions in place, for the bumpers to capture their sterns. Garlanded ephebes manned the shoring blocks awaiting *Antiope*. A pinging metallic clatter began to assault the deck. The people were throwing money. Boys swarmed over the gunwales and scrapped with their mates for the showering coins.

Where the Northern Wall abuts the Carriage Road, that dolorous highway I had trekked alone years past, returning from Potidaea; there where the hovels of the damned had sprawled during the Plague; now this gauntlet of horror had metamorphosed into a boulevard of joy. Cavalry mounts awaited the commanders. Their hooves trod a carpet of lavender. Though the other generals rode in prominence, the mob paid no heed but rounded only to behold Alcibiades. Fathers pointed him out to sons, and women, elder matrons as well as maidens, clutched at their bosoms and swooned.

He was borne to the Pnyx, where the hillsides overflowed with celebrants, roosting even in trees, like birds. There had been a ceremony on the way before the Eleusinium. Here at the hour of Alcibiades' banishment, the King Archon had mounted before the multitude to ordain the striking of the expelled's name from the *katalogos* of citizens and a stele of infamy erected, that the people never forget his perfidy and treason. Now advanced a new *basileus*, trembling, to present to this same man the reconstituted title to his holdings, within the city and his horse property at Erchiae, which had been confiscated at the time of his exile, and a suit of armour, the belated award of his prize of valour for Cyzicus. The stele had been broken apart, the archon pronounced, and cast into the sea.

Throughout these rites Alcibiades had maintained a bearing so stern and remote as to evoke in the people a species of dread. For the man before whom they now danced in supplication was no longer that princeling discharged so stonily beneath their whim but a war-scored

commander at the head of such a fleet and army as at a word might seize
the state and make dice of them all. The congregation searched the
thunderheads of his brow, as children caught at mischief sound their
headmaster as he grasps the rod. And when he suffered the multitude's
recantations with impatience and even disdain, handing off to aides the
various encomia and bills of praise without even a glance, the crowd
rustled in deepening trepidation.

In the square before the Amazoneum the triumphal wagons caught up
with the procession, bearing the ensigns and warpeaks of the enemy, his
rams, and the shields and armour of his generals. In the crush it would
take hours to reach the High City where these trophies would be
dedicated to the Goddess, so here, by gesture, since his voice could not
carry above the tumult, Alcibiades bade these prizes be set down. This
siting was unpremeditated; it so chanced, however, that this cargo of
glory found its rest beneath the great marble of Antiope, namesake of
his flagship, whose facing bears these verses to Theseus:

> And he with gifts returning
> Did to those come,
> Whose hatred first had
> Cast him from his home.

At the Museum, beneath the statue of Victory, his sons and the sons
of his kinsmen were presented to him, in their white ephebic robes,
bearing willow wands and crowned with myrtle. This sight surely, the
people anticipated, must make the darkness of his bearing relent. Yet
the opposite obtained. For the sight of these whose childhood had flown
unwitnessed by him, for his exile had endured now eight years, only
amplified the estrangement of his heart and the bereavement he felt of
those absent and lost. His immediate family, all long dead: mother,
father, and wife, infant daughters, brother and sisters fallen to plague
and war, elders wasted by age in his absence. Now, following, were
presented those of his extended clan, babes unborn when last he saw the
city, maidens now brides with infants of their own, and beardless lads
waxed to manhood; most he could neither nominate nor recognize so
that, as the herald tolled each name, the publication seemed to wring
his heart,

*as those beholding, face to face,*
*voked neither nurture nor embrace.*

The daughter of his cousin Euryptolemus was directed forward, a bride of sixteen, bearing her infant son, she garlanded with yew and rowan as rendering the Kore, her babe in violet for Athena. Advancing before the multitude, the girl, unnerved, could not recall her stanzas of welcome and, faltering, flushed and began to weep. Alcibiades, taking her elbow to uphold her, was overcome himself and could no longer contain the tears.

At once the dams of all hearts burst, as each, whelmed itself, induced capitulation in its neighbour, till none may withstand that which swelled, possessing all. For the people, who had either feared Alcibiades' ambition or dreaded his vengeance – in other words, had confined their concerns to self-interest – now beheld upon their prince's face, as he supported the sobbing girl, that grief he had borne in isolation all these years apart from those he loved. They forgot the evils he had brought and remembered only the good. And recognizing that this moment constituted that pinnacle of reconciliation at which city and son stood at last reunited, all concern for their own slipped their hearts, supplanted by compassion for him and joy at their mutual deliverance at his hands. By acclamation the Assembly appointed him *strategos autokrator*, supreme commander on land and sea, and awarded a golden crown.

He spoke while yet weeping. 'When I was a boy in Pericles' house, I would steal with my mates on Assembly days into those *peuke* trees there, upon the Pnyx's postern brow, and attend all day to the discourse and disputation, till my chums had grown bleary and begged me to depart with them to play; yet I alone remained upon my perch, attending the argument and debate. Even then, before I possessed command to articulate it, I felt the city's power, as if she were some great lioness or beast of legend. I marvelled at the enterprise of so many individual men, of such disparate and conflicting ambitions, and the engine of it all, the city, which by sublime alchemy yoked all to all and produced a whole greater than her parts, whose essence was neither wealth nor force of arms nor architectural or artistic brilliance, though all these she brought forth in abundance, but some quality of spirit, intangible, whose essence was audacity, intrepidity, and enterprise.

'That Athens which exiled me was not the Athens I loved, but another, failing of her nerve, dread-stricken before the exposition of her own greatness and banished from herself by that dread, as she in turn banished me. This Athens I hated and set all my energies to bring low.

'I was wrong. I have worked grave harm to her, this city I love. There stand no few here this day whose sons and brothers have lost their lives because of actions advanced or undertaken by me. I am guilty. Nothing may be said to exonerate me, unless it be that some dark destiny has dogged me and my family, and that this star, driving me apart from Athens and Athens from me, has reduced us both by its sinister designs. Let that bark take upon itself our transgressions, mine and yours, and bear them away upon the seas of heaven.'

Such a cry acclaimed this phrase, and such pounding of feet and hands, as to make the square tremble and the very columns of the sanctuary seem to quake. The people cried his name again and again.

'My enemies for years have sought to sow fear of me in your hearts, my countrymen, claiming that my object is rule over you. No fabrication could be more malign. I have never sought anything, my friends, but to merit your praise and to bear to you those blessings as would induce you to grant me honour. Yet that expression is imprecise. For my conception has never construed the city as a passive vessel into which I, her benefactor, decanted blessings. Such a course would be not only insolent but infamous. Rather I wished, as an officer advancing into battle at the head of his men, to serve as flame and inspiration to her, to call forth, by my belief in her, her birth and rebirth, altering with Necessity's command, but always advancing towards that which is most herself, that engine of glory which she was and is and must be, and that exemplar of freedom and enterprise to which all the world looks in awe and envy.'

Deafening acclamation made him hold long moments.

'Citizens of Athens, you have tendered me such surfeit of honours as no man may alone requite. Therefore let me summon reinforcements.' He motioned his fellow commanders forward, who had attended thus far in silence upon both hands. 'With pride I present to you, your sons whose feats of arms have brought about this hour of glory. Let me call their names and may your eyes feast upon their victorious manhood. Absent Thrasybulus, but present: Theremenes, Thrasyllus, Conon, Adeimantus, Erasinides, Thymochares, Leon, Diomedon, Pericles.'

Each in turn stepped forward and, elevating an arm or executing a bow in salute, elicited such cascades of citation as seemed must never end.

'These stand before you not alone for their own marks but in the stead of thousands yet on station overseas before whose might, we may state at last and acclaim its truth, the enemy has been swept from the seas.'

The roar of acclamation which greeted this eclipsed all which had preceded it. Alcibiades waited until the tumult had subsided.

'But let us not overextol the moment. Our enemies occupy half the states of our empire. Their Persian-provided treasury is ten times ours, nor is their fighting spirit attenuated but by our victories over them recharged and reinspirited. But now and at last, my friends, Athens possesses the will and cohesion to withstand them and prevail. Let us only be ourselves and we cannot fail.'

Such a clamour now arose that the very tiles on the roofs began to clatter and spill. Someone shouted, 'Let him see his home!' and at once the tide engulfed the platform, catching up the party and sweeping it towards Scambonidae, to Alcibiades' former estate, restored now by motion of the Assembly and refurbished in anticipation of his return. The scale of the swell choked the square, prodigious as it was, and the gates, capacious enough even for the great procession of the Panathenaea, could not contain the crush and jammed up in a merry mob.

At the peak of this jubilation, a citizen of about sixty years emerged and shouted towards Alcibiades: 'Where are those of Syracuse, thou treasonous villain!'

Angry cries commanded the elder to break off.

'Their ghosts are not present to cheer thee, godless renegade!'

At once the old man's form was swallowed by the mob. All that could be seen was the pack's rising and plunging fists, then their feet assaulting him, defenceless, on the earth. I turned to reckon Alcibiades' response but could not glimpse him, other figures intervening, but Euryptolemus's countenance rose proximate beside me. Upon his features I beheld such an expression of woe and foreboding as to blight the sun itself upon a cloudless noon.

# THIRTY-FIVE
# BEYOND THE REACH
# OF ENVY

FIVE DAYS LATER THE *PRYTANEIS* CALLED THE ASSEMBLY. MUCH BUSINESS had been prepared by the Council, as to the treasury, nearly bankrupt; reassessment of tribute from the empire; renewal of the *eisphora*, the war tax; imposts from the straits; plus business of the fleet and army, decorations of valour, courts-martial and charges of dereliction and peculation, and the further prosecution of the war. The docket was jammed, yet none would speak. The Assembly only buzzed until Alcibiades appeared, and when he did, the people addressed him with such unction and adulation that no business could be transacted, as each time a bill or measure would be put forward, someone would interrupt with a motion of acclaim. Nor did the derangement abate the day following or the session after, for each time an issue would be set forward by the *epistates*, the presiding officer, all heads would swivel to Alcibiades, awaiting his remark or that of his companions. None would cry yea till they saw him vote affirmative, or nay till they glimpsed him frown.

The Assembly had become paralysed, its deliberative function rendered impotent by the lustre of its most celebrated member. Nor did this aberration confine itself to public debate. Those private individuals like Euryptolemus and Pericles who were perceived as possessing influence with Alcibiades found themselves besieged, not alone by fawning petitioners but simply by friends and associates offering congratulations and proffering their services.

The Assembly consisted only of partisans of Alcibiades. There was no opposition. Even as he beseeched the college to voice dissent without fear, yet individuals seemed to rise only to second that which his votaries had moved or, anticipating such motions as they believed would find favour, bring only these forward. When Alcibiades absented himself, seeking to encourage debate, the assembly simply got up and went home. What was the point of being there if Alcibiades wasn't? When he vacated for dinner, the people did too. He couldn't get up to piss without a coalition reaching beneath their robes, competing to relieve themselves at his elbow.

His triumph of Eleusis followed. That holy procession in honour of the Mysteries whose passage by land had been broken off for fear these years of Spartan siege and been compelled to make its way ingloriously by sea, Alcibiades now restored to splendour, his cavalry and infantry escorting the novices and initiates along their twelve-mile trace, while enemy armour tracked the pilgrimage at a distance, powerless to intervene. I was there and saw the faces of the women as they pressed about their saviour, tears sheeting, calling upon the Two Goddesses, whose wronging at his hands had been the genesis of all this evil, to behold his strong arm shielding them and bearing them honour. So that it seemed now he possessed all favour, not alone of men but of heaven.

One presumed the madness would abate, but it didn't. Crowds pressed about him everywhere, in such numbers as to make Samos and Olympia look like children's games. Once passing along that alley called Little Speedway, by which one may approach the Round Chamber from the rear, his party was overwhelmed by such throngs as to wedge against the wall of the lane Diotimus, Adeimantus, and their wives, who happened to be with them, with such force as to make the ladies cry out in terror of suffocation. The marines in escort must shoulder through the shuttered front of a private home, effusing apologies for the invasion, while the diplomats and their wives fled through the rear egress, leaving the housewomen staring dumbstruck at Alcibiades, upon a bench in the court, his face in his hands, unstrung by the hysteria of the press.

We chased importunists from latrines, rooftops, the tombs of his ancestors. Idolaters came in the night, serenading. Petitions and poems were flung over his wall, wrapped about stones and blocks of wood, descending at times in such a downpour that the servants must evacuate all breakables and children play indoors, so as not to get brained by these projectiles of adoration. Vendors hawked images of him on plates and eggcups, bossed onto medallions, woven into headbands and dust rags, pennants and paper kites. Ikons called 'luck-catchers' were purveyed on every corner, little mast-and-mainsail geegaws with *nu* and *alpha* for Victory and Alcibiades. Models of *Antiope* sold for an obol. Everywhere the guileless hearts of the commons erected shrines of devotion; through the doorways of their flats one glimpsed the sill of gimcracks, laid out like an altar to a demigod.

Delegations presented themselves to him from brotherhoods and tribal councils, cults of heroes and ancestors, veterans' associations, craftsmen's guilds, and fellowships of resident aliens; all-female groups, all-elder and all-youth, some applying for redress of some grievance, others declaring their allegiance, still others appearing to present him with the supreme honour of their sect, some preposterous bauble which the marines must label and heave in a box and cart to the warehouse. But mostly they came for no reason at all, just to be there and see him. In fact it was a point of honour to come for no reason, spontaneously and unannounced, as any calendared agenda smacked of covetousness or self-interest. Therefore they came; the joiners at dawn, the Sons of Danae at the market hour, then the Curators of the Naval Yards and the potters and on and on, serving up the same confection of bombast, abjection, and self-congratulation. Critias, who would himself be tyrant one day, even set such sentiment to verse.

> From my proposal did that edict come,
> Which from your tedious exile brought you home.
> The public vote at first was moved by me,
> And my voice put the seal to the decree.

Nowhere could be discovered any who had voted against him or served on a jury that condemned him. These must have vacated to Hyperborea or hell. Nor could the delegations' encomiasts complete their panegyrics, as cries of '*Autokrator, autokrator!*' interrupted, ascending ad lib from the throng. They wanted Alcibiades master of the state, subject to no constitutional curbs, and in the evening more sober fraternities would second these sentiments, of the Knights' class and the Hoplites', the men of the fleet and the tradesmen's guilds, and plead with him to put himself beyond the reach of envy. Each coterie warned of the fickleness of the *demos*. 'They' would turn on him, 'their' devotion would prove unsteadfast. When that hour came, these partisans of obeisance admonished, Alcibiades' purchase on authority must be absolute. Nothing less was at stake than the survival of the nation.

On the twelfth evening, the most earnest and influential company yet convened at the home of Callias the son of Hipponicus. Critias himself was its spokesman. If Alcibiades assented, he declared, he would the following morning place the motion before the people. It would be enacted by acclamation. At last the city would stand beyond its own self-devastating pendulations of passion. The war could be prosecuted and won.

Alcibiades made no response. Euryptolemus spoke for him. 'But, Critias,' he observed, in a tone flat with understatement, 'such a motion would be contrary to law.'

'With all respect, my friend. The *demos* makes the law, and what it says is the law.'

Still Alcibiades did not speak.

'Let me be sure I understand you,' Euryptolemus continued to Critias. 'Are we to agree that this same *demos* which banished and condemned my cousin unconstitutionally may now, with symmetrical lawlessness, anoint him dictator?'

'The people acted in madness then,' declared Critias with emphasis. 'They act with reason now.'

# THIRTY-SIX

# A DISREFRACTING GLASS

ALCIBIADES SPURNED CRITIAS'S SUMMONS, AS YOU KNOW, CITING THE poet's admonishment that

> *Tyranny is a splendid roost*
> *but there is no step down from it*

and when report of this self-regulation reached the people, his popularity soared to yet more unprecedented heights.

Nor did his enemies wait long to find means to exploit this. It was a sight of pungent irony to observe such miscegenated bedfellows as Cleophon, Anytus, Cephisophon, and Myrtilus, the zealots of the oligarchs, leaping into wedlock with the radical democrats, not only stepping forth in concert but advocating those policies most likely to find favour in Alcibiades' quarter; in other words, to become his most ardent and obeisant toadies, their strategy being, as the comic poets later elucidated, to 'over-Alcibiadize' the people until he lodged in their craw and they spat him out.

No-one perceived this peril more keenly than Alcibiades himself. He drew about him now those companions of youth and war – Euryptolemus and Adeimantus, Aristocrates, Diotimus, and Mantitheus – who he felt loved him for himself and did not perceive him, in the phrase of the poet Agathon, through the disrefracting glass of their own hope and terror. I as well found myself drawn more closely into his confidence.

He entrusted me with assignments of increasing import and subtlety. I was sent to address groups of the bereaved of Sicily, to serve on the committee seeking a site for the memorial. I officiated at sacrifices, represented the fleet marine force at official occasions, entertained prospective allies, and attempted to suborn or intimidate potential foes. I found these chores excruciating and begged to be released. He wished to know my objection.

'They acclaim me not for myself, but for some imagined "Polemides", and address themselves to me as if I were he.'

He laughed. 'Now you're a politician.'

Until that time I had managed to keep clear of political connivance. This now became impossible. Life was politics. A man encountered may not be greeted as mate or fellow, but must be assessed as partisan or adversary and dealt with by this criterion alone: what can he do for our side, this day, not later, while he simultaneously took our measure, and in the same coin. One no longer talked but negotiated, spoke not but represented. The deal was everything; one breathed only to close. Yet such proved elusive as smoke. For many could say no but only one yes, and without yes you had nothing. The worth of each man rose or fell as a ram in the livestock market, according to that currency which is neither coin nor *khous* but influence. I never smiled so much nor meant it less, nor met such friends to whom I was nothing. In all things, perception superseded substance. You could not demand accountability of others, nor give your own pledge to any undertaking, however trivial, but always options must be kept open till the last instant, at which point all bets were off and if you'd given your word to a friend, you now broke it at the orders of another friend and leapt as fast as you could upon the main chance. At dawn I stood garlanded, sacrificing to the gods; by night I cut deals with stooges and back-stabbers. This was not my style. I detested it. Compounding all were the tremendous stakes of these affairs, so that I must think, and indeed did, not only how our party might outpolitick those opposed but in the crunch how we might put them by. I missed not only my bride but her brothers and father and the straightforward landsman's ways of these who had become to me, I realized now apart from them, my hearth and family.

Now I myself became ensnared in politics' web.

I had taken residence with my aunt at Melite. To her I confided my plans to secure exemption or retirement from service and with my wife and child repair to Road's Turn. It was my ardent wish that my aunt make her home with us. I would build her a cottage; she could play the matriarch and lord it over all. She said she had always fancied a cottage. I took her hands in mine. It seemed happiness lay beyond one final bar of shoal.

I went to the Registrar to record my intent to build on our land at Acharnae. To my shock the clerk informed me that a claim had been placed against it. What was this, a joke? The recorder displayed the documents. One Axiomenes of Colonus, of whom I had never heard, had filed a petition of decedent estate, citing my death overseas, and the demise of my brother and father prior, and laying claim to the property. He had even deposited the *parakatabole*, equal to a tenth of the estate's value.

Dawn found me before the archon's clerk, scheduling a *diamartyria*, that hearing at which witnesses known to the court would testify that I was indeed my father's son and legitimate heir. That should put a period to this nonsense, I thought. But when I rode out to the farm at noon, I discovered labour gangs at work upon the site. The sons of the afore-mentioned Axiomenes chanced to arrive at this juncture, three in number, and, comporting themselves with insufferable arrogance, dis-played their papers and proceeded to order me off my own land. I was in military kit, it chanced, with a ceremonial sword at my hip. Perhaps an evil *daimon* took hold of me. My hand flew to the weapon's hilt, and though self-command was reasserted before I could bare its blade, the act itself and the fury behind it sent my antagonists backpedalling in fright and outrage. They withdrew with oaths and pledges to eviscerate me in court. 'And do not run to your patron, Alcibiades,' the eldest squealed. 'For not even he stands above the law.'

A man of politics would have grasped at once the covert design understationing this ruse. I did not. My distress was such that I took counsel with a number of friends, including my commander, the younger Pericles, who, guileless as myself, accompanied me to address this Axiomenes at his home. I begged the fellow's pardon and, maintaining a tenor of temperance, restated my position which was unassailable: I had not been slain in war; the farm was mine; let us put this affray behind us. I would make restitution, I promised, for my unfortunate outburst.

'Indeed you shall,' this villain responded. He had filed an impeachment against me before the Council.

On what charge?

'Treason.'

He had done his homework, this rogue, and unearthed the particulars of my deliverance from the quarries at Syracuse. I was, the denunciation of *eisangelia* professed, an 'agent and instrument of Sparta'. My schooling in Lacedaemon was cited, my repatriation to that country after Sicily, my service with Alcibiades in Asia 'in league with the enemies of Athens', and even the derivation of my own and my father's names, along with diverse other perjuries, slanders, and falsehoods.

This was serious business; not only did the charge carry the penalty of death, but the object of such a motion was liable to *apagoge*, summary arrest. I might not close my eyes without fear of enemies snatching me at swordpoint.

I resolved to settle this without plaguing Alcibiades. But he heard of it on his own and called me to him. This was at his horse property at Erchiae, where he rode early for exercise and to clear his head. 'This action,' he declared at once, 'is not aimed at you, my friend, but me. It is not the only one.'

Some forty lawsuits, he reported, had been filed over the prior eleven days, all targeting colleagues and sharing the same theme: converse with the enemy. The cumulative effect, his opponents hoped, would be to enlarge mistrust of Alcibiades and portray him as in secret complicity with Sparta. My case was small beer. This Axiomenes, Alcibiades imparted, was a flunky of Euthydemus of Cydathenaeus, an uncle of Antiphon and member of the cult of Heracles of that district, an ultra-oligarchic political club, allied with scores of others in their hatred of Alcibiades and resolve to bring him down. 'I'm sorry your affairs have got mixed up with mine, Pommo. But our enemies may have unwittingly handed us a stroke in a greater game. Do you trust me, old friend?'

He could put me to use, if I would consent.

He would interdict the petition of vacancy by bringing a *dike pseudomartyriou,* a suit for false witness; after which he would contrive to have the farm placed in provisional stewardship of any kinsman I wished, to be held over for me until I returned.

'Returned? From where?'

'Meanwhile, Pommo, you must not contest the other charge, the impeachment for treason, but act in fact as if it were true. You must flee.'

I could think only of my bride and aunt. How would I explain this to them? How care for our child? If I absconded under indictment, Aurore and the babe could not come to Athens. As for me, would I not be confirming my guilt by flight and risking banishment for ever?

'Have I ever failed to shield you, Pommo?' Alcibiades assured me that so long as he ruled, no action of man or law would work harm to me or my family. He would set all to right, and with interest.

'Our foes wish to paint you a partisan of Sparta. Very well. We'll let them.'

He wished me to go over to the enemy. Make my way to Ephesus, the Spartan bastion of the Aegean, now under Lysander, newly elevated to fleet admiral. Lysander's prior acquaintance of me, supplemented by these credentials of the charges lodged against me, would open doors to his person. At large I was to represent myself as a private individual only but apart, when summoned by Lysander for interrogation, which summons was certain, disclose my charge as envoy from Alcibiades. I was to attest the good faith of his overtures of alliance with the Spartan and stand by as courier for such communications as Lysander wished to rejoin.

As for any sentence passed against me at Athens, Alcibiades would simply issue a pardon in his capacity as *strategos autokrator,* supreme commander.

'Then do that for me now,' I demanded.

My commander drew up. His eyes met mine, neither cold nor malign, yet intractable.

'These are great affairs, Pommo.'

'Your great affairs.'

'I am as constrained by them as you.'

He had an additional wrinkle to my defection. Some ten days previous, several companies of war prisoners had been brought in from Chalcidice. Among them was my old mate Telamon. I had got him released; he was in hospital now, recovering from wounds. I had not informed Alcibiades or any of my superiors, deeming it beneath their notice. Of course he knew. 'Prise your man out of the sawbones' shack. Make your easting together, as if to advertise your availability as assassins. This will further enlarge your credibility with Lysander; he may even seek to employ you as such against me.'

I would go. What else could I do?

'I take no joy in exploiting your predicament, Pommo. But desperate straits require desperate measures. You care nothing for such sentiments, I know, but this chore, if it succeeds, will alter the fate not alone of Greece but of the world.'

'You're right,' I said. 'I care nothing.'

Euryptolemus and Mantitheus chanced to return at that moment from their own rides in the hills. My predicament was remarked, and the ordination of our commander's coercion. By all means, Euryptolemus attested, I must bolt this charge of treason; I must not let myself be packed off behind bars. Months could pass before trial; who could predict the *demos'* disposition then? It would be madness to tempt fortune before an Athenian jury, particularly since those who would be my defenders must, like myself, depart to war again, and soon.

'Cheer up, Pommo, this rounds out your résumé.' Our commander's cousin laughed and placed a hand upon my shoulder. 'Don't you know, a man may not account himself a true son of Athens until he has been exiled and condemned to death!'

# THIRTY-SEVEN
# A HUNT ON PARNES

MY PLIGHT HAD BEEN BROUGHT ABOUT AS A BY-PRODUCT OF A stratagem Alcibiades had put in play some days prior. The campaign of actions at law was an element of his foe's reply. You have kinsmen and colleagues, Jason, who were present on the evening to which I now refer; no doubt you recall its occasion. Let me relate it as memory serves:

Some days after his return to Athens, not long subsequent to his triumph at Eleusis, Alcibiades organized a hunt on the slopes of Parnes, inviting not only those disposed in his favour but a number of personal and political enemies including Anytus and Cephisophon, the later tyrant Critias, also Lampon, Hagnon, and your own uncle Myrtilus, the latter trio representing the extreme wing of the 'Party of the Good and True', who had been the most virulent of Alcibiades' prosecutors during the affair of the Mysteries. Cleophon and Cleonymus stood for the zealots of the radical democrats. Charicles was invited as well, who with Peisander had inflamed the people against Alcibiades in those days and, among other measures during the reign of terror their stridency had abetted to foment, had proposed repealing the decree banning the torturing of citizens. This hunt on Parnes, Alcibiades put about, was an extension of the olive branch to his former foes. He wanted to make peace with them.

The hunt itself was a grandstand gesture by its host, as considerable

Spartan elements still infested the region, the fort at Decelea lying only seven miles east, and this audacity on Alcibiades' part seized the imagination of the city, as not even the keenest hunters had dared take a party into those hills in years. So thoroughly had the invaders made the place their own, in fact, that Spartan rangers had at seasons set up digs in the lodge itself, stocking the larder and even rebuilding the stone chimney when it toppled in a quake. One could not say no to such an invitation, not with the city buzzing and volunteers of the cavalry trooping forth to provide protection. In addition of course all were aflame to learn what Alcibiades had up his sleeve.

The elements proved wildly inclement; downpours drenched the party both days. The hunting was grand, however, and it may be recounted of the hunters – returning to the lodge to strip their sodden tunics and hang them steaming before the fire, soaking their aches in the great cauldron baths, to be followed by rubdowns with warm oil and then leisure to indulge in the notorious red vintage of the region with pears, figs, and cheese – that no complaints were posted, nor did the meal of game hen, venison, and roast goose engender distress. At last the weary but replete guests settled upon couches in the great hall whose four copper-belled flues each accommodated two hearth fires. Stalkers, beaters, houndsmen, and servants having been dismissed, save those personal attendants whose confidentiality could be relied upon, there remained some thirty gentlemen. Euryptolemus, Adeimantus, Mantitheus, Aristocrates, and the younger Pericles constituted the cabinet of our host, with Theremenes, Thrasyllus, Procles, Ariston, and his party making up the moderates, and those cited above forming the opposition. The distinction of inclusion had done much to disarm hostility. All seemed softened up when their host, clad in huntsman's cloak, arose beside the hearth and began.

He launched without preamble, proposing at once an end to the war and alliance with Sparta. While his guests still goggled at this, he proposed the joint undertaking of war against Persia, its object not limited to liberation of the Greek cities of Asia Minor but, that accomplished, to press inland against Sardis, Susa, and Persepolis. In other words, to conquer the empire entire, clear to India.

The temerity of such an undertaking was so breathtaking that several of the listeners, recovering speech, laughed outright, while others enquired if their host had taken leave of his reason.

Alcibiades addressed first the practical benefits, the most immediate of which was getting the Spartans out of Attica and all back to our estates. That alone would accomplish prodigies: propitiating the hostility of the rich and abating their intriguings against the democracy. Restore them to their vines and horses and they'll give back on over-throwing the state. Nor would the dividends of such an undertaking be confined to the aristocracy. The *demos* would prosper as well, not only our own unpropertied citizens but the unfranchised orders of resident aliens, foreigners, and even slaves, the main of whom are more eager for action than our own citizens. Give them an enterprise of profit and glory, no longer against each other, but barbarians dripping with gold, and they will shut up too.

'This, gentlemen, I call "feeding the Monster". It means providing for our nation's restless factions an object worthy of their aspirations – one that does not set them at odds with each other but reconciles their dis-parate objects. These days the monster has become all Greece, for this war has scraped the moss from every Hellene's backside. They have become Athenians all, even the Spartans.'

He offered a compelling disquisition on the parties at Lacedaemon. That expansionist faction led by Endius would embrace this course with vigour, once satisfied of its authenticity, as would Callicratidas and the old guard who abhor the barbarian and bridle bitterly at grovelling for his gold. The party of Agis and Lysander would oppose us, not because they disbelieved in the enterprise (they would compete for its leadership if they thought it would advance their own self-interest), but because their ambition was bound too tightly to Prince Cyrus of Persia's purse. Private embassies, Alcibiades confided, had long since sounded both parties, and more were on the way; what could not be effected by persuasion might be accomplished by gold.

Persian invincibility was a myth, Alcibiades continued. Their army, composed of conscripts and subject states, would melt away before even second-tier Spartan forces as it had before ours throughout the Hellespontine War, and their navy would prove as paper against the fleet of Athens. He portrayed the Persian system of independent satrapies and the division fostered among them by the King. Darius's health failed; succession struggles would sunder all Asia. Thrusts by our armies into her belly would tear the empire apart. He made it sound so plausible as to be inevitable, particularly allying ourselves with the Macedonians and Thracians, whose princes were favourably disposed to him, and the Greek cities of Ionia whose end had always been independence and would rise as one beneath the banner of their united homeland.

His listeners were professional politicians and knew to distinguish purpose from enactment. To this Alcibiades now addressed himself. 'Consider the predicament, gentlemen, in which this proposal places the Spartans. They have rallied the allied states by their slogan of "freedom", which means no more than getting rid of us. Now we ourselves would commandeer this high ground, constraining them to make a choice which will shake their state to its foundation.

'Consider next the reaction of the independent Greek states. Each shrinks to follow a power as Sparta or Athens lest she be gobbled up and made subject, or fears that that Greek alliance of foes will defeat her outright. But to join an alliance of these two against non-Greeks presents a far less daunting prospect. If affairs fall out, she can always back one power against the other; if the enterprise fails, she has set only men and ships at hazard, not her own sovereignty, and if it succeeds, she may reap wealth and glory unimagined.

'Lastly, gentlemen, ponder the effect upon the Persian. The Spartans are his allies. Even if they reject our offer, the Mede cannot but wonder, as each new admiral comes out from Sparta, where this fellow stands and how far he is to be trusted. So that even if we must continue this war, we have sown disunity among our enemies, and at the cost of nothing to ourselves.'

Now came the main stroke: 'I want you to make this proposal, Cleophon, and you, Anytus and Charicles. Not me.

'Such a measure must be put forward by my enemies. Hear me, please, and weigh these considerations. If I or any of my party place this plan before the people, it will be perceived as recklessness born of pride. I will be accused of partisanship in favour of the Spartans owing to my past associations with them, or, worse, being bribed by them, and this will be followed by the predictable indictments of treason, ambition, self-interest, and so forth. You yourselves will no doubt put these forward. On the other hand, if your parties, gentlemen, whose enmity for the Spartans is known to be implacable, advance this proposition, it will at once achieve credibility and, more, be greeted as one of vision and daring. You will gain the credit. And I will back you with all I possess.'

He was speaking to no fools. All perceived at once the genius of this plan and its corollary, that is, of having his enemies propose it. Should Anytus and Charicles of the oligarchs or Cleophon of the radical democrats do as Alcibiades proposed and advance the measure in their own names, he would have either achieved his object, if this in fact was his intent, or, more likely, have set his foes up for a double cross, should he instead denounce the project as treason and themselves as traitors, claiming never to have heard of such a plan and demanding that its progenitors receive hard justice. Should his enemies on the other hand attempt to pre-empt this by betraying him first to the people, represent-ing the plan as his own, themselves rejecting it, they ran the risk of discovering the *demos* in support and themselves cut out by their own cravenness and perfidy. Either way they were ruined. And he, Alcibiades, would appear as the generous and all-embracing statesman who had offered even to his enemies this chance for glory they had so short-sightedly spurned, or as the blameless patriot stabbed in the back by the same villains who had deprived the city of his genius once before. Only if the people rejected Alcibiades' plan would his opponents come off unscathed. But who could risk that now, in the supreme hour of his ascendancy?

Charicles rose, the would-be torture master. 'Why go to such extrava-gant lengths to ruin us, Alcibiades? Why not simply employ murder? We would.'

Alcibiades laughed. 'That would not be as much fun!' Then with an expression sober as stone repeated that he stood in absolute earnest about the plan.

'Balls!' rejoined his foe. 'I'll stand with you in hell before Persepolis.' And he stalked from the stage.

Debate protracted far into the night, with much propounded by Critias, Cleophon, and Anytus, arguing their separate points of view, Critias as expected favouring alliance with Sparta but apprehensive about the people's response and Anytus attacking the plan as 'un-Athenian' and in fact treasonous, meaning he believed Alcibiades trod the city as a stone to grander ends, and in fact cared nothing for Athens save as 'a bauble with which to encrust your tiara'. To Anytus's credit he spoke this straight out to his foe, nor censored candour in any form.

Past midnight I retired with the younger Pericles to the cubby hole we shared. For some time voices could be heard from the hall; at last the lodge fell silent. Sleep after such a symposium proved elusive, however; waking with an appetite, my roomfellow and I crept down to raid the larder. To our astonishment Alcibiades was awake, in the kitchen, alone save his secretary, dictating correspondence. 'My dear Pommo and Pericles! What calls you forth, a late supper or an early dinner?'

He rose at once and, drawing benches to the great table, insisted on serving as chef's apprentice, to prepare us a snack of cold meat and breads. He dismissed his weary secretary and, enquiring of our welfare and that of our families, set to his task.

'I couldn't summon the pluck to enquire in the presence of the others, Alcibiades,' our host's kinsman seized the moment to venture, 'but can you truly be serious about this Persian business?'

'Sober as a shroud, my friend.'

'Surely you can't expect this night's synod to remain privileged. It wouldn't surprise me if reports were speeding now on the road to Athens.'

Alcibiades smiled. 'Tonight's caucus was for many audiences, Pericles, least of all those assembled to receive it firsthand.'

Alcibiades drew up and, his speech altering into that tenor of con-fidentiality which may not be dissimulated, addressed us as a master his acolytes or a hierophant his mystae. 'Understand what may be accom-plished. Victory over Sparta is a chimera. Persian treasure or no, her army remains invincible. Nor would one wish to overthrow her even if one could, lest such a consequence, in Cimon's phrase,

*make Greece over lame and rob Athens of its yoke-fellow.*

What, then, is possible? Not peace. This, Greece has never known and never will. Rather a nobler war. A war that will not alone turn the Monster from devouring her own vitals but set her upon a stage of such scale and moment as may permit the meanest to mount to prominence and the greatest to undying glory.'

Alcibiades served the bread and meat. We both wondered at the daring of his vision and the extravagance of his ambition.

'One perceives your purpose, sir. But in all candour, can such an adventure succeed?'

'It must and it shall.'

He sat then and, remarking Pericles' expression of incredulity, rejoined with a dissertation so extraordinary, and so revelatory of the configuration of his intellect, that this officer took the extraordinary measure upon return to our quarters of setting it down, as close to verbatim as he and I could recollect. I have the notes yet, in my sea chest.

'Most men believe,' Alcibiades began, 'that what they call waking life is our only existence, while dreams are such substanceless apparitions as visit our slumbering selves at night. The wild tribes beyond Bithynian Thrace warrant the opposite. To them true existence takes place in sleep, while this, waking life, they dismiss as phantom and illusion. They can locate wild game, that is, predict the site of its appearance, based on dreams which they claim to summon the night in advance. I have hunted with them and I believe it. They enter and exit dreams at will, they testify, and fear nothing more than to die in their dreams, while death in the flesh they account as nothing, the dream enduring absent even that vessel which housed it.'

'What nonsense!' Pericles exclaimed. 'If you die in a dream you don't wake up dead. But perish in real life and you'll dream no more!'

Alcibiades only smiled. 'One senses a world beneath this one. Not a dream exactly, but a possibility. That which is not yet but which may be. And which we may summon. As a boy lies in the grass at the brook edge, who may break the surface with his hand to snatch a pebble from the bottom. This is how one lives, is it not? A beast sees gross substance only, but a man sees dreams.

'I have dined on dreams. Not alone to sustain myself but to set a feast before others. This is how the great identify one another and how the commander of vision leads free men. Ah,' Alcibiades continued, 'but not any dream will do. Only one, and that, like the pebble in the stream, has long been nominated. This pebble has a name. It is called Necessity. Necessity is the dream. That which cries out to be born and summons all who would call themselves commanders to draw it forth.

'As a boy I often observed this of the elder Pericles: that he was capable, through no force beyond that of his own person, of defining present and future not only for himself but for others. He could tell them what they saw and make them see it, perceiving no longer with their own eyes but with his. By such means he held the city, and the world, in thrall.

'Lovers perform this service for each other, the elder elevating the younger by donating his nobler and more far-reaching vision. For all boys, and most men, are profoundly imperfect not only in themselves but in their aspirations, which are mediocre, vain, and self-interested. This was Socrates' gift to me, to exalt my aspiration, and I perceived of the power by which it held me that this was man's supreme gift to his fellows and also his mightiest instrument of ambition. For what may raise a man higher in his countrymen's esteem than to bear to them happiness and prosperity?

'Socrates,' he continued, 'considers politics inferior to philosophy, and in this I concur. What educated man wouldn't? But philosophy could not exist without politics. By this measure politics is the noblest calling of all, for it makes all others possible. And how would one define politics except the bringing forth of a vision for the people, that vision which is their destiny but which they sense only imperfectly and by part.'

'That is no politician, Alcibiades, but a prophet!'

'The prophet perceives truth, Pericles, but the politician brings it into manifestation, for his countrymen and often in the face of their bitter opposition.'

'And in the case of Athens,' this officer put in, 'that of our subjects and enemies.'

Here was a point I myself wished to question.

'Suppose, Alcibiades, that Justice were seated at this table and were to call you short, saying, "My friend, you have left me out of your equation. For what you call Necessity, others name Injustice, Oppression, and even Murder." How would you respond to the goddess?'

'I would remind Justice, my friend, that Necessity is elder to her and was made before even the earth. Justice, as she well knows, may not prevail even in heaven. Why should she, therefore, among mortals?'

'This is a stern philosophy, Alcibiades.'

'It is the philosophy of power and those who possess it. The philosophy of empire. And we have all embraced it who hold our subject states, Spartans and Persians as well as Athenians. Otherwise let them go! But then we fall, and fail, and slight our destiny. This to my mind is a far weightier crime than injustice, particularly our own benign species, which in fact brings greater security and material blessing than our subject states would be capable of providing for themselves without us.

'But here is the point, my friends. Our so-called subject states are not subject in the deeper sense, that is, held down by force, but are instead compelled to emulate us, at our greatest, by their thralldom to our excellence. Otherwise why do their sons flock to our city and our fleet, even in her most embattled hours? Their destiny ascends with ours and is indivisible from it, as that of all those slumbering states whose armies will fall in freely and joyfully at our side when we advance against Asia.'

'Then you see not just for Athens, Alcibiades, but for her subjects and enemies as well?'

'And the wide world!' Pericles put in.

Alcibiades responded with a peal of irony light as spindrift. He indicated the plates and platter before us.

'I merely set out the banquet and stand aside while my companions dine.'

Returning to our billets, we passed those of Anytus, Critias, and Charicles, yet astir and hissing with conspiracy. Alcibiades' enemies intrigued for a device by which to bring him low. They did not reckon that that agent which would despoil him, and themselves, had already at that hour debarked at Castolus in Ionia, under guard of the Caranedion, the Royal Horse of Prince Cyrus of Persia.

# BOOK EIGHT

# THRICE
# NINE YEARS

# THIRTY-EIGHT
# THE GRAVITY OF GOLD

HAVE YOU EVER SEEN A CARTLOAD OF GOLD, JASON?
It doesn't look like much. Just two ingots, swathed in fleece and
no bigger round than firestand logs, but so heavy, the escort officers
informed Telamon and me, permitting us a glimpse outside the treasury
at Ephesus, that they must be loaded by tackle up a rollered incline.
Each bar has to set directly over an axle or the weight will break the
wagon's back. Such a burden must be drawn by oxen; draft horses or
mules could pull it on the flat, but not up a grade.

Prince Cyrus had conveyed nine of these to Castolus with instructions from his father, Darius of Persia, to supply the Spartans with
everything they needed to destroy the fleet of Athens. Past this, reports
said, the prince had pledged his personal fortune and vowed even to
break up his golden throne. This was five thousand talents in all, ten
times the treasury of Athens. You tell me, my friend, what won the war
for Lysander.

Sailors of Athens were drawing three obols; Lysander paid four. An
Athenian crew was three-quarters foreigners then; some ships listed as
few as twenty citizens. Lysander's recruiters could sell these lads hard.
And the Spartan paid 'on the bollard', full wages each month, not a
third only, as our own paymasters, the rest held back till you made home
port . . .

A T THIS POINT PRECISELY – I RECALL BECAUSE MY NOTES BREAK OFF IN
mid-sentence – a commotion from the Iron Court interrupted
Polemides. A turnkey appeared with the report that a woman claiming to be
the prisoner's wife had forced her way into the jailer's station and was, in the
most scabrous tongue, demanding entry to him. This could be none but
Eunice. 'What shall I tell her?'

'That I am otherwise occupied.'

We could hear her oaths, rivalling any boatswain's, as the porter conducted
her from the yard.

'The lone privilege of incarceration,' Polemides observed. 'Privacy.'

His concentration had been broken, however. I had other obligations;
we cut the session short. Though at this juncture, my grandson, I may prof-
itably interject, to continue Polemides' train, several documents of my own
possession.

These are captain's logs of the younger Pericles, commanding Calliope at
that time, deposited by him into my care following the trial of the generals of
Arginousai. They make a sketch of the early campaign against Lysander.

8   Hecatombaion, Mycale straits. Beleaguering the Pedagogue.
[The Athenians called Lysander this, as well as Schoolmaster and
Professor.] He will not come out to play.

12   Hec. Blockading Ephesus. Prof's 76 won't stick nose out to
face our 54.

27   Hec. Raid villages east of Elaeus. 60 taken, mostly women,
worth barely a mina. 6 wounded, 4 severely. Pay: 40 days arrears.

3   Metageitnion, Imbros. Chased 2 sq of 6 and 8 all day from
Myrina. They drag ashore, flee by night.

11   Meta. Aenus, Thrace. Pillage. 4 wounded. No pay.

14   Meta. More villages. No pay.

2   Boedromion, Samos. Indomitable in. Alcib with 3 sq has been
chasing Lys from Aspendus. Still no action.

*This was the Spartan navarch's answer to the supreme pitch of readiness possessed then by his enemies. He refused to be brought to battle. He would not fight.*

*Pericles writes to his wife, Chione:*

It is one thing among commanders to grasp Lysander's strategy and steel oneself with patience for its overthrow, and another entirely to sell this to the men. The crews discharge their frustration not on Lysander, but on us.

*To his son Xanthippus, already schooling the lad to the commander's trade:*

... money remains the naval officer's bane. Nothing, not even a horse-breeding establishment, eats cash like a ship, and none gobbles it more greedily than a trireme. The replacement of a single plank with its mortise-and-tenon joinery requires the vessel to be careened, girdle unshipped, and often a complete section of hull replaced and refitted, a task of such complexity as to require the skills of master ship's carpenters, not to mention the right wood of the right age in the right dimensions, and where can you find any of these when you need them? But the main loot-devourer is the men, who spree every spit the instant they touch it, and who can fault them, breaking their backs in all weathers at constant peril of their lives? Try telling them, after ten days of eighteen-hour pulls, cold chow, no sleep, all of it up and down a hostile shore, that you can't come up with their wages!

The trierarch expends the capital of his credibility every time he puts his men off, which he will covet sorely when next they see action, and if he's rich, which he must be (or so the men believe) or the city would not have lumbered him with command of a vessel of war, then the bitching oarsmen want to know why he doesn't dip into his own coffers now, for their sake, and recoup it from the treasury later. Of course many do, to their ruin. For once a captain has funded his crew from his own purse, he can never say them nay again. He has ceased to be their commander and become their slave.

Foremost among Alcibiades' aptitudes, and the element by

which he has held the nearly bankrupt fleet together for so long, is his mastery of extracting treasure from a city or rural district against its will. For believe me, these planters can bury their goods deeper than you can dig to find them, and to put their feet to the fire only doles to the enemy exactly what he wants. Alcibiades alone can make them cough the loot up on their own. Contributions. He charms or swindles them or writes his notorious W.C.s – Warrants of Compensation. The fleet may send no-one else to perform this wizardry. They can't pull it off. This produces a further liability, for Alcibiades must be drawn from command purely to raise money. This eats like acid at morale, but the fleet possesses no alternative and Lysander knows it.

Our commanders, driven by the hard pinch, must make acquaintance of the terrible chore of pillage. Its cardinal mischief is the hazard at which it sets the men. Seamen are equipped neither physically nor constitutionally for land warfare; it unnerves them. Those who are leaders on ship fall back as the column presses inland, while the bullies and blackguards mount to the fore. It is not the oarsman's forte to assault palisades, drive off sheep, or round up for the slave dealers urchins and grandmothers. If a village puts up resistance, the men squat, sullen, and refuse to attack. If the foe caves in, they run amok. Atrocities. The officer dreads this before all. For every maiden raped means another hamlet handed on a plate to the foe and, of more immediate peril, the massacred victim's kin roused to vengeance, harrying our passage back to the ship, bronzeheads and stones raining on our rear guard, javelin-slinging zealots making rushes at us, on horseback, while the very loot we've risked our hides to bag must be dumped willy-nilly as we lighten loads to flee.

The party always comes back with wounded, and this works hell on the ship. Even one man gutted and wailing turns every other's bowels to water, and it's worse if he's blinded or burned. God forbid a man catch iron in the privates; his mates huddle dread-stricken and only action, at once and to save their skins, keeps the aspiring demagogues among the crew from whipping the men to the brink of mutiny. You can flog them. You can hawsehole them. You can have the marines single out one and make an example. But a ship of war runs on heart as much as sweat. There must be love among the men or you're finished.

# THIRTY-NINE
# BAWLERS AND CRAWLERS

IHAD A NUMBER OF OTHER OBLIGATIONS THAT DAY [GRANDFATHER continued], *several relating to Socrates, whose date of execution stood apart only four risings of the evening star; it was well past midnight when at last I reached home. To my astonishment, Eunice awaited, alone in the fore-court, with a mantle about her shoulders against the chill. She had been there all day, she reported, since vacating the prison. My wife had given her supper and set at her disposal an attendant to conduct her home, but the matter upon which she called was urgent, she declared, so she had elected to remain. She must speak to Polemides. It could not wait.*

*I was exhausted and desired nothing more than a bowl of wine and a warm bed, but I sensed a chance at last to get to the bottom of things.* 'Who has filed this murder charge against Polemides?' *I demanded in a manner both sudden and truculent.* 'Not the name on the indictment – I know that – but the real prosecutor. Who is behind this, and why?'

*Eunice rose with indignation, disclaiming all intelligence. She commenced pacing, then muttering, at once breaking into a spate of profanity.*

'At what house are you staying?' *I demanded, employing not* oikos *but* oikema *for its connotations of the brothel.*

*That of Colophon, she replied in anger, the son of Hestiodorus of Collytos. This was, I knew, a nephew of Anytus, who was prosecuting Socrates and the bitterest foe of Alcibiades in the past. It was Colophon's brother Andron who had taken the prosecutor's oath that he was a phratry-mate of the victim, and* had sworn out the writ of elapsement to permit prosecution after passage of time.

'And do you share this Colophon's bed as well?'

The woman wheeled in anger. 'Is this a law court? Since when am I on trial?'

'Who wants your husband dead, Eunice? Not this rogue or his brother, who will be content to snatch his land and pack him off to exile. Some other wants his finish. Who?'

She met my eyes with an expression I will never forget. I felt myself stumble, as one, in Hermippus's phrase,

who stubs his toe upon the truth.

It was she. How? I insisted. By making a powerful man your lover? Or did you seek out those you knew possessed motive to eliminate your husband and only lead them to the crimes they needed to effect his arrest?

She wept then. 'You cannot know, sir, what it is to be a woman in a man's world . . .'

'Is this how you excuse murder?'

'The children are mine. He will not take them from me!'

She sank upon the settle and began to sob. At last the tale gushed forth. Its seed was her boy, named Nicolaus after Polemides' father. The lad was sixteen and bursting with the venturesome sap of youth. As boys raised with numerous 'uncles' in their mother's bed, Nicolaus had come to idealize the father whose society he had shared only intermittently, a sire moreover whose proximity to great events had rendered him the more glamorous in his issue's imagination. Nor was this notoriety diminished by his father's imprisonment for murder.

The lad, Eunice revealed now, had run away and enlisted twice, under false names with counterfeit papers. Collared by the Guardians of the Yards, he fled again, into the harbour lanes of Piraeus, where his father shared a bed with the widow of a mate of the fleet. To this site Eunice had tracked her son, but could not make him come home. Some hard-up outfit would take him; it was only a matter of time before he would ship out, certainly to his death. Only his father could dissuade him. I must help. I must!

The uproar of this plea had drawn the watchman, on this eve the cook's boy, a bright lad named Hermon. It was late and cold. 'You must eat, lady. Please. Come inside.'

I instructed the boy to lay a fire in the kitchen grate. Eunice I assisted within, fetching a fleece for her feet and placing a chair for her beside the brazier. You know this quarter of our compound, my grandson; it is a snug harbour; the charcoal makes it toasty in moments.

I may have failed, in my narration, to do justice to this woman and the empathy her person evoked. For though her speech was rough, it was straightforward. One must admire her survival if nothing else. Heaven only stood witness to the trials she had endured, raising her children in barbaric precincts at the limits of the earth. Even her present object, to shield her son from war, could be called noble if one made allowance for the means. Nor was she uncomely, it must be said, but possessed that species of fleshy concupiscence that a woman acquires sometimes past her prime, when the toll exacted by hard experience has settled her at ease within her own skin. A sailor would say she still had the goods. I found myself drawn in sympathy to her. I could picture her and Polemides together. Perhaps it was not past my powers to effect a reconciliation, even at this hour. I confess, watching her settle in before the grate, that for moments I wished I had known them in their heyday (and my own), them and their mates of the coop and the harbour.

Eunice broke the silence. 'What part is he up to?' In his story, she meant. I told her Samos and Ephesus. She chuckled darkly. 'I'd give a lot to hear that string of fiction.'

The lad brought bread and boiled eggs; this seemed to fortify Eunice. She had abated somewhat her hostility and suspicion. 'What if I could get the charges dropped?' she offered. 'I'll screw anyone I need to, and I have cash for bribes too.'

Too late. The trial date was set. 'Polemides knew all along, didn't he? That it was you behind the charges.'

The woman's look acknowledged this likelihood.

'He doesn't hate you, Eunice, I'm certain of that.' I promised to employ all my efforts to get him to help; I believed he would. Yet sorrow clouded her features. I felt moved and wished to comfort her.

'May I ask a question, madam?'

'You've done little else, Cap'n.'

I enquired of her life with Polemides. What had been the best time? When were they happiest together? She eyed me sceptically. Did I mock her? 'The best for us was the best for Athens. Samos and the Straits. When Alcibiades brought his victories.'

At last she settled, and applying the fleece across her lap in such a way as to permit the brazier's glow to warm one side and the wool's heft the other, she took a sip of wine and began.

'We had a cottage at Samos. Pommo brought us out from Athens, me and the kids. It was a pretty place, called the Terraces. Every door on the lane was full; the men was all with the fleet. It was swell days, Cap'n. Swell mates. The way the cottages was carved into the hill you could cut out little gardens, that was why they called it Terraces. We grew melons big as your head, and flowers; pansies and bluejackets, shepherd's capes and wildhearts. The chimneys had those ironwood ptera on top, wings, that turn like weathercocks and make that sweet moan when the wind pipes through 'em. I hear that sound now, it breaks my heart.

'You never saw so many little boogers. All the girls was carrying or just dropped; there was bawlers and crawlers underfoot everywhere. You wanted kids, 'cause you never knew how long you'd have your man. And they was beautiful, Cap'n. Not just my Pommo, though he was at his pick and prime, but all of 'em. So young, so brave. They was always carrying wounds. Ashamed not to be. A man would row with a broken leg or blinded, a 'starfish' across his gut, you know this, sir; that's how set they was never to let their mates down. They called fractured skulls "headaches". I remember the docs' advice to one concussed cross-eyed: "Sit down."

'We had a pot on our lane. You put your money in; who needed took and put back when he had it. No-one stole. You could leave it out all night. If a mate died, his funeral come from that pot. There was no gangs or cliques; everyone was your friend. You didn't need no amusements. Just to be together with such mates. Nobody cheated; nobody owed nothing. We had all we needed – youth and victory. We had the ships, we had the men, we had Alcibiades. And wasn't that enough, Cap'n? Wouldn't that be good enough for most men?'

Eunice peeled an apple as she spoke this; she slung the skin sizzling into the grate.

'Not Polemides of Acharnae. Not him. He found another woman, did he tell you? Not a tramp. A lady. That's right, he married her, and had the cheek to tell me to keep off from the wedding. What do you think of that? He turns over his pay to me, half a duck a day, as if that sets all square. A boy and a girl, his own, and he chucks 'em without so much as a kiss-my-arse.

'He would be a gentleman farmer, see, like his father. There's a laugh! He

tried working the land with me and didn't know pig shit from pork sausage.
But he tells me now that's his dream; he'll make it pay this time.

'I killed a man with an axe for him. Did he tell you that, Cap'n? At
Erythrae. Split this whore's son open, blind soused and coming after Pommo.
Gimme that axe again, I'll sling it into the soup.'

She fell silent and for long moments held stationary, one hand holding the
fruit absently beside her cheek, the other arm wrapped about herself, like a
child.

'But why am I working myself up? She's under the ground and he'll be too.
They'll pit him for Alcibiades, and no wriggling free this time.'

I asked if she loved Polemides.

'I love everyone, Cap'n. Can't afford not to.'

The hour was late. Clearly Eunice was as spent as I. I assured her I would
speak to Polemides about his son and do all I could to secure her own entry to
him, to exhort him in person. I recalled the fee she had left unclaimed and
proffered it doubled. Was she certain she wished to brave the street at this
hour? I could easily have a room made up for her. She thanked me, but no,
better she not distress those with whom she resided. At the gate as I assigned
an attendant with a torch to accompany her way, impulse prompted a query.

'Can you enlighten me, madam, with a woman's view of Alcibiades? How
did he strike you, not as a general or a personage, but as a man?'

She turned with a smile.

'We race of women crave glory, Cap'n, just as you men. But where does
our greatness come? Not from him we conquer but him we bear.'

I was seeking, I said, to understand Timaea of Sparta – the queen who had
not only permitted herself to be seduced but boasted of her infidelity.

Eunice discovered no mystery to this occasion. 'There wasn't no woman in
the world, not Timaea of Sparta or Helen herself, who could stand before that
man and not feel the god's command crying from her belly. What children his
seed would give me! What sons!'

The woman drew her cowl; then, lifting the veil to set it in place, she paused
and turned back.

'Do you really want to know about Pommo?'

I assured her most earnestly I did.

'His heart opened twice in his youth,' she spoke, her glance no longer
towards myself but averted soberly aside. 'His sister and his bride. When the
Plague took 'em, he buried their bones, but not their memory. What woman

of flesh can compete with that, sir? And them both dead, so she can't even talk 'em hard.

'That's him, Cap'n. And it's Athens too. Plague and war took her sons' hope. Yourself too, sir, unless I misread your eyes.'

I absorbed this gravely, struck by its toll of truth.

'If you need anything, madam, make no shame to call. That which I can, I shall.'

She set her veil in place and, turning, made ready to step off.

'Alcibiades gave 'em hope, didn't he, Cap'n? They felt it in their bellies like women, looking past all his faults and crimes. He had eros. He was eros. Nothing less could take the city and make her over new.'

# FORTY
# THE RED RAG OF SPARTA

IT WAS AUTUMN [*POLEMIDES RESUMED*] BEFORE TELAMON AND I REACHED Miletus, via Aspendus and the Coast Road through Caria. I counted the calendar differently now; not by days, but by Aurore's term. She was due in forty-three days, by the ticks carved in the haft of my nine-footer. I warned my mate not to count on me, for when the hour came I'd be at Samos by her side.

'Hope is a crime against heaven,' Telamon reproved me as we trekked the gale-buffeted highway, where you lugged your shield inboard at morning and outboard after noon and which rumbled at all hours with enemy caravans transporting war matériel and regiments of cavalry and foot. Every bridgehead was being outposted, every landing site fortified. 'You were superb once, Pommo, because you despised your life. Now hope has made you worthless. I should quit you, and would but for our history.'

The coast towns through Caria were all Spartan-garrisoned. They had changed, Miletus most of all. Under Athens the city had celebrated a festival called the Feast of Flags. Housewives draped the lanes with jacks and standards; guilds and brotherhoods massed in the squares; the town was gay nightlong with street dances and torch races and the like. Now that was over. Housefronts squatted, sallow and stark. On the docks men worked their business and nothing more. You wore red, everyone, some rag or kerchief to show obeisance to Sparta. The greeting was no longer

'Artemis', the goddess's blessing, but 'Freedom!' as from Athens' tyranny. This salutation was compulsory.

The Spartan garrisons ruled under martial law, with a curfew, but the affairs of the cities were run day to day by the Tens. These were political committees of the wealthier citizens, estate holders and such, which answered not to Sparta, but to Lysander. Under Athenian rule, civil cases must be tried at Athens, where the vultures of the courts picked the colonials clean. Now such shenanigans looked benign. In Lysander's courts each civil trespass was reckoned a crime of war. Breach of contract was dereliction, laziness treason. Even if the Tens wished to be fair, in a boundary dispute, say, between a crofter and his landlord, a lenient judgment might set them up for denunciation as democrats, partial to Athens. The fist must fall hard.

All Ionia had become a camp of war. Lysander had made dead ends of all other trades. Nor did he abide indiscipline within his company. Corporal punishment dominated; every quay sprouted its stocks and whipping post. One heard the boatswain's cry, 'Fall in to witness punishment'; the lanes rang with the swish of the birch and the crack of the cat. Along the wharves laggards must labour in twenty-pound collars or shuffle about, hobbled by ball-and-chain. Delinquents stood at attention daylong with iron anchors on their shoulders.

We saw Lysander gallop past once, on the Coast Highway south of Clazomenae. His party was a dozen, preceded by a guard of Royal Persian Horse, Prince Cyrus's men. You had to salute as he passed, or the buck cavalrymen would rough you up. Telamon admired Lysander. He was a professional. He had whipped this mob of civilians into a corps of fighters and taught them to fear him more than the foe. 'Freedom!' We greeted mates on the street, a red rag round our necks.

Lysander had moved his bastion to Ephesus. The place was magnificent. Telamon sought out his old commander Etymocles, in whose service he technically remained. This officer's term had expired, however; he had been rotated home, replaced by Teleutias, who would later raid the Piraeus to such brilliant effect.

'Are you spies?' was the Spartan's opening query.

'Only him,' replied my mate.

'Blast! I had hoped to spit you both.'

Teleutias had other foxes to harry; he despatched us straight to

Lysander. The *navarch*, it turned out, had intelligence of both our cases, including my indictment and flight. I had been convicted, he informed me. I had not known this. He laughed. He was handsome, I had forgotten how much so, and his self-assurance, abundant in the days when he served without portfolio, appeared amplified tenfold by his accession to supreme command.

'You are sent by Alcibiades,' he observed without rancour. 'With what instructions – my assassination?'

'To attest, sir, the fidelity of his call for alliance against the Persian and the faith of his overtures to you.'

'Yes,' Lysander observed, scanning his papers, 'I have this from Endius in detail, and two other covert embassies from your master.'

His glance searched mine, marking offence at that terminal word. With effort I governed my aspect. As for Telamon, the insult hadn't been coined which could induce him to renounce self-command.

How were we fixed for cash? Lysander scribbled a chit. He ordered his Persian aide, in Persian, to secure us accommodation, at the six level, for colonels.

'The Games of Artemis will be celebrated the day after tomorrow; I will address the army. Be in attendance. Alcibiades shall have his answer at that time.'

Ephesus, as you know, is one of the great harbours of the East. That massive seawall called the *Pteron*, the Wing, is a wonder of the world. At that time eight hundred of its ultimate eleven hundred yards had been completed, broad enough topside for two teams to pass abreast. Scaffolding sheathed the entire extent of construction, with coffer-dams at intervals to sink the footings. The sea was white with mason's dust fifty yards out.

Here was the fruit of Lysander's regimen. Purses were flush; morale was high. The discipline which the Spartan had enforced was acknowledged, even by those who must endure it, as indispensable. Nor did he spare his own person. The commander could be descried before dawn at the gymnasium, training hard. Nights he laboured, late as Alcibiades. He bore himself as if victory were his already and himself not commander but conqueror. Shit rolls downhill, soldiers say, but so does confidence. You could see it down to the lowliest corporal.

The new theatre, west of the *temenos* of Artemis and overlooking the sea, was grander than that of Dionysus at Athens. There the corps assembled in the sequel of the Games, fifteen thousand within the amphitheatre, another twenty thousand ascending the slopes, with heralds relaying their commander's address. Prince Cyrus took the admiral's box, compassed by the nobles of his guard, the Companions. From the theatre's twin risers, the Ears, you could see the Athenian squadrons, commanded by Alcibiades, at their blockade stations picketing the harbour.

Lysander spoke: 'Spartans, Peloponnesians, and allies, the sight of your manly vigour today brought joy not only to the cities in whose cause of freedom you labour but to the gods, who prize above all such enterprise and devotion. Yet I recognize that many among you chafe. You behold the warships of our enemies advancing with impunity to the very chain which seals our harbour and you burn to give them battle. Why must we continually train? you demand of your officers. Every day more skilled oarsmen come over from the foe. Every night our ranks swell as theirs diminish. Let us attack, you cry! How long must we idle? I will answer, comrades, by recounting to you the distinction between our race, the Dorian, and the Ionian strain of our foes.

'We, Spartans and Peloponnesians, possess courage.

'Our enemies possess boldness.

'They own *thrasytes*, we *andreia*.

'Pay attention, brothers. Here is a profound and irreconcilable division. These points of view represent hostile and incompatible conceptions of the proper relation of man to God and, in this, foretell and foreordain our victory.

'In my father's house I was taught that heaven reigns, and to fear and honour her mandates. This is the Spartan, Dorian, and Peloponnesian way. Our race does not presume to dictate to God, but seeks to discover His will and adhere to it. Our ideal man is pious, modest, self-effacing; our ideal polity harmonious, uniform, communal. Those qualities most pleasing to heaven, we believe, are courage to endure and contempt for death. This renders our race peerless in land battle, for in infantry warfare to hold one's ground is all. We are not individualists because to us such self-attention constitutes pride. Hubris we abhor, defining man's place as beneath heaven, not challenging her supremacy.

'Spartans are courageous but not bold. Athenians are bold but not courageous.

'I will detail for you, friends and allies, the character of our enemy. And call me short if I lie. Shout me down, brothers. But if I speak true, then acclaim my address. Let me hear your voices!

'Athenians do not fear God; they seek to be God. They believe that heaven reigns not by might, but by glory. The gods rule by acclaim, they say, by that supremacy which strikes mortals with awe and compels emulation. Believing this, Athenians seek to please heaven by making clay gods of themselves. Athenians reject modesty and self-effacement as unworthy of man made in the image of the gods. Heaven favours the bold. And experience, they believe, has borne them out. Bold action preserved them from the Persian twice, brought them empire, and has maintained it since. Athenians are peerless at sea because boldness wins there. The warship accomplishes nothing holding the line but must strike her enemy. Boldness is a mighty engine, friends, but there is a limit to its reach and a rock upon which it founders. We are that rock.'

Tumultuous acclamation interrupted Lysander's address. A wave rose from those near enough to hear unamplified, augmented by a second crest, as the heralds relayed their commander's words to the thousands upslope, and enlarged yet again as the rearmost at last received the heralds' resonation.

'Our rock is courage, brothers, upon which their boldness breaks and recedes. *Thrasytes* fails. *Andreia* endures. Imbibe this truth and never forget it.

'Boldness is impatient. Courage is long-suffering. Boldness cannot endure hardship or delay; it is ravenous, it must feed on victory or it dies. Boldness makes its seat upon the air; it is gossamer and phantom. Courage plants its feet upon the earth and draws its strength from God's holy fundament. *Thrasytes* presumes to command heaven; it forces God's hand and calls this virtue. *Andreia* reveres the immortals; it seeks heaven's guidance and acts only to enforce God's will.

'Hear, brothers, what kind of man these conflicting qualities produce. The bold man is prideful, brazen, ambitious. The brave man calm, God-fearing, steady. The bold man seeks to divide; he wants his own and will shoulder his brother aside to loot it. The brave man unites. He succours his fellow, knowing that what belongs to the commonwealth belongs to him as well. The bold man covets; he sues his neighbour in the law court, he intrigues, he dissembles. The brave man is content with his lot; he respects that portion the gods have granted and husbands it, comporting himself with humility as heaven's steward.

'In troubled times the bold man flails about in effeminate anguish, seeking to draw his neighbours into his misfortune, for he has no strength of character to fall back upon other than to drag others down to his own state of wickedness. Now the brave man. In dark hours he endures silently, uncomplaining. Reverencing the round of heaven's seasons, he does what must be done, sustaining himself with the certainty that to endure injustice with patience is the mark of piety and wisdom. This is the bold man, and the brave. Now: what is the bold city?

'The bold city exalts aggrandizement. It cannot remain at home, content with its portion, but must venture abroad to plunder that of others. The bold city imposes empire. Contemptuous of heaven's law, it makes of itself a law unto itself. It sets its ambition above justice and acquits all crimes beneath the imperative of its own power. Need I name this city? She is Athens!'

Such an ovation acclaimed this as to resound throughout the harbour and roll, as thunder, even to the Athenian ships at their stations.

'Look there to sea, brothers, to those squadrons of the foe which flaunt their supposed supremacy at the very portals of our citadel. They have accounted our inexperience at sea and deliberateness of action, which they deem liabilities and by which they hold to overturn us. But they have not reckoned their own impatience and restiveness, which are their flaws, and fatal. Our deficiencies may be overcome by practice and self-discipline. Theirs are intrinsic, indelible, and irremediable.

'Alcibiades thinks he blockades us, but it is we who blockade him. He thinks he is starving us, but it is we who starve him. We starve him of victory, which he must have, which the *demos* of Athens must have, because they do not possess courage but only audacity. And if you doubt the truth of these words, my friends, remember Syracuse. The world knows how that game played out. They err fatally, our enemies, in their conception of the proper relation of man to God. They are wrong and we are right. God is on our side, who fear and reverence Him, not on theirs, who seek to shoulder their way up Olympus and stand as gods themselves.'

Citations interrupted Lysander so repeatedly that he must make interval now at nearly every phrase and wait for subsidence of the uproar.

'Our race, brothers, has set itself to study courage, and we have learned its source. Courage is born of obedience. It is the issue of selflessness, brotherhood, and love of freedom. Boldness, on the other hand, is spawned of defiance and disrespect; it is the bastard brat of irreverence and outlawry. Boldness honours two things only: novelty and success. It feeds on them and without them dies. We will starve our enemies of these commodities, which to them are bread and air. This is why we train, men. Not to sweat for sweat's sake or row for rowing's sake, but by this practice of cohesion to inculcate *andreia*, to lade the reservoirs of our hearts with confidence in ourselves, our shipmates, and our commanders.

'Men say I fear to face Alcibiades; they taunt me for want of intrepidity. I do fear him, brothers. This is not cowardice but prudence. Nor would it constitute bravery to confront him ship for ship, but recklessness. For I reckon our enemy's skill and observe that ours is yet unequal. The sagacious commander honours his enemy's might. His skill is to strike not at the foe's strength, but at his weakness, not where and when he is ready, but where he is lax and when he least expects it. The enemy's weakness is time. *Thrasytes* is perishable. It is like that fruit, luscious when ripe, which stinks to heaven when it rots.

'Therefore possess your hearts in patience, brothers. I tell you: I am glad we are not ready. Were we, I would seek pretext to hold even longer. For every hour we deprive the foe of victory is another we turn his own strength against him. Alcibiades in his godless vanity flatters himself that he is a second Achilles. Well, if he is, boldness is his heel and, by heaven, we will strike that heel and send him sprawling!'

More acclamation, deafening and unbroken.

'Lastly, men, let me tell you of this Alcibiades, and what I know of him. Brave men tremble at his name, so many are the victories he has brought his nation. Yet I tell you, and stake my life upon it, that he will fade away, by the hand of heaven or his own countrymen's. He must; his own nature calls this fate forth. For what is this man but the supreme embodiment of Athenian *thrasytes*? His victories have all come from boldness, none from courage. Let him strike us with terror and we will hand him his triumph. But only hold firm, brothers, undaunted by whatever flash and dazzle he throws at us, and he will crack and his nation with him.

'I know this man. He slept under my roof at Lacedaemon when he had fled there, condemned by his own countrymen for outrage against heaven. I loathed him then and despise him now. Before God I swore a mighty oath, that if He brought this man before my prow, I would break his pride and free Greece of his blasphemy and the tyranny of Athens with which he seeks to enslave us all.

'I plant my trust in you, brothers, in our arms and our *andreia*. But before all I place it in God. Nor is this wishful thinking but objective observation of heaven's laws, for I perceive these faithworthy as the tides and immutable as the transit of the stars:

'Boldness produces hubris. Hubris calls forth nemesis. And nemesis brings boldness low.

'We are nemesis, brothers. Called into being by heaven's outrage at this would-be tyrant's pride, and at his city's presumption. We are the Almighty's right arm, God's holy agent, and no force between sea and sky may prevail against us.'

## FORTY-ONE
# FIRE FROM THE SEA

THE ALARM SOUNDED DEEP INTO THE THIRD WATCH. I WAS FAST
asleep, in the villa at which Telamon and I had been billeted,
which housed a dozen other officers and their women. These staggered
now into the street. 'Is it a drill?' one bawled from a terrace. The harbour
lay a quarter mile below; you could see fire ships pouring in over the
chain and, in their flare, Athenian triremes pulling fast in two columns
with tow arrows and flame catapults arcing fire in all directions.

We armed and raced down the hill. You know the city, Jason. Mount
Coressus overstands the eminence, her shoulders embracing the sprawl
of suburbs spilling back from the port. The great seawall, the Pteron,
spans the harbour mouth. Behind its base extend the commercial
wharves, the Emporium, and beyond these the Toll, the inner fortifications, and the naval bastion, Huntress's Hood. The river Cayster
debouches, dense with silt, between the temple of the Amazons and the
great square of the Artemisium, with the dredging works and the marsh
on the south side, the cavalry grounds, and more suburbs outside the
walls. These are all on hills and were all ablaze.

It was clear to any who understood Alcibiades' frame that this assault
was his answer to Lysander's speech and a leap upon the main chance of
Prince Cyrus's presence on-site. Given the audacity of his generalship,
he could have landed every regiment he had or even called in his
Thracians, heaven help all who must face them. 'I'm not too keen on

this,' I shouted to Telamon amid the waterfront crush, meaning I was in no mood to go epitaph-hunting for either side. 'Let's find a rat hole and sit this son of a whore out.'

We cracked into a warehouse adjacent the Armourers' Lane. You could see the fire ships as brilliant as daylight now; crewless galleys stacked with pitch and blazing like Tartarus. I had never experienced an attack of Alcibiades from the receiving end. It struck like a terror show of shock and thunder, and it was beating the shit out of the Peloponnesians. Twelve-oared longboats towed their incendiary trailers at a furious clip, sidescreens up to shield the oarsmen from the missile fire of the defenders, so far conspicuous only by its absence. A clutch of Spartan six-stickers hauled to intercept the lead towboat. We could see the attacker cast off her line; two enemy sixes struck her just as her fire ship, loosed now, ploughed into the roadstead where a dozen Spartan triremes rode at anchor. The impact snapped the incendiary's booms; they crashed thunderously, dumping their cargo of pitch and sulphur onto the decks of the foe.

Now a second line of fire ships lit up astern of the first. The eruption of these, invisible heretofore, produced among the Peloponnesians a disseverment of the senses both palpable and paralysing. 'Don't mill about like bloody sheep!' A Spartan colonel waded into the press. 'Launch ships, curse you!'

At this instant Lysander himself thundered into the lane, on horseback, compassed by his lifeguard of Knights. We could see the colonel dash before him, informing him of his order. Lysander countermanded it. Peloponnesian infantry were pouring onto the site. Athenian pinnaces continued to rake the ship sheds, slinging pinwheels and hello-theres. Shall we rush the Pteron? the colonel cried to Lysander, meaning make for the seawall to repel the landing.

Lysander rejected this as well. One must give the bastard credit. Any other of his race would have hurtled mindlessly into battle's maw, seeking victory or glorious death. Lysander knew better. As he had baited Alcibiades, now his rival baited him. Lysander would not bite. He hauled towards the Artemisium and the great parade ground fronting the city. 'Draw back! Marshal on the square!'

Lysander had built walls dividing the residential quarter of Antenoris from the dockyards, an undertaking scorned even by his own officers as make-work and folly. Now one perceived its brilliance. The ramparts funnelled seaborne attackers – those striking from the Pteron, as the Athenians had – onto the Exposition Road, quayside, with water at one hand and wall at the other. Here was a pen made for slaughter. All Lysander need do was wait.

Where Telamon and I hid had become no-man's-land. From seaward rushed the Athenians and allies; landside marshalled the Spartans and Peloponnesians. They would clash in the rock-hemmed pound before us, and our troops would be massacred. So futile, however, are all designs of war. All at once sprang an overthrow from the last quarter Lysander could have projected, for the lone motive against which he could not contend.

This was Prince Cyrus, on fire for glory.

We heard hooves on the Lane of the Armourers; into the open thundered a cohort of Royal Persian Horse. The troop galloped onto the square of the Artemisium, parting the massed Peloponnesians. The prince reined in before Lysander. The lad himself was but seventeen and slight as a stalk, yet so fired by the nobility of his blood and the impulsion to emulate the deeds of his ancestors that he seemed lit as though aflame.

'The enemy is there, Lysander! Why do you hold?'

Meet him! Attack!

The prince wheeled and spurred. His Guard thundered at his heels. Peloponnesians and allies could not be held; the throng flooded onto the Exposition Road. Our warehouse sat right in its path. Athenian rangers who had advanced thus far now spun and bolted, slinging their brands into every eave and alley.

Telamon and I peered about our coop. Paint. Our rat hole was a hive of pitch and encaustic. We flushed from this covert the instant she exploded. I felt hair and beard erupt; flaming turpentine spewed upon me. I careered into the lane, beating at the flames with my cloak, but it, too, was drenched with oil and blazing. Telamon pitched me into a mound of pumice, annexed to a construction site, moments before the hordes overran it. A Peloponnesian sergeant rounded upon us, beating at us with his staff to join the affray. My entire left side had been incinerated; I could not see, nor feel of my face aught but charred meat. Telamon defended me. 'By the gods, this man cannot fight!' He drew on the sergeant. 'Go!' I propelled him, before he got himself arrested or worse.

Down the Exposition Road Prince Cyrus galloped with the troops from the Artemisium, above thirty thousand, while Lysander in fury drove his Knights in the youth's train, to deliver the lad from his own mad valour . . .

POLEMIDES CONTINUED HIS NARRATION, TO WHICH WE SHALL RETURN. However, his object for the remainder of this action was clearly neither to participate nor to report, but to preserve his life. Let us shift narrators, then.

It was the younger Pericles' assignment, under Alcibiades, to command the wave of assault ships succeeding Antiochus', those vessels which Polemides recounted as breaching the harbour chain and carrying the assault to the waterfront. I have drawn already from these logs, given me by his wife after his trial following Arginousai. In addition she placed in my care several of the journals Pericles penned in those hours, for his children, that they might not credit the slanders of his accusers, and also, I believe, to preserve his reason during that ordeal, whose chronicle I shall relate in its course. But to return to Ephesus, and Pericles' journal:

THE PLAN WAS ALCIBIADES', DRAFTED IN A SINGLE NIGHT BY THE trierarchs and squadron commanders working under his direction. Its impetus was receipt of the transcript of Lysander's address at the Games. Here was the Spartan's rejoinder, final and beyond appeal, to Alcibiades' overtures of alliance. He would slug it out to the finish, would Lysander, putting his faith less in God, as Alcibiades observed, than in the impatience of the Athenian electorate. Lysander understood this monster as well as his rival. Victories in the hinterlands, even the sack of mighty cities, would not slake the beast's rapacity, not now, inflamed as it was by expectations of its all-conquering commander. Alcibiades must attack, and attack Lysander. No meaner object would serve. The monster would have its enemy's head, or his who failed to produce it.

Such was the strategic objective. Tactical were three: to raze the ship-yards and repair facilities; to destroy or carry off as many battleships as possible, in as spectacular a manner as possible; to capture the Pteron and despoil its superstructure. The assault was an amphibious operation comprising twelve thousand four hundred troops, ninety-seven capital ships, and a hundred and ten support vessels. It involved the co-ordination of eleven assault elements across a front of twenty miles. Forty-six objectives were assigned. The signal rolls were as thick as your wrist.

Preliminary movements had commenced two days prior. A squadron of twenty-four under Aristocrates and another of twenty-eight under Adeimantus embarked from Samos, manned not by conventional crews, but by armoured infantry doubling as oarsmen, with slingers and javelineers, as many as the vessels could bear without betraying their numbers by their draught, prone topside behind sidescreens. Aristocrates' squadron made southeast as for Andros, Adeimantus' north to the Hellespont. Both permitted their movements to be observed by Lysander's lookouts on Mounts Coressus and Lycon. They stood out to sea, beyond sight, doubling back on the second night to land their companies, Aristocrates in the planters' country between Priene and Ephesus, Adeimantus north at the resort colony called the Crook, deserted in this season on account of the Etesian winds.

The horse transports crossed by night from Samos and Lade, putting ashore at an inhabited cove called the Crescent. Alcibiades commanded these. Detaining all who might dash ahead with the alarm, the units proceeded by back tracks across country, linking with Adeimantus' companies landed at the Crook. From there Alcibiades advanced on the city. So swiftly were all pickets overwhelmed that he was into the suburbs before any warning apprised Lysander.

Aristocrates' companies landing to the south not only cut the causeway by which reinforcements could be brought up from the city but released the canal gates, flooding the plain. They cut the chain at Fort Cylon. Swimmers captured the twin islets, the Yolk and the White, which comprised the suspensors of the cable. By this time the first incendiaries were lighting up the suburbs. Erasinides' marines broke apart the gate north of Exposition Road. Antiochus' battleships swept past Cylon into the harbour. My twenty-four lay-to seaward of the chain. Should Antiochus be repulsed, we would form the bulwark through which he would withdraw. Should he signal the advance, we would strike in his wake with everything we had. Bonfires at Cylon and the Yolk lit the channel. No more need be told of the ravagement than this: the blazes set upon the shipyards, seawall, and Emporium were on such a scale that their flare could be seen from Chios, sixty miles away.

Alcibiades at this time, one learned later, was very nearly losing his life in the following manner. His cavalry had swept through the suburbs, outpacing Adeimantus' infantry, and were making for the northern gate to link with the marine companies landed on the Pteron by Antiochus and Erasinides. They had a guide, Alcibiades' troop did, who led them through the maze of lanes and alleys which constitute that quarter. They emerged to a square. Astonishingly a corps of women had seized this choke point and, barricading its lone egress with benches and over-turned wagons, made bold to defend it. These were no Amazons but women of the district, marshalling to preserve their hearths and infants.

The women attacked Alcibiades' cavalry from the rooftops, hurling tiles, bricks, and stones with fabulous daring. Nor did they give back beneath the return volleys, but kept up a din of such profane contumacy as, the troopers testified, evoked sterner terror than any phalanx of Spartans or horde of shrieking savages. Alcibiades himself was struck by a brick on the shoulder. The blow fractured his collarbone; he must be assisted from the fray by Mantitheus, fighting as ever at his side. Alcibiades, as was his habit, fought helmetless; a handsbreadth more and the missile would have staved in his skull.

In the city, the foe's battalions swept along the Exposition Road. Now came the struggle for the Pteron, the great seawall upon which men and horses and ships were duelling, it seemed, for every yard. Scaffolding ascended on both flanks, all pine and all blazing. Coffer-dams abutted the final furlong, spiked with construction debris, brick and timber, mortar sleds, pumpworks, and great piles of iron fittings which made them jagged death pits. Horses and men were tumbling into these in numbers as ghastly as they were uncountable.

Antiochus made signal: 'Advance!' I had stationed Calliope at the left of the line, to pass close abeam of the Pteron to evaluate the situation. We returned signal and kicked off.

The riot upon the seawall was absolutely spectacular. Alcibiades with the cavalry and heavy infantry had punched through now, though we did not know this yet from our vantage. Their lane of advance down

Exposition Road had been blocked by masses of the foe, a hundred shields across and what looked like a mile deep. Some four or five thousand of the enemy, including cavalry, had got aboard the seawall before Alcibiades and Adeimantus and now hacked and heaved towards the Windlass House at the extremity. They were going for the cable, to reseal the harbour and trap the vessels inside. Defending the final furlong of seawall were the Athenian marines who had taken the Quay and cut the chain. Flanking these, Erasinides' engineering vessels had set themselves broadside against the seaward palisade and were applying winch and tackle to the enemy's submerged stakes while simultaneously disembarking more marines from transports moored outboard hull-to-hull. Passing the terminus of the Pteron aboard *Calliope*, I could see in the van of the foe a personage magnificently mounted and apparelled, compassed by a guard of knights.

This could be none but Lysander.

At once I determined to strike for him, forswearing all other objects. I resolved to sacrifice my own life and all my crew if I must. I signalled to my second, Lycomenes, aboard *Theama* to take the squadron forward on his own, then made to Damodes, trierarch of *Erato*, these signals: 'Follow me' and 'Land marines.'

I could see Damodes called the Bear upon his sternpeak. He, too, had spotted the foe and hopped with frenzy to get at him. As these turns eventuated, Antiochus' *Tyche*, within the harbour, had had her stem staved in and must withdraw. He brought her out stern-first, backing water, and now approached the Pteron from the landward side. To moor a triple against a twenty-foot seawall is no mean feat in broad daylight. Under fire *Calliope* came in like a refuse boat helmed by a drunk. Antiochus simply rammed *Tyche* stern-first between two coffer-dams and, slinging the last of his hello-theres, mounted behind a screen of fire.

The struggle aboard the Pteron had reached that state of compaction where even the most elementary tactics may not be implemented, such is the press of mayhem. The enemy had five thousand on the wall, massed shield-to-shield, with thousands more pressing from the land. The main of our cavalry fought dismounted now, as the foe in his swarm carved the horses out from under them. These unfortunate creatures wailed in agony upon the block, hooves thrashing, wounding others, while more struggled in the water, drowning. My foot slipped mounting a dam and I fell hard, all my weight plus armour, beating my helmet crown-first into the stone. I blacked both eyes and tore thumb's web so that it still has not knitted. In this shape I clambered at last onto the Pteron, seeking the Spartan.

It was not Lysander but the prince.

Cyrus of Persia, who had sworn to break up his very throne to bring low the might of Athens. Cyrus! Cyrus!

Our men cried his name and hurled themselves at the champions who defended him. The prince's knights duelled with breathtaking valour, the riders' prowess exceeded only by that of their mounts, specimens trained to maintain cohesion flank to flank and to rear and strike both with forehooves and the spiked armour on their chests. The look in their eyes I shall never forget.

'Kill him!' Antiochus bellowed from *Tyche*'s stern.

Now through the mob punched cavalry and heavy armour, Alcibiades and Adeimantus. Marines pressed about, crying that they had Prince Cyrus trapped. At once an alteration overcame our commander both wondrous and profound. Though beneath his breastplate his scapula had been fractured, as we learned later, such an injury as would carry away any man with incapacity and pain, he straightened and elevated his eighteen-pound shield upon that forearm above which the bone had been shattered.

He went after the prince. So did everyone. We were driven, all, before that tide which was the mass of flesh and armour being propelled towards the Pteron's extremity by the advancing press of Spartan and Peloponnesian reinforcements surging from the shore.

Now came Lysander at these battalions' fore. He called to Cyrus to make for him. Break through, I will preserve you! A space separated the two, packed shield-to-shield with Athenian marines, such orphans as myself off marooned men-of-war and our commanders, Alcibiades and Adeimantus, with the last of the cavalry. Ships roared, afire port and starboard; warhorses' muzzles seemed to belch live steam; men's cries ascended in a din ungodly.

'Do you see, men of Greece?' Alcibiades cried towards the foe. 'A Spartan fights at the barbarian's shoulder!'

'For freedom from thee, prideful villain!' Lysander bawled back.

The Spartan dug his knees into his mount and slung, so proximate across the press that the shaft of his javelin traversed barely thrice its length before seating with thunderous concussion upon his enemy's shield. Alcibiades took the stroke flush on his shattered arm. The warhead tore through the bronze and split the oak beneath, penetrating to a handsbreadth of his flesh.

'He is wounded!'

Men of both sides cried in exigency, Spartans and Persians rallying to press for the kill; Athenians and allies closing yet more densely, if that were possible, to erect a wall of their own flesh before their commander. An infantryman at Alcibiades' side elevated before him the shield his strength could no longer bear. Darts transfixed the hero's back. Shafts riddled Alcibiades' mount. Clouds flew about his head.

Lysander's knights heaved upon him. Alcibiades slung his axe across a sward of plumes and pike blades. I myself was within feet of the Spartan, so close I could see his beard beneath the cheek pieces of his helmet, as he beat the weapon apart with his shield.

'Sling there, Lysander!' Alcibiades bellowed, indicating Prince Cyrus. 'Sling there and stand with Leonidas!'

He meant of course the Spartan king who had fallen with such valour at Thermopylae, two generations past, defending Greece from the Persian.

Lysander frothed with fury. 'Can you court the crowd even now, thou actor!'

'He is here, thy king Leonidas – and marks thee traitor to Greece!'

Our marines made a last rush for Cyrus. Missiles rained from ships and seawall; prince and knights fell back. 'Kill him!' Antiochus trumpeted above the mêlée. The youth gave place towards the Pteron's end, driven by the Athenian press.

'Men of Persia,' Cyrus cried in his tongue (or so it was translated for us later), 'it is up to you now to decide if your prince will live or die.'

Without a heartbeat's demurral Cyrus's champions flung themselves and their steeds upon the spearpoints of the Athenians, driving these back by their magnificent sacrifice and creating an interval for their master. Cyrus spurred. Prince and mount broke through, lapped in deliverance by the bronze of Spartan knights.

Here came the terminal push. Mass against mass, each division straining to hurl the other into the sea. All utterance ceased. Men did not shout or even groan. Even the horses no longer made cry, but that sound arose which constrains all who have known battle to start from their slumber in terror.

The foe were too many, we too few.

We fell back. The ships took us off. The assault was over.

Alcibiades got off aboard *Tyche*. Men pressed about him, Antiochus recounted to me later, motioning towards the conflagration and acclaiming his triumph.

He rejoined nothing at that hour. Only past dawn ashore at Samos, bathed and bound by the surgeons, did he summon to his side, in confidence and apart, Adeimantus, Aristocrates, Antiochus, Mantitheus, and myself. We must take thought now, he admonished, for our lives apart from him.

'With this night,' he said, 'my star has fallen.'

There is an anecdote of Lysander in the aftermath of the battle. It is recounted that on remuster at the Artemisium, when reports accounted forty-four of eighty-seven triremes burned or destroyed, with the ship-yards, repair works, and all construction ramparts of the Pteron, he was confronted not alone by Prince Cyrus, who must account the produce of his father's gold, but by representatives of the Spartan ephorate, technically his superiors, who chanced to be present from the home government.

'And what do you call this, Lysander?' these officers demanded of their admiral, indicating the ruin of the port.

'I call it what it is,' Lysander is said to have replied. 'Victory.'

# FORTY-TWO
# THE CHORE OF PILLAGE

THESE JOURNALS OF *THE YOUNGER PERICLES* [GRANDFATHER CONTINUED] it has been my honour to preserve, along with this ensign of Calliope, sacrificed subsequently in the fight at the Blue Rocks, and Endeavour, whose helm was his at the Arginousai Islands. This was the last command he ever held. But such, my grandson, we shall get to presently.

To return to Polemides, whom we left at the inception of the raid.

He had successfully fled Ephesus, he told me, exploiting darkness and the disorder wrought by the assault. His burns and their attendant shock caught up with him, however, in the country south of the city. He must seek cover.

In the raid's wake Lysander's coast guard had doubled watches and patrols. Rewards were posted for all stragglers of the Athenians; locals, boys, and even women swelled the manhunts. Polemides survived on the flesh of mice and lizards spiked in the canals in which he had gone to ground, and leeks and radishes grubbed at night from the kitchen gardens of housewives. Warships of Athens transited on night reconnaissance; he made signal and once attempted swimming out, but his strength failed. He hid, he said, like a rat.

The term of his bride Aurore came and went. He had a child now or so presumed, but did not dare daylight, seeking a ship or even to post a letter. Though he declined as ever to confide to me such as he deemed overpersonal, it took scant imagination to conceive his distress, in terror for his life, whose preservation he now sought most desperately for the sake of his bride and child; with the consternation of being unable to reach her side for the birth; and the grief he had occasioned her, who could not know if he even still drew breath.

I was at Athens then. The city was sobered and chastened, groaning awake with a hangover from its bout of passion with Alcibiades. As a respectable matron adjusts her girdle and reclaims her dignity after the excesses of the Dionysia, so did the city of Athena shudder and splash its face, embracing collective amnesia. Did we really say that? Do that? Promise that? Those who had capered most shamelessly to their new master's pipes now came to themselves and, repenting this licence, snapped out to the bracing chill of abjuration. So that, the more abjectly a man had grovelled for Alcibiades' favour or donated resources to his cause, the more he now affected indifference and swore himself superior to such slavishness.

As men reckoned how near they had come to forfeiting their freedom, their resolve redoubled never to hazard such derangement again. The oligarchic element closed ranks, fearing the mania of the multitude; the democrats scourged themselves for their eagerness to offer up their liberty. The mob's code was as concise as it was common: any shoot lifting its head beyond another must be mown down. The new radicals, championed by Cleophon, would not prostrate themselves before Alcibiades or anoint any omnipotent over themselves, the sovereign people.

It became clear now to what extent Alcibiades' rule had depended on his personal presence. The main of his ministers had embarked with him with the fleet, while those who remained – Euryptolemus, Diotimus, Pantithenes – possessed no specific programme or philosophy to implement. Alcibiades had left the city with no agenda other than its adulation of himself, and without his celebrity about which to construct a consensus, a vacuum arose. Into this flooded his enemies.

Despatches detailing the raid at Ephesus, considered a great victory, failed to ignite the city's joy. Daily from the fleet arrived pleas for money. I served then on the Board of Naval Procurement. We were ten, one from each tribe, with an epistates, a presiding officer, serving each day in rotation. Only myself and Patrocles, son of the officer of the same name who had perished in Sicily, voted faithfully to fund the fleet. Our colleagues resisted, from legitimate concerns of economy but primarily under pressure from the foes of Alcibiades: to strangle him of cash and bring him down.

Formerly correspondence was received by the board only from the Curators of the Yards or the College of Architects, the Ten Generals, or the tribal taxiarchs. Now we admitted appeals, twenty a day, from squadron commanders and even boatswains and marines, begging for money. Here, a motion proposing citizenship for all aliens who manned benches with the fleet. Now a plea to slave owners, who had let out their chattel as oarsmen, to forgo their commission, permitting wages to the man 'on the stick', to hold him from deserting. Then a petition to enfranchise these as well.

Now Alcibiades' enemies' hundred suits at law began to take their toll. Each associate, as Polemides, accused of commerce with the foe added another razor's nick. Why had Alcibiades failed to take Ephesus? What other than his friendship with Endius and past association with Lysander? His enemies seized this moment to put abroad Alcibiades' scheme for league with Lacedaemon against the Persians. What could this be but a device to sell out the city to the foe?

In my own family debate protracted, of fear for the nation. Ruinous as was the intemperance of the radical democrats, one dreaded their accession little less than that of Alcibiades. A figure on his scale, even a noble one, emasculated the internal intercourse of the state. Even those who loved him, or like myself acclaimed him as a commander and man of vision, came to fear his return, with victories or without.

But the element that worked him the most grievous injury was his notorious W.C.s. These Warrants of Compensation, which he had issued in Athens' name throughout the Hellespontine War and which had succeeded spectacularly in lieu of plunder in securing the contributions that had maintained the fleet . . . now these came due. Of course they could not be paid; the treasury was bankrupt. But their very existence lent credence to the allies, poormouthing in return, when they inverted the cash box and shook out the terminal moth. Alcibiades' enemies seized upon the W.C.s to denounce his regime as barren and corrupt. And when his victories stopped coming – when he failed to reduce Andros, when Lysander's enterprise reinvigorated the Peloponnesian fleet, when desertions proliferated among our islander oarsmen, drawn off by Cyrus' gold – the whispers became murmurs and the murmurs cries.

That spring I was assigned my seventh command, the trireme Europa, and despatched to Samos to join the squadron under the younger Pericles. Strife commenced before we had hauled down the slipway. A score of slave oarsmen deserted in port and twice that of foreign nautai at Andros when we touched to assist in the siege, so that we arrived at Samos 'at half-stick', so undermanned as to get only two oar banks in the water. Alcibiades was not there.

He had been absent for two months, in the Chersonese trying to raise money.

There is this about sailors, my grandson: they must have drink. More even than women, whose use they require for physical release, they must have the psychic purgation of euphoria and stupefaction. In my judgment this is less a vice than a fact of nature. Sailors need wine when they're in action and need it more when they're not. The hardship of the seaman's life is well accounted; what is understood less is the toll of fear. The landsman thinks sailors love the sea or feel at home upon it. This is erroneous. Most are in terror of the salt element even at its mildest; in a blow they must be driven to their benches by the lash. Nor has the architect's hand crafted a vessel less seaworthy than a trireme. Her freeboard to the thalamites' port is less than a yard; in the least swell, seas are shipped without let-up. The trieres is built for speed, not strength. In a hammering sea she buckles; her planks start. In a running swell she bellies and hogbacks. Her ram ploughs under driven before a gale, her perilous trim makes her hell to handle in a wind from abeam, and her long slender profile threatens to broach her to in a blow of any kind. To survive a gale leaves the seaman less hardened to hazard than in terror of the next. Add fear of the foe to the dread of death on the featureless waste, and you manage a brew of terror that few may endure, even over the short haul, and next to none, season upon season.

Alcibiades, fleet gossip declared, was skimming loot from the plunder. His mistress Timandra, now styled by the seamen 'the Sicilian' for her birth at Hyccara, was said to have cached above five talents, which she used to secure sanctuaries in Thrace for her lover, should affairs compel him to slip the cable. The men's disgruntlement went past bitching. 'That's our drink and our pussy,' they complained, and they were right.

Want of funds drove Alcibiades to recklessness. With the princes Seuthes and Medocus he raided the Thracian interior. But the tribesmen proved of such warlike disposition and so adept at concealing their goods that casualties outstripped profit ten to one. The men refused to march a step from the ships. Alcibiades could no longer 'borrow' from friendly districts or merchandise his W.C.s. As Lysander tightened fortification of the coastal cities, it became a task of peril even to land for water or to take the midday meal.

Our squadron was despatched to reinforce Alcibiades' at Phocaea. My log records putting in on the way at Thercale. Villagers in the hundreds lined the landing beach; these first stoned the ships, hurling curses; then, when after much remonstrance we had disabused them of any hostile intent and were at last permitted to land, the women flocked about us weeping. Alcibiades' troops had razed four towns, they claimed, carrying off money and cattle. Pericles assured the women they must be in error; the pirates could only be Lysander's men, impersonating Athenians to sow insurrection.

We pressed north. Smoke could be seen on the hills; fishing smacks repeated the refugees' story; columns of displaced villagers, they said, were fleeing to the interior. We encountered Theama and Panegyris, triremes under Alcibiades, returning to Samos with hostages. These were children of our allies, held for ransom. Had straits become so desperate? We caught up at Cyme. You know this city, my grandson. Its flavour is Eastern and easygoing, its siting above a charming harbour called the Saucer.

Alcibiades had demanded twenty talents of the district. The inhabitants had pleaded poverty and begged his sufferance, citing the prodigious levies contributed heretofore, which had left them barely eking survival. He countered that the fleet's needs superseded all. When the citizens could not pay, they took the step of barring the gates to him. He attacked. It became a fiasco. Athenian units balked at aggression against allies; several refused orders. The only corps which followed Alcibiades without qualm were his Dii, those most savage of the Thracians. In the aftermath such atrocities were revealed as could not be covered up. The city was taken. Treasure was extorted.

Our squadron arrived in the immediate sequel. Courts-martial had concluded; four Athenian officers and sixty-one men had been convicted. The charges, arising from an action under naval command, could not be reduced to simple insubordination. This was mutiny. The penalty was death.

Alcibiades had contrived to free a number under sundry pretexts and look the other way as more escaped. But nine oarsmen, led by one Orestides of Marathon, refused to ratify their blame by such expedients. They were guiltless, they maintained. It was their orders that were criminal.

It was afternoon, blistering and sere under a fierce Etesian wind. The accused were being held in a saddler's shop just off that common called the Square of Truth. Alcibiades was drunk, not so as to derange his reason but only, one felt, to dull the sensation of this ordeal. He sought only a measure to get these men off the hook. He could not compromise his authority by negotiating with the mutineers in person; he despatched Pericles instead. I accompanied my friend on my own.

We spoke with the man Orestides and his companions as they were being led out by marines and bound to execution posts. The fellow was as *honourable as any I have ever known. We wept to hear him state his case, and his men's, with such conviction, so absent artifice. He was running no bluff. Such was his honest outrage at the state of the fleet that he and his mates would, in his words, 'forsake our lives before our purpose'.*

*Alcibiades ordered the execution. The marines refused. I have never witnessed such a scene of grief and consternation. Alcibiades had two companies of Thracian tribesmen, Dii. He ordered them to do it.*

*They did.*

*Such outrage now swept the fleet, that free Athenians be massacred by savages, that Alcibiades must stand offshore all night aboard* Indomitable *in fear for his life. Next dawn he ordered the plunder of Cyme, which had been collected in the bowls of two shields, laid out by the paymasters along the beaching strand. The men were marched past the tables. Not one would take his pay.*

*That night came report of Notium.*

*A sea battle had been fought there, two days past. Lysander's squadrons had routed ours, commanded by Antiochus, whom Lysander had slain. Fifteen Athenian ships had been sunk or captured – no great loss in numbers, but calamitous in morale.*

*Alcibiades raced back to Ephesus, drew the fleet up at the harbour mouth. But Lysander was too shrewd to come out. The now-completed Pteron sealed the bastion tight. Spartan and Peloponnesian troops held every foot of shore.*

*Sixteen days later came this report from Athens: the vote for the new year's Board of Generals had been tallied. Alcibiades had not been re-elected.*

*Two dawns later he addressed the fleet in farewell.*

*He dared not return home for fear of trial; he must retire, to Thrace perhaps if the rumours of strongholds acquired by Timandra were true. He dismissed* Indomitable's *crew, permitting each man to seek another berth. One hundred and fifty-four oarsmen and marines volunteered to share Alcibiades' fate; they would stick with him.*

*That night my vessel,* Europa, *drilled beyond the breakwater, the Hook, conducting signal exercises with several Samian corvettes and despatch runners. We came in late, making our reversion by cresset-light. As the craft swung stern-to, preparing to beach, we remarked a warship launch from the strand and gather way, under half-stick, against the tide.*

*We peered. The vessel bore neither running lights nor signal lamp;*

*her crew rowed in silence, stroke sounded only by the tapstone. She was* Indomitable.

*It had been eleven months to the day from our fleet admiral's apotheosis at Athens to this skulking decampment to exile, by the dark of the moon.*

# BOOK NINE

# TIDES
# OF WAR

# FORTY-THREE
# BETWEEN THE EARTH
# AND THE SEA

THE EXIT OF ALCIBIADES WAS HAILED AT ATHENS [GRANDFATHER continued] *with a relief verging upon the ecstatic (or so my wife reported by letter received at Samos that autumn), such had become the people's trepidation, not alone of that tyranny they imagined they had so serendipitously eluded but of the unaccountability of a single all-powerful commander whose conduct of the war had become at best idiosyncratic and whose style of generalship, the hallmark of which had become the conspicuousness in high places of his cronies and his lover, had begun to border upon the regal. The Assembly replaced Alcibiades with a college of ten generals, to impede any attempt at concentration of power, and sent out as well a supplementary body composed of the ten tribal taxiarchs, serving as ships' captains, to act as a further check on recurrence of excess. If these curbs were not enough, the Assembly buttressed the fleet by drafting a number of past generals to command single ships. Illustrious names now bedizened the trierarchs' roster. Europa made a passage in convoy to Methymna; two vessels ahead sailed Alcyone, commanded by Theramenes, while to flank rowed Indefatigable under the great Thrasybulus.*

*It succeeded. Command was now dispersed across the entire political spectrum; rivalry receded; order was restored. Scarcity and hardship chafed less, shared by such a company. So many crack foreign sailors had deserted to the enemy that for the first time a fleet of Athens must advance to battle inferior in seamanship to the foe. This sobered the force further. Crews trained with a will; discipline was enforced internally, by shipmates, not imposed by officers. I may say of all my overseas tours this aggregation of ships and men was, if not the most brilliant, certainly the most able.*

*The departure of our supreme commander had as well profound consequences for Polemides, who learned of it, he told me, while yet in hiding in the aftermath of Ephesus.*

*With Alcibiades out of power, Polemides could not go home. Road's Turn would be lost if it wasn't already, and with it all means of support for his brother's children and his own. His conviction for treason would stand. He was a hunted man now, by both sides. Even to cross to Samos to join his bride and child carried grave risks. He was caught, as the poet says, between the earth and the sea.*

T HE ESTATE OF MY FATHER-IN-LAW, AURORE'S FATHER [POLEMIDES *recounted*], comprised some twenty acres in the hill country remote from the port of Samos, on the north slope above Pillion Bay. One approached from the city side via the Heraion Road. I had chosen to land, however, at the island's most remote point, on the bay side, while it was yet dark, a headland called the Old Woman's Tit. I had got from the mainland to the islet of Tragia, then at last, a month and more past the time of my bride's term, ferried the final leg by a lad of fourteen named Sophron in his father's bumboat he had stolen. The boy asked no payment, nor even enquired my name, undertaking the hazard, he professed, purely for the adventure of it.

I mounted via the back track, steep and stony, and had worked a lather by the time the sun, and the welcome tiles of the farmhouse roof, hove into prospect above. One could see the compound from a distance: the pair of stone steadings, the hillward trace between, and the lane of camphor trees that mounted to the house itself. The family tombs were sited upon this track, and as I passed I noted, hung upon the lintel, two *epikedeioi stephanoi*, the wreaths of tamarisk and laurel offered in the islands to Demeter and Kore in intercession for the dead. Has the old man passed off? I wondered. Perhaps Aurore's grandfolk, who inhabited cottages of the downslope enclave. I hurried on, minding myself not to permit my own joy at this much-behindhand homecoming to obtrude upon another's grief. From the distance of a stone's sling I spied my brother-in-law Anticles, with his dog Ironhead, striding into view from the corner of the steading. Two drystone dikers waited upon him with their mawls and stringers. 'Has the garden wall taken another tumble?' I called in salute. Anticles turned and saw me. Such an alteration deformed his features as to choke my greeting in midbreath. His elder brother Theodorus turned into view from the hillward trace. He took one look, bent in midstride, and, seizing a stone in each fist, advanced upon me.

'You.'

This was his solitary word.

'What has happened?' I heard myself cry.

Stones screamed past my ears. 'You are not welcome here.'

I let fall kit and arms and, spreading palms wide, beseeched clemency in the name of the gods.

'May hell take you,' Anticles spat, 'and the evil you have brought upon our house!'

Both brothers advanced. Even the dikers rose. I could hear the dogs clamouring.

'Where is Aurore? What has happened?'

'Get out, thou villain!'

A stone of Theodorus struck my hip.

I begged the brothers to tell me what had happened. Let me speak to Aurore. 'She is my wife, and the child my own.'

'Attend them there.' Theodorus indicated the tombs.

All who have been soldiers know these, Jason: such hours when pain of flesh or spirit surpasses the heart's capacity to endure it. I shook myself, as in a nightmare. How could these, my brothers, advance upon me with such hatred? How could those wreaths be for them I so loved?

'Leave this country!' Anticles strode upon me, brandishing his staff. 'By the gods, if you cross again within my sight, that hour will end your life or mine.'

I withdrew. Where the farm's limit fell away to the bay, two lads of the neighbour's were clearing brush. From them I learned that my bride had succumbed two months previous. Poisoned. The child in her womb had perished with her.

Somehow it had become afternoon. I mounted the hill again. At the fence the dogs cut me off in a pack. Anticles roared down, on horseback.

'What may I do, brother,' I beseeched him, 'to requite this woe . . .'

He made no answer, only wheeled his mount in place, regarding him who stood beneath with such rue as one may donate not to another of humankind, but to a wraith or spectre, life-fled yet present, denied repose beneath the earth.

'You have stolen the sun from our sky, you and he who sent you. May your days, and his, be ever as lightless as you have made ours.'

# FORTY-FOUR
# A WITNESS TO MURDER

POLEMIDES BROKE OFF AT THIS POINT AND WAS UNABLE FOR LONG moments to continue. When at length he recovered himself, he declared that he had had a change of heart regarding his trial. He no longer wished to contest the charge; he would plead guilty. He had been deliberating upon this for some time, he acknowledged, but had not until this moment come to it as the course of honour. His lone regret was that his affairs had consumed so much of my time, proffered, he acknowledged, with such generosity and regard. He begged my pardon.

I was seized with outrage at this defection and lit into the man in fury. How dare he exploit the empathy of my heart and defame by enlisting it in his cause the memory of beloved comrades? Did he think I undertook this chore lightly? Because I admired him or deemed him worthy of deliverance? I despised him and all he had done, I declared, and had donated my advocacy only that the narration of his self-dishonourment might serve as a manifest of infamy to our countrymen. His cause had ceased to be his own the moment he sounded me to assist him; how dare he break off short of the mark? Yes, die, I heard my voice exclaim, and good riddance! I strode to the door and pounded upon it, calling for the turnkey.

Naught but echo met my halloo. It was the hour of the man's supper, I realized; he would be across the way at the refectory. I could hear our client behind me, chuckling. 'It seems you have become a prisoner as well, my friend.'

'You are a cur, Polemides.'

'I never pretended otherwise, mate.'

I turned back, already recognizing beneath wrath's receding flush how profoundly I had come to care for this villain. The veteran's features declined into a smile. He acknowledged the aptness of the verdict I had pronounced upon him, remarking that its single shortcoming was its failure to go far enough.

He continued not with words, but by withdrawing from his chest two articles of correspondence which, one could not but infer from the way he handled them, he had re-perused recently and whose contents had affected him profoundly. He passed them to me.

'Sit down, my friend. You're going nowhere for a while anyway.'

The first item was a letter from him to his great-aunt Daphne, dated some months subsequent to the final destruction of the Athenian fleet at Aegospotami, that calamity which made inevitable the city's capitulation and, after twenty-seven years, her defeat at the hands of the Spartans and their Persian and Peloponnesian allies.

At that time Polemides, he told me now, stood in the service of Lysander, with convictions for treason and murder imposed from his homeland. He writes to his aunt at Athens, instructing her to prepare for the siege and surrender to come:

. . . factions among our countrymen will nominate themselves to procure what they will call the Peace. The nation's sovereignty will be given over; her fleet destroyed; Long Walls torn down. A puppet government of collaborators will be imposed. Acts of reprisal will follow. Perhaps by my return I may mitigate, at least for you and our family, the effects of the lawlessness which is certain to ensue.

You must get out of the city, Aunt, to the land. Take Lion's children. Can you locate my own? Please, get them to safety. The seal on this letter is that of Lysander's staff. It will protect you, but don't use it unless the issue is life-and-death, for others, our countrymen, will make you pay later.

Lastly, my dear, do not be present when Lysander's squadrons enter the Piraeus or you will see that which no patriot like yourself may bear without heartbreak: the child you raised, in the scarlet of the foe. I am beyond love of country and long past shame. I act only as others will and have, to preserve my own.

*His aunt replies:*

Thou shameless soul! How dare you apply care for my person as pretext for your perfidy? I wish you had perished in the quarries, or in some nameless scrape where you could still be called your father's son and not the agent of infamy you have so wickedly shown yourself to be. God grant I never look upon your face again. You no longer exist for me. I have no nephew.

*I passed the correspondence back to Polemides. His aspect conveyed clearly that he shared this condemnation articulated by his aunt, and to such a depth as to preclude contravention, at least now, at this hour. I felt him slip from me as a corpse upon dark water, when the boat hook fails of purchase and one's vessel, driven by its way, passes on, to put about no more.*

*The jailer returned; I was released. I crossed the Iron Court to Socrates' cell and passed, in that company, the remainder of the evening. Our master's days were now down to three. The sacred ship returning from Delos had been sighted off Sounium that morn; her arrival at Athens would put a period to the reprieve which had thus far postponed his execution. One anticipated the vessel this night. She did not turn up, however. A dream of Socrates had predicted this. A fair woman in white robes had appeared to him, he recounted to us gathered that evening, and addressing him by name, declared,*

To the pleasant land of Phthia
On the third day shalt thou come.

*A terrible despair gripped my heart, communicated in part from Polemides, whose recollection of the hours of our country's fall coincided with the pending execution of my master, which to me stood as a second and more calamitous overthrow, for it forecast, I felt, not alone the passing of our sovereignty but the ideal of democracy herself.*

*I passed out of the prison last of all that night. I had made up my mind to speak in person with Polemides no more, nor even convey his wishes to the authorities. He had made his choice; let him enact it. The passageway out* stood silent save for a carpenter framing a door in the prison shop. I glanced in. The iron bands I took at first for some sort of hinge or brace. At once I recognized the instrument.

It was no door.

It was the tympanon, upon which Polemides would be executed. He would be affixed to the plank, naked, the instrument itself then elevated upright with the man bound upon it. No-one would be permitted to approach, or bring aid of any kind; only the executioner would remain, to apply the torment prescribed by the court and to certify the condemned's demise. The carpenter haled me in, yarning amiably as he worked. He must, he imparted, fabricate a fresh device for each execution. 'You'd not believe what runs out of a man's guts, sir. The dead comes off light as a doll.'

He showed me how the instrument worked. Four cramp irons imprisoned the victim's limbs, a fifth yoke of chain cinched his throat. Turning pegs tightened this, choking the breath. No blood, that was the apparatus's strong point.

I asked if this particular device was for Polemides. The joiner didn't know; it was not his practice to enquire. One convicted of treason, though, he observed, may not be buried in Attica or 'any land of which the Athenians are masters'. The corpse would be cast out, unburied, for the dogs and crows.

The carpenter considered this appliance the latest in humane treatment. 'Better than chucking 'em into the Dead Man's Pit, like the generals after Arginousai. That was bloody frightful. My father made the traps for that. No-one had never done six at once, so three had to wait. That was horrible, 'cause you could hear the sound as the first three hit. The younger Pericles and Diomedon went off without no shroud. None of 'em spoke a word, just Diomedon. "Let's get it over with."'

Best of all things, Theognis says, is never to be born

> . . . but being born, best then to speed
> straightway to hell and there sleep
> under the weighty shield of earth.

Some days previous, succeeding my second interview with Eunice, I had summoned my bloodhounds Myron and Lado and, proffering a premium, spurred them to redouble their efforts to discover the particulars of the murder with which our client was charged. Nor did my spies tarry, but presented themselves two mornings later. They had found a man, a sailor at the time.

*An eyewitness. He would not testify in person as he owed money and did not wish to advertise his presence in the city. For a consideration, however, he would dictate an affidavit and swear an oath to its truth.*

*Here is that document. The man identifies himself as a citizen of the district of Amphitrope and former petty officer of the fleet:*

... this was at Samos, in that kind of dive they call a 'soda'. The Pennyroyal. Mates off certain ships congregated there; it was their place. Polemides' tart Eunice was aboard that night, and about a dozen others from the lanes; kids too, it was that kind of joint. A rain had got up, the roof had sprung gushers; there was pots on tabletops, that sort of thing ...

Polemides stalks in. He don't look right or left, just makes straight for the woman Eunice and lays violent hands on her, to snap her neck. Two or three leaps on him and hauls him off, they go to brawling. Polemides kicks free. He snatches up an iron kettle, set out to catch the rain, and goes after the woman again. This fellow Philemon tries to block him. Polemides swings the kettle, the man goes down – dead before he hits the deck.

Polemides stares at him, and at the woman Eunice, and his own brats, gaping up like he's gone raving. The sight of the whelps snaps him out of it. He wheels and stalks out. The whole stunt didn't take half the time it needs to tell it. No-one had spoke a word, start to finish.

The dirt comes out later from the girlfriends. This Eunice, it turns out, is a gale-force hellcat. She had got belladonna into the gentlewoman Polemides had married. Poisoned her. Knocked-up she was, the bride, so the kid in her belly snuffed it too. That was the gossip anyway.

That's what happened, Cap'n. Polemides planted this luckless bastard Philemon, not from malice, just 'cause he got in his way as he was going after his woman to settle her. That's the truth. I was there and I saw it.

# FORTY-FIVE
# AN ADVOCATE AT
# THE GATE

TWO DAWNS REMAINED BEFORE SOCRATES MUST DRINK THE HEMLOCK. *One could not sleep but thrashed nightlong, only to doze as in a nightmare at dawn's pallor.*

*It was at this hour my attendant knocked, reporting a young man at the gate. The lad refused to give his name, but importuned my attendance most earnestly. The youth had a sum of money, my servant recounted, which he wished to deliver into my keeping.*

*Curiosity drew both my sons with me to the threshold. The lad, when we opened to him, appeared just a stripling, sixteen at most, and slight as a stalk. I invited him within.*

'No thank you, sir. I come only as a representative of certain concerned citizens. Quite a body, if I may say so.'

*The child was so earnest that one almost laughed, his oration offered with the stilted solemnity of one composed in advance and committed to memory.*

'I wish,' *he declared,* 'only to place these funds in your hand, Captain, on behalf of Polemides the son of Nicolaus of Acharnae, for you to employ in his defence as you see fit. I am young, sir, and have no experience of the courts. One cannot but imagine, however, that certain expenses may arise . . .'

*That which he proffered was no mean sum, but above a hundred drachmas. A run of silver tetras, newly minted, struck me at once, and my sons, as stolen in a lump.*

'How does a twig like you come up with a load like this?' my elder enquired.
'It rings, don't it?'

His accent was a double for Eunice's, his brow and eyes hers as well.

So this was the runaway.

'Indeed it does, young man.' I hefted the money. 'And what shall I use it for – to bribe the jurors?'

'Those I represent, sir, accede to your wisdom.'

'And these concerned citizens . . . what precisely is their interest in this case?'

'Partisans of justice, sir.'

One began to assimilate details of the youth's lineaments. His cloak was that overlong type called a 'street-sweeper', and though it had been brushed perhaps as recently as last evening, the dusty stain of its hem gave it away. Beneath its folds no doubt the boy's feet were unshod.

'Have you had dinner today, young man?'

'Indeed, sir. A gut-buster!'

Both my sons laughed. 'Mind a stiff puff doesn't strike you broadside!'

Again I invited the boy in. Again he declined. I held out the money. 'Why not take this to Polemides yourself?'

At once the child began to stammer and withdraw. Clearly we had strayed from the turf of his prepared presentation.

'I think you should,' I insisted. 'A prisoner in distress will be much heartened to learn of friends who uphold him in his cause.'

'Just take the jack, Cap'n.'

'I'll tell you what I'll take, young man.' At a gesture, my sons seized the lad. 'I'll take you and this sum to the magistrate and let him decide where you got it.'

'Let go, fuckers!'

The youth fought like a wild beast; it took both my boys, outstanding wrestlers, to pin him. 'Now, my young friend. Will you come with me to Polemides, or shall we knock at the archon's gate?'

Approaching the prison, the boy became agitated. 'Will they search me, sir?' And he stripped a dagger from beneath his arm and a Spartan xyele from a sheath on his thigh.

In the corridor approaching the cell I halted. The boy's face went to chalk. 'Ain't you coming in, Cap'n?'

'You've played your part manfully thus far,' I reassured him, and, *setting a bolstering hand upon his shoulder, prompted him forward.*

*From where I stood I could not see Polemides within the cell, but only the boy at the threshold as the turnkey opened and the lad hesitated, peering in as if at a caged brute he feared might rush upon him. I confess that, when the child found courage and vanished within, I discovered my eyes burning and a thickness about my throat.*

*Father and son remained all morning, or at least beyond the hour I waited, across the way at the refectory of my ancient comrade, the marine archer Bruise. My sons had gifted the boy Nicolaus with a packet of kit articles, including shoes and a new tunic, ostensibly to be passed on to his father but, we hoped, one that his pride would permit him, out of our sight, to retain for himself.*

*Instead by noon the kit was returned to our gate, intact, with a note thanking us, and no more.*

# FORTY-SIX
# ACROSS THE IRON COURT

LEAVING SOCRATES' CELL THAT NIGHT, THE PARTY OF HIS COMPANIONS crossed the Iron Court to the chambers of Lysimachus of Oa, Secretary of the Eleven. The master's execution would be tomorrow. The hemlock, at his request, would be administered at sunset. The secretary showed us the bowl, plain wooden with a cover; apparently the juice altered composition, exposed to the air. It must be consumed at once, in a single draught if possible.

The executioner, a physician of Brauron, chanced to be within the prison on another errand; he was kind enough to donate an interval with us, myself and Critobulus, Crito, Simmias of Thebes, Cebes, Epigenes, Phaedo of Samos, and the others. The practitioner, whose name was not revealed and who was unknown to us by sight, wore a plain white chiton as we all. He apprised us that tomorrow he would appear in the robe of his office; he wished to forewarn us that the sight might not, by its unexpectedness, evoke dismay.

We would be permitted to remain in the cell with Socrates until the end and to claim his body as soon as death had been pronounced and the certificate recorded. There would be no 'final repast', as the subject's belly must be empty; nor might wine be taken later than noon, as its effect acted in contravention to the poison.

Crito asked what we may do to render our friend's passage more endurable. Hemlock was painless, the doctor declared. Its effect was a progressive loss of sensation, commencing from the feet, the subject remaining alert and lucid up to the final stages. Nausea might be experienced as the drug reached the midsection; thereafter accelerated numbness, followed by loss of consciousness and, ultimately, cessation of heartbeat. The drug's deficiency was that it took time, often as long as two hours. It was best if the subject remained quiet. Stimulation could impede the poison's effect, necessitating a second dose and even a third. 'He will feel cold, gentlemen. You may wish to bring a fleece or woollen mantle for his shoulders.'

Our party exited in silence. I had forgotten entirely about Polemides (who by now had no doubt filed his attestation of guilt) and would have departed without another thought had not the porter hailed me as we crossed the court, asking after the designated claimant for his, the assassin's, body. For a moment I feared sentence had already been carried out; I was seized with grief and anguish. But no, the official informed me, Polemides' execution would be tomorrow, at sunset, as Socrates'.

Death would be on the tympanon. He could not say how long they would drag it out. The assassin – so clever was he, the porter observed – had confessed not to treason, but to 'wrongdoing'. By this technicality (as that was indeed the specific charge against him) he had ducked the disgrace of having his body dumped unburied beyond the borders of Attica; the corpse would be transported to the Funerary Depot beside the Northern Wall, where it could be recovered by his kinsmen. 'A boy has been round, sir, claiming to be the prisoner's son. Absent another, may the officers release the body to him?'

'What does the prisoner say?'

'He says to ask you.'

It was now well after dark; I had been up for a day and a night and could look forward to the same tomorrow. Yet clearly I could not go home. I hailed a 'skylark' and, pressing a coin into the lad's hand, despatched him with a message for my wife that I would be delayed.

When I entered Polemides' cell, he was writing. He rose at once, in hale spirits, clasping my hand in welcome. Had I been with Socrates? Of course. The prison could speak of nothing else.

I had thought I would chafe at this chore and discover myself in anger at him, for the labour he had put me through for nothing. To my surprise the opposite obtained. Immediately within the cell, I felt the weight of distress lift from my bones. It was bracing, the assassin's acceptance of his fate. It shamed me.

'What are you writing?'

'Letters.'

*To whom?*

'One to my son. One to you.'

*At once tears sprang; a sob wrenched from my throat. I must hide my face.*

'Sit,' *the prisoner bade.* 'There's wine brought by my boy, take some.'

*I obeyed.*

'Just let me finish this. I won't be long.'

*He enquired, as he wrote, of Socrates. Would the philosopher exit on shanks's highway? Would he* 'mount the midnight mare'? *Polemides laughed. No secret endured long within these walls, he observed; he had overheard all the getaway schemes, of Simmias and Cebes hiring horses and armed escorts; he knew which officials had accepted bribes, and even how much. Sundry informers had already put their blackmail to Crito and Menexeus and been paid off to come down with lockjaw.*

'He won't run,' *I said.* 'He's as stubborn as you.'

'Well, you see, we're both philosophers.'

*Polemides reported that he had yarned several times with Socrates, when they chanced to be granted exercise at the same hour. What had they talked about?* 'Alcibiades, mostly. And a bit of conjecture on life after death.' *He laughed.* 'I'm to be boxed on the Whore, did you hear?'

*He had learned he would be executed on the* tympanon.

*He asked what we prated about, who closeted all day about our master. Customarily I would not speak of this, yet now . . .* 'We talked of the law and adherence to it in the face of death.'

*Polemides considered this gravely.* 'I would like to have heard that.'

*I watched as the assassin scripted his valedictory. His hand was firm and sure. When he paused periodically, seeking a word, one could not but be struck by the recollection of Alcibiades, possessed of the identical trait, so charming when he spoke, of drawing up until the proper phrase presented itself.*

*In the lamplight the prisoner looked younger than his seasons. His trim waist, product of years of campaign, made it no task to envision him as a lad at Lacedaemon, with such hopes, more than thrice nine years gone. I was struck by the irony, the inevitability, of his passage, and Socrates', to this enclosure and this end.*

*Might I importune him for the conclusion of his tale? Did it matter? Surely no longer to mount a defence. Yet that wish persisted to hear what remained, from his lips, to its period.*

'You must tell me first,' he replied. 'A fair trade. What Socrates said today about the law . . . in return for my tale to its end.'

I resisted, for much of our master's matter was commendatory to me.

'Of course it was, Jason! Do you think I muster with any but the noblest?'

I told him then. It had gone like this:

Our circle had gathered in Socrates' cell. A number continued to urge escape. I added my voice. With an escort at arms our master need fear nothing on the highway. He could travel to any sanctuary we, or his friends of other nations, could provide him.

I had been foolish enough to look for a direct answer. Of course the philosopher accorded none. Rather he addressed himself to Crito's son, youngest among us, who sat at his knee along the wall.

'Advise me, Critobulus, may one make distinction between justice and the law?'

A groan escaped my lips of such violence as to evoke mirth from all, not least Socrates. Again I put my case. The time for philosophical debate was over! This was life-and-death. One must act!

It was not Socrates who admonished me, but Crito, his oldest and most devoted friend. 'Is that what philosophy is to you, my dear Jason? A pastime for the parlour, with which we divert ourselves while fate clasps us in clemency, but in the hour of extremity cast aside?'

I told them to chastise me all they wished, only heed that course I exhorted. Socrates regarded me with patience, which infuriated me the more. 'Do you remember, Crito,' he continued, still not addressing me, 'the oration our friend Jason put to the people during the trial of the generals?'

'Indeed I do. And a fire-breather it was!'

Please, I urged our master, do not mock me. For the issue of that day proved my point precisely.

'And how is that, my friend?'

By miscarrying justice! By putting good men to death in madness. 'The demos may summon you back from Elis or Thebes, Socrates, but not from hell.'

'Yes, there's the fire, Jason! The flame you showed that day and the brightest you have burned in all your life. I was proud of you then as of few others before or since.'

This abashed me. I fell silent.

'You spoke of law and charged the people not to despoil it, following

Euryptolemus, who had made such an intrepid speech in defence. This was the crime you charged the people with, if memory serves: you declared that jealousy drove the meaner man to destroy the better. Is this correct? I only wish to reiterate precisely, that we may examine the matter and perhaps gain illumination.'

I acknowledged that it was, desiring, however, to return to the matter of escape.

'I believe what distresses you now,' our master resumed, 'is that you feel such miscarriage recurring. My own conviction, you warrant, has arisen not from merit of the case, but from hatred felt by men towards one who styles himself their better. Is this correct, Jason?'

'Is this not exactly what has happened?'

'Do you believe the people capable of ruling themselves?'

I replied in the negative, emphatically.

'And who would govern best, in your view?'

'You. Us. Anyone but them.'

'Let me phrase the question differently. Do we believe that the law, even an unjust law, must be obeyed? Or may the individual take it on himself to decide which laws are just and which unjust, which worthy of obedience and which not?'

I protested that it was not justice which Socrates had received, and thus its disallowance was legitimate.

'Let us hear your opinion, Jason. Is it better to perish through injustice inflicted upon one by others, or to live, having inflicted injustice on them?'

I had lost patience with this and remonstrated vehemently. Socrates inflicted injustice on no-one by taking to flight. He must live! And by the gods, each of us would move heaven and earth to secure this!

'You forget one, Jason, upon whom I would be inflicting injustice. The Laws. Suppose the Laws sat among us now. Might they not say something like this: "Socrates, we have served you all your life. Beneath our protection you grew to manhood, married, and raised a family; you pursued your livelihood and studied philosophy. You accepted our boons and the security we provided. Yet now, when our verdict no longer suits your convenience, you wish to put us aside." How would we answer the Laws?'

'Some men must be set above the laws.'

'How can you strike this posture, my friend, who argued with such fervour, that day, the contravening course?'

*Again abashment took me. I could not stand in the face of his conviction.*

'Let me restore your memory, my dear Jason, yours and those of our friends who stood present that day, and bring to these here, who were then too young, enlightenment afresh.

'After Alcibiades' banishment following the defeat at Notium, the city sent out Conon to assume command. That authority not be concentrated in the hands of one man, however, the Council compassed him within a corps of ten generals, among whom were our friends Aristocrates and the younger Pericles. Under this collegial command, the fleet engaged the enemy in a great battle at the Arginousai Islands, destroying seventy of their warships, including nine of ten Spartan vessels, while losing twenty-five of our own. You were there, Jason. Do I recite accurately? Correct me please if I miscarry.

'At this hour, the close of fighting, all fortune had favoured the Athenians. But in battle's aftermath a blow arose with terrible swiftness, as storms do in those seas at that time of year, so I am told, and the men in the water – our men, from those ships holed and sunk – could not be recovered. Those assigned by the generals, among them Thrasybulus and Theremenes, proven leaders, could not master the tempest. All in the water were lost. These comprised the crews of some twenty-five vessels, five thousand men. The city, when it learned of this, was riven in conflicting directions, the first in rage and horror clamouring for the blood of those who had failed to rescue the ship-wrecked seamen, the second straining to absorb the calamity as one must all in war, acknowledging the severity of the storm, which was ratified by all reports, nor failing to recollect the greatness of the victory.

'It chanced, however – you who were there cannot but recall – that the Feast of the Apaturia fell proximately after the battle, that customarily joyous season when the brotherhoods assemble to rededicate their bonds and enrol the youths entering their fraternities. It happened, I say, that so many were the gaps in the ranks vacated by those sailors and marines lost at sea, that men broke down to behold the magnitude of the loss. And this despair, inflamed by the rhetoric of certain individuals, some of legitimate motive, others seeking to deflect blame from themselves, erupted to a conflagration. The city clamoured for blood. Six of the generals were arrested (four received warning and fled first). The people proceeded against them at once, trying them not individually as the law prescribed, but in a block, as one. Pericles, Aristocrates, and the other four were made to defend themselves in chains, as traitors. Do I say true, Jason? And you, Crito and Cebes, who were there, draw me up if I narrate imprecisely.'

All concurred that Socrates' depiction was faithful in spirit and fact.

'The generals were tried in open Assembly. My tribe held the prytany; the lot of epistates chanced to have fallen to me. I was president of the Assembly, the lone occasion of my life on which I have held so lofty a post, and for one day only, as the laws prescribed.

'The prosecutors spoke first; then the generals, one after the other in their own defence, but refused by the mob's impatience the prescribed interval of the law. Only two spoke in their defence. Axiochus first, then Euryptolemus, nor did he or any of his family ever honour their name more than by his gallantry in that hour. He confined his arguments, shrewdly in the face of the mob, to an exhortation to give each general his day in court. "In this way you may be sure of exacting the fullest measure of justice, punishing the guilty to the maximum while avoiding the terrible crime of condemning those who are blameless."

'The people listened, and even carried his motion, but then Menecles lodged an objection on a technicality and the motion was about to be put to a second vote, that vote which in fact overturned Euryptolemus' plea and doomed Pericles and the others. Before this ballot could be taken, however, you arose, Jason. I, as chair, recognized you, though many attempted to shout you down, knowing the fellowship you bore for the younger Pericles, not to say your own record of valour with the fleet. Will you permit me, friends, to attempt to recapture the character, if not the text, of our comrade's plea? Or shall I quit this line of recital?'

The others desired most ardently that our master continue. He glanced once in my direction, then returned to them in sober mien.

'You spoke as follows, Jason:

' "You are impatient, men of Athens, to conclude this matter. Allow me then to propose a course. As you have determined already that these men are guilty, sparing the state expense of trial or deliberation, let us so name them. Let us agree that in violation of the ordinances of gods and men, they forswore their duty to their comrades in peril. Are we agreed? Then let us advance upon them in a pack now and tear their throats out with our bare hands!

' "You howl at me, gentlemen. We must do it by law, you cry. Which law is that: the one you overturn at your whim or the one you make unto yourselves? For tomorrow when you awaken, defiled with these innocent men's blood, no canon or statute will cloak your wickedness.

' "But you will contend, and those prosecutors speaking in your name have so contended, These accused are murderers! You will paint, as your indictors have painted, the soul-rending portrait of our shipwrecked sons crying for that aid which did not come, until, strength at last failing, they gulped the salt element that overwhelmed them. I have fought upon the sea. We all have. God help us, to perish on that field is the most piteous death a man may suffer, where not his bones, nor the shreds of his garment, may be restored to find rest beneath his native soil.

' "Yes, our sons' blood cries for retribution. But how shall we exact it – by dishonouring the very law they gave their lives for? In my family we call ourselves democrats. Within my father's vault reside commendations inscribed by the elder Pericles, father of one who stands here accused today, and my friend, as all know. These artefacts rest revered beneath our roof, talismans of our democracy. Now in holy assembly we gather, Athenians, as our fathers and theirs before them. But do we deliberate? Is that what you call this? My heart perceives a darker spawn. I peer into your faces and ask, Where have I seen this aspect before? I will tell you where I have not seen it. I have not seen it in the eyes of warriors facing the enemy with fortitude. That is another look entire, and you know it.

' "What unholy imperative, men of Athens, compels you against all reason and your own self-interest to strike down those who are best among you?

' "Themistocles preserved the state at her most imperilled hour; yet him you exiled and condemned. Miltiades brought you victory at Marathon, yet you bound him in chains and ravened to cast him into the Pit. Cimon, who won you empire, you hounded to the grave. Alcibiades? By the gods, you didn't let his feet warm the very pedestal you had set him upon before dragging it and him to earth and dancing with glee upon the sundered stones. Acid and bile are mother's milk to you. You would rather see the state ground to dust by its enemies than preserved by your betters and be compelled to acknowledge this to their faces. This is the most bitter fate you can imagine, men of Athens. Not vanquishment at the hands of those who hate you, but accepting grace from those who seek only your love.

' "When I was a boy, my father took me to the yard at Telegoneia where his cousin, a master shipwright, constructed a boat. The hull had been founded and within her bowl we reclined, enjoying our dinner and anticipating the pleasure of seeing the craft rise to completion. In sober tone my father's cousin remarked of the necessity, now, to remain with the vessel even at night.

Perceiving my perplexity, he set a hand upon my shoulder: 'Beware the saboteur.'

' " 'Men are jealous,' the ship's master instructed my innocent heart. 'Of all affairs beneath heaven, they may bear least success in a friend.'

' "Our enemies watch us, men of Athens. Lysander watches us. If he could slay in battle all ten of his enemy's generals, how wouldn't his countrymen honour him? Yet we propose to do this for him!

' "What madness has seized you, my countrymen? You who claim above all peoples to oppose tyranny; you yourselves have become tyrants. For what is tyranny but the name men give to that form of governance which spurns justice and acts by might alone?

' "I had come to this platform fearing you. In my wife's bed last night I trembled and required her gallant heart, and those of my comrades this day, even to mount the stand to address you. Yet now hearing you howl, I feel no terror whatever, save that gravest of all: terror for you and for our nation. You are not democrats. Turn to the fleet for those. You will find none there who condemns these men. They saw that storm. I saw it. The men in the water were dead already, God help them. Yet that is not the crime for which you prosecute these commanders. They are guilty of another. They are your betters and for that your craven hearts may never acquit them.

' "Yes, bay at me, men of Athens, but know yourselves for yourselves. Don't be hypocrites. If you intend to overthrow the law, then by Chiron's hoof, do it like men. You there, tear down the steles of ordinance. And you, seize chisel and mawl and efface the constitution stones. On our feet, all! Let us march as the mob we are to Solon's tomb and there cast to hell his holy bones. That is what you do, to condemn these men against all law and precedent."

'These words, my dear Jason, or others very like them, you spoke that day. You heard the mob roar at you then, as they did at me moments later, when I refused as president of the Assembly to put to the vote their unconstitutional motion. They cried for my head, threatened my wife and children. Such rancour I have never heard, even in battle from the blood-mad foe. But I had sworn my prytane's oath and could act in no way contrary to law. It availed nothing, as you know. The people simply waited one day, till my term expired and the new presiding officer acceded to their will.

'The point, however, my dear Jason, is that in neither case – the conviction of the generals or my own – were the laws to blame. Rather the people *overturned the law. Wherefore I believe you were right to defend the law then, and I am right to adhere to it now. Please, my friends, may we at last set aside the issue of flight or evasion?'*

I yielded, chastened. Socrates placed his hand kindly upon my shoulder. He spoke to me, but addressing all.

'Can the demos rule itself? It may perhaps ease your mind to recall, my friend, that those ideals to which the lover of wisdom aspires – the precedence of soul over body, the enquiry after truth, the mastering of the passions of the flesh – are to the common herd not only abhorrent but absurd. The main of men seek not to govern their appetites, but to gratify them; to them justice is an impediment discommoding their cupidity and the gods but vacant tokens, invoked to mask their own actions taken out of fear, expediency, and self-interest. The demos may not be elevated as the demos, but only as individuals. In the end one may master only oneself. Therefore let us leave the throng to its own.

'What distresses me far more, Jason, is your despair and its issue: estrangement from philosophy. It is as if you could endure all, holding fast to our calling, but this blow, the loss of myself, your heart cannot bear. Nothing could cause me greater grief or make me fear more that my endeavour, and in fact my life, have been in vain.'

I wept now, yet could not command myself to subscribe to his posture.

'Do you remember when the trial of the generals was over,' Socrates resumed, 'how we gathered, friends of the younger Pericles, outside the precinct of the Barathron, the Dead Man's Pit, and claimed his corpse from the officers?

'Pericles' kinsmen Ariphron and Xenocrates had arranged for a carriage to bear his body home. His wife Chione, "Snow", overruled them. She despatched her sons to the harbour to fetch a public handbarrow. You know these, my friends. They may be found on any quayside, two and three in a bunch, set out as a courtesy to returning sailors, to take their gear to waiting carts. The barrows are marked Epimeletai ton Neorion – Property of the Admiralty.

'Upon this simple seaman's cart we bore our friend's corpse home. We were twenty, in a body, as we felt we must be in fear of the mob. None molested our way, however; their lust for blood had been sated. Pericles' son Xanthippus was the bravest. Only fourteen, he strode before the party erect and dry-eyed. He dressed his father's corpse, in apprehension yet that the*

Eleven might order it expelled from Attica, and that night sheared his mother's hair and bound her in the cowl of mourning. The order had already been served, confiscating Pericles' property. Do you remember? We gathered to take into our own homes whomever and whatever we could. Yet what fell out was this: within two days the people had come to themselves and discovered their derangement. Collective contrition seized the city, as men discerned the outrage they had wrought and lamented bitterly their own passion and overhaste.

'Now Chione refused to confine herself to the women's quarters. "Let them stop me," she declared. Draped in mourning, she strode abroad, veilless, with her shorn locks, in reproach to all and any. To those few who summoned courage to approach she addressed not a word, day upon day, but only displayed her cropped hair.

'Do you understand, Jason? She was a philosopher. Untutored, her valiant heart grasped the requirement of the hour and endowed her with the intrepidity to act. Neither Brasidas nor Leonidas, not Achilles himself, ever evinced greater fortitude or more selfless love for hearth and country. How then may I, friends, who claim love of wisdom my calling, how may I permit myself an action unworthy of it or of her? I may step off the precipice, so to say, as in silence the younger Pericles, her husband, did. And you, friends, may walk abroad with shorn heads, as his wife.'

I finished.

Polemides said nothing for long moments, absorbed in meditations of his own.

'Thank you,' he spoke at last.

He smiled then and, producing a document from his chest, passed it to me.

'What is it?'

'Take a look.'

I glanced at its prologue. It was my defence of the younger Pericles, the very address I had, in Socrates' redaction, just recounted.

'Where did you get this?'

'From Alcibiades, in Thrace. He admired it greatly, as do I. It was not the only copy among that army.'

Again my throat thickened, recalling those loved ones, Polemides' as well as my own, of whom we could claim naught but memory. The night was well advanced; the porter's steps could be heard below retiring to his cubby hole. It would require a racket now to accomplish my release. Let it go, I thought. My *wife will not fret, but think me overnighting with one of our company. I turned to my companion, who, alert as well to my predicament, regarded me with amusement.*

*'Now you must keep your bargain, Pommo, to conclude your tale aloud. Or are you too wearied to see it through?'*

*An odd expression animated him.*

*'Why do you smile like that?' I asked.*

*'You've never addressed me as "Pommo".'*

*'Haven't I?'*

*Indeed it would be his pleasure to finish, he said. He confessed he had feared that I myself had lost interest, absent the need to prepare for trial. 'Let us bring the ship to port, then, shall we, and secure her safely, if the gods will.'*

# FORTY-SEVEN
# THE TALE TO ITS END

I WAS WITH THE SPARTAN COLONEL PHILOTELES AT TEOS [*POLEMIDES resumed*] when reports came from Athens of the execution of Pericles and the generals. The Spartans could not believe it. First Alcibiades deposed, now their best men put to death. Had Athens gone mad? There was a ditty then.

> *Two-eyed the Owl-men*
> *Once polled sound as brass.*
> *Now they ballot with one eye,*
> *The one in their arse.*

Heaven had severed Athens from her senses for the excesses of her empire. Such was the Deity's requital, the street-corner prophets proclaimed, for the hubris of imperial pride.

Spartan morale soared. Desertions from Athens redoubled. I passed along Lysander's quays that autumn; one saw the same faces as at Samos, so many were the oarsmen, islanders, who had come over. Even the ships were the same. *Cormorant*, Lysias' squadron leader, was now *Orthia*. *Vigilant* and *Sea Swallow*, captured at Arginousai from the Cat's Eyes, were *Polias* and *Andreia*. Already in the taverns one heard short-timers' jabber; sailors and marines nervous of some fluke demise before war's end and discharge.

Athens had cobbled together her final fleet. Every jack who could piss standing up had been conscripted, even the Knights. The generals were so shaky they didn't even plunder. One defeat would finish them, while the Spartans, floated by Persian gold, could absorb loss after loss, simply making each good and continuing to fight.

I had put back to Ephesus after Samos. Where else could I go, with murder appended to treason on my proscript? Not that anyone noticed amid the flocks of deserters, turncoats and renegades lining up at the recruiting desks beneath the red rag. I refound Telamon. A new generation of officers had come out from Sparta, many mates of my youth. They had won their colonelcies or come East to try.

Philoteles, under whom I now took service, was the lad of my *agoge* platoon, twenty-six years past, who had with such empathy informed me of the burning of my father's farm. Now a division commander, he vowed to make good that long-ago injustice. 'When we take Athens I'll set the title in your fist, Pommo, and see him racked who dares cry foul.'

Here is how I became an assassin. We were training marines, Telamon and I, trying to stay out of trouble. Lysander, who had been recalled to Sparta on expiry of his commission as *navarch*, was back. The ephors had appointed him vice-admiral under Aracus, since no Spartan may hold supreme command twice. Lysander was chief, however, in all but name. Not hintermost among his directives was the elimination of political resistance within the cities. The Spartans are past masters at this, having acquired the practice from the subjugation of their own helots. Now Lysander recruited these themselves, the *neodamodeis*, the freed Spartan serfs, to carry out his campaign of terror.

These helots do not make bad troops in units under Spartan officers. On their own, however, they are notorious. Atrocities began coming to light. Philoteles approached Telamon and others, myself among them, who could be entrusted to act with restraint.

We were called 'summoners'. It worked like this. We were issued warrants, called 'writs of remission'. The names upon these were of officials and magistrates, naval and army officers, any who had held positions of responsibility under Athenian rule and whose sympathies might lie opposed to 'freedom'. In Spartan eyes these were traitors, plain and simple. The bills were death warrants. Arrest was followed by execution, at once and on the spot.

We endeavoured to be clement. A man was granted time to shrive himself or scribble his testament. If he'd fled to the interior and we'd had to chase him, we brought him back. The flesh was spared, as much as possible, and bodies released for burial to kin. There was a science to it, this state-sanctioned slaying. It was best to take a man in the street or the marketplace, where dignity restrained him from putting up a fuss. A good arrest was civilized. No weapons were drawn or even exposed. The man himself, recognizing his position, sought decorum. The bravest summoned quips. One could not but admire them.

You ask, how did one feel about this? Was he shamed, schooled in the honourable profession of arms, to discover himself a butcher?

Telamon for his part lost not a wink and scorned all who did. To him this work, though distasteful, was as legitimate an aspect of the warrior's trade as siege operations or the erection of ramparts. As for the victims, their graves were dug. If not us to speed their luckless passage, others would perform it and with far less craft.

Athens' grave was dug too. For my children and my brother's, my aunt and sister-in-law and Eunice if she cared, I must be there when the city fell, and possessed of sufficient station to manage their preservation. Of such self-exoneration is participation in terror comprised. I knew. I didn't care.

One day Telamon and our party were on a spree, with women, on the coast, when a man-of-war beating north hailed us to put ashore prisoners. When the longboat came in, I noted the warrant officer's red hair and hazel eyes.

It was Forehand, Endius's man.

There was grey in the fellow's beard and a cloak of scarlet about his shoulders. No longer a youth in service, he had been freed and enfranchised. I congratulated him with all my heart. 'And where bound, beating north this time of year?'

'To Endius, on the Hellespont. He is there now, treating with Alcibiades.'

# FORTY-EIGHT
# THRACEWARD

W E RETURNED TO TEOS, TELAMON AND I, TO DISCOVER OURSELVES
fallen from favour with the Spartans. Purges must be made from
time to time of those undertaking such errands as we. Philoteles got us
out one jump before the next rotation, with orders to trek north to
Alcibiades' new domains and 'assess the situation'.

Alcibiades had three castles near the Straits, at Ornoi, Bisanthes, and
Neonteichos. These were the strongholds bought for him by Timandra
with loot skimmed, it was said, from the Samos fleet. We beached on the
same strand of Aegospotami into which, in less than a twelvemonth,
Athens' final blood would drain.

The Odrysian Thracians detain without exception every foreigner
landing on their soil. They impound your kit and compel you to get
drunk. Their drink, *coroessa*, is a syrupy liquor, potent as fire, which
pours like resin and which they imbibe neat. One must not resist its
effect but yield and become as arseholed as possible. This is how they
determine your *aedor*, 'wind' or 'breath', which is to them the supreme
and all-defining attribute of a man. We underwent this ordeal with the
passengers of two ferries beached before us. Three gentlemen apparently
lacked breath. The Odrysians packed them off with the next boat; they
simply would not let them in.

Escorts arrived from the interior to take us on. These were
youths, spectacular horsemen with foxskin boots and bridles of silver.

'What prince do you serve?' Telamon asked, admiring their spirit.

'Prince Alcibiades,' our guide declared.

The lad boasted that his master's fortune, got from raiding the tribes east of the Iron Mountains, exceeded four hundred talents. If this was true, Alcibiades held more wealth than the treasury of Athens, bereft now even of her final emergency reserve. Spartans and Persians paid court to him, the youth bragged, and Prince Seuthes himself stood his sanction. We enquired what type of troops he commanded, expecting peltasts and irregulars, tribesmen who would melt away at the first snowflake. '*Hippotoxotai*,' the youth replied in Greek. Mounted archers. We exchanged a glance at this wild tale. Some miles farther our guide reined us in, overstanding a heathland valley. There across an expanse that would have swallowed Athens whole the turf stretched sundered by hoof strikes and littered end-to-end with camp debris, through which women and dogs ranged, scavenging. Great barrows had been thrown up for sacrifice; we saw stands before which troops had passed in review and dikework ponds where streams had been dammed for the watering of horses in the thousands.

'*Hippotoxotai*,' the youth repeated.

We rode all day. This part of Thrace is treeless. Rather the ground is swarded with species of low flowering hedges which find the cold hospitable; these heatherlike ivies produce carnelian berries, quite pretty, and provide a carpet over which horses may gallop at speed and upon which one sleeps, wrapped in one's pelt mantle, with the bliss of an infant. Peaty rills gush beneath beetling prominences, so cold a draught numbs your teeth and leaves fingers sensationless. Tribal territories are bounded by these courses. To water one's horse on the land of another is a declaration of war, and that in fact is how they do it.

Fleas abound in Thrace, even in winter. They infest every covert from beards to bed-wrappings; nothing short of a plunge into ice may dislodge them. Horses are runty, tough as rawhide; they can carry their own weight all day and fear nothing save the swell of the sea's edge, or perhaps the salt stink of it, which makes them mad with fright.

For myself, I debarked in the country upon as doleful a frame as I had ever known. The place cheered me. It was like dying and going to hell. Nothing could be worse, so you might as well perk up. I believe it exercised a similar tonic on Alcibiades. The people had a vigour. Their gods were refreshingly uncouth. And the women. In raiding cultures a man carries with him all he wishes not to lose. These flea-biters ranged with sisters, mothers, daughters, and wives, all itching for trouble. One would think a man of my history would lose appetite for the female. But such is the ungovernable nature of that captain between our thighs that life, or heat at least, does implausibly return. I found myself content to be on campaign again. The soldier's life agreed with me. I was watching a Thracian woman milk a bitch (they mix dog's milk with millet to make a porridge for their babes) when it struck me that I was interested in something. The supreme mystery of existence is this: that, perceiving it for what it is, we yet cling to it. And existence, despite all, discovers measures to reanimate our despoliated hearts.

The words for wind and sky are one in Thrace: *aedor*, a god's name, which is neither feminine nor masculine but of such antiquity, they say, as to antedate gender. Thracians believe the world upheld not by earth, but sky, elemental and everlasting. They chant this hymn:

> Before earth and sea was sky
> And sky endures, them past.
> In you too, Man, breathes aedor first
> And takes leave last.

Wind is of profound substance in the protocol of Thrace. The natives are never unaware of its 'beat' or 'nose', as they call the quarter from which it blows. No man-at-arms may stand upbeat of his better. The nobler takes the beat at his back; the lesser endures it in his face.

Camps are laid out by wind, and a prince's retinue forms up by beat. With Seuthes this was above a hundred, each stationed about his principal in a hierarchy as elaborate as the court of Persia. Only one foreigner ever mastered the nuance of the knights' order of Thrace. Need I name him?

We had bypassed his coastal castle, seeking him inland beyond the Cold Ford, the second tier of mountains, where he had gone, our buck informed us, on a *salydonis*, a combination hunt and rite by which a lesser lord pledges fealty to a greater and upon which the Spartans, Endius's legation, had accompanied him as a way of assessing the troops Alcibiades and Seuthes proposed to ally with them. For two days we encountered no-one, not even herders for the sheep, whose fleeces in that remote province are undyed by their holders, as the code of hospitality permits any to take what he needs. Then at midmorning a solitary rider appeared on the skyline, a thousand feet above us, advancing across our vision with the fearless grace of a young god. The rider descended the slope by traverses as we mounted towards him.

When the prince came closer, however, we realized it was a girl, in hide buskins like a man. One was struck by the gloss and amplitude of her mane, shiny as sable, which she wore tied in a knot at the crown, while tendrils flew about her face in the wind.

'Stay here,' our guide commanded. 'Face into the beat.' He trotted to greet her. The foot-bearers overhauled us. 'Who's this sparrow?' Telamon enquired.

'Alexandra,' one cub replied.

This was Seuthes' woman, no mere bed companion but his bride and queen. She did not deign to acknowledge our party's existence but parleyed apart with our guide. I asked if women travelled alone in Thrace.

'Who offends her, sir, makes himself a banquet for crows.'

We had been warned never to stare at another man's woman. In this case it was impossible. The princess's hair shone, glossy as a marten pelt, and her eyes mated it like jewels. Her horse, too, complemented her colour as if she had selected him, as a city woman a gown, to set off her eyes and skin. The beast seemed to sense this as well, so that the two, animal and woman, constituted one creature of spectacular nobility, and both knew it.

We reached Alcibiades' camp that night. Endius was there, with a party of Peers, colonel or higher. Seuthes had ridden to the interior, raiding. Alcibiades commanded four nations, thirty thousand men, the greatest army west of Persepolis.

We rode out next day to observe the training. The horse troops present were Odrysian and Paeonian, five thousand, with another ten thousand Scythian archers and peltasts. The Greek officers who served as cadre had rigged a mock fort on a strongpoint of the plain, which expanse spread calf-deep in snow, and across which ranged that army of wild dogs which track the Thracian hordes, scavenging their scraps. The exercise called for two wings of cavalry to assault from the south, upbeat, while the third struck from the north, supported by the infantry. In no time it broke down to blood madness. The Thracians could not grasp the concept of practice. They began firing in earnest and must be waved off by frantic Greek officers. The savages possessed one object only: to impress their princes with their individual daring and horsemanship. One espied any number standing on their mounts at full gallop, slinging lances and axes; others clung side-style, firing arrows beneath their animals' necks. Only a miracle prevented a bloodbath, and now, drill aborted, each wanted his weapons back. Into the fracas these desperadoes descended, brawling merrily over their kit while calling in kin and kind to back them.

The carousal and copulation after dark defied depiction. Bonfires made boulevards across the plain, ringed with figures capering ecstatically to tom-tom and cymbal. One could not but fall in love with these wild, free fellows. But as one picked one's way across the camp, stepping over the forms of sodden fornicating louts, one understood why these, the most numerous and valorous warriors on earth, had never carved a scratch on the waxboard of history. Their dogs possessed more discipline.

I returned with Endius and Telamon to the *podilion* where Alcibiades remained awake. These huts of hide and turf are circular, low and wonderfully commodious, excavated so that one descends as to a badger's den. A soup-pot fire keeps them cosy even in a blizzard. Mantitheus and Diotimus were there, with the Cat's Eyes, Damon and Nestorides, now fur-swathed, and about a dozen I recognized as officers, good ones, of the Samos fleet.

'Welcome, outlaws and pirates!' Alcibiades greeted the party. The politics went on all night. I snoozed between two bearhounds. At last near dawn the parley broke, and Alcibiades, ascending through the smoke, motioned me outside to the air.

He had learned of my bride's decease and my own warrant of murder. There was nothing to be said and he didn't try. Rather he tramped at my side on the ground frozen to iron. I have never experienced trepidation, in battle or at hazard of any kind, as in his presence. Despite all, one feared disappointing him. Do you understand, Jason? His will was so formidable, his intelligence so keen, that one must summon all resource just to take counsel and not play the booby. He indicated the men in slumber about the camp. 'What do you think of them?'

'As what?'

His laugh shot a plume upon the air.

'As fighters. As an army.'

'Can you be serious?'

He made his case as we walked. The element Athens has lacked, debarring her from exploiting her success at sea, is cavalry. You forget money, I appended.

'Cavalry produces money,' Alcibiades retorted. 'Give me Sardis and I'll coin money, enough to bear us to Susa and set us in camp before Persepolis.'

Now it was I who laughed. 'And who will train these invincible battalions?'

'You of course.' He set his hand upon my shoulder. 'And your mate Telamon and the other Greek and Macedonian officers I have here already and those who will come.'

We had climbed to a summit from which, across forty miles, could be glimpsed the lightening sea. Two forces contended for the Aegean, Alcibiades testified: Athens on one hand, Persia and Sparta on the other. 'Here is a third force – and irresistible. Which nation out-numbers the Thracian? Which is more warlike? Who possesses more horse, or may strike more swiftly? Thrace brings all these, lacking only . . .'

'You.'

A third power allied with either side must tip the balance, he declared. He was in secret negotiation now with the Persian Tissaphernes, who had had his wings clipped by Cyrus and burned to pay him back. 'Tissaphernes hates Lysander and will sow that malice with the Crown, against which Cyrus must advance, as is self-evident, the instant of King Darius's death. This is why the prince wraps himself in Lysander's mantle. But his plan will miscarry. Spartans may take Persian gold but never Persian service; here is a draught not even Lysander can make them swallow. He has earned Endius's gall by throwing him over for Agis. Neither can move without Athens, and Athens, rid of me, possesses none with the stomach to speak aloud the name Lacedaemon. Each for his own reasons must look to a third power, or conjure one if it did not exist.'

But how would he bring in Athens? 'This is a bridge twice burned,

Alcibiades. The *demos* will never accede to a regime, of whatever might or promise, presided over by you.'

He did not answer at once, rather glanced over the camp, across whose frost-bound sprawl squires, arising, began now to beat the snow from their master's tents, while grooms, thumping limbs across fleece-mantled chests, spread fodder for the horses and transport beasts, which in turn set up that cacophony of bawl and bray which is to the campaigner as the cock's crow to the husbandman.

Any other, scanning this hyperborean stadium, must query that fate which had driven him, after twenty-six years of war, to these barrens at this remove from civilization's quick. Yet for him such a notion was so alien as to be unthinkable. That site on which he stood was ever, and must be ever, the hub and axis of the universe.

'One has no need of Athens. I will draw her best to me, one man at a time, as I have drawn you. Look there to the camp. I already claim the ablest marine cadre in the world, the boldest cavalry commanders, the most skilled shipwrights. Money will buy sailors. Seuthes' timber will build ships.'

Yes, if you can control him.

'Seuthes is keen, Pommo, but he is a savage in awe of me. Where I have moved throughout the war, the nexus of enterprise has followed. Now it will follow me to Thrace; I will compel it. Seuthes cannot summon it on his own and he knows it. For the time being this affords me influence. The army may be his, but mark to whom it turns for command.'

He indicated the awakening camp.

'Alcibiades!'

'Commander!'

Captains hailed him; mounted officers spurred his way; others advanced at the double to receive his orders.

'We will take the straits,' Alcibiades continued, meaning the Hellespont at Byzantium, which conquest he had already accomplished with a tenth of these numbers. 'But we will not cut off Athens' grain or exact concessions, rather continue to supply her at our whim.'

He would do it, I could see, and I must with him. But who will hold these savages, who worship the wind and come and go as ungovernably? 'Even yourself, Alcibiades, are not so vain as to imagine they will stick for you.'

He regarded me wryly. 'I'm disappointed in you, old friend. Can you be as blind as these Thracians to what stares you, and them, in the face?'

And what would that be?

'Their own greatness.'

He meant he would lift them to it. 'They will not stay for my destiny, Pommo, but their own. For their nation poises like an eagle at the brink of the sky, lacking only the daring to launch and ascend. I will give them that. And when they have seized it, by all the gods, the feats they will perform will transfigure the world.'

You have heard the stories, Jason, which say he had gone mad, or native. He danced all night, men claimed, to cymbal and timbrel. Liquor taken neat had stolen his wits. I myself saw his horse tethered in an alder copse alongside Alexandra's. It was fact that Seuthes grew distant, then hostile. Athens wooed the prince shamelessly, granting citizenship to his sons and despatching to his court poets, musicians, even hairdressers. Towards the end, reports claimed, such irregularities infiltrated Alcibiades' speech as 'the alchemy of acclaim' and 'the plain of intercession', the latter constituting, he averred, that field upon which gods and mortals mingle and convene. He warranted to rule by 'commanding the *mythos*' and designated his philosophy 'the politics of *arete*'.

He began to refer to himself in the third person, they said, and invoke his own spirit as if it were a god. Sorcerers and warlocks sat to each hand. He declared it achievable to stop the sun. His flesh he mutilated, some recited, scorning the stuff as but a mantle to transcend or discard. I witnessed him sacrifice all night, more than once, to Hecate and Necessity. They say Timandra was his mentor in such deviation, a succubus herself and no woman but hellspawn. In thrall to her, men alleged, he debarred all from his society to dream and convoked wizards to divine these phantoms' import. He claimed once that he could fly, and had soared to Phthia on wings of quicksilver, conferring there with Nestor and Achilles.

In spring he sent me to Macedonia to procure masts and ships' timbers. There chance set in my path Berenice, Lion's camp woman, by heaven's grace in sheltered circumstances, wife of a wagoner. She had endured unimaginable sufferings since Syracuse, yet through all had preserved her lover's *historia*. This she restored to me, with the chest, the same which holds it now, carved by her new husband. I liked the fellow. He was an unplaned plank, much as his predecessor. He had come from work 'down south', carting goods in secret out of Attica. Athens' own generals were caching their movables, he reported, so certain were they of the ruin to come.

I was still there, at Pella in Macedonia, when report came of the final calamity at Aegospotami. In the days before the battle, after Lysander had taken Lampsacus and drawn up his two hundred and ten battleships across the strait from Conon's hundred and eighty, he came down from his castle, did Alcibiades, to the strand where his countrymen's fleet lay. He was garbed in fox skins, they said, hair unbound and falling down his back. Forty horsemen of the Odrysians provided his lifeguard, accoutred more savagely than he. He would bring fifty thousand horse and foot, he pledged, and strike Lysander by land, if Athens' generals would ferry him. Lampsacus he would recapture for them, entreating nothing. But they drove him off.

'You command here no longer, Alcibiades.' This was the speech of the general Philocles, that villain whose concept of the warrior's code included putting forward the motion, carried so infamously by the Assembly at Athens, to strike off the hand of every enemy sailor taken captive.

Thus was Alcibiades, for the third and final time, banished from the society of his countrymen. Sixteen months later, as that party which bore his murder trekked in his trace upon this selfsame sand, Endius with sorrow remarked that derangement which was at once Alcibiades' curse and genius, and to which, unforswearing, he held true all his life.

'Nations are too puny for him. His self-conception supersedes statehood, and they are dwarves in his eyes who will not step in his train off the precipice of the world. He is correct of course; that is why he must be made away with. For his vision is the future, which the present uncompelled may not now, or ever, abide.'

# FORTY-NINE
## AEGOSPOTAMI

THE EVOLUTION OF OUR TALE [*POLEMIDES CONTINUED*] NOW mandates address of that defeat which broke our nation. It would make a better story to appoint it a mighty conflagration, with tides of battle alternating between throw and overthrow and the issue in doubt to the ultimate hour. As you know, it had been lost years before.

Give Lysander credit. This victory, devoid of honour, was yet informed by masterful cunning and forbearance, evincing such discipline and self-restraint, and such shrewd assessment of his enemy's weaknesses, as to render the event itself anticlimax. Lysander waited; the fruit fell. None may take this from him, that he gained for his country and her allies that triumph which no other had proved capable of securing over thrice nine years of war.

I remained in Thrace through much of the winter preceding the battle. We heard of Lysander's agents overthrowing Miletus, putting all democrats to the sword. He took Iasus in Caria, an Athenian ally, executing all the males of military age, selling the women and children into slavery, and razing the city.

During that final winter Alcibiades suffered a serious fall from a horse. For months he could not walk; to rise from his chair left him white with pain. Savage peoples possess no patience for incapacity. Medocus took his army and decamped; Seuthes followed. The prince, who should have hated Alcibiades for his offence with Alexandra, proved his most steadfast upholder. He had him borne by litter to Pactye, sent him a falconer, beasts for sacrifice, and his own doctor. He gave him five towns for his meat, wine, and necessities. When asked what he lacked for sustenance of his spirit, Alcibiades requested three regiments, which he put under Mantitheus, the younger Druses, and Canocles. These he trained as a type of mobile élite unknown heretofore, who could both row and fight as heavy infantry, each carrying his own kit and armour, independent of squires or commissariat. When Medocus made sport of these as inconsequential numerically, Alcibiades declared he could triple their ranks in a month and not put out a penny. He simply outfitted them in colours of war and marched them through the Iron Mountains. So many were the youths drawn by the splendour of this outfit that he raised ten thousand and must turn away ten more.

At last in the spring his back was better. He could ride. The Thracian clans gather at the rising of Arcturus, and at this festival Alcibiades competed in the horse trials and took the crown, aged forty-six. I believe this put him back in fettle.

Lysander had captured Lampsacus, so close across the strait you could see it on a hazeless day. Now to the foreshore beneath Alcibiades' stronghold, summoned by what perverse destiny, came Athens' final fleet, commanded by Conon, Adeimantus, Menander, Philocles, Tydeus and Cephisodotus.

POLEMIDES' REPORT OF THIS ACTION WAS NECESSARILY ABRIDGED, forasmuch as he himself had been absent, despatched to Macedonia for ships' timbers, and because he addressed one, myself, already amply acquainted with the consequence. For your sake, my grandson, let me 'take up the line' then and flesh out that which our client had passed over in his account addressed to me.

Aegospotami lies dead across the Hellespont from Lampsacus. It is not a harbour, barely an anchorage. There are two small hamlets, no market. Wind is out of the northeast, steady and strong; a rip current runs adjacent the strand, making it difficult to launch and more so to beach, as the vessels of course must put in stern-first. The beach itself exceeds ten furlongs, abundant extent for the ships and camp for thirty thousand men. These, however, must hike four or five miles to Sestos to secure their dinner. There is good water at

Aegospotami except at high tide when the creeks run salt; one must track inland a quarter mile to fresh. It seemed folly to encamp on this inhospitable spit, with the allied city of Sestos so near. Yet to withdraw to that site, as many urged, including Alcibiades, would be to concede Lampsacus to the enemy, and this the generals dared not, recollecting the fate of their predecessors after Arginousai. The commanders burned to draw Lysander to battle. Whatever Aegospotami's liabilities, at least it sat square across from the foe. Lysander could not slip away; sooner or later he must come out and tangle.

Here, from the Council inquest in the aftermath, this affidavit of my old mate Bruise, who served aboard Hippolyta upon that strand:

'He come down from his castle. We all turned out, crowding about him. It was Alcibiades, all right, but got up like a savage. You know, sirs, how he took on the colours of them he slept with. The generals wouldn't let him address the troops, but every word he spoke spread like fire through the camp. He didn't say nothing that the men hadn't heard over and over: that this patch was a death trap, put back to Sestos. You're vulnerable, he said, scattering across miles to get your grub. What if Lysander attacks sudden-like? But we couldn't move, or Lysander'd scoot. What would come next, but the Salaminia putting in from Athens, calling the generals home to be tried for dereliction? We all knew how that would end.

'Alcibiades brought food, but the generals wouldn't let the men take it. He'd provide a market, he swore, or even get us fed, free, off the country. He had his Thracians, he said, ten thousand, trained for foot, horse and sail. Seuthes was coming, and Medocus too. Another fifty thousand. He would hand these over to Athenian command, taking no share for himself.

'If they wouldn't take his troops, then give him one ship. He'd serve under any commander they named. But they couldn't do that neither. To give him a nibble was to hand over the whole cheese. Beat Lysander and all glory goes to him; lose and the shit rains down on us. How could the generals say aye to that? They'd be executed the second they set foot in Attica.

'He proposed service not as a ship's captain, but a common marine. They drove him out of the camp. He was too big, see? He made 'em all dwarves beside him. And they was right. In the commanders' eyes he was Athens' worst enemy; they feared him more than Lysander.'

For four dawns Lysander drew his force up in midstrait in battle order. For four days the fleet of Athens set up opposite. Each noon Lysander pulled back to Lampsacus; each noon the Athenians withdrew to Aegospotami. Each day *our men must disperse for their meal, while Lysander's, with a city at their back, had theirs to hand beside their ships. The fifth noon Lysander ran the same drill: draw up, draw back. Athens' fleet followed suit. But this day, when our sailors scattered to fetch their dinner . . .*

*'They came down on us stripped and at the triple – two hundred and ten men-of-war, forty-two thousand men. I don't have to tell you what chance we had. There's only one way to board a trireme – by companies, in order. But how do you do that with crews flushed over four miles of shell and pebble? Hippolyta got off with one bank manned. On our flanks Pandia and Relentless didn't muster even that. No-one even tried to bring the ship to bear. We just ran for it. They holed us fore and aft. Whoever was in the water was dead. The rest the Spartans took apart on the strand.*

*'Lysander had drilled them for it; they knew the ground and cut off both creeks and every out-track. Their ships got iron into ours and towed 'em off. Lysander was smart; no heavy infantry to bog down in the sand, just peltasts and javelineers. And they didn't come charging wildly, but formed up in companies, quartering the field like hounds. You looked back and saw scarlet everywhere.*

*'He collected twenty thousand, did Lysander. Sold the islanders and slaves, hanging on to only Athenian citizens.'*

These were carried in captivity to Lampsacus, drawn up before a tribunal, and executed as oppressors of Greece. By the time of the Council inquest, the galleys had begun arriving at the Piraeus, bearing the cargo of this slaughter. Lysander restored to Athens the corpses of her sons, that none may impute impiety to him, but more to break the city's heart. For though she no longer possessed a fleet or sufficient manpower to fit one, yet many had vowed to resist to the end, with bricks and stones if necessary, from the top of the Acropolis, precipitating themselves sooner than submit to the foe.

Lysander transported the bodies naked, shorn of all identifying articles and garments. This was to compel the officers to lay out the dead en masse, as a necropolis, that the people, to identify sons and husbands, must tread among lanes and boulevards of the fallen, peering into each face, seeking their own. By this ordeal Lysander sought to appal them with the issue of defiance and render their hearts vitiated of the will to resist.

His corps now comprised the whole of Greece, backed by Cyrus's limitless gold. Agis's army besieged the city; Lysander's fleet blockaded her by sea.

On the sixteenth of Munychion, the same date upon which Athens and her *allies had at Salamis preserved Greece from the tyranny of Persia, Lysander's armada entered the Piraeus unopposed. That party headed by Theramenes turned over the city. Two battalions of Theban heavy infantry seized the Areopagus and shuttered all government vocations. A Corinthian regiment grounded arms in the agora; divisions of Elis, Olynthus, Potidaea and Sicyon broke down the gates and began demolishing the fortifications of the Piraeus, while others of Oeniadae, Mytilene, Chios, and the empire, now liberated, commenced to the music of flute girls the dismantlement of the Long Walls. Two brigades of Spartan and Peloponnesian marines, including* brasidioi *and the freed helots, the* neodamodeis, *under Pantocles, took possession of the Acropolis. They sacrificed to Athena Nike and made their camp upon the stones between the Erechtheum and the Parthenon. The last division, composed of Lacedaemonian marines and mercenaries of Macedonia, Aetolia and Arcadia, took possession of the Round Chamber and the Assembly site on the Hill of the Pnyx. Among these was Polemides, clad in scarlet.*

# FIFTY
## UPON ROAD'S TURN

Mʏ ᴀᴜɴᴛ *[POLEMIDES RESUMED]*, ᴅᴇsᴘɪᴛᴇ ʜᴇʀ ʟᴏᴀᴛʜɪɴɢ ᴏғ ᴍʏ conduct and myself, did not debar me from hoisting her belongings onto a carter's flat and herself upon the driver's seat. She moved to Acharnae with me, to take up residence at Road's Turn. In the city tyranny reigned. The Thirty, as they were called, backed by a Spartan garrison, consolidated their power through the courts and by acts of terror. I sought repeatedly to evacuate my brother's former wife and children; but Theonoe was a town woman and would not come. For two months my aunt and I provided each other's sole company; I at work on the land, she cooking, washing, mending, and in all ways commanding the household, servantless, as she had her husbands', staffed by scores.

The lawlessness in the city at last convinced my sister-in-law to vacate; she came to us on the first of Hecatombaion, Lion's birthday, with her daughter, my niece, and the lass's two babes (her young husband missing with the fleet). Her son, my nephew, had fled to exile; he was nineteen and a partisan, vowing never to reconcile to his nation's vanquishers. Theonoe brought with her a boy, nine, and a girl, seven, issue of her second marriage to a mate of the merchant fleet, lost in another nameless action. Eunice I had tracked to a tenement at Acte. She would not let our children near me, fearing my influence upon the boy.

In town the democracy had been abolished, the citizenry dis-
enfranchised and disarmed. A new constitution was being drafted, or so
the Thirty assured the people. Months passed and no article appeared.
Instead there were lists. Your name appeared on one and you were seen
no more.

What had been the popularly elected executive, the Board of Ten
Generals, no longer existed. The Areopagus did not convene. Exiles
were brought home, meaning those banished heretofore as enemies of
the democracy. These were now either recruited to the Thirty or
engaged as their agents. The courts were shuttered for civil litigation,
which matter was perceived as forwarding the cause of the commons;
when they opened again, it was as engines of persecution. As under all
tyrannies prosecutorial legitimacy was extended to the pre-emptive. A
man could be executed not alone for acts committed but for those he
might commit. Nor were such arraignments confined to political targets.
The Thirty went after anyone with money. The toll was fifteen hundred
and counting. Those democrats who escaped the executioner were
packed off to Lysander's service, the front lines.

Telamon rode out to Road's Turn one day, bearing wine and parched
barley, most welcome. I asked him what he would do, now the war was
over. He laughed.

War is never over.

He had come to recruit me. To no specific employer; just back on the
tramp. Surely I reckoned that my tenure on the land bore an expiry.
Sooner or later, if only from her own want of allies, Sparta must lift her
heel from Athens' throat. The democracy would revive. Such swallows
as myself who had roosted under the conqueror's eave would find themselves back out in the storm. We would either be butchered in the street
by our neighbours or called to execution by due process. My luck consisted in this, Telamon observed, that my kin were women and children.
Its revenge sated upon me, the *demos* would leave these innocents
alone.

I regarded my mentor as he put his case. How youthful he looked! He
had not aged a month, it seemed, down twenty-seven years of war. 'Give
us the secret of your immortality!'

He would lecture me, I knew, on vices. Three he abhorred – fear,
hope, and love of country. He abominated only one beyond these:

contemplation of past or future. These were offences against nature, Telamon maintained, as they bound one to aspiration, to a result whose issue was adjudicated by forces, above the earth and beneath, which mortals could neither alter nor apprehend. Alcibiades was guilty of these, my mate observed, and of another violation of heaven's law.

Alcibiades perceived war as a means. In truth it was an end. Where our commander claimed to honour only Necessity, Telamon served a divinity more primordial.

'Her name is Eris. Strife. All things are brought forth through Strife, my friend, even ourselves torn from our mothers' wombs. Look there to those hawks on the hunt; they serve her, as even these weeds at our feet, whose roots duel beneath the earth for each square fist of dirt.

'Strife is life's oldest and most holy fundament. You tease me, my friend, that I have not aged. If this be true, it arises of obedience to her, this woman at once ancient as earth and youthful as the morrow's dawn.'

I smiled. 'Do you know how many times I have heard this sermon?'

'Yet still you do not learn.'

War waged for advantage yields only ruin. Yet one may not disown war, which abides as constant as the seasons and eternal as the tides.

'What world is it you seek, Pommo, that is "better" than this? Do you imagine like Alcibiades that you, or Athens, may elevate yourselves or anyone to some loftier sphere? This world is the only one that exists. Learn its laws and obey them. This is true philosophy.'

Perhaps to him. Yet I was not ready to don the perennial soldier's kit and enlist, beyond hope, in Strife's battalions.

I stayed.

How my aunt despised me! We worked the lambing together, barefoot in aprons. 'Don't credit yourself with preserving us. We would all be here just the same, absent your intercession.'

'Thank you, dear.'

At table she had assumed the patriarchy, abdicated by myself, and employed this pulpit to decant at full strength for the innocents' edification love of freedom and enmity of tyranny. I knew how desperate her patriot's heart had grown when one day from her harangue arose the name Alcibiades. 'By the Holy Twain, none remains but he, possessed of the bowels to resuscitate the state.'

In the country markets one overheard kindred sentiments. Grovers enquired of merchants from the city, did Alcibiades yet live? Had we driven him, by our repudiation, apart from Athens' cause for ever?

To me this was madness. He had gone over to the Persian now. God knows what robes he swathed himself in and what fictions he wove to preserve his hide. Let Athens, like her waste and weary lands, set her own store in order. Let it rest! Let him!

I trekked in to the port one day with my nephew and a vintner of the overhill farm. Cresting the track at Butadae, one could see the city walls, untouched and imposing as ever. Then we made the turn above the Academy, where the Carriage Road and the Northern Wall conjoined.

There was nothing left.

The quarter west of Melite had been levelled to the distance of a furlong. We passed Maroneia, the played-out silver mines, where these bricks and stones had been dumped. The rubble covered acres, deep enough to bury a fleet, which in the truest sense it had. When we passed the Legs themselves, the walls that had linked city to port, you could see from one side to the other, so utterly had the fortifications been obliterated. Far gone as I thought I was, this sight chilled my heart. My companion, the vintner, wept.

My aunt Daphne died on the twenty-third of Boedromion, final day of the Mysteries.

My son had come out, as on several prior occasions, run off from Eunice. I must restore him to her, but let him stay for now. He seconded me at the old lady's obsequies. We sang the Hymn for the Fallen, the first time in our family for a woman. She had earned it.

Some days later a party of deputies from the city appeared at Road's Turn. I was coming in from the fields and saw them before they saw me. Should I run? What good would it do? They took me into town to an abandoned private home two blocks off the Sacred Way. Windows had been bricked, all furnishings removed. Where the hearth had stood, the stone squatted dark with blood.

I was led into a back room. There were other men, armed, and a plank desk, behind which sat two, unknown to me, but by whose demeanour I recognized as agents of the Thirty.

'Your name has come up on a list,' the taller asserted.

'Which list?'

He shrugged.

The shorter passed two documents across, enquiring which I wished him to sign. The first was my death certificate, the second a warrant of Athenian citizenship for my son and daughter.

'We have a job we want you to do.'

Before any spoke, I knew what it was.

'I call him friend,' I declared, 'and the last hope of our country.'

A sound came from the side door; I rounded towards it. Telamon filled the frame to the lintel, in his kit of war. I turned back to the agents.

'That is why,' the taller spoke, 'you must kill him.'

ALCIBIADES HAD FLED THRACE BY SEA TO PHOCAEA, HEADING EAST into the Empire. That country is vast but roads are few; it is no chore to track a man once on his trail. From Smyrna one makes Sardis in two days; three more carry one to the Lydian city of Cydrara and another to Colossae and Anaua in Phrygia. Roadhouses, called 'ordinaries', terminate each trek. Every fifth day is an inn, where it is the custom of the country to lay over two nights to rest one's stock. Other troopers gave report of him. He travelled with his mistress Timandra and a party of Mysian mercenaries, fewer than five, serving as bodyguards.

Others hunted him as well. Darius of Persia had deceased that spring, succeeded on the throne by his son Artaxerxes. Alcibiades, aware that the Thirty at Athens were applying pressure to Lysander to procure their countryman's end, had approached the satrap Pharnabazus, against whom he had won many victories but to whom now he proposed friendship. He wished, Alcibiades did, to offer his services to the throne of Persia and had intelligence to impart concerning certain perils, namely Prince Cyrus, abetted by Lysander, who, no longer vexed by Athens, would turn about and make his own run for the Crown. Alcibiades could be of great use to the king in this campaign and, he assured Pharnabazus, advance the satrap's standing as well. Pharnabazus, dazzled by his new friend, provided an escort and sent him on to the Interior. It was then that envoys arrived from Sparta. These informed the Persian that if he wished to avoid incurring Lysander's wrath, not to say full-scale war, he would rethink the hospitality he had vouchsafed to the only man living who constituted a threat to Spartan hegemony in Greece. Pharnabazus did not need to hear music to know when to dance. He despatched riders to overhaul and assassinate Alcibiades. Alcibiades evaded these, slaying several. His Mysians vanished and so did he.

A second pursuit party was organized at Dascylium under Susamithres and Magaeus, Pharnabazus' deputies and kinsmen. It was to this posse that Telamon and I became attached. This was at Callatebus. Endius accompanied this cohort, with two other Peers of Sparta, under orders of Lysander to confirm the kill.

Reports put Alcibiades on the track to Celaenae. The party pushed to Muker and the Stone Mounds, beneath which the Phoenix is said to have deposited two eggs, to hatch on that day when the race of men tames its unpacific heart. Privateers scoured the trail. The price on Alcibiades' head, one told us, was ten thousand darics; another quoted a hundred thousand. Between Canae and Utresh are no towns, only a staging area, a coop, called the Tailings. At this site we encountered five brothers of the Odrysians, likewise in pursuit of Alcibiades. My horse had developed an abscess and was suffering terribly; one of these brothers possessed skill with the lancet; he performed the veterinary's service and would take no money. I spoke aside with him.

Alcibiades had dishonoured the brothers' sister; the maid had taken her life. Such an outrage is called in the Thracian tongue *atame*; it may be requited only by blood. The brothers claimed to have scoured the dozen overnights to the east; their prey, they swore, was behind us; we had overrun him. They would spur in that direction; their youngest in fact made off that night. Our guides informed us that no Odrysian may exact blood vengeance, *inatame*, absent his prince's permit, in this case Seuthes'.

Alcibiades had rendered himself fugitive, thus, from Spartan, Athenian, Persian and Thracian.

Our party pressed on. A peculiar bond had evolved between myself and Endius, as on occasion when one journeys in company great distances by horse. Each rode daylong at the other's shoulder, neither speaking nor glancing in his companion's direction yet each attuned to the other's mood and preoccupation. In camp Endius kept to his mates of Lacedaemon, then with morning's trail fell in again upon my flank. 'Will you indeed murder him, Polemidas?' he enquired one nooning, his first words all day.

'Will you?'

'I give thanks to God such is not my charge.'

Of that troop he and I alone seemed alive to the enormity in whose service we trekked. On another day he edged his mount alongside mine. 'If you bolt ahead, or attempt to deal him warning, I shall kill you.'

I enquired if he made this threat in his own name or that of Lacedaemon. To my wonder he began to weep. 'By the gods, what a catastrophe!' And he spurred, in tears, away to the van.

There is in Phrygia in the district of Melissa, where the Ephesus–Metropolis road bears east towards the central provinces, a place called Elaphobounos, Deer Hill, blessed by nature and the ordering hand of man. The prospect from the village, Antara, excellently contoured and cultivated, is among the most delightful in the world. Encamped at this site one evening, my course came clear to me.

I could not perform this slaughter. I would make off this night, informing none including Telamon, that he escape implication. That which I could do for my children, I would, to carrying them with me on the tramp. I had set my resolve and even commenced transferring my goods from the pack stock to my own mount when a great commotion arose across the valley.

A compound was afire. Men of the estate rushed upon our site in terror. We saw the boy, youngest of the five Odrysian brothers, dismounting breathless. Their party had doubled back from the west, the tale burst from him, having picked up the prey's trail, and skirted our camp in the night to beat us to him. '*Etoskit Alkibiad!*' the youth cried, gesturing towards the flames. 'Alcibiades is taken!'

All sprang to their horses' backs. The party raced at a gallop, at terrific hazard to the animals and ourselves as the ground had been staked to receive vines and was pocked with trenches and voids. One saw a house. A farm cottage. The brothers had apparently encircled it in darkness and piled faggots against its walls. The place blazed like a tinderbox. No doubt the flames had driven the quarry forth from his bed to such exposed position as permitted the hunters to shoot him down without hazard to themselves. My heels beat the ribs of my mount. The party raced onto the site. You could not see Alcibiades (he was obscured by the wall of the forecourt) but only the brothers. Two were on horseback, at the gate, pouring bowfire point-blank from their elevated vantage. The others, and their attendants, occupied positions on and behind the wall; these slung javelins and darts. The brothers, even at this remove, stood so flush upon the conflagration that their garments and hair caught and smoked.

I was first upon the court. The heat was monumental. My mount balked and pinwheeled; I sprang to earth.

Now I saw Alcibiades. He was naked, save shield and short *xiphos* sword. His back was charred like meat. Shafts and missile bolts made a stubble field of his shield. The woman Timandra sprawled flat at his heels, a carpet or some heavy garment over her, cloaking her from the flames.

As our party roared upon the site, the brothers did not break off but intensified their attack, ejaculating in their savage tongue that the prize was theirs and they would slaughter any who sought to rob them of it. The Spartans and Persians overran them at once.

Endius, Telamon and I rushed to the gate. The holocaust howled, sucking the breath from our throats. The Spartan dashed in first, snatching up the woman and bearing her from the court. She clutched at her lover's limbs, crying something we could not hear. Telamon and I, elevating cloaks to our faces, ploughed in next. Alcibiades turned towards our sound, as if to attack, then dropped the way a dead man does, not breaking his fall with the strength of his arms, but pitching face-foremost. His shield crashed first and then he, forearm yet within its sheath, plunged upon it. His skull struck like a stone. I have never seen a man shot through with so many bolts.

We hauled him from the inferno. I propped him upright on the far side of the wall. I had no doubt he was dead. My intent, deranged no doubt, was that these cowards not behold their prey stretched forth in the dust.

He was alive and sought to rise.

He cried Timandra's name, in such anguish as I have never heard. She responded in equal affliction, from Endius's arms bearing her clear. Alcibiades relented, reckoning her safe. His hand clutched me by the hair.

'Who is it?' he shouted.

He was blind. The flames had taken half his face. I called my name. He could not hear. I cried louder, at his ear. I was riven with such distress as words may never compass. Behind, the Thracians put up a clamour ungodly, claiming their prize. The cottage continued collapsing by sections. Again I shouted into his ear. This time he heard. His fist held me like a griffin's claw. 'Who else?'

I told him Endius and the Persians.

A terrible groan escaped his breast. It was as if this was what he had expected and, expectation fulfilled, he recognized his fate. His grip clenched me fast.

'The woman . . . she must not be left undefended in this country.'

I swore I would protect her.

His great shield, the same he had borne down thrice nine years since our first blooding beneath those cliffs called the Boilers, rested yet across his chest and shoulders. I had set it thus to cover his nakedness. He shifted now, straining against its weight. With what strength remained he declined the bronze, exposing the flesh of his neck and throat.

'Now, my friend,' he said. 'Take what you came for.'

POLEMIDES HERE ELEVATED HIS GLANCE AND MET MY EYES. FOR A *moment I thought he could not continue, nor was I at all certain I wished him to.*

LYSANDER HAD SAID OF ALCIBIADES THAT IN THE END NECESSITY would bring him low. Perhaps she did, but it was my hand which drove the fatal blade. Nor did I slay a general or statesman, as history will memorialize him, but a man, hated by many and loved by more, myself not last among them. Set aside his feats and felonies. In this I honour him: that he drove the vessel of his soul to where sea and sky conjoin and contended there, without fear, as few before, save perhaps only your master, his first instructor. Who will sail so far again?

And I, who took upon myself such freight of self-condemnation for my acts of the Plague and after, discovered myself experiencing on Deer Mountain, to my wonder, no such grief or remorse. I did not act so much

as enact. Do you reckon the distinction, my friend? I was Alcibiades'
own arm, as I had been since that night of our youth upon the storm-
bound strand, striking that blow which he himself called down. Who is
guilty? I and he, and Athens and all Greece, who have fashioned our
ruin with our own hands.

*Polemides finished. It was enough. No more need be narrated.*
*Later, within his sea chest, I discovered this correspondence in Alcibiades'*
*hand. It bore no salutation and was salted with misspellings, indicative of a*
*preliminary draft – to whom one may only guess. By its date, the tenth of*
*Hecatombaion, it may be the last he ever wrote.*

. . . my end, though it come at the hands of strangers, will have
been purposed and paid for by my own countrymen. I am to them
that which they esteem most and may endure least: their own like-
ness writ large. My virtues – ambition, audacity, emulation of
heaven rather than prostration before it – are but their own,
amplified. My vices are theirs as well. Those qualities which my
constitution lacks – modesty, patience, self-effacement – they too
despise, but whereas my nature has preserved me unfettered by
these, theirs has not. They both fear and worship that brilliance to
which my example summons them, but which they possess insufficient spirit to embrace. Athens, confronted by the fact of my
existence, owns only these options: to emulate or eliminate. When
I am gone, she will cry for me. But I will never come again. I am
her last. She will produce no more as myself, however many hoist
the jack and ensign.

# FIFTY-TWO
# A MAGISTRACY OF MERCY

I PASSED SOCRATES' FINAL DAY [GRANDFATHER CONTINUED] IN HIS CELL with the others. I was exhausted and dozed. I had this dream:

Weary and wishing to attend our master with the clearheadedness he deserved, I hunted through the prison for a recess in which to catch a catnap. My search delivered me to the carpenter's loft. There, horizontal, spread the tympanon on which Polemides would this day meet his end. 'Go ahead, sir.' The carpenter motioned me in. 'Take a snooze.' I lay down and fell at once into a blissful slumber. I awoke with a start, however, to discover officers binding me to the instrument. My wrists and ankles were fettered beneath the cramp irons; the chain strangled me about the throat. 'You've got the wrong man!' I shouted. But my cry was throttled by the iron. 'I'm the wrong man! You've got the wrong man!'

I snapped to to discover myself in Socrates' cell. I had cried out and disquieted him. He had taken the hemlock already, I was informed, and, awaiting its effect, had settled to rest upon his pallet, compassed by those who loved him, his face shrouded beneath a cloth. I begged the company's pardon. It was clear that agitation was the last thing our master needed. In distress I excused myself and hastened from the cell.

It was late in the day. As I emerged at the head of the Iron Court, I glimpsed a woman and a boy vacating towards the vestibule. Eunice. This was odd, as Polemides had thus far refused to see her. Had something happened?

At once the lad reappeared. Polemides' son Nicolaus. He had not been departing, only assisting his mother upon her way. He strode straight up to me and took my hand, narrating his gratitude for my exertions on his father's behalf. A sea change had overtaken the youth. Though lank and cranelike as ever, he had acceded to manhood. He greeted me equal-to-equal, so much so that I found myself abashed and, seeking to allay what I imagined to be his distress, addressed him to this effect: that though his mother had been the engine of this grief, he must recall that her object was his own preservation, that is, to keep him from harm, running off to war.

The boy regarded me queerly. 'That is not how the land lies at all, sir. Has my father not told you?'

His mother, the lad insisted, had not engineered anything. She was no instigator of this prosecution but its pawn. That perjurer Colophon who had brought suit against my father, the youth said, acted as stooge for those who had hired him, Polemides, during the reign of the Thirty, to assassinate Alcibiades.

'These villains, learning of my father's return to the city, feared exposure for their crimes. They have put the squeeze on my mother, reckoning her vulnerable as a noncitizen, and compelled her to provide particulars of that accidental murder in Samos, years past, by which the rogues have secured my father's sentence of death.'

Polemides had delivered his confession, the lad informed me, in return for a warranty of citizenship for Eunice and the children, made to him in secret by his prosecutors, who apparently possessed the sway to pull it off. He had been loath to reveal this to me lest I, in outrage at the cost to himself, seek to expose it.

There is a bench beside the steps which lead from the Iron Court. Weariness now overcame me. I must sit. The lad took the place at my side. Darkness fell. Brands were lit and set within their hangers.

I came to myself after some while, roused by a commotion across the cloister. The keeper stood in heated skirmish with Socrates' dear friend, Simmias of Thebes, who had this moment been summoned apparently from the cell. Had the master expired? I crossed at once with the boy. The porter now joined this affray, whose core of contention was, to my puzzlement, horses. 'You may have hired them, sir,' porter and keeper protested to Simmias, 'but it's our necks if they're found out.'

Simmias tugged me aside in consternation. 'By the gods, I have cocked up, Jason.'

Some days earlier, he explained, confident of securing Socrates' assent to a design of escape, Simmias had engaged several gentlemen of dubious reputation to hire mounts and purchase the silence of guards and informers. This course he had set in motion, Simmias recounted, before Socrates had with such finality repudiated it. 'Can you credit it, Jason? With all else the scheme has slipped my mind entirely!'

'I don't understand, Simmias.'

'Horses and escorts are here! What shall I do?'

Simmias was clearly distraught; no doubt he had been fetched from Socrates' cell only moments prior, by the porter in a state of alarm and demanding immediate action. Simmias failed yet to rally his reason. All that animated his purpose, clearly, was to return at once to our master's side and, above all, not to stand truant at the hour of his passing.

'Leave this to me, Simmias.'

'By heaven's mercy, Jason! Will you manage this for me, my friend?'

There are frontiers one crosses, our client had once observed, without understanding of what he does. This was not one of them. To Polemides and to our master the demos had debarred clemency. Now by fortune's hand a fresh magistrate had been appointed, and that arbiter was myself. Who would reprieve the transgressor, if not I? Who would accord him absolution, when he himself had cast the black pebble? Perhaps heaven had granted, through his surrogateship, occasion to pardon all, myself included.

I turned to the lad. 'Your father claims he has made peace with his own execution.'

'Yes, sir.'

'Can you change his mind?'

The boy seized both my hands in his. 'But what of you, sir?' He feared that informers, learning of my part, would set my life at peril.

'Whose silence must be bought, has been bought.'

The keeper had overheard all and now nodded his concordance. I released the lad's grip. Away he tore to his father's side.

Should I, too, seek Polemides, for farewell, or track Simmias' footsteps to our master's chamber? I regarded the porter. He was already despatching his own prentice to communicate to the escort riders, who awaited no doubt in some abutting starless lane, the change in plans. I asked if this discommoded him. 'Horses is horses,' he replied. 'Who sits 'em is no account to me.'

The porter had become anxious, however, and the keeper as well, as any upon the instant of felony's commission.

'Best if you begone, Cap'n.'

And leading across the court, he conducted me without.

## FIFTY-THREE
# THE HOLM OAK'S BLOOM

OUR MASTER'S BODY WAS RELEASED NEXT DAY TO HIS COMPANIONS; WE interred his bones within his ancestors' tomb at Alopece. I cannot cite that date as the one upon which I lost all heart for politics; any man of reason had despaired for years of the demos's capacity to rule itself. Within the twelvemonth I had quit the city, with wife and daughters, and taken up residence in the country at Holm Oak Hill. Here I have remained.

For thirty-nine years from my twentieth birthday, I donated all of flesh and treasure to our nation. Youth and manhood I accorded, and broke my health in Athens' cause. Three sons I sacrificed to her corps at arms, and two more she stole in paroxysms of civil derangement. Through pestilence and privation she robbed two wives of the measure of their days.

As a naval officer I performed the trierarchy seven times. I have served as Councillor, magistrate, and minister. My country I have represented on deputations abroad and affixed my name in her cause to instruments of peace and war. Once I tallied our clan's contributions to the state. The toll came to eleven talents, roughly the produce of all our holdings over twenty years. I do not repent such impost and would gladly bear all again in the cause of our country. I still call myself a democrat, though, as my wife, your grandmother, would have it, a heartsore one.

I heard nothing from Polemides for above three years. Then one morning a lad came racing with report of a stranger at the gate. I hastened down. A man awaited in blistered leather, shouldering a mercenary's kit. I had never seen the

Arcadian Telamon yet knew at once this was he. He would not stay but delivered into my hand a pair of letters. He had carried them from Asia two years.

Polemides was dead, he reported. Not of war but mishap; an iron spike trodden upon and gone to lockjaw.

I beseeched the fellow to remain. 'You have trekked leagues, sir, to render us this service. Please stay for supper, for our sake if not your own, or at least come in and wash off the dust.'

The man assented to enter as far as the copse that shades the steading spring. There is a pleasant bench there, as you know. He sat. The girls brought wine and alphita bread and an excellent opson of salt fish and onion. While the man ate, I scanned the letters.

The first was from Polemides, dated two years prior. He is well, he says, and hopes I am the same. He remarks the slender margin of his reprieve from the tympanon and chaffs me for joining him among 'the gallery of rogues'.

> . . . I trust, my friend, you harbour no illusions as to my reform-
> ation. I dance ever to the time-fixed tune. As all abhorred of
> heaven, my luck continues brilliant. Nothing can kill me and the
> girls scratch out each other's eyes for a berth beneath my bed
> sheets.

The second was from his son. They served together, the mercenary noted, beneath the Spartan colonel Philoteles, in Agesilaus' brigades fighting the King of Persia. Nicolaus informs me of his father's death. This was in Phrygia, the valley of the Maeander, not sixty stades from Deer Mountain.

> . . . as to the contents of my father's sea chest, he would deem it a
> meed of honour, sir, if you would hold them as your own. I would
> not know how best to use them. I am not the kind.

The chest had been delivered to my door a month after Polemides' escape by my old shipmate Bruise, who, you may recall, ran the refectory in the lane opposite the prison. Bruise had this tale of that final night.

It was he who had contracted the horses for the getaway and, following my departure, had brought them round to the alley abutting the court. The keeper meanwhile had released Polemides, and, with his son, the trio descended to this egress. As they stepped into the lane where Bruise and the horses waited, three men turned the corner into view – Lysimachus, Secretary of the Eleven, and two magistrates – come to check on the disposition of the executions.

The officers' placement was such as to easily intercept the absconders. A cry would summon the prison's complement. Bruise himself, he declared, nearly pissed on the paving stones with fright. What went through their minds, these magistrates enjoined by the demos to carry out the execution of the noblest of their countrymen? Did they, who were but men and fellows of his race, grasp the enormity? Perhaps by some measure they came to perceive this gentleman turned villain, Polemides, as a surrogate, if not for Socrates, then themselves. He was as guilty as they, not alone for those acts with which he had been charged but for a thousand more, unwitnessed and unarraigned, down thrice nine years of war. Perhaps their silence now confessed such conviction as my own. Let him live, for our sake. Let us once play Zeus and tender clemency, through this man, for all those evils of our own devising.

For whatever motive, the officers stood aside. In heartbeats Polemides and the boy made off. The man's parting prayer to the keeper was that his chest be released to my care, when this could be performed without setting me at hazard.

Here let me insert, my grandson, one final document. I discovered this in our client's chest only days ago, seeking another I wished you to see. It is a transcription of that address delivered by Alcibiades to the men of the Samos fleet upon his second farewell, following Notium, that estrangement from which he never returned.

. . . what I say now I address to your generals and officers, gentlemen, who must command you scrofulous rabble, may the gods help them. Shall I tell where I learned to lead such men as you? In my father's stable, from his horses. And I call upon our friend Thrasybulus to back me, for he stood at my shoulder when as lads we marvelled at those champions on racing day. No-one had to teach them to run. Buying a horse, we learned to remark carriage and posture before length of bone or power of ham. Will you agree that a racer may possess nobility? And what is nobility that a beast may own it as well as a man? Is it not that capacity of soul by which one donates oneself to an object greater than one's own self-interest?

How lead free men? Only by this means: the summoning of each to his nobility.

When I was a boy, my tutor took me down to Piraeus to watch the racing shells sculling from Acte to the Silent Harbour. My child's eye imagined that one creature drove each boat, a single splendid beast with multiple pairs of arms. But when the shells pulled in, I saw that men propelled them. Will you believe me, friends, when I say that I broke from my pedagogue to touch them with my hand, to see they were real? How could six, I begged to know, row as one? 'Look there, little cousin, and see a hundred and seventy-four do the same.'

A trireme on the wing: by the gods, here is a sight of splendour! Nobler still a line at the advance and noblest of all, that symphony, a fleet. And you, my friends, of all who ever sailed or ever will, you are the finest. When sorrowful age has wrung us in its grip, what shall remain? Fathers and mothers, wives, lovers, even our own children, all will fall away, I believe, leaving only these, our comrades with whom we have made trial of death. They are enough, my friends. They are that which few ever feel or know.

You do not need me, brothers. No force on earth can stand up to you. May the gods bear you from victory to victory. The last sight I behold as hell hauls me down shall be your faces. Thank you for honouring me with your comradeship. And now goodbye, my friends. Fare you well.

*I studied the mercenary Telamon as he finished his feed. Though calculation put his years well past fifty, his aspect was so lean and weatherworn as to tell thirty-five or even fewer. I wished earnestly to interrogate him, of Polemides' final seasons and his own.*

*One look told he would endure nothing of the sort. I enquired only where he was bound. To the harbour, he replied, to ship out on campaign.*

*I had a pair of boots in the barn and a woollen mantle far superior to that threadbare article he wore. He would take neither. He rose, shouldering his kit.*

*Upon the bench he set a coin.*

*I protested that he offended the farm's hospitality.*

*He smiled. 'It's from Pommo, Cap'n. He thought you might find the piece of interest.'*

I picked it up. It was a gold daric of Phrygia, a month's pay for an infantry-man. The reverse bore a trireme and a winged Victory; the obverse Athena Triumphant framed by an owl and olive branch.

The coin was called an 'alcibiadic', Telamon reported. It was a favoured piece, good across all Asia.

The lane passing out from the farm bisects the central compound. The hands' kitchen and service stalls mark the west, as you know, adjacent several cottages and a transients' barracks. Equipment sheds stand across, with that steading upslope we call the Crease, and the stock pens beyond. As the mercenary trekked down towards the gate, a huddle of gawkers tracked him with their gaze, arrested by his appearance and his kit. This following was comprised not alone of lads but of maids and even husbandmen and women breaking off from their labours. As he approached the gate, two boys dashed ahead, that he not be put to trouble by the latch, and would have trailed him a distance down the lane, or to the sea itself, had not their fathers hailed them back.

I, too, was held by this apparition, unable to turn away until he had vanished along the avenue of holm oak, whose blossom yields that scarlet dye which ever colours the soldier's cloak of war.

# A NOTE ON SPELLING

For persons and places which have been widely known in the English-speaking world through their Latinized versions, I have respected the tradition. Thus Alcibiades does not become Alkibiades, nor Jason Iason. Similarly Piraeus is not Peiraieus and Potidaea is not Potidaia.

However, for less well-known names, and in particular Greek terms, I have retained the Greek spelling transliterated into English; thus *homoioi* does not become Latinized to *homoii*, nor *toxotai* to *toxotae*.

# GLOSSARY

**ACHARNAE**   A *deme* or district of Athens, about seven miles north of the city.

**AEGOSPOTAMI**   Site on the Hellespont (Goat Creeks) where in 405 BC the Spartan navy under Lysander defeated the fleet of Athens, sealing victory in the Peloponnesian War.

**AGEMA**   The élite corps of king's defenders in the Spartan army.

**AGOGE**   'The Upbringing'; the Spartan educational regimen.

**AGON**   Contention; competition.

**AGORA**   Political and social centre of Athens and other Greek cities, housing the marketplace, civic buildings, temples, etc.

**AKATION**   The smaller 'boat sail' of a trireme, as differentiated from the mainsail.

**ALPHITA**   Barley bread.

**ANASTROPHE**   Countermarch.

**ANDREIA**   Courage; manly virtue.

**APAGOGE**   Summary arrest.

**APATURIA**   Festival of the Brotherhoods at Athens.

**APELLA**   The Spartan Assembly.

**APOSTOLEIS**   Senior administrators of the Athenian fleet.

**ARCADIA**   Region of the Peloponnese noted for producing great fighters, particularly mercenaries.

**ARCHITECTONES**   Architects.

**ARCHON**   One of nine senior magistrates at Athens, elected each year for a one-year term.

**AREOPAGUS**   The senior Council at Athens, composed of ex-archons.

Also the hill west of the Acropolis, the 'Hill of Ares', upon which they met.

*ARETE*   Excellence; virtue.

ARGIVES   Men of Argos.

*ARISTOI*   The nobility, 'the best'.

ARTEMIS ORTHIA   Temple of Artemis Upright at Sparta.

*ASPIS*   A shield of the heavy infantry; pl. *aspides*.

ASSEMBLY   The sovereign body of Athens, open to all adult male citizens. Also, *ekklesia*.

ATTICA   The region of which Athens is the principal city.

'THE BARBARIAN'   To a Greek, any non-Greek; usually in reference to the Persians, whose speech sounded like 'bar-bar' to Greek ears.

*BASILEUS*   The 'King Archon' at Athens; his duties were primarily to officiate at religious events.

BOXER'S STONE   Olympic pugilists fought tethered to a heavy stone so they could not duck away from opponents.

*BRASIDIOI*   Helot troops who had won their freedom fighting under the Spartan general Brasidas.

'BREAKTHROUGH'   Naval manoeuvre, the *diekplous*, in which a warship shoots the gap between enemy craft advancing in line abreast, then wheels to attack from the flank.

CANTHARUS (*KANTHAROS*)   The Goblet; the main harbour of Piraeus.

CATHEAD   On a trireme, a stout beam structure projecting laterally just aft of the prow, supporting the outrigger.

CHOMA   The ceremonial jetty at Piraeus from which a fleet embarked to war.

CIMON   Athenian general, son of Miltiades; his victories in the mid-fifth century drove the Persians from the Aegean and established Athens' hegemony at sea.

'CONCENTRIC'   A naval tactic, *kyklos* or 'circle', whereby one fleet literally rowed rings around another, probing for a weak spot to strike.

COUNCIL OF 500   At Athens the deliberative body which prepared business for the Assembly.

CUIRASS   Armour breastplate.

'CUTBACK'   Naval manoeuvre, *periplous*, whereby a warship shoots past an opponent to get astern of her, then turns about to strike from aft or abeam.

*DAIMON*   Inhering spirit; in Latin, *genius*. Socrates' *daimon* always warned him when he should not do something, but never when he should.

DARIC   A Persian gold coin called after King Darius.

DEAD MAN'S PIT   The *barathron* at Athens, into which criminals were thrown. Scholars are divided over whether the condemned were precipitated alive, to be killed by the fall, or simply dumped as corpses, having been executed at another site by other means.

DECELEA   A site in Attica which the Spartans fortified during the latter, or Decelean, phase of the war.

DEME   A ward or district of Athens.

DEMOS   The electorate of a democracy, 'the commons'.

DEMOSTHENES   Athenian general (*not* the orator of the fourth century), victor over the Spartans at Pylos/Sphacteria; leader of relief expedition to Sicily.

DIKE   Civil lawsuit.

DIKE PHONOU   An indictment for murder.

'DOLPHIN'   A heavy weight elevated upon a spar or boom, to be dropped onto an enemy warship's deck to hole her.

DRACHMA   Coin, a 'handful', about a day's pay for an armoured infantryman.

EIRENOS (EIRENE)   A youth-captain of the Spartan *agoge*, twenty years old, in charge of a *boua* ('herd') of boys.

EISANGELIA   A formal procedure under Athenian law for making a variety of grave charges, often treason, before the Council or Assembly.

EKKLESIA   The Assembly of the people.

ENDEIXIS   A type of indictment or denunciation at law.

ENDEIXIS KAKOURGIAS   At Athens an indictment for 'wrongdoing', a category covering everything from petty theft to murder. *Kakourgoi* = criminals.

EPHEBE   At Athens, a youth in military training, eighteen to twenty years old.

EPHOR   A senior magistrate of Sparta. A board of five was elected each year for a one-year term; they were the real power, superseding even the kings.

EPIBATAI   Marines; armoured infantrymen who fought from the decks of ships.

EPIMELETAI TON NEORION   At Athens the Overseers of the Port and Naval Establishment.

EPINIKION   Victory ode.

EPIPOLAE   'The Heights' overlooking Syracuse.

EPISTATES   At Athens the chairman of the executive committee of the Council, chosen by lot to serve for one day only.

EPITEICHISMOS   Military tactic of establishing a fort in enemy territory, from which to ravage the countryside and to which the foe's deserters and slaves could flee.

EUROTAS   The river of Sparta.

GRAPHE   A public lawsuit or indictment.

GYLIPPUS   Spartan general; victor over the Athenians at Syracuse.

'HEDGEHOG'   A sunken stake, part of a naval palisade, meant to tear the bottom out of an attacking ship.

HELLAS   Greece.

HELLENE   A Greek.

HELOT   A Spartan serf.

HERMAI   Blocky stone statues of Hermes – messenger of the gods and benefactor of voyages – which stood before private homes and public buildings. Herms usually sported erect phalluses. Regarded as good-luck pieces.

HETAIRAI   Courtesans.

HOLY TWAIN   At Athens the goddess Demeter and her daughter Persephone, the Kore. At Sparta the Dioscuri or 'twins', Castor and Polyduces.

HOMOIOI   The officer class of full-citizen Spartans; Peers or Equals.

HOPLITE   Armoured infantryman, from hoplon meaning 'shield'; one who owned a full panoplia.

HYBRIS   Hubris, pride. Also 'outrage', punishable at Athens by death; an act of wilful and malicious abuse intended to humiliate someone irreparably.

IMPIETY   At Athens a crime punishable by death; the charge under which Socrates was condemned.

IRONHEAD   Arrow.

KATALOGOS   Roll of citizens at Athens, from which men were drafted for military service.

KEELSON   Keel timbers of a ship.

KHOUS   A liquid measure; about 3½ litres.

KLEROS   At Sparta, a Peer's agricultural landholding. The ancient lawgiver Lycurgus divided the state into nine thousand equal allotments, each to support one warrior and his family.

KOPPA   The archaic letter Q.

KYRIOS   Legal guardian. At Athens a male citizen who protected the interests of the women, children, and slaves of his household, since they did not have political rights.

LACEDAEMON   The region of Greece of which Sparta is the principal city; Laconia.

LAMBDA   Greek letter L. Lacedaemonian infantrymen bore a *lambda* on their shields.

LENAEA   An annual festival at Athens.

LEONIDAS   King of Sparta and commander of the Three Hundred who sacrificed their lives defending the pass at Thermopylae against the Persians, 480 BC.

LOCHOS   A Spartan regiment; pl. *lochoi*.

LONG WALLS   Fortifications linking Athens to the harbour at Piraeus.

LYCURGUS   Ancient lawgiver of Sparta.

MEDES   Usually a synonym for Persians; actually another warrior race, of the kingdom of Media, conquered by Cyrus the Great of Persia and incorporated into the empire.

MILTIADES   Athenian general, victor at Marathon against the Persians, 490 BC.

MINA   100 drachmas.

MONTHS   The Athenian year started in midsummer: Hecatombaion, Metageitnion, Boedromion, Pyanopsion, Maimacterion, Poseidion, Gamelion, Anthesterion, Elaphebolion, Munychion, Thargelion, Sciriphorion.

MOTHAX   A 'stepbrother' class at Sparta, often bastard children of Peers, permitted to train in the *agoge* under sponsorship of full citizens; pl. *mothakes*.

MYSTERIES OF ELEUSIS   Festival of Athens, lasting nine days, in honour of Demeter and Kore. Each year during the month of Boedromion (September) neophytes and initiates made the pilgrimage to Eleusis. During the war, Spartan occupation of Attica compelled the procession to travel ignominiously by sea, until restored by Alcibiades.

NAUTAI   Sailors; oarsmen.

NAVARCH   A Spartan admiral.

NEMESIS   Goddess who personified divine retribution, usually for the human sin of pride, *hybris*.

NEODAMODEIS   'New citizens'; Spartan helots manumitted as a reward for military service.

NEORION   The works and administrative establishment of a port or naval base.

NIKE   Goddess of victory.

OBOL   One-sixth of a drachma, a 'spit'.

OIKOS   A household.

OLIGOI   Aristocrats, 'the few'.

OPSON   A 'relish' at dinner; that which one dipped one's bread into.

OTHISMOS   In ancient warfare, the scrum or shoving match that occurred when two close-ranked formations clashed.

PAEAN   Hymn sung by Dorian infantry – Spartan, Syracusan, Argive, but not Athenian (who were Ionian) – as they marched into battle.

PALAMEDES   Greek warrior of Trojan War, accused unjustly by Odysseus; emblematic of the man wrongfully charged.

PANATHENAEA   The great festival at Athens in honour of Athena.

PANOPLIA   Full armour for a heavy infantryman: helmet, breastplate, shield, greaves (shin guards). You had to be fairly well off to afford a panoplia.

PARAKATABOLE   Fee deposited at Athens in arbitration of inheritance cases, equal to one-tenth the value of the disputed property.

PEER   A full citizen of Sparta.

PELOPONNESE   The mainland of southern Greece, literally 'isle of Pelops', an ancient hero.

PERICLES   Athenian statesman and general of the mid-fifth century, 'the Olympian' presided over the Golden Age of Athenian democracy, empire, and artistic achievement. Kinsman and guardian of Alcibiades.

PERIOIKOI   The 'neighbours' or 'dwellers-around' of the allied towns outlying Sparta. Autonomous but of noncitizen status and required to follow the Spartans 'whithersoever they should lead'.

PHARMAKON   Painkiller, pl. pharmaka.

PHARNABAZUS   Persian satrap or governor of Phrygia and the Hellespont. Capital at Dascylium.

PHOINIKIS   The scarlet cloak of Lacedaemon.

PHRATRIAI   Brotherhoods of kinsmen at Athens.

PHTHIA   Achilles' home region in Thessaly.

PILOS   A cap of felt, often worn as padding beneath the bronze helmet.

PNYX   A hill southwest of the Acropolis on which the Athenian Assembly met, in the open air, to conduct its deliberations.

POLEMARCH   'War leader'.

*POLIS*   City-state; pl. *poleis*.

*PORNE*   Whore; pl. *pornai*.

*PROSTATES*   Bow officer of a trireme; 'he who stands forward'.

*PRYTANEIS*   The fifty 'presidents' at Athens who represented their tribe in the Council of five hundred. Each group served for a tenth of the year, a prytany, as the executive committee of the Council and Assembly.

*PSEUDOS*   A lie.

*PYTHIOI*   Spartan priests of Apollo; warriors themselves, who also performed the priestly offices of battle.

ROUND CHAMBER   The *Tholos*, where the executive committee of the Council, the *prytaneis*, met at Athens.

*SAMOS*   Island of the Aegean and staunch ally of Athens; her overseas naval bastion throughout the war in the East.

*SCIRITAE*   Spartan rangers of the district of Sciritis.

*SICELS*   Non-Greek inhabitants of Sicily.

*SKYTALAI*   Message sticks. As a means of encrypting despatches, the Spartans issued a dowel-like *skytale* of a specific circumference to their commanders sent abroad, maintaining a duplicate at Sparta. To send a message a strip of leather was wound obliquely about the home stick; the message was written on it, then unwound and despatched, decipherable only when wound again about an identical-size *skytale*.

SOLON   Athenian sage and statesman of the sixth century; he wrote the laws that laid the groundwork for the democracy.

*SPARTIATAI*   Spartans of the officer class, Peers or Equals; anglicized as 'Spartiates'.

*STADION RACE*   A straight dash covering one *stade*, about two hundred yards.

*STRATEGOS*   An Athenian general or war commander; or one of the Board of Ten Generals elected yearly, roughly the executive branch of the democracy.

*SYKOPHANTAI*   Informers and extortionists who preyed upon the litigants in Athenian law courts.

TALENT   A weight of silver worth roughly 6,000 drachmas. It took about a talent a month to keep a warship in action.

TARTARUS   A sunless abyss below Hades, where Zeus imprisoned the Titans. An anvil, dropped from Olympus, would fall nine days before reaching Earth – and another nine days, beneath the earth, till it reached Tartarus.

*TAXIARCH*   Each of the ten tribes at Athens was required to supply an infantry regiment, a *taxis*, to the state. Its commander was a *taxiarchos*.

*TECHNITAI*   Craftsmen.

*TEMENOS*   Sacred precinct surrounding a temple or sanctuary.

*TETRAS*   A group of four.

*THALAMITAI*   Trireme oarsmen of the lowest row; holdsmen.

THEMISTOCLES   Athenian statesman and general, victor over Persia in the sea battle of Salamis, 480 BC. Fortified Piraeus, initiated construction of the Long Walls, set Athens on the course of sea power and empire.

THERMOPYLAE   Pass in central Greece at which three hundred Spartans and their allies held off for six days the advance of the Persian myriads under King Xerxes, 480 BC.

THE THIRTY   Puppet government at Athens following surrender to Sparta in 404 BC, headed by Critias. Known for its tyrannical acts of repression.

*THRANITAI*   Trireme oarsmen of the topmost bank, who rowed through an outrigger.

*THRASYTES*   Boldness.

TISSAPHERNES   Persian satrap of Lydia and Caria. His capital was at Sardis.

*TOXOTES*   A marine archer; pl. *toxotai*.

*TRIERARCH*   A trireme captain. Wealthy Athenians were conscripted to command, and bear the financial burden for, a warship for a term of one year. This could prove a white elephant, as anyone who has owned a sea-going vessel can testify.

*TRIERARCHY*   At Athens the civic obligation to serve as a *trierarch*.

*TRIERES*   A trireme; pl. *triereis*.

TRIREME   The primary ship of war, propelled by three banks of oars, crew of about two hundred.

'TWO-AND-ONE'   On a trireme, resting one bank of oarsmen while the other two row.

*XENOS*   Stranger; also 'guest-friend', a privileged bond between families of different states.

*XIPHOS*   The short Spartan-style sword.

*XYELE*   A sicklelike weapon carried by Spartan youths.

*ZYGITAI*   Trireme oarsmen of the middle row, between the *thalamitai* and *thranitai*.

# ACKNOWLEDGMENTS

Any work set in the era of the Peloponnesian War begins and ends with Thucydides. Not to mention Plato, Xenophon, Plutarch, Aristophanes, Diodorus, Andocides, Antiphon, Lysias, Aelian and Cornelius Nepos. A pretty stellar lineup to say thanks to.

Of modern scholarship I must single out the works of Irving Barkan, Jacob Burckhardt, Walter Ellis, Steven Forde's *The Ambition to Rule*, Peter Green for *Armada from Athens*, Donald Kagan, D. M. MacDowell, J. H. Morrison and J. F. Coates for *The Athenian Trireme*, Barry Strauss, and Jean Hatzfeld for *Alcibiades*, with special thanks to Dr Christine Henspetter for translating the latter for me (longhand no less) from the French.

Among friends and colleagues, Dr Ralph Gallucci and Dr Walter Ellis have applied a most excellent chisel and mawl to the manuscript. Thanks, above and beyond the call of duty, to Dr Ippokratis Kantzios, who has been my indispensable counsel from the first and also a great and true friend. And to the Baronessa C. S. von Snow, my companion and cartographer to antique lands.

My profound gratitude to my editors at Doubleday and Bantam, Nita Taublib, Kate Burke Miciak, and Shawn Coyne, and especially Shawn, who did what old-time editors used to do in plunging in, shirtsleeves up, to whip what was a sprawling monster of a manuscript into what we both hope is a work suitable for literary consumption.

Finally *Tides of War* is fiction, not history. I have taken liberties with events and chronology and interpreted historical characters, hopefully in a higher cause. For the book's faults and shortcomings the responsibility is entirely mine.